ETERNITY ROW

A StarDoc Novel

S. L. Viehl

A ROC BOOK

ROC
Published by New American Library, a division of
Penguin Putnam Inc., 375 Hudson Street,
New York, New York 10014, U.S.A.
Penguin Books Ltd, 80 Strand,
London WC2R 0RL, England
Penguin Books Australia Ltd, Ringwood,
Victoria, Australia
Penguin Books Canada Ltd, 10 Alcorn Avenue,
Toronto, Ontario, Canada M4V 3B2
Penguin Books (N.Z.) Ltd, 182–190 Wairau Road,
Auckland 10, New Zealand

Penguin Books Ltd, Registered Offices:
Harmondsworth, Middlesex, England

First published by Roc, an imprint of New American Library,
a division of Penguin Putnam Inc.

First Printing, September 2002
10 9 8 7 6 5 4 3 2 1

Copyright © S. L. Viehl, 2002
All rights reserved

Cover art by Jerry Vanderstelt
Cover design by Ray Lundgren

ROC REGISTERED TRADEMARK—MARCA REGISTRADA

Printed in the United States of America

Without limiting the rights under copyright reserved above, no part of this
publication may be reproduced, stored in or introduced into a retrieval
system, or transmitted, in any form, or by any means (electronic, mechanical,
photocopying, recording, or otherwise), without the prior written permission
of both the copyright owner and the above publisher of this book.

PUBLISHER'S NOTE
This is a work of fiction. Names, characters, places, and incidents either are
the product of the author's imagination or are used fictitiously, and any
resemblance to actual persons, living or dead, business establishments,
events, or locales is entirely coincidental.

BOOKS ARE AVAILABLE AT QUANTITY DISCOUNTS WHEN USED TO PROMOTE PRODUCTS
OR SERVICES. FOR INFORMATION PLEASE WRITE TO PREMIUM MARKETING DIVISION,
PENGUIN PUTNAM INC., 375 HUDSON STREET, NEW YORK, NEW YORK 10014.

If you purchased this book without a cover you should be aware that this
book is stolen property. It was reported as "unsold and destroyed" to the
publisher and neither the author nor the publisher has received any
payment for this "stripped book."

For my sister, Kimberly Anne,
who knows all about making peace,
and has walked in beauty
every day of her life.
I'm so proud of you.
I love you.
Stay with us, sweetheart.

PART ONE

Contentions

CHAPTER ONE

The *Sunlace*

... and [I] will abstain from every voluntary art of
mischief and corruption, and further from the
seduction of females or males, bond or free. ...
                    —Hippocrates (460?–377? B.C.)

Hippocrates must have never gotten the wife in the
family way, I thought as I felt something tickle my
foot. Or he definitely would have covered baby-sitting
in the oath.

"Okay." I gazed around my operating table. "Who
forgot to secure the door panel?"

That startled the sapphire-skinned Jorenian nurse
manning the prep tray beside me. "Your pardon,
Healer?" Although her eyes were solid white—no
pupils or irises—she wasn't blind.

Neither was I. I pointed down.

Everyone looked down.

A fold of white surgical linen twitched, then someone small and unauthorized giggled.

The whole team tried to keep their blue faces
straight, but if there weren't big grins under every
mask in the room, I was a Hsktskt.

Serving as a thoracic surgeon on board the star vessel *Sunlace*, crewed by my adopted Jorenian family,
HouseClan Torin, was never dull. Squilyp, my boss
and the ship's primary physician/surgeon, had alter-

nated shifts with me and two senior residents so he could devote more time to training the junior residents and interns on staff.

And usually, that wasn't a problem. Usually.

Stuff like this *never* happened to my boss, of course. If the Omorr had been attending, the patient would already be cut open and the procedure half done. That was because Squilyp was still a bachelor and didn't have to deal with inquisitive progeny sneaking in during his operations.

For me, it was the third time that week.

"Marel." I crouched down and flipped up my eye lens to stop my cortgear from recording. "Come out of there."

Another fold moved. "Doan see me. I dibisibow."

I sincerely hoped not. "I have to work now, baby. You can be invisible for me later."

A perfectly perceptible blond head popped out from under the linen. Like me, she was small, Terran, and used to getting her own way. "Be dibisibow *now.*"

I heard a suspicious, choking sound, and whipped up my head. My team became instantly preoccupied with studying the upper deck.

"This is surgery, people, not day care." I lifted the edge of the drape. "Marel, come out of there. *Immediately.*"

She crawled out, stood up, and tried to see over the edge of the table. "Who dad? I see, Mama?" She stretched up her arms. "Me up!"

"No touching." Her small, eager hands were the reason I'd had all the laser rigs raised another foot off the deck. I stripped off my gloves, then pointed to the door panel. "Out."

She planted herself and gave me The Pout. "No, sday."

The Pout usually preceded The Tantrum, so I saved time and everyone's eardrums by picking her up. That ruined my scrub, but she'd already contaminated the entire field. Which reminded me—how had she gotten in here before we'd activated that? By riding on the bottom of the patient's gurney?

"Deactivate sterile field." The bioelectrical bubble enclosing us abruptly vanished. To the team, I said, "Repeat patient prep and give me five minutes."

Marel abandoned The Tantrum and resorted to The Wriggle. Fine blond hair flew in my face, scented with a floral cleanser that always reminded me of Terran vanilla. "Me down!"

"Not a chance, kid." I'd gotten over being afraid I'd drop and break her, but I still kept a firm grip. She was really good at The Wriggle. "What happened to Daddy? Did you conk him over the head with something?"

Mentioning her favorite Terran male turned her into The Dictator. "See Daddy! You dake me, Mama!"

"Oh, we're going to see Daddy, all right." Among the other things I intended to do to my husband. "He should have picked you up from school two hours ago."

She folded her little arms. "Daddy did."

"Yeah, but he lost you again." I didn't have to use a console to find Duncan. The cortical-optical receiver/transmitter—cortgear—I wore was the latest medical tech-wear from Joren. It not only recorded everything I did, but could transmit that to any console on the ship. Very handy, if I wanted to watch an appendectomy from the comfort of my own quarters, but Squilyp was using them mainly as a teaching device. I flipped the lens down and relayed to my quarters.

No answer.

At my second signal, an austere, masculine Omorr face appeared on the inner surface of the lens, an inch from my eye. Handsome, if one preferred males of the tall, pink, and alien variety.

"Yes, Doctor, what . . ."—my boss's dark eyes rounded as I looked at Marel, then the shrouded patient and surgical team behind us—"oh, no. Not again."

Marel giggled and waved at my face.

"Again." I adjusted my daughter's weight on my hip. Though I considered Squilyp partially responsible—after all, he *had* saved Marel after I miscarried by transferring her to an embryonic chamber—he wasn't on after-school duty today. "Where's the guy who did this to me?"

My alien colleague's prehensile gildrells undulated like a long beard of white snakes. "I'll find him."

"Find him fast, Squil. My bilateral hernia can't wait all day."

I removed my cortgear, then carried my daughter out of surgery and sat her down on an exam table. The ward nurses, all of whom were my daughter's personal slaves, wisely stayed away. "Now, Madam, you and I are going to have a little talk."

She tried The Adorable Smile, which displayed all nine of her seed-sized teeth. "Dawk domorrow?"

"Today." I stripped off my mask and surgical gown and tossed them into a nearby disposal bin. "You promised me you wouldn't sneak into surgery anymore, remember?"

Marel nodded slowly.

One of the new Jorenian residents hovered nearby, but he could wait. "What happens when you break a promise?"

"Can pway with 'Sawa." Tears welled up in her big

blue eyes. Fasala Torin, the ClanDaughter of Salo, Chief Operational Officer and Darea, the Head of Administration, was Marel's unofficial big sister. "For a week."

"That's right." Being doused with hydrochloric acid would have been easier than watching her cry, but one glimmer of sympathy and she'd mow me down. "You can't be in surgery when I'm operating on someone. It could make my patient very sick."

"Why?"

That was her favorite word these days. The runner-up was "No."

"Because." I tapped the end of her nose. "You bring germs in with you. We've talked about that, too, so don't claim amnesia."

The resident caught my eye again—one of the new guys, since I couldn't place him. Like ninety-nine percent of the crew, he was over six feet tall, blue skinned, and black haired. Young, too—not a single line or wrinkle marred his handsome face, and no age strands of purple in his long, tidy queue. A modest, silver pictoglyph symbolizing something important and Jorenian hung attached to the side of his vocollar. His immaculate tunic fitted him like he'd been born with it on.

He was also definitely watching us. Why?

"Why?"

Distracted by Marel's echo of my thoughts, I almost grinned. Almost. "The amnesia? Because you haven't figured out how to properly fake the symptoms yet."

Behind her, a door panel opened, and a lean, fair-haired Terran male in plain black garments strode in. The ship's linguist wasn't as tall as the new resident, nor half as bulky, but he moved with a silent, ominous efficiency that made felines look gimpy. An equally lean, one-legged Omorr male followed in his wake, displaying his own rather odd elegance of movement. If you could call all that bouncing my boss did elegant.

"Okay. Here comes the cavalry."

Marel turned to see two of the three males she adored most on the ship, then knuckled her eyes and spontaneously burst into tears. "Daddy . . . Uncwip . . ."

The Heartbroken Sobs had a killer effect—both men looked like she'd hit them over the head with a sledgehammer. My one-man fan club, on the other hand, seemed even more fascinated, and took a couple of steps closer.

The dangerous-looking guy in black was the first to crumble, and had Marel in his arms before I could blink. "It will be well, *avasa*." To me, my husband said, "How did she get in there this time?"

I took a moment to appreciate the picture of tough, battle-scarred Duncan Reever holding our delicate little daughter. "I haven't a clue. She was hiding under the table, a foot from the enviro intake vents." I had nightmares about Marel's fingers getting caught in them, but that wasn't bothering me. The guy now standing just behind my husband was.

"Excuse me," I said to the curious resident, "do you need something?"

"Not directly. Your pardon, ClanCousin, I only wished to inquire about the patient in surgery."

ClanCousin was what most of the Jorenian crew called me, but we'd all served together for a long time. This guy, however, was brand new, and his familiarity bugged me. " 'Healer' will do fine. So will the patient. Why don't you get back to work now?"

He inclined his head and returned to the nurses' station. By then my daughter had worked herself up pretty well, and had both of her slaves trying in vain to calm her down.

"Hush, child, no one is angry with you," Squilyp said, rubbing her back with one of his spade-shaped membranes and a few stray gildrells. He'd come a long way from the guy who had nearly gotten killed after suggesting a half-dead child be disciplined more stringently to prevent future injuries. "We are only concerned with your safety."

Marel hiccuped through a sob. "Why?"

"Don't start that again," I told her.

"Senior Healer, perhaps you could erect some type of barrier outside the entrances to the surgical suites," Reever suggested.

"I've tried several." The Omorr sounded a little annoyed. "They've never even slowed her down."

"Well, think of a solution, *Uncwip*. I can't keep stopping in the middle of cutting because she's sneakier than all the grown-ups on the ship." Marel's sobs dwindled, and I stroked the back of her blond head. "Sweetie, you go with Daddy now. I'll see you tonight."

Reever covered my hand with his for a moment, then carried our daughter out of Medical.

"I'll stay and assist," Squilyp muttered as he stomped over to the cleansing unit with me.

I felt like I'd traded one kid for another. "I think I can be trusted to invert a couple of hernial sacs without perforating the patient's bowel."

That got me a scowl. "Don't be touchy."

"You first."

"I am not . . . I apologize." He stuck his membranes under the sterilizer. "Allow me to assist, if you would."

"It's your show, boss." What had put his face in a mesh? "I just work here."

Our patient, Yarek Torin, was a data archive analyst and lifelong warrior-instructor. Over the years, his dedication to teaching weekly classes in swordsmanship had earned him a great deal of respect from the crew. Waving around all those heavy Jorenian multibladed swords had also given him a pair of direct inguinal hernias, bilaterally opposed on either side of his pelvic bone.

"Reinitiate sterile field," I said as we stepped up to the table and donned our cortgear. "Vitals?"

My assisting intern checked the monitors. "Stable and holding steady, Healer Cherijo."

"Excellent." I powered up the laser rig. "Let's try this again, shall we? Clamp."

Squilyp seemed content to observe, so I made the primary incisions. There were only a few areas on Jorenian bodies that weren't protected by a subdermal layer of cartilage, but unfortunately both sides of the lower pelvis were among them.

"Nurse, a little suction here, please." After opening the patient's external oblique muscle and separating the cord structures from the first hernia sac, I stepped back to let the Omorr make the call. "Invert, or excise?"

He made a huffy sound. "Excise."

I winked. "Just checking."

Once I'd removed the protruding viscera, Squilyp took over and reinforced the site with biomesh, to strengthen the abdominal wall and prevent reoccurrence. The other hernia wasn't large enough to merit excising, so I inverted it and did the same patch work myself. We worked without speaking, except to ask for instruments, but I could almost hear the gears whirling around in the Omorr's busy head.

As we finished suturing up our respective sides of Yarek's lower abdomen, Squilyp finally got chatty. "Let me talk with Marel later. Perhaps I can influence her behavior. She has always responded well to me."

Was that the hair up his olfactory channel? I looked at the Omorr over the edge of my mask. "She's fine, quit worrying. Wait until next revolution—on Terra, we call that stage of development 'the terrible twos.'"

"What do you call the threes?"

"Nothing. We're too busy thanking God we survived the twos."

"I can see why."

I finished the last suture and powered down the laser rig. "Done." I watched him finish, then stripped off my gloves. "Nice work, everyone. Let's move him into post-op now."

As the assisting nurse wheeled Yarek out of the suite, a Lok-Teel oozed down the wall and went to work on the deck. The ambulatory fungus we'd discovered on a slaver depot world had become very handy in Medical. The Lok-Teel absorbed almost any kind of waste and secreted a natural antiseptic by-product that sterilized the surrounding surface. The one we'd brought back had happily divided until its offspring populated every deck, and had integrated themselves into everyday life on the ship.

"Cherijo, I think we should test Marel," Squilyp said as we went to clean up.

Since emerging from Squilyp's prototype embryonic chamber, my daughter had been conspicuously healthy—no viral or bacterial infections, not even a little sniffle. Marel carried half of my bioengineered genes; genes that had doubtless enhanced her immune system.

Among other things. Things I wasn't sure I wanted to find out. "For what?"

The Omorr misinterpreted my reaction. "I would never do anything to harm her."

"I know that. God, she's practically more your kid than mine." I tugged off my outer gear. "I'm serious, what kind of tests are you talking about?"

He removed his cortgear and pulled down his mask. "It would not hurt to run a full series. Her growth rate is two percent below average for a Terran female."

"She has a short mother." Squilyp was famous for becoming obsessively meticulous under stress, but I had a feeling Marel wasn't responsible for his present bad mood. "All right, let me talk to Reever about it."

Once we'd stripped, cleansed, and checked on Yarek, who was doing fine, we retreated to the Senior Healer's office. I dialed up some tea for us and sat in the uncomfortable chair in front of his console. "I hate this chair."

"So does everyone else." He accepted the server with an absent glance. "I'll have it replaced."

I nodded through the viewer at the strange resident, who was updating charts with one of the nurses. "Who's the guy with the pretty necklace?"

"Qonja Torin, a psychiatric resident."

I raised my brows. "We need a psychiatrist around here?"

"They usually serve a portion of their medical rotation in space." He frowned. "Is there a problem with him?"

"No, he's just . . . new."

"After the retrofit on Joren, we obtained more than thirty new crew members—replacements for the crew who chose to stay onplanet." He gestured toward the viewer. "I can assign him to another shift."

"No, I'll get used to him." I steepled my fingers.

"Now why don't you tell me what's got your beard in such a scramble?"

Squilyp seemed surprised by that. "Nothing."

"This is me, Squid Lips. I've seen you go on these Mr. Wonderful binges before, remember?" I grinned at the indignant reaction. "Come on, I'm serious—are the students making you nuts? Need me to take over training for a few rotations?" My first attempt at instructor duty hadn't worked out so well, but I could try again. "I won't browbeat them, I promise."

"That would be rather difficult," he said, "but the interns are not a problem. Neither are the residents. Vlaav is ready to complete his final year requirements, and Adaola shows great natural talent for microsurgery."

I'd thought we'd left all the competitiveness between us in the past, but maybe Squilyp still had some issues. "Is it me?"

"Of course not." He set his tea aside, and spread one appendage end out on his desk. "It's a personal problem unrelated to work." Something made him look, for a moment, very young and unsure of himself. "You wouldn't understand."

I felt sorry for him, but I couldn't let that last part stand. "Squilyp, I'm a fugitive genetic construct on the run from basically everyone in the galaxy. My adopted family are lovely blue people who eviscerate anyone who threatens their relatives—handy in my case, but often nerve wracking. My father was a monster, my genetic twin, and experimented on me for twenty-eight years. My alien-raised husband until recently had no human emotions, and you incubated my daughter in an artificial uterus." I laced my fingers together and rested them on my knee. "Believe me when I tell you, there is *no* personal problem I can't handle."

He eyed me with speculation. "I suppose you'll badger me until I do."

"My reputation"—I shrugged—"has to be upheld."

He began tracing circles on the surface of the desk with one edge of his membrane. "I've been considering pursuing an alternative to my current situation. Certain biological imperatives are involved."

I became immediately wary, with good reason. A certain Jorenian biological imperative had gotten me accidentally betrothed. Twice. Everyone knew Reever and I were exclusive to each other, but it never hurt to be cautious. "Could you be a little more specific about the imperative part?"

"Acting as surrogate father to Marel these past four cycles has given me great satisfaction. It made me realize I've been denying my own personal needs in pursuit of my career."

"And you need . . . ?" I spread out my hands.

"More than I have." He rested his head against the high back of his chair and closed his eyes. "It's time I went home, Cherijo."

Home. I checked on our patient one more time before heading in that direction myself. Yarek was awake, comfortable, and talking with his bondmate, who gladly agreed to my instructions not to let her spouse lift anything heavier than an eating utensil for the next three weeks.

My quarters were on level nine, two decks below Medical, so it was a short walk. Before I reached my door panel, it opened and something small, fast, and blond came darting out.

"Mama! Mama!"

I found my arms full of twenty-two-and-a-half

pounds of Terran kid. "How did you know it was me? It could have been Salo."

"CanUncaw woves me," Marel said with the absolute confidence of a much-adored child. "Daddy knew id you."

My husband came to stand in the doorway. Somehow he always knew it was me, too. "Daddy's radar is pretty neat, isn't it?"

Reever gave me one of his rare, spontaneous smiles—something Marel had taught him. "She has been asking me to signal you every five minutes for the last hour."

"Miss Impatience," I said as I went into my husband's embrace. Marel wiggled and laughed between us. "So what's for dinner?"

While Reever prepared our meal, I took a quick shower and dressed. As I came to the table, I thought of what Squilyp had told me.

He can't quit and go home. We need him.

Over dinner, we talked about work, and Marel informed us what she'd done in day school. Once we'd finished, our resident Lok-Teel oozed over to clean up the scraps while we went into our living area for family time. Marel had already begun tackling the elementary Terran reading texts at school, so we listened to her read every night.

" 'See Max run.' " Marel traced her fingertip over the display of a little Terran dog. "Mama, we ged a Max?"

"No, sweetie. We've already got Jenner and Juliet," I reminded her, nodding at the two felines presently curled up under the table at our feet. My Terran cats had wasted no time in consummating their brief romance, and as a result Juliet had a nice, fat tummy. "They don't like Maxes."

She pouted a little. "I wan one."

"You, Madam, want everything." I tugged her into my arms. "How about a bath instead?"

Marel caught my neck in a stranglehold. "With buh-buhs?"

"Absolutely with bubbles."

Bathtime was another task that required full-family participation. Reever's job was to keep Marel, the bubbles, and her bath toys in the small oval tank we'd recently installed. Mine was to apply cleanser where needed, scrub, and rinse.

Marel's job was to make all this as difficult as possible.

Finally, glowing pink and yawning, our daughter toddled off to her room. Both cats were already waiting on her small sleeping platform to curl up with her.

"Sleep well, *avasa*," Duncan said as he kissed Marel and tucked her in. "You are my delight."

"You mine wide do, Daddy." Marel peeked over the edge of the bright blue linens at me. "Sorry I noddy doday, Mama."

"No, you're not." That made her giggle, and I smoothed some fine golden strands back from her now-green eyes. "Good night, baby."

We turned down the optics as we went out and I dropped on the sofa. "How did she get away from you today? Was she even at school?"

"I picked her up as usual, then put her down for her afternoon sleep interval. When I checked on her a few minutes later, she was gone." My husband eased down beside me, and began unwinding my braid. "I went to see if she had slipped out to visit Fasala."

I rubbed my cheek against his hand. "Can't we put a bell on her or something?"

"We used bells for the cats." Reever's mouth

touched my cheek, then drifted over to my ear. "A small proximity transmitter would be more efficient."

"Get some. I'll attach them to her play clothes." I pulled open the front of his tunic as an image of Marel and a little Omorr playing together flashed behind my eyes. *Wouldn't that be something to see.*

Duncan stopped kissing me and drew back. "Squilyp wants a child?"

"Hey." I whacked his bare chest with my hand. "You promised me you wouldn't *do* that anymore."

"I didn't link with you. You projected to me."

"Yeah, right." I glared as I felt him slipping into my mind. Sometimes being married to a telepath was a pain. *Don't say anything about this; he told me in confidence.*

Proliferation is a natural desire. Reever's thoughts echoed inside my head as he completed the link. *The Omorr need not suppress his biological needs, or be ashamed of them.*

It's a little more complicated than that, Duncan. He's been suppressing going into season to avoid this for a couple of years now, and that has to stop. Also, he needs an Omorr female, so he'll have to go home and get one. Not to mention all the endless contract negotiations involved with Squilyp choosing a mate. Apparently, on his homeworld, marriage was about as much fun as working out a cease-fire between warring armies.

You don't want him to leave.

Sheer laziness. I don't want to be Senior Healer again. I worked his tunic off and ran my hands up his arms. *I have other priorities now. Like finding out how you're going to lure me from this sofa to our sleeping platform.*

His hands framed my face as he ended the link. "That will require minimum effort."

"Hey. Maybe I'm not that easy," I said, slightly miffed.

He slid his hands in my hair and pressed his mouth over mine. When we came up for air, my hands were in his hair, and I'd somehow gone from sitting beside him to straddling him.

So I was easy. Big deal.

He stroked his hands over my back, and cupped my hips. "Are you still averse to the thought of moving to our sleeping platform?"

I nipped the edge of his jaw as I rocked slowly against his lap, and the very solid, very enticing anatomical changes down there. "Maybe."

He stood up, lifting me with him. "I will have to convince you to think otherwise."

"Yes." I wrapped my arms around his neck. "Convince me, love."

He would have, too, if a signal hadn't come in over the console.

I sighed. "It could be Medical."

With gratifying reluctance, Reever put me down so I could answer it. The image that appeared on the vid wasn't relayed from Medical Bay, however. Complex navigational equipment appeared behind a stern blue face. Like many of the crew, my ClanBrother Xonea Torin wore his long black hair in a warrior's knot. Unlike them, he got to wear a dark gray Captain's flight-suit.

"You were to report to my office after your shift," he said, sounding mildly peeved.

"Sorry, I forgot." And I was—I'd been making an effort to be more punctual lately. "Can we reschedule for tomorrow morning?"

"That would be when you are to report to the departmental staff meeting." His white eyes shifted and focused on a spot behind me. "Perhaps Duncan can persuade you to program a reminder alarm."

"I will see to it. Good night, Captain." Reever reached over and shut off the console.

"That was kind of rude," I said as he picked me up again.

"If Xonea wishes courtesy, he can signal our quarters at a more reasonable hour." He dropped me on our sleeping platform before securing the door panel and joining me. "It seems you require a great deal of persuasion in several areas."

I forgot about the Captain and arched under his hands. "Then you'll just have to put in a little overtime."

I made up for missing the appointment with Xonea by making it to the staff meeting on time. Barely.

I smothered a yawn as I sipped my herbal tea and took my place at the oval conference table. Department heads from every section on the ship gathered here to discuss everything from reassignment of personnel to proposed sojourns. As Senior Healer, Squilyp should have been here, not me, but Xonea had specifically requested I attend.

Individual departmental requests were presented first, and my attention drifted. I thought about the Omorr's decision to leave the ship, and how everyone would assume I'd take over Medical. Only problem was that my life and my priorities had changed since the first time I'd joined this crew. Becoming Senior Healer meant more time away from Marel, and we'd already been separated since her birth. I didn't want to miss any more of her life than I had to. And then there was Duncan.

"Cherijo."

I dragged my thoughts back to the meeting I was supposed to be paying attention to, and noticed everyone seated around the table was staring at me. "Sorry, what?"

Xonea gestured toward the star chart he'd holoprojected in the center of the room. "This is our intended route to reach the Liacos Quadrant. What say you our first sojourn be for Taerca?"

There were two other stops planned on our journey, but I had some reasons to want to delay those. "Sounds good to me."

"I know little about my father's homeworld." My half-human friend Hawk, who had given up life in the alien underground to help me and Reever escape Terra, sounded uneasy. Then again, it was hard to sit in a chair when you had fifteen-foot wings to contend with. "Perhaps we should make the journey another time."

That meant jaunting to Dhreen's homeworld, Oenrall, or trying to find Maggie's homeworld, Jxinok. Dhreen's people were suffering from some mysterious disease he still hadn't defined for anyone, and Maggie—the only mother I'd ever known—was a manipulative alien who had implanted subliminal messages in my brain and possibly meddled in my creation. "I vote for Taerca."

"It is the logical choice." Salo, Fasala's ClanFather and second in command, punched up another, more convoluted route on the chart. "Should we jaunt to Oenrall first, we would have to double back, adding ten rotations to our journey." He glanced at the empty chair where Dhreen should have been sitting. "I would not advise we linger in this region. League traders have established trade routes in this quadrant."

The same League who would pay major credits to anyone who captured me.

"Let them attack," Xonea said, sitting back and studying the chart. "We are well equipped to deal with whoever challenges us."

Maybe my vocollar wasn't translating right. "Excuse me, but I thought our policy was *not* to deal with these people."

"The Ruling Council has ruled in favor of retaliation."

This was news. I knew my ClanBrother preferred to stand and fight, but now he had his homeworld's blessing? "What kind of retaliation are we talking about, Captain?"

Xonea nodded to Salo, and a schematic of the *Sunlace* replaced the Liacos star chart. "The retrofit we underwent on Joren included the installation of aft and stern sonic cannons. Secondary buffers now reinforce each level, and Engineering has relocated the stardrive, helm, and weapons control, which have also been fitted with autonomous power and fuel cells. All engagement-response systems now have alternate backups duplicated in a different area of the ship."

Cannons. Secondary buffers. Engagement-response systems. Nice way to refer to tech created solely to destroy life. I didn't like it, but the Jorenians had the right to defend themselves. Especially since I was the magnet drawing all those bounty-hungry mercenaries toward the ship.

"So the new policy is what? We defend ourselves, disable the other guys, and leave?"

"We will not turn our backs to our enemies," Salo said in that quiet, ominous warrior way. "Not before the House, in the flesh or in space."

The Captain nodded. "Thus decrees the Ruling Council of Joren."

Something twisted in my stomach. I knew a lot

about Jorenian customs, and this new policy went way beyond what had been permitted before. "They said you could declare ClanKill on attacking ships?"

"In essence, yes. The decision remains solely a Captain's prerogative." Xonea smiled, and it wasn't pleasant. "I shall decide whom we pursue."

"Terrific." The one guy on the ship with the biggest chip on his shoulder as far as the League was concerned now had his government's blessing to hunt down and destroy his enemies. With a ship that had over a hundred children on board.

Including mine.

CHAPTER TWO

Engagement Response

Reminding everyone about how vulnerable we were with children on board had defeated Xonea's pro-military agenda before; maybe it would again. "What about our kids?"

"I anticipated your concern." Xonea made a slightly ironic gesture. "Combat training and battle drills for the crew and their young ones will be held on a regular basis."

"Warrior training for the children?" My voice climbed an octave. "Do you have a head injury I don't know about?"

"They will be taught to defend the House." My ClanBrother gave me a stern look. "As will you, Healer."

Before I could pick my jaw up off the conference table, Salo helped the Captain railroad me. "Training schedules shall be decided at our next meeting, after the related programming has been examined." He passed down a stack of discs to me. "Healer Cherijo will perform the inspection."

Healer Cherijo was about to perform some lobotomies. "I'll get out my white gloves."

That left only the unfinished discussion of where to go, and everyone voted to head straight for Taerca. The meeting adjourned, but Xonea left before I could corner him. Not that I was worried. People who avoided me usually regretted it.

Combat training. For children. For Marel. I stalked out. *Over my dead body.*

Hawk caught up with me outside. "You are upset, Cherijo?"

Steam should have been pouring out of my ears. "My daughter is only a year old, Hawk. I'd rather she not learn to rip out someone's intestines until she's done cutting her baby teeth."

"Let me carry those." He took the discs from me. "The Captain can't teach that to the children. Marel is not large nor strong enough to kill."

I scoffed. "You've never witnessed one of her tantrums."

"I have, ClanCousin." The new resident, Qonja, caught up with us. "Such sophisticated methods of manipulation as she displayed yesterday, at this developmental stage—"

"Wait." I held up one hand. "Who are you talking about?"

"I was speaking of your ClanDaughter." He made a gesture used to display concern for a close family member. One he had no business flashing at me. "I have several theories regarding her behavioral aberrations."

"Do you?" My temper, never a very shy or retiring thing, had been tugging at its mental chains all morning. Links began to snap. "You know, I'd love to hear them, but there's just this one problem."

His brow furrowed. "What is it?"

"I was having a *private* conversation here. As in, it's none of your business. Go *away.*"

Now he looked completely baffled. "Your pardon, but I merely wish to point out—"

All the chains snapped. *"Get lost!"*

Hawk's wings arched as he moved in between me and the psych resident. "Shall I notify Security?"

"That is not necessary." For a Jorenian, Qonja seemed extraordinarily obtuse. "I believe I have valuable insights to contribute to this dialogue."

"I don't. Take a hike." With that I spun on my heel and strode away with Hawk. Once I made sure our shadow hadn't followed us, I sighed. "That guy is really obnoxious. How can he be from Joren?"

"He seems very eager for your approval."

Perhaps that was all it was—a little misplaced hero worship. "Speaking of approval, why are you so jittery about going to see your dad?"

"He left Terra before my birth." His troubled expression returned. "My mother died soon after, and my grandparents despised him."

"Terrans are xenophobes," I reminded him. "Why did he leave?"

"The Planetary Residential Commission deported him. My mother forced my grandparents to vow to care for me." He hesitated. "Cherijo, why is the Captain doing this?" I thought Jorenians avoided violence."

"They do, unless someone attacks their kin. Then they hunt them down and kill them—no matter how long it takes. No second chances, no mercy." I thought of the ritual ClanKill I'd seen performed in the past, and shuddered. "This ruling takes it to a whole new level."

"Is that bad?"

"Xonea has permission to go after an attacking ship, with possibly thousands of people on board. People who are simply doing their job. He won't stop until he kills them all."

"Oh." He fluttered his wings for a moment. "The Jorenians are truly obsessed with revenge."

"It's just a little thing." I waved a hand. "When they're not disemboweling an enemy, they're really very nice people." I thought of the nosy resident. "With a few exceptions."

I left Hawk at his duty station, and checked my wristcom. I had another couple of hours before my shift, but I felt too restless to go home to my empty quarters.

"Cherijo."

I watched as Xonea approached. Apparently, it was my morning to be annoyed by everyone. "That was some meeting."

He studied my expression. "I thought you might be angry with me."

"Aren't you psychic?" I took a deep, cleansing breath. "Let's do this later, when I don't feel like knocking you through a wall panel."

"I will give you a brief demonstration of the combat training we intend for our younger crew members, and all will be well between us."

"You can do the show-and-tell for Squilyp." I shoved the discs in his hands. "I am *not* going to be involved with this inspection nonsense."

He didn't like that, and shoved them back. "You refuse to understand my point of view."

"I'm a doctor, Xonea. I understand perfectly." I planted my hand on my hip. "Most of the surgery I performed when I was Senior Healer was as a result of attacks on this ship. Actually, I don't know why I'm complaining—if you kill everyone before they get to Medical, I can take some vacation time."

"You are part of HouseClan Torin, Cherijo."

So now it was down to emotional blackmail. "I took an oath to do no harm first."

"Your oath will not protect your daughter."

Somehow he knew my maternal instinct was just as ferocious as the Jorenian need to protect the House-Clan. But then, they hadn't elected Xonea Captain for nothing.

"All right." I gave up. "Show me what you've got."

Thirty minutes later, Xonea finished running the last of the juvenile combat-training simulations in the environome, and shut down the program. "What say you now, ClanSister?"

"Besides uncomplimentary things about your lineage?"

He grinned. "You would not insult our ClanParents so."

"Don't push me, pal." I finished skimming over the last of the training text from a data pad. "Okay, I'll admit, they're very clever."

Rather than try to fight, each child would be assigned a "safe place" where they would go during an attack on the ship. If someone boarded the ship and tried to grab them, they could disable their attackers by hitting them with a pressure infuser disguised as a wrist ornament. To prevent accidental injections, the wrist units would only function after an activation signal was sent out from Command.

However, the compound used *in* the wrist units was the reason why Xonea needed Medical's blessing.

"Tell me one thing—why use drugs instead of some kind of zap ray or toxic poison?"

"Your report detailing the methods you used to liberate the Hsktskt slave depot inspired the idea." My ClanBrother popped out the program disc and handed it to me. "I thought you might approve, as this method does not kill the attacker."

"No, it only paralyzes and renders them completely helpless for several hours. Convenient, if you want to rip their intestines out without a lot of fuss and mess." I wondered if Squilyp would sign off on this, and how much trouble I'd get in for punching out my boss if he did. "What if the attacker simply tries to shoot the kids?"

"All children will be assigned a drone unit, which will be programmed to escort them to their safe place, secure, and guard them." At my expression, he made a quick gesture. "I know it is not infallible, but it is the best we can do at present. Will you test the adult program with me now?"

I certainly felt like beating up something. Might as well be the guy responsible for that. "Sure." When he put on cortgear, I frowned. "Do you have to record it?"

"Indulge me."

Another hour passed—this one much more attention intensive—then I finally pushed myself up from the practice mat and called it quits. "What are you doing to me? I don't remember it hurting this much when I sparred with you two years ago."

Xonea dried the sweat from his face and chest with his tunic. "I am throwing you harder."

My abused muscles made me groan. "Gee, thanks."

"Your physical condition has improved." He helped me to my feet. "Stretch. It will help."

As I went through the limbering exercises that obsessed him, Xonea walked around me, sizing me up. "You have regained the weight you lost, and your muscle tone appears more defined."

"That mean I'm in better shape?"

"Yes. Your reflexes and response time have improved." He took off his cortgear. "Have you spoken to the Oenrallian about the crisis on his homeworld?"

"Not yet."

Dhreen, the alien pilot who had taken me to my first offworld position at the colony on Kevarzangia Two, was not in my good books altogether yet. He'd started out pretending to be my friend while spying on me for Joseph Grey Veil. Although he had redeemed himself by helping me and Reever escape Terra, I still had my doubts.

So did Xonea. "He has been avoiding staff meetings since returning to the ship from Terra. Talk to him, if you would, and discover what you can. Report back to me."

Xonea and Dhreen had been good friends, once upon a time, but the Oenrallian's deception had put him on the Torins' persona non grata list. "If it turns out to be safe for us, do you still intend to go there?"

"As long as the sojourn presents no threat to the crew, yes."

I wiped a streak of sweat from my cheek. "And this combat training? You're really going to make me do it?"

"You serve as a member of my crew." He tossed me his tunic. "As such, you will fulfill all training requirements."

I blotted my face. "I liked pilot training better, and I was awful at that. I mean, look at me." I waved a hand around. "I'd make a lousy warrior. You *know* that."

"Your size remains your greatest disadvantage. If you would agree to train with bladed weapons—"

"She already knows how to use them."

I swiveled around to see Reever standing just inside the door panel. "Only when I can't get my hands on a lascalpel. Hi, Duncan. What are you doing here?"

"Looking for you," my husband said as he leaned back against the panel and regarded my ClanBrother. "Why is my wife wiping her face with your garment, Xonea?"

"We're just sparring," I told him.

Now he looked at me. "For what purpose?"

"I'm going to be inspecting the new combat-training programs Xonea has lined up for the crew." I nodded toward the console. "This was just a trial run."

"I will need the inspection completed within the next week," my ClanBrother said.

Reever folded his arms. "Indeed. Have you relieved Cherijo of her Medical duties, to provide time to complete the assignment?"

Xonea glanced at me. "I was not aware that I needed to."

"I'll talk to Squilyp about switching some shifts with me." I walked over to the door panel, and took my husband's arm. "Let's go. See you later, Xonea."

For a moment, I didn't think Reever was going to budge. Then, with a small nod toward my ClanBrother, he left the environome and entered the gyrlift with me.

As soon as the doors closed, I started on him. "Correct me if I'm wrong, but I get the impression you don't think I can handle this."

Reever stopped the lift. "Xonea knows you are already overloaded with your responsibilities in Medical, and yet he gives you more work."

"Xonea isn't the issue here. I am. I'll take care of my job." I started the lift again. "I'm not your slave anymore, Reever. Try to remember that."

"You were never any good at it when you were." He touched my cheek with one finger, tracing something. "I do not like seeing his bruises on your skin."

"Good thing I heal fast, then." The lift stopped, and

I got off with him. "Look, these programs are going to be used for training the children. I need to make sure they're safe. Plus, it wouldn't hurt for me to learn a little self-defense."

"I will protect you and Marel."

"Uh-huh." My mouth curled. "And what about when you're tied up saving someone's planet or something?"

He dropped his hand. "I will show you what to do."

I didn't want that. Reever and I had spent too many years at odds with each other already. Sparring together would only create a whole new set of problems. "Xonea plans to make everyone undergo this training. Like the pilot program. You had no problem with me learning how not to crash a launch."

He stopped in front of the computer archives section, where he was currently working on updating the ship's linguistic database. "I was scheduled to report for duty five minutes ago."

"So you're late. Let them give you a tardy slip."

"I have much to think about, *Waenara*. May we discuss this later?"

I'd lived with him long enough to know the polite formality was a smoke screen. I'd loved him long enough for it to hurt when he shut me out like this. "Duncan—"

He rested a finger against my lips. "I am not angry with you, nor do I think of you as my property. I am only concerned with Xonea's intentions."

That thawed the rest of my internal frost layer. "He only wants what's best."

"As do I." He kissed me, the way he would Marel, on the forehead. "Until tonight, wife."

As I watched him go, I heard someone else moving away from me in the opposite direction. I turned my head in time to see someone in a resident's green tunic disappear into the unoccupied gyrlift.

I confronted Qonja Torin in his quarters a few minutes later. Having to wait for another gyrlift hadn't improved my mood.

The resident, on the other hand, acted very surprised to see me. "Healer Cherijo." He stepped aside and indicated I should enter.

I did, and waited for the door panel to close before I attacked. "Why are you following me?"

He went over to the food prep unit. "Would you care for tea? I have programmed some Terran blends."

"I'd like an answer. Now."

"Of course. Just a moment." Qonja prepped a single server, then came over to sit in front of me. Very natural, as if he stalked people every day. "I am interested in crew behavior."

Ice chips wouldn't have melted in his mouth. "But you're not following *them* around."

"You are a prepossessing subject." He took a data pad from the table between us. "I have been observing and recording your interactions for some time. It is most engrossing."

I wondered how engrossing he'd find having a server dumped over his head. "Really."

"Your parenting methods, for example." He switched the pad to "display," and turned it to show me. Jorenian pictographs crowded the small screen. "Your approach is quite unique."

"You're *documenting* all this?" I swiped the pad and checked the file. He had pages of notes. "Why?"

"As I have said"—he spread his hands out—"I find you absolutely riveting."

Either he was joking, which wasn't funny, or he was

serious, which was worse. I pressed a key, erased the entire pad, then tossed it back to him. "Don't ever do this again."

"I mean no harm to you, ClanCousin."

I went to the door panel. "You're here to study medicine, resident, not me. Is that clear?"

"As you wish." He came after me. "May I make one request?"

"No." Out I went.

As Marel was still in school, I opted to change out of my sweat-stained tunic before I talked to the other problem child on the ship.

I found Dhreen in central launch bay, working beneath one of the shuttles. Kneeling by his feet was Ilona Red Faun, the Navajo girl who had once been my clone-brother's lover.

"Is he making you hand him the tools?"

Beautiful dark eyes that had been adoringly fixed on Dhreen's oversized feet flashed toward me, and filled with feminine suspicion.

"No, patcher. I offered to help."

We weren't friends, Ilona and I—more like uneasy allies. After Jericho had nearly beaten her to death for betraying his underground to the League, I'd saved her life and hid her from my clone-brother. She and Dhreen had subsequently become lovers, but I secretly doubted there was any love on her side of the arrangement. Ilona Red Faun had been raised to do whatever it took to survive, and evidently she thought that required belonging to a man.

Oh, knock it off, Cherijo, one of my inner voices chided. *Like you and Reever are role models for normal relationships.*

"You'd better watch him—he'll make you work overtime."

"I will remember that." The graceful Indian girl rose to her feet. She'd traded her customary two-piece Navajo *biil* garments for a pilot's flightsuit, and had looped her two long dark braids into a gleaming, woven crown. Dhreen's promise-to-marry earring, according to Oenrallian custom, sparkled at the top of her right ear, where she'd pierced it through the auricle. "What brings you here?"

"I need Dhreen for a minute, if you can spare him."

The Oenrallian was already crawling out from under the shuttle. Like Ilona, he also wore a flightsuit, but grime and some kind of blackish fluid spattered his. Short, pumpkin-colored hair stood on end around two short, red nubs that served as his ears. Sort of. He had pallid skin with the faint, yellowish tinge of good health, and big, innocent-looking amber eyes. A less-sparkly, male version of Ilona's ear bauble encircled one of his almost-ears. For some reason, every time I saw it, I thought it should be looped through his nose.

Dhreen grabbed a cloth as he got to his feet and wiped his hands, but his spoon-shaped fingers needed a thorough scrubbing. "Hey, Doc." He flashed a grin. "What's developing?"

"I need to discuss the situation on Oenrall with you."

His grin faltered for a moment, then he scanned the area. There were a handful of other crew members working around us. "We should chat in my accommodations."

A need for privacy. Not promising. "All right, but if this is another song and dance, Dhreen, I'm going to strangle you."

"Give me another blip. I have to cap off this beam emitter. Ilona, go inside and shut down the power cells." He crawled back under the hull. "Doc, would you hand me that hand welder?"

I looked down at the pile of tools beside his footgear. "What's a welder?"

"It looks like one of your suture lasers."

I picked up a black-handled tool that vaguely resembled the medical instrument and bent to show it to him. "This thing?"

"That's it." He reached out to take it, his spoon-shaped fingers closing around mine.

Without warning, the ship destabilized, and the tilt threw me forward against the shuttle. Something blew, then a burst of light and heat swept up my arm as Dhreen shouted. Smoke poured out from under the shuttle, and Ilona staggered out just as the ship righted itself. I was flung backward onto the deck.

"Healer, shut it off!" she shouted.

The tool in my hand was busily burning a hole into the shuttle's hull, but before I could react, the beam shut off by itself. I put it down, then saw a narrow stream of orange blood seeping from under the shuttle.

"Dhreen!"

Ilona crouched down beside me. "What have you done to him?"

"Nothing. Something exploded." I crawled under, coughing on the smoke. Dhreen wasn't moving. "Come on, help me get him out!"

Between us, we managed to drag him out onto the deck. The front of his tunic was smoldering, so I tore it open, and found a two-inch entry wound in his right lateral chest. Dark-orange arterial blood pumped out onto his abdomen and formed a spreading pool under his shoulders. "Signal Medical—hurry!"

"You shot him!" She jumped on me instead, wrapping a strong arm around my neck and jerking my head back by the hair. "I'll kill you!"

Having my air cut off made protecting Dhreen's body and breaking her hold a challenge. "It . . . was . . . an accident!" I dug my hands in, breaking the choke hold, then pushed hard with my legs. It threw us both backward, with me landing on top of her.

I scrambled up, panting and furious, and when she launched herself at me again, I grabbed her by one braid and slapped her as hard as I could. By that time the launch bay crew had rushed over to us. "Somebody take her and signal Medical for me!"

She held a hand to her face and muttered vile things in Navajo as one of the engineers led her away.

I went back to work on Dhreen. In the background, I heard a voice say, "Medical, emergency, central launch bay. Pilot Dhreen has been wounded."

One of the other pilots knelt beside me. "How serious are his injuries, Healer? Shall we transport him to Medical for you?"

"Really bad, but wait for the team." I pressed my ear to his chest. Judging from the gurgling breath sounds and the irregular cardiac rhythm, whatever had blasted the hole in his chest had also punctured the Oenrallian's lung/heart on the right side. I kept one hand jammed down on the wound as I rolled him onto his side. From the size of the exit wound, it must have nailed the right hepatic lobe, too. "Signal Medical again. Tell them to prep a cardiothoracic team."

"You're not operating on him," Ilona hissed from several feet away. "You did this to him!"

"Someone had better, and soon, or he's not going to make it."

The Senior Healer and a medevac team got to the launch bay at about the same time I'd slowed the bleeding with makeshift pressure dressings on either side of the wound.

Squilyp bent down to help me transfer Dhreen onto the gurney. "Gods, Cherijo. How did this happen?"

"Something hit him with a point-blank pulse blast to the lower lateral chest with a thirty degree up angle. Massive cardiopulmonary trauma and liver damage. Scan him." Beneath the fingers I had pressed to his throat, I felt Dhreen's pulse fading. "He's flagging. Move it, people!"

Ilona abruptly went nuts, and flung herself at me again. "You've killed him!"

One of the engineers dragged her away. Then the Omorr and I pushed Dhreen's gurney out into the corridor. On the way to Medical, I initiated the infuser line as Squilyp continuously scanned his vitals.

"Extensive residual pressure damage in the soft tissue and viscera of the upper torso," Squilyp said, and handed me a syrinpress. I injected Dhreen with adrenalisine to help his traumatized lung/heart keep pumping. "What was he working on?"

"Some emitter thing under a shuttle, but I was handing him a laser tool when the ship rocked. It may have accidentally gone off." We guided the gurney around a corner and through the main entrance panel to Medical. "Surgical team prepped?"

"Scrubbed and waiting for you."

"Us. I can't patch up this many holes by myself." Sweat stung my eyes. "We've got to work fast, too."

"Go scrub." Squilyp nudged me toward the cleansing unit. "I'll get started in surgical and trans him to the machine." He paused. "Put your cortgear on. We need to make a record of this."

"Your students can read a text."

"It's not for my students," he said, then hopped away.

As I passed my hands under the sterilizer port, I was shocked to see them trembling.

I thought of OverSeer FurreVa, the Hsktskt guard who had become my friend during my days as a slave doctor on Catopsa. I'd lost her to the same kind of injury, after she'd taken a blast meant for me.

No way was I letting Dhreen go that way.

I remembered the cortgear and clamped the unit over my head as I rushed into the surgical suite, where the team had the Oenrallian on the procedure table. Squilyp was transitioning Dhreen's body from his own lung/heart to the machine which would perform the same functions for him while I repaired the damage.

He looked so damn young, lying there. Like a little boy. And I could smell him—that not-quite pineapple mixed with chocolate smell filled my head. I clenched my hands into fists for a moment, then gloved. "Report."

"Hypoperfused but prominent jugular venous distention," the Omorr said. "I can't get him over on the machine."

I stopped feeling guilty and became furious. "He's going into cardiac shock. God*damn* it." I yanked the table scanner over his chest. "Compression's coming from the pericardium. Great. Cardiac tamponade. Just what we needed."

"Fluid bolus?" the Omorr asked me.

"No time. Number four chest aspirator." I held out a hand, and the instrument nurse slapped the big needle onto my palm. With a hard push I stabbed it through the wall of Dhreen's chest until I penetrated the smooth membrane surrounding his lung/heart. Immediately the aspirator's empty reservoir began to fill up with bloody fluid. So much had accumulated inside the pericardium that the membrane was literally crushing the organ that it was supposed to protect.

Once I finished the aspiration, I withdrew the needle. "Make sure we've got plenty of Oenrallian whole blood synthesized; we're going to need it." I looked toward the head of the table. Vlaav was manning the anesthesia rig. "Status?"

"He's leveling, Doctor, but his vitals remain borderline," the Saksonan said.

"Can't be helped. Squilyp?"

"Almost there." The Omorr finished inducting the arterial lines that would supply Dhreen with oxygen and pump his blood. "Ready."

I powered up the lascalpel rig and made the initial midline incision with one stroke. Every order I gave was clipped with impatience. "Clamp. Get those ribs out of my way. Suction."

Once the blood and tissue fragments had been cleared from the chest cavity, I stopped Dhreen's cardiopulmonary organ and switched him over to the lung/heart machine, then inspected the damage. A large, clean perforation ran straight through his liver and into his lung/heart on the cardiac side. Because Oenrallians breathe with the same organ that pumps the blood through their bodies, he had in essence collapsed both lung and heart.

"Dhreen, you'd better not die on me," I told his unconscious face, "because you still owe me a hundred credits for that last whump-ball game I won."

My boss took a position on the other side of the table and studied the mess. "Acoustic inhomogeneity refracted the blast wave, judging by the tissue displacement."

"We'll deal with that later." I carefully suctioned the

pooled blood out of his delicate cadiac sacs and began removing several bits of scorched tunic that had lodged in the wound. "You'd better get that bleeding in the liver under control. Cauterize and suture if it's clean."

Plugging the holes in his lung/heart wasn't enough. I had to piece back together the internal bronchial structures that had been ruptured by the point-blank shot first. He'd lost too much tissue for a normal repair job on the cardiac structures as well. "I'm going to have to use a pericardial graft to fix the ventricular sacs and install a triventricular assist device for the interim." I glanced down at Squilyp's membranes, which were busily sewing the two halves of Dhreen's liver back together. "How's it look?"

"The shot exited the liver through the hepatic flexure." He tossed aside a suture laser and asked for suction. "I've debrided and litigated the enterotomies. Left lobe is intact and functional." Squilyp peered into his scope. "I can't resect the flexure."

"You'd make a defect the size of Texas if you did. Anastomose with the primary and tertiary hepatic vessels."

The Omorr lifted his face from the viewer. "The tertiary's too narrow."

"Damn." I finished removing a piece of the smooth membrane surrounding Dhreen's lung/heart for the graft and set it on a sterile procedure tray before stepping around the table to look in the endoscope myself. "Do it anyway. We'll find a way to keep it functional until I can clone a new liver."

Behind his view lens, one dark eye narrowed. "That is very risky."

"Have you got any other options?" I flung a hand toward the open cavity. "I mean, show me what *doesn't* have a hole blasted through it!"

Vlaav cleared his throat. "Doctor. Vitals are falling into red range."

"Right. Plug them together for now, Squilyp." I trotted back around the table to perform the cardiac graft. "Suture laser."

Several hours later, Squilyp and I trudged out of the surgical suite, both of us liberally splattered with Dhreen's blood. Although he was out of immediate danger, we had a real problem on our hands.

Dhreen's lung/heart had been badly damaged, but his liver was basically totaled.

"Even with the TriVAD in place, those sacs may atrophy," the Omorr said as he cleaned up at the scrub unit beside me. "The anastomosis won't keep his liver functioning more than a few days. How long to clone a new organ?"

"A week. Maybe two." I stripped off my gloves and splashed my face with cold water. "He won't survive that long, which means we have to find a transplant."

"With the ship two weeks away from Oenrall? Unlikely." Squilyp shook off his membranes. Someone made a polite sound behind us, and he straightened. "What do you want, resident?"

"Some manners," I muttered as I brushed past Qonja and headed for the Omorr's office.

The Senior Healer conferred with the psych resident for a minute before he joined me. "It's a shame you couldn't bring back one of the hypercellular injectors from Terra."

"Yeah, I know." I thought of Reever. "You should have seen how those cells rebuilt Duncan's kidney." I decided not to tell the Omorr about my little chat with the resident. Though the Boy Shrink and I might need

to have another one. Soon. "Why don't we try to construct one ourselves?"

Squilyp finished fastening his fresh tunic. "I can
biopsy your husband's organ and perform a microcellular analysis. The device itself would be simple to
duplicate; all we need are the organic components of
the replacement cells."

I tried to imagine Reever agreeing to that. My husband was only squeamish about one thing, and it just
happened to be surgery. "I'll talk him."

My boss left to check on Dhreen, while I stayed behind and wrote up the surgical notes. Xonea came in
when I was about finished. Flanking him were two
armed security guards. All three appeared mildly distressed. "Problem, Captain?"

"Ilona Red Faun claims you shot Dhreen."

"Did she?" I went around him and sat behind the
desk. It was better than kicking it across the room. "I
didn't know she had X-ray vision. Or is that shuttle's
hull transparent on the bottom? Because she was inside
it when Dhreen was injured."

"Cherijo." Xonea made a gesture of frustration. "Tell
me what happened, and all will be made simple."

I sighed. "I'm not sure. Dhreen was working on
something, and asked me for a laser welder. When I
handed it to him, the ship tilted, and I was knocked off
balance. Who rocked the ship, by the way?"

"A stabilizer failed. The problem was corrected immediately."

"Not soon enough for Dhreen." I thought of the hole
I'd burned in the hull. "It's possible I triggered that
welding tool by accident. I'm not sure."

"The Terran female claims she heard you threaten
Dhreen just before the incident."

I recalled my threat to strangle him. "It was a joke, Xonea."

Xonea seemed really miserable now. "Cherijo, in light of Dhreen's condition, I must treat the threat as serious."

After everything we'd been through, he really thought I'd shot Dhreen. "For God's sake, I was handing him a tool! Besides, if I wanted him dead, why would I spend the last six hours working on him in surgery?"

Squilyp came in, carrying a stack of charts. "Cherijo, I have a—" He skidded to a halt when he saw the armed guards and Xonea. "What is the meaning of this?"

"Stupidity should be painful, and I should get a job in the galley." I chuffed out some air. "Guess who they think tried to kill Dhreen?"

"You? That's ridiculous; it was an accident." The Omorr thumped down the charts and treated the Captain to one of his iciest glares. "We're physicians. We don't shoot people. We heal them."

"Thank you. Nice to know *someone* has faith in me." I folded my arms and turned to Xonea. "What happens now? You put me in restraints? Throw me in a cell?"

"I must investigate the scene and interview Dhreen." The Captain gestured toward the critical care unit. "When will he recover from his injuries?"

"Hard to say. Today. Tomorrow. Never. Read it and weep." I pushed Dhreen's chart across the desk. "He has multiple systemic damage that we couldn't fix. The temporary repairs we made won't last more than a few days. We were just discussing how to save his life before you showed up to arrest me for attempted homicide."

"Doctor." Squilyp put a gentle membrane on my

shoulder. "This is all a simple misunderstanding. The patient has regained consciousness, and is fairly lucid. Captain, you may speak with him now, if you keep it brief."

We all went in to see him. Adaola, who was monitoring Dhreen, jumped up when she saw the guards. "Healer? Is something amiss?"

"Plenty." I took the scanner she handed me and performed a thorough pass over Dhreen's chest. Our repairs were sustaining him—barely. "Dhreen, can you hear me?"

Hazy amber eyes focused on my face. "Doc?"

"My alibi is awake." I stepped to one side to allow Xonea access to the jerk.

"Pilot." The Captain spoke softly, but with intense dislike. "How is it that you acquired these injuries?"

Dhreen closed his eyes. "I don't know."

I was watching his vitals, which unexpectedly began to spike. "All right, calm down. Just tell Xonea what happened in launch bay."

Guileless amber eyes went from the Captain to me. "What launch bay, and who is Xonea?"

CHAPTER THREE

Necessary Compromises

"He's lying."

"No, he has trauma-induced global amnesia." I sat back and rubbed a tired hand over my eyes. I wasn't happy with my present situation, but I had to be professional. "He can't lie. He can't even remember his own name."

Reever didn't respond to that, but then, he was too busy pacing back and forth in front of the detainment cell I occupied.

I watched him for a minute, then shifted Marel on my lap. She'd been there for an hour, without moving. "Are you tired, honey? Daddy will take you home and get you settled down for a nap."

"No." She put her arms around my neck and pressed her cheek against my breast. Like me, she was watching her father. "Sday wid you, Mama."

The guards had already violated the Captain's orders by allowing my daughter in my cell, but not even the toughest, battle-hardened Jorenian warrior could deny my daughter when she turned on the tears.

Not while her extremely agitated father was in close proximity, anyway.

"Xonea should have confined you to quarters. This is ludicrous." Reever stopped once more in front of the inhibitor webbing. "He can't keep you here. I'll attest to your innocence through a mind link."

I'd already suggested that, but the Captain had shot it down. I repeated to Reever what he'd told me. "Under Jorenian law, bondmates cannot testify for or against each other. I think there was a law like that on Terra, once, before they legalized polygraph drones."

He gripped the webbing with both hands, and something ripped. "We are not Jorenian."

"You're not. I was formally adopted and granted residential status. Which includes planetary citizenship, being subject to their laws, getting tossed in the brig when I'm under suspicion of attempted murder, et cetera." I put Marel down and walked her over to the barrier. "You'd better take her home."

"I'm not leaving you here like this."

"Squilyp will straighten it out." More webbing tore, and I quickly laced my fingers through his. "Duncan. Please."

His thoughts blasted into mine, along with images of what had happened to me in Joseph's lab. *Do you know what it does to me, to see you confined like this?*

Yes. Do you know what seeing her daddy lose it will do to our kid?

He glanced down at the little girl on the other side of the barrier, and closed his eyes for a moment. *Very well.*

I squeezed his hand, then called out, "Guards. My daughter is leaving."

Marel kicked the webbing. "Mama weave do."

"Soon, sweetie." I knelt down to get on her eye level. "You take care of Daddy for me until I come home, okay?" As the web slid to one side, I stood up and handed her over to Duncan. Then I touched his face. *Don't worry. And don't get into this with Xonea. He's only doing his job.*

He kissed me before I could think another word. *Don't get comfortable.*

I eyed the mostly empty cell, with its single console and spartan sleeping platform. "No problem."

Since I might be in detainment for a few days, I decided to use the time to get some research done. Squilyp had already transferred all of Dhreen's and Reever's medical records down to my console, so I could work on replicating the hypercellular injector.

Several hours passed as I roughed out a schematic for the injector device. One of the guards brought me a meal I didn't eat, then later interrupted me again. "Healer, there is an urgent signal from Medical for you."

"Transfer it to my console."

Squilyp's face appeared on my screen. "Cherijo, I just completed the kidney biopsy on your spouse."

That was news. I'd asked Reever to donate some cells, but hadn't expected him to do it so quickly, considering the patient I needed it for had inadvertently gotten me thrown in jail. "Everything go okay?"

"Marel's presence persuaded him to stay out of the critical care unit, but he indicated to me he'd be back to speak to Dhreen tomorrow."

I winced. "You'd better post some guards up there, just in case."

"I've already contacted security." He did something to the console. "Downloading the microcellular results to you now."

I watched as the scan data appeared. "Hold on, Squilyp, these aren't the right tests. The patient has two kidneys." Reever had only been born with one.

"Wait for the download to finish."

I waited. I'd performed a follow-up exam on my husband a few days after we left Terra, and that file appeared. Duncan Reever, Terran male, one kidney. His individual DNA pattern provided the file ID. I split the screen to show Squilyp the other test belonged to someone else, then nearly fell on the deck. The file ID tags were the same.

Reever, Duncan. Male, Terran. One kidney, two kidneys.

That was absolutely impossible, unless— "Squilyp, have you been performing transplants behind my back?"

"No."

I sat back and rechecked the DNA patterns. Then I ran a comparison test via the computer, just in case I was hallucinating.

"Send me the renal imaging, split screen." I leaned forward as my vid divided and the internal scans of two Terran torsos appeared. One had one kidney. The other had two.

Both torsos were Reever's.

I didn't want to believe my eyes. "It's not a tumor? You checked?"

"I checked. It's not."

I stared at the budding mass tucked away under the right side of Reever's liver which, until a few weeks ago, had never existed. "Terrans don't spontaneously regenerate organs."

"Nevertheless." He rotated the view for me. "It's another kidney, Cherijo."

I magnified the normal-size, healthy left kidney. "No abnormalities detected from the hypercellular procedure?"

"Other than some unusual microcellular structures, none."

Back on Terra, Reever had taken a deep stab wound to his kidney, which had required me to perform surgery under the worst conditions. I'd only been able to repair it enough to keep it working for a few weeks. When it subsequently failed, I'd even managed to rig a hemodialysis machine. But in the end, I had gone back to my deranged creator, Joseph Grey Veil, to beg him to save my husband's life. He'd used an experimental technique to restore function to Reever's dysfunctional kidney.

But no technique in the world could produce a second one—or so I'd thought, until today.

Squilyp's image reappeared. "His counts are unremarkable. Textbook Terran, in fact." He stroked his gildrells. "What is your opinion?"

"I'm thinking these hypercells Joe used to repair the damaged kidney may be acting like a carcinoma, and spreading."

Once upon a time, Squilyp would have scoffed at a wild theory like that. But we'd been through a lot medical science couldn't explain, and now he just nodded. "If these engineered cells were modified to act like cancer, they may have been derived from some form of the disease. They may *be* an entirely new form of the disease."

And Reever could end up with an abdomen full of extra kidneys. "Jesus Christ."

My boss tried to look sympathetic. "I must perform more tests at once. I must also discuss the scan results with Duncan."

I was tempted to ask him not to until we found out why Reever had grown another kidney, but my conscience kicked me, hard. *No more secrets between us.* "Let me tell him. In the meantime, check your equipment and repeat all the tests."

"I will, but this is not my area of expertise." Squilyp

rubbed a membrane over his eyes. "We have to get you out of there, Cherijo."

"I have to prove I didn't deliberately shoot Dhreen first."

I spent most of the night thinking about how I could do that. The next morning, I pulled up specifications for the laser welder. From what I read, the tool could easily be calibrated to be used as a weapon, but was generally employed at a much lower setting.

I signaled the chief engineer on duty in central launch bay.

"Dhreen said he needed to cap off this emitter he was working on. What does that mean?"

"That would involve disabling the exterior port and severing the power relays, Healer." The older Jorenian male gave me a sympathetic look. "We are all most distressed over your present circumstances."

"I'll be fine. Why would he have to disable it?"

"That particular unit was found to be malfunctioning during the shuttle's routine maintenance sweep." The engineer consulted another screen. "Conductor control between the power cells and the converger showed some random pulse instability."

"He was working on a *pulse* emitter." When he nodded, I sat back. "Another one of Xonea's new war toys, I suppose."

"It is not suitable for young ones, Healer."

"I don't imagine it is." I pressed my fingers against my temples, trying to keep from screaming with frustration. "What's the difference between getting shot with a tool and getting fried by a weapon?"

"Well, the laser welder employs concentrated light, while the emitter utilizes sound and energy."

What had Squilyp said during surgery? *Acoustic in-homogeneity refracted the blast wave, judging by the tissue displacement.* "They'd create different wounds, wouldn't they?"

"They would." He smiled at me. "Data on the specific disparities may be available from the medical database."

"I bet there is." I grinned back. "Thank you, engineer."

I terminated the signal, tapped into the medical system, and found a dozen cases of injuries resulting from both pulse fire and using the laser welder. Dhreen's injuries showed a distinct pattern of displacement that was only possible if he'd been hit by pulse fire—not a laser.

Which cleared me completely.

I wrote a summary report, then removed the recording disc, and went to the barrier. "Guards? Would one of you mind taking a little present to the Captain for me?"

Qonja Torin appeared in front of the web, and took the disc before I could yank my hand back in. "Allow me, Healer."

"Hey!" I swiped at him, but he stepped out of reach.

"I will see that the Captain reviews it as soon as possible." He turned and left.

Both guards, much to my disappointment, refused to shoot him in the back.

Qonja apparently kept his promise and delivered the disc to Xonea, who personally came down to let me out of the brig. My ClanBrother was, understandably, apologetic.

"I cannot make exceptions for any member of the crew." As he spoke, his hands moved through a half dozen gestures of regret and sorrow. "Even my own ClanSister."

I felt I had to rub it in a little. "The same ClanSister who bailed you out of a detainment cell once, as I recall."

"I would have taken your place, if I could have," he said, sounding wounded.

"Just do me a favor and remember this the *next* time I'm accused of murder, okay?" I swept past him and entered the gyrlift.

My first stop was at my quarters, where I found Alunthri baby-sitting my daughter. Marel had refused to go to school, and now sat in a miserable huddle on the sofa, clutching Jenner in her arms.

"Hey, is this any way to celebrate my parole?"

Alunthri grinned. "Cherijo!"

"Mama!" Marel slid off the cushions.

"Mrrrow!" Jenner jumped down and sauntered over to sniff at my footgear. *About time.* Indignant blue eyes glared up at me. *She's had me in that death grip all morning.*

"Miss me?" I bent to scratch Jenner's ears and catch my daughter as she got to me. "Hi, sweetie."

"Mama." She patted my face and head with her little hands. "CanUncaw Xonea's nod mad ad you anymore?"

"No, honey, now he's mad at himself." I picked her up and turned to Alunthri. "Reever draft you into doing this?"

Alunthri's pointed ears flicked, and it looked a little uneasy. "Duncan signaled me earlier this morning. He mentioned he had to talk to someone."

"In Medical?" Alunthri nodded. "Marel." I put my daughter down and crouched in front of her. "Would you stay here with Alunthri while I go stop Daddy from messing up my work?"

"You come back, Mama." It wasn't a request.

"I will."

I didn't stop to signal Squilyp, but went straight from my quarters to Medical. Good thing, too. I could sense trouble brewing before I went through the door panel.

Inside, the Senior Healer was the only thing keeping my husband out of the critical care unit. It may have been because Reever's fist held him suspended a half foot off the deck. My husband was ignoring the two security guards holding their weapons aimed at his head, and Qonja, who was evidently trying to reason with him.

Only one person could reason with Reever when he got like this.

"Cherijo." Squilyp had never sounded more relieved. "Thank the gods."

Reever turned around. "Xonea released you?"

"I proved my innocence. Put the Omorr down."

Slowly, my husband returned my boss to the deck.

"Thank you." Sometimes I didn't know who was worse—Marel or her father. "Squilyp, I'm sorry. Reever, get on an exam table. And you." I planted a hand on Qonja's chest and shoved him out of my way. "You're relieved of duty. Get out."

His friendly smile evaporated. "You can't do that."

"Squilyp? Got a problem with this?" My boss shook his head, and I beckoned to security. "Escort this man to his quarters. Or an open airlock. Whatever's convenient."

The guards exchanged a glance, shouldered their weapons, and left, guiding the seething psych resident between them.

"I don't require an exam." Reever was staring at Dhreen through the clear plas wall in the same way he would a small bug he wanted to squash.

The Senior Healer straightened his tunic and resumed his usual expression of grave dignity. "I've been trying to convince him to do exactly that."

"You just have to use the right words." I went over and took one of Reever's hands in mine. Tenderly, I pressed it to my cheek, making him focus on me. "Duncan. Sweetheart. I'm okay. It's over. Now get on that exam table before I tranquilize you."

Reluctantly, he turned away from his intended victim. "I don't want to be examined."

"You mean you're not going to let me expose your magnificent body and make all the other girls jealous? I'll cry." I led him over and tugged on his sleeve. "Tunic off, please. Squilyp, you repeat those tests?"

"Twice. Results were identical, both times."

"Okay." I went on to explain the findings to Reever as we prepped him for a thorough examination.

When I was finished, he said, "You didn't want to tell me."

"Not really, but I know better." He'd taught me on Terra that we were partners, in every sense of the word. And partners didn't hold out on each other. "In return, you can do me a favor and leave Dhreen alone."

His eyes went from dark green to crystal gray. "I want to ascertain the level of his memory loss for myself."

He wanted to pound him into the deck.

"Duncan, give it a rest. He's not faking it."

"He acquired this amnesia before you could learn about the conditions on Oenrall." His mouth became a thin line. "That seems very convenient."

"I'm sure his memory will return in time." I calibrated the table scanner. "If it doesn't, I'll go down to Oenrall by myself. My immune system can handle anything Dhreen's people dish out."

Squilyp prepared the biopsy tray. "I don't think it's wise, Cherijo." He gloved before placing the monitor leads on Duncan's chest. "The Oenrallian has many connections within the League. There may be no health crisis at all."

"No. Whatever this thing is, it was more important than making money to him." I thought of how he'd bargained with my creator, trading his services as a spy for Joseph's promise of aid. "More important than our friendship."

"And Jxinok?"

He was referring to my promise to stop by Maggie's homeworld, which was supposed to be in the same quadrant. "We still need to work on that one." I gloved and masked, then caught that silent, masculine communication thing my husband and my boss did over my head. *"What?"*

"I don't trust Dhreen," Duncan said.

"Nor do I trust this Maggie person," Squilyp added for good measure.

"Guys. *Guys.*" I activated the scanner arm, which slowly began mapping out Reever's internal organs. "None of this is a big deal. I find out what the problem is on Dhreen's world, and we fix that—I owe it to Dhreen. We go to Maggie's world—assuming we can *find* the damn thing—and see what little present she left for me. Then we outrun all the mercenaries and lizards and find a nice, quiet non-League world to settle down on. Piece of cake."

"You are not indebted to Dhreen," Squilyp said. "And I am not too sure we can outrun the Hsktskt."

"He got us off Terra, and I gave him my word." I moved over to the other side of the table, and inspected the long, hair-thin biopsy needle. "As for the Hsktskt, playing war games with the League will keep them tied up. Now, shall we find out why Reever has cornered the kidney market, or chat all day?"

Since my hands were steady, but my stomach wasn't—I'd been forced to operate on Reever back on Terra, and twice had been more than enough—I had Squilyp take the biopsy. As soon as he extracted the tissue sample from the budding organ, I prepared a slide and popped it in the electroniscopic unit.

"Here we go." I peered in the scope, and saw what appeared to be healthy, fully functioning kidney cells. I stepped back, then fed the data into the diagnostic unit. A moment later, the screen confirmed my diagnosis.

"According to known medical science, it's absolutely, positively a functional kidney." I went over to the table, dressed the small biopsy puncture, and handed Reever his tunic. "Which is improbable, if not completely impossible."

Squilyp hopped over to the scanner and had a look. "I can't see any formative abnormalities. Even the arterial connections are exactly where they should be."

"That in itself belongs on the impossible list." Seeing Duncan's frown, I explained, "It's not just that you grew an extra kidney, honey. It's hooked itself up to your circulatory system, and organs don't do that without me or Squilyp doing a lot of cutting and sewing."

The Omorr lifted his eyes from the scope. "Nothing *but* surgery can do this."

I wished I could feel as certain. "Run a microcellular repeat on both kidney samples. I'm particularly interested in the bio-organic structure of the right side cells."

Duncan finished fastening his tunic. "I will see Dhreen now."

It finally hit me, why he was so determined to have

a go at the Oenrallian. "You want to try to link with him."

He eyed the isolation unit. "You can stay in the room, if you like."

"Oh"—I folded my arms—"I'm definitely staying."

The Omorr frowned at my husband. "His condition is extremely serious, Duncan. I do not want him agitated."

"The minute he agitates, I'll kick him out," I assured my boss.

When we entered the critical care unit, I saw Dhreen was sleeping. Adaola, a former nurse and now one of Squilyp's surgical interns, was changing his dressing. She saw Reever behind me and immediately stepped between him and the berth.

"He's going to be on his best behavior." I nudged him. "Right, sweetheart?"

"I will not injure him."

The intern stepped aside, but stayed close enough to intervene if necessary. I picked up Dhreen's chart and reviewed his vitals, which showed no deterioration, but no improvement, either.

"Will he die?"

"Not if I have anything to say about it." I looked up and saw Reever had turned completely white. He'd endured slavery, torture, and endless deprivations, yet he still got squeamish about something like a draining chest wound. "Let Adaola finish dressing his chest, or you're going to throw up."

We let the intern complete her work, then Duncan took hold of Dhreen's hand. He was still a little pale, but seemed calmer and more in control.

"Dhreen." He bent over the berth as the Oenrallian's eyelids flickered, then opened. "Do you know where you are?"

"In a hospital." Drugs made his voice slur the words. "On a ship."

"Think of the last thing you remember," Duncan said, then he went still and his eyes lost their focus.

I monitored Dhreen's vitals, but there were no changes beyond a slight elevation in his blood pressure. Reever stayed silent and motionless for a few minutes, then placed Dhreen's hand back on the linens and straightened. The Oenrallian smiled a little as he drifted into sleep.

I let out a breath my lungs had refused to release. "Well?"

"His thought patterns are a jumble of disordered fragments." He turned and took my hand. "You were right; he is not making a pretense of this. I apologize."

I made an impatient sound. "Apologize later. What did you see?"

"Nothing that made sense. Discarded toys. Oenrallians dancing on a street. Rooms filled with empty beds."

Before I could interpret any of that, there was a huge *boom* outside the starboard hull panel, and we were thrown to the deck.

The main medical display chimed an emergency signal. "Alert. Exterior hull damage to levels nine, ten, and eleven. All crew members to engagement-response positions."

"I'll check on Alunthri and Marel on my way to Communications." Reever pulled me close for a brief, hard kiss, then looked into my eyes. "Be careful."

I pressed my hand against his cheek. "You, too."

As the door panel opened, I heard Squilyp shouting, "Secure Yarek and the other patients! Cherijo—"

I stuck my head out. "Give me a minute in here."

Dhreen's eyes fluttered open and widened as I bent over to grab the berth restraints. "What happened?"

"The ship is under attack." I stripped away his top linens and removed three Lok-Teel from various parts of his body—the housekeeping mold evidently had taken a real liking to the Oenrallian—and adjusted the tilt of the berth. "I'm going to put you in sleep suspension, to protect your wounds."

He tugged halfheartedly at the straps. "You'll rouse me when it's through?"

"I might even bring you breakfast in bed." I positioned the suspension shroud over his face. "Don't worry, this feels just like taking another nap."

"All I do is sleep."

"We can swap jobs anytime you want." I calibrated a syrinpress. "Now close your eyes and relax."

Once Dhreen was hibernating, I went out to help Squilyp with securing the rest of our patients and getting the staff prepared to triage incoming casualties. I paused long enough to signal Alunthri and check on Marel myself.

"Duncan is on his way, and I'll be down as soon as I can," I told the Chakacat, and reassured my daughter as best I could. "Listen to Alunthri, sweetie, and I'll see you soon."

"I nod 'fraid, Mama." Marel showed me a wrist unit. "CanUncaw Xonea give me dis."

ClanUncle was going to get his large blue jaw broken by me, as soon as this was over. "That's great, baby." When she wandered far enough away from the screen, I added, "Alunthri, get that thing off her, if you would."

As more blasts hit the ship, we began setting up as many empty berths as the wards could hold. I started one of the nurses on the blood synthesizer, and another four prepping ortho and wound instrument trays.

"Cherijo." Squilyp waved me over to the main display, where he had punched up an exterior view of the *Sunlace*. "It doesn't look like a League ship. Are they mercenaries?"

"No." I watched as the fast, heavily armed alien star vessel came about and flew toward the starboard side of the ship. "It's a Hsktskt raider, gstek class."

I grabbed the console as it fired another displacer salvo at the *Sunlace*, sending more shock waves through the hull.

The Omorr rocked on his foot. "Obviously not a scout vessel."

I pushed a handful of hair out of my face. "What is Xonea doing? We've got to transition out of here."

Before I could signal Ship's Operational and demand to know why we were sitting around letting the lizards blast holes in our hull, a brief, high-pitched screech blared through the air.

I clapped my hands over my ears. "*Ah!*"

Squilyp, whose auditory membranes were ten times as acute as mine, made a horrible sound as he doubled over in agony. A couple of nurses rushed over to help me support him.

If that wasn't bizarre enough, my daughter appeared out of nowhere, ducked between my legs, and grabbed the edge of the Omorr's tunic. Her small hand shook as she touched the pink and white streaked blood draining from Squilyp's ears. "Uncwip!"

"I am well, child," he said, taking her hand in one of his membranes.

"Let go, Squilyp." When he did, I grabbed Marel and held her for a moment. Alunthri was nowhere to be seen. "Baby, how did you get in here?"

"I wanded you."

"Healer, look." One of them pointed to the display screen.

A silent, light-bending ripple appeared in front of the *Sunlace*, spreading out in all directions. As the Hsktskt raider came about for a third pass, it ran into the ripple. I squinted as a huge flash of white light obscured the screen. When it cleared, the Hsktskt ship had been reduced to a pulverized cloud of debris.

It was so unexpected and lethal that, for a moment, all any of us could do was stare, openmouthed.

"Mama, wad dad?" my daughter whispered.

I swallowed. "A bad thing, baby. A very bad thing."

"The Captain's celebrated sonic cannons, I presume." Squilyp's face had gone pale pink, but he mopped up the blood on his cheeks and neck with steady hands. "Most proficient."

"Dear God." I'd never seen a weapon that could do that to a ship with one shot. Then I glanced down at my kid. "Intern, could you take Marel back to Alunthri for me?" I paused long enough to remove her wrist unit and stick it in my pocket before handing her off. "Go with ClanCousin Adaola now, baby. I'll see you later."

I watched her go, then turned to Squilyp. "Bend down here for a minute and let me check you."

Blood filled the Omorr's tympanic channels, which I evacuated, but there were only slight perforations which I quickly treated with a topical anesthetic. He claimed to have no lingering pain or hearing loss, so we went back to work. I signaled Alunthri to make sure Marel had returned home. It reported she was shaken by what she'd seen, but otherwise fine.

"I am sorry, Cherijo." The Chakacat seemed confused. "I do not know how she got away from me. One moment she was there, the next . . ."

"She does it to everybody, pal. Don't blame yourself, just lock down the door panel." I saw a number of wounded stream in through the main entrance, and grimaced. "Looks like I'll be tied up for a while. Would you stay with her until Duncan gets home?"

"I will stay as long as you like," the Chakacat reassured me.

I went to help with the triage, which went smoothly, until Dhreen's girlfriend showed up and demanded to see him.

"You can't go in there," I said as I herded her away from the critical care unit. "He's in sleep suspension, and he's also too weak to resist infection from the germs you're carrying."

"I have washed, thoroughly." She spit the words out through clenched teeth as she tried to go around me. Although Xonea had made it clear to her that I hadn't been responsible for Dhreen's wounds, she still treated me like a leper. "He does not like to be alone. He needs me at his side."

"He doesn't need the bacteria that exist in places you can't wash." I saw the desperation in her dark eyes, and tried again. "Ilona, more than anything right now, he needs to stay under suspension."

"So you say, patcher." She stalked out.

More crew members reported with injuries, but all were thankfully minor, and Squilyp told me to leave.

"Everything here is under control. See to your family, Doctor."

Marel burst into tears the moment she saw me, convinced her beloved "Uncwip" was hurt. It took a lengthy explanation, a signal to Medical so she could speak to Squilyp herself, then two bedtime stories before she calmed down enough to sleep.

Alunthri lingered, and seemed very upset, by the way it paced around our quarters. "I do not understand it."

"I'm telling you, it's like a hobby with this kid. Don't let it bother you."

"It's more than that, Cherijo." It stopped, and stared at Marel's door panel. "I tried to track her, but I couldn't find her scent path."

Given the Chakacat's extraordinary olfactory senses, that seemed a little strange. "Maybe you're congested."

"Perhaps." Its whiskers twitched. "I will leave you now."

"But—" I sensed it was upset and needed some space, so I let the topic drop and walked it to the door. "Thanks for helping out."

The cats were also agitated; an extra server of dried cod bits soothed Jenner, but Juliet wasn't interested in eating. My husband came in about an hour later, his face set in remote lines.

"I take it you saw what Xonea's big gun did to that raider," I said as I brought him a server of tea.

"Yes." He stared down at the steaming liquid.

Now for the hard part. "Marel saw it, too. There was no warning, or I wouldn't have let her near the console, but . . . she saw everything."

He glanced at her room. "Is she all right?"

"I think she will be, but we'd better expect more nightmares."

He abruptly handed the server back to me. "I need to cleanse."

As Duncan spent an extended interval doing that, I sat and thought. Although I had no love for the Hskt-skt, and several million reasons to despise them, watching that ship being reduced to space dust had sickened me. I could just imagine how much it shook our kid.

As for Reever, he'd spent a number of years with the Hsktskt, first as a captive slave, then working for the Faction. He'd never gone into much detail about that time in his life, but I knew he had been friends with at least one of the big lizards. He had to feel as bad as I did. Probably worse.

What if TssVar was on that ship?

Jenner stayed curled up on my lap, but I noticed Juliet had gone back to pacing restlessly. They might have been frightened by the cannon blast, too, I thought, stroking my cat's silvery head. Juliet disappeared into a narrow gap in the doors of a storage unit, the one where I had set up a kittening box for her. I thought she'd gotten stuck inside, but when I opened the door, I saw her squatting and straining with her tail up.

Whenever there's mass destruction, life still came barging in to remind us that all is never lost. Tears blurred my eyes for a moment as I knelt down and gently felt her abdominal muscles contracting.

"Your timing is incredible." I smiled as she nipped my fingers, then shook her head and yowled. "Settle down, Mom, I'm here to help."

The first kitten emerged shortly after that, headfirst, still partially encased by a sac of membranes. Juliet expelled the placenta a moment later, while I broke the sac over the kitten's face and began rubbing it with a soft cloth as soon as it wriggled and mewled.

She delivered four more in fifteen-minute intervals, which I separated from her into a small warming basket while she finished her delivery. The final kitten was presented breech, but I was able to turn it before it emerged. As soon as Juliet had finished, I sterilized the kittens' umbilical cords and allowed their mother to consume one of the afterbirths before moving the rest aside for the Lok-Teel to absorb.

"Very nice, Miss Juliet. Tell me something—why is it every time I deliver babies they come in fives?"

I sat back on my heels as Juliet inspected and cleaned each of her kittens, and felt someone hovering behind me. I looked up to see Reever holding Jenner, and both had such expressions of masculine anxiety that I had to chuckle.

"Mom and kitties are doing fine, guys." I rose and stepped back to take my cat so Duncan could see the new additions to the family. "Time for Jenner to move in with Salo and Darea for a few days, though."

The proud father's eyes met mine, and I could have sworn he was dazed. *Hey, I did that.*

I laughed. "Wait 'til they keep you up all night, wanting to play."

When I returned from placing Jenner into temporary exile, I found Duncan sitting on the deck beside the storage container, watching a now-content Juliet nurse her new family. He glanced up at me as I put a hand on his shoulder.

"How are you doing?"

He ignored that. "They seem healthy."

I scanned them. "They are."

He lapsed back into a brooding silence, so I went over to the console to put on a disc of Nat Adderly, whose warm, clear jazz coronet solos always gave me a boost whenever I felt depressed. Maybe he'd do the same for my husband.

As if on cue, Duncan came over as the music began and took me into his arms. "Dance with me."

We danced, or rather, we held each other and swayed to the music. After a few songs, Duncan pulled me over to our favorite chair and sat down with me on his lap. *Forgive me.*

I pretended to be surprised. *For what?*

For not protecting our daughter better.

I think that's my line. I rested my cheek against his shoulder, and thought of the one Hsktskt who had tried to protect me.

TssVar was not on the raider.

How do you know?

I once served on that vessel. A brief memory stream from his years in the Faction crossed the link, and I saw the image of a rather dignified-looking lizard wearing a flightsuit. *I knew the OverLord who captained it. He was a good commander, one who treated me fairly.*

"Then I'm sorry that you lost a friend." I curled my arms around his neck. "Duncan, maybe we should get off the ship. Take Marel and disappear on some non-League world."

He seemed startled by that. "Do you really wish to leave?"

"No," I admitted. "I love the Jorenians, and they have done a lot to help us. But as long as we're on board this ship, it'll be a moving target, and our friends and our kid will be in danger."

We talked into the night, considering a number of alternatives to staying on board the *Sunlace*, finally agreeing to make our decision after we took care of our sojourn commitments in the Liacos system.

It hurt to think of leaving the Torins, but I had to be practical. "You know, I think I've seen enough killing to last me several lifetimes," I said, just before I fell asleep in his arms.

"So you have," he said, and held me close. "As have I."

CHAPTER FOUR

New Additions

When Marel woke up the next morning and discovered Juliet's litter, she planted herself next to the storage container and refused to budge.

"So diny, Mama." She admired the blind, squirming kittens as they bumped and crawled into each other. I saw no indication she was still distressed over what had happened in Medical. "Can I hold one?"

I carefully held her eager hands with mine. "Not right away, sweetie. Juliet might get upset." Her disappointment made me add, "Besides, don't you want to signal Alunthri and Fasala and tell them the big news?"

I left her happily manning the console with Duncan, sending signals to practically everyone on the ship, while I kept an overdue appointment in Command. On the way, I passed repair crews working on areas damaged by the attack. Everyone seemed immensely satisfied with the results of the skirmish, but they were Jorenian. Crushing an enemy who threatened the HouseClan was practically instinct for them.

Yet even the most basic instinct could be overcome.

A pair of engineers, waiting outside the Captain's office, graciously allowed me to go ahead of them, and when the door panel opened, I strode in.

"Cherijo, I had not expected you today."

"You'll get over it." I refused Xonea's offer of a seat

and got right down to business. "Didn't waste any time invoking the Council's new codicil, I see. How many Hsktskt died yesterday?"

"Raiders carry a standard crew complement of four hundred." He sat back in his captain's chair and looked a little smug. "Perhaps now the Faction will have second thoughts about attacking Jorenian ships in the future."

"The Faction will want to know how deadly your new weapon systems are." I could have slapped the smile off his face. "You know the Hsktskt love efficient death machines."

"I do not fear the Hsktskt."

"Really." I planted my hands on his console. "Xonea, I was barely able to keep those lizards from invading Joren before, and to do that, I had to give them four hundred League ships. If they find out about your sonic cannons, nothing will keep them out of Varallan or off Joren."

"We developed this particular technology in direct response to the attack on Joren." He stood up, seven and a half feet of pure warrior. "The ground to space cannon installations were completed two cycles ago, and the planetary stations have ten times the sonic output capacity." He showed me all his pretty Jorenian teeth. "Let them come and attempt to invade our homeworld again."

"Good attitude. Pretty soon you'll have your own little war going." I straightened. "Tarek Varena would be proud."

Mentioning the father of Jorenian journey philosophy had the exact effect I wanted. "ClanJoren Varena desired to end the conflicts between primitive House-Clans." He made a sharp slash with one hand, one of the more basic Jorenian nonverbal insults. "He did not have to stave off intergalactic slavers and mercenaries from a thousand worlds, bent on destroying every civilization in their path."

"I know. All poor old Tarek had to do was end the hostilities between, what, forty or fifty measly warring HouseClans?" I made a *tsking* sound. "Not much of a job. They were just fighting a bunch of stupid territorial wars in which they enslaved, raped, and murdered other Jorenians, right? Bet he never even broke a sweat."

Xonea saw where I was going. "It is not the same."

"It is *exactly* the same, you thickheaded dolt!" I flung a hand toward the wide vista of stars outside his viewer. "Who are you taking on with your sonic cannons? The slavers and the soldiers and the hired killers aren't any different than the ones Tarek Varena brought to the peace table. There's just more of them."

"I am not a philosopher!" He slammed his fist into his console, leaving a deep depression in the surface.

I drew back a step. "No, you're not. You're a warrior. A warrior who killed four hundred beings with one blow yesterday. That makes you an aggressive leader. And a mass murderer. Bravo, ClanBrother."

The words hung between us for a moment.

"One more thing." I took Marel's wrist unit out of my tunic and slapped it on his console, hard enough to shatter the infuser port. "Keep my baby out of your war."

He gathered up the pieces, and tightened his fist over them until a trickle of green blood ran down his arm. "I will defend this vessel and our HouseClan, Healer."

"You do what you have to do." Unmoved, I watched him bleed. "Next time *you* can explain to my daughter why the big ship went *boom*."

"Marel witnessed what happened?" He came around the desk. "You allowed this?"

Now I wanted to *make* him bleed. "No, Xonea, I try not to deliberately traumatize my kid. She came to Medical and saw it happen on the screen, like the rest of us."

He got in my face. "You should have removed her!"

"You shouldn't have blown it up!" I shouted back.

For a minute, only an inch separated us, and I could have sworn he was going to take a swing at me. Just like the old days. But this Xonea hadn't been drugged into mindless aggression, and quickly regained his self-control.

"I regret that my ClanNiece witnessed this."

"I believe you." Time to play my final card. "Tell me why you've got Qonja watching me."

His expression went blank, but not before betraying a flash of wary surprise. "I don't know what you mean."

"This psych resident spends more time following me around than he does in Medical," I said. "Next thing you know he'll be sleeping between me and Duncan. What's going on, Xonea?"

He dragged a hand through his black hair, messing up his warrior's knot. "Qonja has not received orders from me to keep you under surveillance."

I knew he was telling the truth—Jorenians are lousy liars—so why did I still sense he was hiding something? "Then you should have no problem with ordering him to stop it."

"I will speak to him."

I waved at his bloody fist. "Report to Squilyp to get that treated. If I have to suture it, I may sew it over your mouth."

"As honest as you are blunt." He bowed his head for

a moment, then leveled his gaze with mine. "You must understand, Cherijo: An enemy allowed to live will return to attack again. That is the way of war."

"Is it? What if you don't? Maybe they won't attack. Maybe, just maybe, they'll come back to find out why you didn't destroy them when you had the chance." I went to the door panel. "When that happens, it's called something else. The way of peace."

I reported to Medical to take over from Vlaav, who had relieved Squilyp during the night. The Senior Healer appeared in time for morning rounds, and reluctantly allowed me to give him a brief follow-up auditory exam.

"No aftereffects from the sonic blast?" I peered into the narrow, flat apertures that served as his ears. The perforations had nearly closed.

"Only a slight headache." He hopped off the exam table. "I understand you have five new feline companions."

"For a couple of weeks, anyway." I gave him a speculative look. "I was thinking—"

"No." He backed away, shaking his head, holding up all three appendage-ends. "No kittens. I beg you."

I scowled. "Coward."

We decided to keep Dhreen in sleep suspension while we went back to work trying to slow the rate of deterioration in his liver. Ilona showed up again, demanding to see him.

"We did this yesterday." I gestured behind my back at Adaola to come and help me. "You can't go in there."

"I will see him today."

"Weaver Red Faun!" Adaola distracted the Terran girl by admiring the striking black-and-yellow tunic she wore. "What a lovely garment! I am going off duty now. Perhaps you would accompany me for a meal interval and discuss its making with me?"

"Chief Xonea will hear of this." Not quite finished, Ilona shot me a look of sheer dislike. "The men on this vessel understand a woman's duty."

I couldn't help the chuckle. "Jorenians don't subjugate their females, Ilona. They'd get their teeth knocked in if they so much as tried."

She didn't like me laughing at her, either. "Regardless, I shall return."

"I'll hold my breath in anticipation," I assured her.

Squilyp called me over to perform morning rounds with him, and we discharged most of the inpatients who had come in with injuries from the brief Hsktskt attack. Several signals came in from Qonja, which we both ignored. Our double-hernia patient, Yarek, proved to be healing rapidly and anxious to return to duty.

"Other archivists must work double shifts to compensate for my continued absence," he said as he tried to talk us into discharging him. "Surely I can sit at my duty terminal and run analysis programs without risking physical injury."

"Oh, sure, no problem. And when you're off duty, of course you wouldn't teach any classes, or lift so much as a throwing dagger to demonstrate something for your students, right?" I watched the telltale shift of his white-within-white eyes. "That's what I thought."

"You are a tyrant, Healer."

I batted my eyelashes at him as I completed my scans. "Flattery will not get you discharged, Clan-Cousin."

One of the nurses interrupted us with her concern over Dhreen's monitors, which were showing unusual cardiopulmonary fluctuations, and Squilyp decided to take him out of sleep suspension long enough for a full examination. He left me to finish rounds, which I continued until crashing sounds came out of the critical care unit.

"What now?" I ran in.

Squilyp was holding Dhreen down by pinning him to the berth with his body. The Oenrallian struggled wildly, tearing at the monitor leads with scrabbling hands.

"Stop that!" I pushed between the two males and hauled a restraint strap over Dhreen's chest. "Squilyp, get his legs!"

"Let me out of this contraption," Dhreen said, then coughed up some blood. "I need some air."

Between us we got him restrained, but I already knew what the problem was from the heat emanating from his skin. I turned and grabbed a syrinpress and a scanner. "Temperature's spiking. One hundred fifteen degrees. He'll stroke out on us."

"I can't breathe! Get off!" the Oenrallian yelled as his wavering fist connected with the side of my head.

Squilyp turned and bellowed, "Nurse! Coolant paks, stat!"

Fever in an Oenrallian was much more lethal than in humans, as their lung/heart organs automatically valved off blood circulating to the extremities. It rendered the feverish patient irrational, then unconscious. A healthy Oenrallian body would kick-start itself by reopening those arterial valves once the internal temperature dropped to a normal one hundred and five degrees.

Dhreen's tattered lung/heart, on the other hand, couldn't stand that kind of strain.

"Cardiopulmonary rate falling. Thirty-two cycles." Squilyp reattached the leads, then grabbed a chest tray and brought it over. He shoved a mask over Dhreen's nose and mouth and placed him on pure oxygen. "Blood pressure still dropping. One-sixty over forty."

Our patient shouted through the mask, the gist of which suggested Squilyp and I attempt something anatomically unlikely with our respective heads.

"Gee, Dhreen, I find the Omorr attractive, but that kind of thing would really upset my husband." I injected the Oenrallian with an aggressive analgesic, yanked off the berth linens, and tore open his patient's gown. Dhreen's suggestions went from obscene to vile. "Where are those paks?"

As if conjured, three nurses appeared beside us and began slapping the plas-encased coolant gel onto his limbs and torso.

I kept a chest scanner on continuous as I watched the monitors. "Come on, come on. Body temp's still rising. One-sixteen. One-seventeen."

Someone yelled from outside the unit, then the door panel slid open and a black-and-yellow blur hurtled toward the berth. "Dhreen! What are you doing to him? Dhreen!"

She landed on top of the Oenrallian, who got an arm free and grabbed at her head. "Get off!"

Ilona cried out in pain as Dhreen ripped the ring from her ear. "No!"

"Nurse!" I pulled her off, and thrust her into capable blue hands. "Take her out, treat her ear, and keep her out."

"Let me go!" Ilona tried to struggle, but it was rather pitiful, considering the Jorenian female was twice her size. "No, I want to stay with him!"

The Oenrallian managed to dislodge his mask by whipping his head to one side. "Get out, you fatuous nuisance!" he shouted at his mate. "You're nothing but an irritant, always suspending yourself from every appendage on my body!" Then he threw the earring at her face, where it left a bloody mark before bouncing off and rolling under the berth.

Ilona stopped struggling to stare at Dhreen with unblinking, tear-filled eyes. The nurse wisely took advantage of the moment and guided her out of the unit.

"I guess you remember who Ilona is." I watched as the indicators began to slow. "Leveling out. One-seventeen. Replace the torso paks with fresh ones." I glanced down at Dhreen again. "What, no more creative propositions for me and Squilyp?"

"You think you're so unique," he said, practically spitting the words. "Your dilemmas are nonexistent collated to mine."

He might be furious, but hearing him mangle Terran delighted me. "At the moment, I have to agree."

As the nurses removed the paks, four Lok-Teel oozed up onto the gurney and onto Dhreen's body. I'd seen them do that before, on Catopsa.

"Leave them," I said when one of the nurses went to detach them. "They're attracted by the toxins in his blood. They'll absorb them out through his skin. Just arrange the new paks around them."

"Take this slime off me!" Dhreen shouted.

Squilyp put a membrane on his brow and bent over. "Try to relax, pilot. Breathe deeply and slowly."

"She despises me," he told the Senior Healer. "You might as well let me expire."

So he remembered me, too.

"No, Dhreen." The Omorr eyed me across the berth. "She's going to save your life."

After an interval that stretched into forever, Dhreen's body temperature slowly began to cool. He began muttering to himself as he slipped into a semiconscious daze. The Lok-Teel remained in place,

steadily removing impurities from the Oenrallian's
bloodstream.

"One-sixteen. Heart rate stabilizing." I glanced up
and saw Dhreen's face grow slack. "One-fifteen. Cerebral pressures?"

"Sluggish, but improving."

A half hour later, we had Dhreen sleeping peacefully
and his body temp back down to normal. More tests
would have to be performed to ensure he'd suffered no
systemic damage, but at least we'd gotten him stabi-
lized again.

"We should put him back in sleep suspension,"
Squilyp said as I ran a complete blood series. "He's at
less risk of infection that way."

"Not a good idea," I said, and nodded at the data on
my screen. "Look at his counts. In his species, fever is a
form of anaphylactic shock. Leave the Lok-Teel in the
unit; they may be able to help."

"What do you think triggered this episode?"

"I'll run an allergen series, but my guess is he's re-
acting to the suspension drugs."

Gildrells turned into spokes. "He couldn't be—he's
a pilot. He's flown dozens of deep space jaunts!"

"Maybe." A chill ran up my spine as I glanced at the
critical care unit. "Maybe not."

"Your pardon, Healer, Senior Healer."

We both turned on Qonja. "You were relieved of
duty, resident," my boss said, his voice matching his
gildrells. "Return to your quarters at once."

"I have been reinstated to my position, and will report for my usual shift tomorrow." He handed the Senior Healer a data pad, gave me one of those irritating,
cheerful smiles, then strolled back out of Medical.

"Did Xonea reinstate him?" If he had, the ship was
going to be minus one Captain.

"No." My boss sounded odd as he passed the pad over to me. "According to this, the Ruling Council on Joren did."

I signaled the Captain, and filed a formal protest to be sent back to the Ruling Council. "I don't know who this guy is, Xonea, but I don't want him around me."

"I will relay your concerns." Xonea made a note on something, then looked up at me. "Report for combat training after your shifts ends."

"Didn't you hear a single word I yelled at you this morning?"

"I have your objections to our defense tactics under consideration," my big brother told me. "You are still required to complete this inspection assignment."

"You said combat training."

"You must undergo the training in order to correctly inspect the programs."

Terrific. "Who's my teacher?"

"I am. Report to environome six." He terminated the signal.

I closed the channel and rested my head against my palms. I needed to find out exactly who this psych resident was, and what was going on with him and my ClanBrother. Meanwhile, if I told Duncan about these lessons, he'd get mad and probably get into it with Xonea. If I didn't, I'd be hiding stuff from him again.

Doesn't this relationship thing ever get any easier?

In the end, I compromised—I sent a relay to my quarters, telling Reever I'd be late for dinner because I had to begin the training program inspections. I didn't mention the words "combat" or "Xonea." It would have to do.

Nine minutes later, I reported for my training, and began warming up. My ClanBrother didn't join me, but took up an observation position beside a table piled with assorted bladed and energy weapons. "You get started without me?"

"No. You have already been through the primary level training program. We shall begin with secondary level exercises."

I wanted to feel flattered, but I was still too steamed about Boy Shrink going over everyone's head and my inability to stop him. "Can I use any of this stuff on Qonja?"

"Try to temper your behavior around the resident until we have a decision from the Council." The door panel opened before I could say what I thought of that, and Xonea's expression lightened. "Thank you for coming, orderly, Doctor."

I watched as Wonlee and Vlaav entered the environome, both wearing sparring garments, then eyed the weapons table. "What are these secondary level exercises, Captain?"

"You will face multiple opponents."

Wonlee, a former League Lieutenant who had become my friend after losing his wife during our enslavement by the Hsktskt, was an Esalmalin. Sharp, thin spines covered virtually every inch of his skin, and he had more claws and teeth than a roomful of Hsktskt.

Vlaav, who was entering his third year of surgical residency under Squilyp's watchful eye, was a Saksonan. Bubbly scarlet hemangiomas crowded his species' skin surface, making him appear like a gigantic, overripe fruit. He had no spines or claws, and his teeth were blunter than mine.

"Them?"

My ClanBrother nodded. "Dr. Irde and Orderly Wonlee volunteered to assist me."

"Could you have picked someone a little easier than Won? Besides Vlaav, I mean?"

Vlaav ducked his head, mumbled something, and headed for the door. Wonlee only grinned at me, displaying most of his pointed teeth.

"Dr. Irde, please stay." Xonea gestured to both males. "You both can contribute greatly to Healer Cherijo's training." He shook his head when I tried to say something. "You will follow my instructions during training, just like any member of the crew."

I was willing to go along with this because of Marel, but even I wasn't that stupid. "I didn't agree to become a pin cushion—no offense, Won."

The Esalmalin inclined his prickly head. "None taken."

"Orderly Wonlee is an expert on League assault techniques and weaponry." My ClanBrother gestured toward the table. "Dr. Irde's species has enjoyed considerable success using alternative weaponry."

"Can we do this without the weaponry? Please?"

"For this session, we will only practice hand-to-hand assault and defense maneuvers." Xonea marched me to the center of the practice quad. "Allow each of them to demonstrate one method."

"I'd better not need bandages after this." I spread my feet and centered my weight. "Okay, Won, let's see what you've got."

"League troop protocol during individual engagement is to initially eliminate enemy mobility." Wonlee dropped suddenly, and the next thing I knew I was facedown on the mat beside him. "Like so."

"Great protocol." I sat up. When he would have helped me to my feet, I shook my head. "Show me how you did that."

Won demonstrated, this time going for Xonea. The

Jorenian merely vaulted over him before the Esalmalin so much as laid a spine on him. Then they made me do it to Vlaav, who proved to be almost as nimble as Xonea. That, or I was too slow and clumsy to nail him.

"Okay, Dr. Irde." I rolled to my feet and went after him. "Let's see why Saksonans are supposed to be such hot fighters."

Vlaav, who looked very serious, didn't move. Just as I got within smacking range, he lifted his upper limbs and slapped them together. Every dermal pocket on the inside of his arms instantly burst, spraying us both with bloody body fluid.

A second later, I was on my knees, sputtering and trying to wipe my eyes clear with the sleeve of my tunic.

"That's—that's *disgusting*!" I yelled, as soon as I'd spit the hemangiomatic fluid from my mouth.

"Let me help." The Saksonan bent down and wiped my face with a piece of cloth Xonea tossed him. "It's disgusting, but harmless," Vlaav assured me. "It was not always so. My people once deliberately infected themselves with various diseases before entering into battle."

"Bacterial warfare delivered via infected body fluid. Very nice." I took the cloth away from him and scrubbed. "Humans don't maintain enough of any body fluids to squirt in the enemy's face. If that much blood comes out of us, we die."

"Such attacks are common among nonhuman species," Xonea said.

He'd done this on purpose. I could feel it. "I've been subjected to a couple of nonhuman species attacks already, thanks. Is the demeaning part a central aspect of the program?"

"Only if the participant is a complete novice in battle."

"Perhaps Duncan should spar with you," Wonlee said, oblivious to the undercurrents flowing between me and my ClanBrother. "He is a well-trained warrior, but Terran, like you."

Won was right, of course. The Hsktskt had taught Reever to fight in a slave arena, and as a result he used their bizarre, nonhuman moves to stomp pretty much anyone who came at him. I'd seen some glimpses of *how* he'd learned to fight when we were linked. It wasn't something I wanted to experience personally.

"It's better if I keep my marriage out of the warrior's quad." I looked at the stains on the front of my tunic, and frowned. "Be nice if I had something like Vlaav does, though."

"You can use a blade as well as any warrior on the ship," the Captain insisted.

I went to the table, and examined the lethal assortment. "I don't mean to kill. To . . . disarm . . ." I picked up what looked like a short black stick. "What's this?"

Won came over, took the stick, and twisted it. Both ends shot out and turned it into a *long* black stick, which he whirled around in a blurry circle. "A *goreu* staff, from my homeworld. It is used instead of a blade during training."

"Kind of long to be a pretend sword." I grabbed it when he tossed it back to me and planted one end on the deck. It appeared to be a good foot taller than me. "It's just a telescoping device, right? Spikes don't shoot out of it or anything, do they?"

Won grinned. "No, it merely elongates."

"Handy." I measured it again by holding it against my body. During a visit to Asia as a Medtech student back on Terra, I'd discovered one form of the martial arts that had briefly fascinated me. When I returned home, Joseph had vetoed training, but allowed me to purchase instructional vids. I'd never really used the lessons I'd learned, but I hadn't forgotten them. "Can you make it shorter? Say, hack seven inches off each end?"

"Of course, but why?"

I turned the staff sideways, dropped down, and slammed it into the backs of his central leg joints. Two seconds later, Won lay on the practice mat and stared at me, shocked.

"That's why." I hefted the staff, thought of Qonja, and nodded. "And take off eight inches."

A few days later, Squilyp and I met to discuss options on how to deal with the ever-increasing problems with our Oenrallian patient. I would have done that over the diagnostic console in his office, but the Omorr steered me out to the corridor.

"We need to take a meal interval," he said, adding when I protested, "you missed at least two today."

Three, but who was counting? "I checked the scaffolding chamber; the clone liver won't be ready for transplant for at least another four days. Since when do you worry about my diet?"

"I am worried about this new resident, but we can't talk in Medical—he listens to every conversation we have. We must also determine how to replicate those hypercells if we're going to save Pilot Dhreen, and perform the necessary test trials."

"I hope we have time to do all that." In the galley, I walked up to the prep unit and dialed up the first thing on my personal menu—mixed Chinese vegetables on steamed rice with almond tea. "What are you having?"

He punched in his own choice. "Vreah stew."

"Does it look like a bowl of live worms?"

"No."

"Good."

As we sat down with our trays, I noticed Salo and a group of engineers making gestures of greeting toward us from several tables over, and waved back at them. Each male wore a warrior's knot in his matte-black hair, which meant they were probably old battle buddies. It was unusual to find Xonea's second-in-command in the galley at this time of night; generally, Salo spent his off-duty time with his bondmate and child.

"Looks like Xonea's bright idea to deploy the cannons has everyone talking." I tasted my tea, and eyed Squilyp's stew. It didn't look like worms, but it was bright yellow, pulpy, and had purple spiny things in it. "Does that really taste better than it looks?"

He sampled it. His species ate using their gildrells like utensils, but Squilyp did it with such elegance that it almost seemed dainty. "The indigenous cephalopods on the Omorr homeworld are tastier, and have more crunch."

"Yum." I turned my head and made a horrible face. "Are you sure you want to go back there?"

He shrugged. "It is tradition, if I wish to secure a viable marriage contract."

I really didn't want to be in charge of Medical again. Especially if Duncan and I decided we'd be better off leaving the *Sunlace*. "Too bad the Omorr don't have mail-order brides. Your parents could buy a wife for you and send her to the ship."

"Terrans order and purchase their spouses, like commodities?" He frowned. "I thought slavery had been eradicated from your homeworld."

I explained the joke, and briefly described the authentic archaic Terran custom behind it.

"Quite a novel idea." He pondered that for a moment. "It is quite possible I could arrange to negotiate my marriage contract here, on the *Sunlace*."

"Squilyp. I was *kidding*." I'd better change the subject, or he'd be signaling Omorr for some single female catalogues. "So what's up with our favorite stalker?"

"I retrieved his personnel data and reviewed it. Before his assignment to the *Sunlace*, Qonja Torin studied as a student of Klarak Adan, at a Medtech in the Lno Province."

"Which means what?"

"The Ruling Council governs Joren from the Lno Province. Coincidentally, Klarak Adan also serves as the Council's Primary Health Advisor."

"Interesting set of coincidences." I tapped a fingertip against my lips. "Either he has friends in high places, or they sent him to watch me."

My boss gave me a worried look. "Why would they do that, Cherijo?"

"Maybe they want my secret recipe for chicken noodle soup." My attention strayed as Ilona Red Faun strode purposefully across the galley toward Salo and his group. The Terran girl put her hand on Salo's arm and bent over to speak to him. The big warrior immediately rose and led Ilona away into the games room. "I should tell you, Squil, Reever and I may take Marel and get out of here. Soon."

"Will the Torins allow you to leave the ship?"

"Xonea won't like it." I tried my rice, which wasn't quite sticky enough. "He and Reever aren't exactly best friends these days."

"I've noticed." Squilyp smiled at the snort I made. "Perhaps they only want what's best for you and Marel."

"Yeah, too bad they can't agree on what that is."

I watched Darea enter the galley, obviously looking for her bondmate. She stopped at Salo's table, then went into the games room. Four seconds later, a woman screamed.

Squilyp and I looked at each other, got up, and ran. We and a couple of crew members had to dive out of the way as a whump-ball table came flying out of the games room and crashed, wiping out several tables and chairs.

"Someone's having a bad day," I said.

Inside, Darea had Ilona pinned up against an interior hull panel, one huge blue hand holding the red-faced Terran girl by the throat. Ilona's feet dangled a good two feet above the deck.

Salo stood beside Darea, apparently trying to calm her down and keep her from snapping the weaver's neck. "It is not what you perceive, my heart."

"Darea!" I rushed forward. "Let her go!"

"She put her hands on my bondmate!" The big Jorenian female shook Ilona like a rag doll. "You *dare* beset what is mine?"

"I— I—" The beautiful face contorted as Ilona tried to get enough air to speak, and couldn't. White showed all around her frantic dark eyes.

I tried again, this time with a softer tone. "Darea, please, put her down. I'm sure she didn't mean to threaten Salo."

He gave me a faintly ironic look. "She was not *threatening* me, Healer."

"Then what . . . ?" The light dawned when I saw a smudge of color on Salo's face—the same color as the pigment Ilona used to redden her lips. "Oh. Oh, no."

Squilyp chose a more direct approach. "Darea Torin, I shield Ilona Red Faun. Release her this moment."

"You cannot shield her, Senior Healer." Despite stating this, Darea released Ilona and watched her thump down on the floor. The Terran girl grabbed her throat and coughed uncontrollably. "She attempts to violate the bond between mates. There is no shielding of such an offense."

I'd never heard what Jorenians did when someone made a pass at their bondmates. Evidently no one had been stupid enough to try it very often. "Darea, she's Terran. In her culture this sort of thing happens regularly—"

She turned her head to glare at me.

"Not that I'm condoning it at all," I quickly added. "She probably didn't know."

"She was given the standard protocol briefing that everyone who joins the crew receives." Darea eyed me. "Would you ever try to violate my bond with Salo?"

"No, but—"

"Yet you come from the same culture as this one." She reached down and grabbed Ilona by the front of her tunic, clearly ready to hurl the girl out of the room.

Salo stepped in and grabbed her hands. "Darea, Cherijo has lived among us before. This female has not, and perhaps she did not understand the protocol. I am certain she will not attempt to do this again. Is this not correct, Ilona Red Faun?"

The Terran girl coughed and nodded.

Darea stared at her bondmate's fingers, curled around her wrists. "Release me. I have the right to instruct as Chosen and bonded."

Salo's jaw sagged for a moment; then he snapped it shut and stepped away.

"What does that mean?" I looked at Squilyp, who only shrugged, as puzzled as I was. "Darea, what's that mean?"

"I will teach this outsider what it means to be

bonded within the HouseClan, and assure she will not make the same mistake again. Tomorrow, at shift commencement." Darea kicked Ilona out of her way and stomped out of the games room. Salo stayed behind and watched as Squilyp and I helped Ilona up from the deck.

"I'd better take her to Medical and treat these contusions," the Omorr said as he put an arm around the Terran girl's waist. "See you in the morning, Doctor. Salo."

That left me standing with Darea's bemused bondmate, who was still staring at the deck where Ilona had fallen.

I cleared my throat to get his attention. "How bad is this, Salo? Can't you talk Darea out of it?"

"Not when our bond has been violated. It is a serious matter." He started for the door.

"Wait a minute." I went after him. "How serious? Don't tell me they fight to the death or something."

"No." He expelled a long breath. "They fight to decide who gets me."

CHAPTER FIVE

Lessons in Protocol

Reever and I discussed the challenge the next morning over breakfast, and I found out he knew a lot more about bond protocols than I did.

I checked the time on our main console. "The fight starts in about an hour. You're sure they don't beat the daylights out of each other?"

He poured me another server of morning tea. "They pit themselves against a series of obstacles to prove their strength and agility."

Darea would win, hands down, I thought as I wiped Marel's face, which she'd smeared with jaspkerry jam. "What happens to Ilona when she loses?"

Marel gave me a cheerful smile. "CanAnn Darea beads da wides owda her."

I glanced at Reever. "Is she right?"

"If she prevails, the bondmate has the right initiate a nonlethal bout, yes."

"Great." Sometimes Jorenian customs made very little sense to me, but this one moved to the top of the list. I rested my aching brow against one hand. "They do this in an environome, I presume."

"Yes." My husband lifted our kid out of her chair and brushed a fine layer of toast crumbs off her tunic. "Go and wash your hands, *avasa*; then I will take you to school."

As soon as she left us, I asked, "Darea wins, maybe beats up Ilona, and that's it, right? No one starts interior decorating with anyone's entrails?"

"That is all, unless Ilona prevails."

That wasn't going to happen in a million, zillion years, but I gulped down the rest of my tea anyway. "If she does, what?"

"Darea must embrace the stars."

"You're kidding." I watched his face, hoping to see one of those rare smiles. No smile. "Jesus. You're not kidding."

"I must take Marel now, then report for duty. I know you will do what you can for Ilona." He reached across the table and took my hand in his. "I missed you last night. Do not work late again today, beloved."

In spite of my current worries, I felt the jolt I never got used to hit me as his fingers entwined briefly with mine. "I'll try not to."

As a precaution, Squilyp sent a couple of nurses with me to monitor the challenge. Half the crew had already crowded into the largest environome on the ship on level fourteen, where Darea was already warming up. I pushed my way through the mob of big blue giants to enter the warrior's quad.

"Darea, got a minute?"

Salo's bondmate stopped stretching and stood up, towering over me. Her hands were in tight fists. "I will not be persuaded to alter my path, Healer."

"Take it easy. I'm not the one messing with your marriage, remember?" I glanced at the other side of the quad. Still empty. Maybe Ilona would have a bright moment and not show up. "My concern is about what happens if you don't win."

Darea flexed her hands, cracking knuckles as the

crowd parted and Ilona hesitantly walked in. "I will prevail."

"Is that what you told Fasala this morning?"

My friend got mad. "You do not understand our customs. Salo Chose me, and I him. Allowing another to come between us would sully our bond forever." She turned a little, looking up at the galley where her bondmate sat. "Bonds are sacred things, Healer. They cannot be made lightly, or taken for granted. Interference in such creates rifts between Chosen, and must not be tolerated."

I thought it was a bit much, even for the loyalty-loving Jorenians, to expect no one to flirt with their spouses. Then I saw Qonja headed my way, and decided to try another approach, fast. "You have to know how much Salo loves you."

She tilted her head. "What does *luhuvs* mean?"

I forgot, "love" didn't translate into Jorenian. "Honors. I meant he honors you. He certainly doesn't want anything to do with Ilona."

"It is not only about Salo. My feelings are of equal importance. What is mine is to be kept mine, and sullied by no other." She stretched her long arms over her head. "How would you feel if that Terran female acted improperly toward Duncan?"

Since I'd gotten into a fistfight with Ilona over pretty much the same thing, all I could say was, "Point taken."

Giving up on persuading the enraged Jorenian spouse to see reason, and determined to avoid the Boy Shrink, I went over to parley with the offender. "Call it off, Ilona. Tell her you're sorry and you'll never do it again. Throw in some begging for mercy while you're at it."

The Terran girl stripped off her tunic. "I am not afraid of her."

I hauled her over to a corner and made her face me. "Look, I know we have our differences, but this is *serious*. If Darea wins, she will pound you into the deck."

"She will not win."

I tightened my grip. "And if that happens, she has to commit ritual suicide."

Ilona didn't blink. "Then Salo will be in need of a new woman, will he not?"

Reminding myself that the little snot had endured a deprived existence on Terra, I clenched my teeth. "What happened to your beloved Dhreen?"

Her confident expression clouded. "You heard him. I am nothing to him but a weight around his neck. If he survives his injuries, he will not care for me anymore." She tucked her arms around her waist. "He has discarded me."

"For God's sake, Ilona, he was *delirious* when he said that!"

Her brows arched. "I must look after my future. Now leave me alone."

I released her and stalked off, but her attitude actually didn't surprise me. Ilona's culture encouraged her to attach herself to the strongest male as a matter of protection and survival. Dhreen's rejection must have made her panic and go after Salo.

Who was the next person I needed to chat with? I spotted him sitting in the front of the gallery Darea had programmed for spectators. Unfortunately, Tall, Blue, and Bothersome got in my way first.

"Healer Cherijo, may I have a word with you?"

I wondered how hard it would be to eviscerate someone with my bare hands. I didn't have claws, so I'd need a blade. "No."

"I've changed my mind—"

"Does the new one work any better?" I went around him and got to Salo. The resident gave me a frustrated look, then left the environome. Which allowed me to concentrate on my friend, not on how much I wanted to throttle the Boy Shrink. "Hey, big guy. This is a real mess, isn't it?"

"Cherijo." He gave me an unhappy look. "Darea has never been so angry."

"I noticed." I sat down beside him. "I tried to talk to both of them, but they're not listening. How about you? Is there something you can do to stop this?"

"Darea is within her rights to demand the threefold challenge. It is an archaic custom, noted only in the books of the First House, but remains valid."

I recalled Salo collected old books. "You should watch what your wife reads. It may end up costing Ilona her life."

"I do not believe Darea will kill her." He didn't sound too certain of that as he gestured toward Ilona. "She brought it upon herself when she chose to violate our bond, although why she did still mystifies me."

Even before Varena brought journey philosophy to his people, the Jorenians had never indulged in infidelity. According to Reever, it was a matter of animal instinct overriding sociological development—whatever that meant. The fact remained: Salo's people mated for life. Even after the loss of a bondmate, they rarely Chose again, so the old Terran vow of "until death do us part" had little meaning for them.

They also had no idea how attractive they were to anyone who appreciated big, healthy humanoid males, and Salo had the bad luck of being one of the best-looking guys on the ship.

"Ilona's upbringing on Terra taught her to form a

sexual alliance with the strongest male in her tribe," I explained as the environome deck cleared of everyone but the two females. "I really don't think she understood the Jorenian protocols regarding personal relationships."

Salo made a faintly commiserating sound. "She is about to be taught the finer details." He went on to explain the first challenge as Darea's program initiated. "Each female proves her strength by disabling a physically superior opponent."

Two images coalesced in front of Darea and Ilona—Tingalean warriors, who reached heights of over eight feet when erect, and whose blood alone was lethal upon skin contact. Both simulated warriors carried traditional tooth-cluster slings, a native weapon that vaguely resembled a Terra bola. Only this alien bola was studded with the Tingalean's own teeth that had been shed and collected since infancy.

"Couldn't Darea have picked something a little easier?" Light gleamed over the rows of razor-sharp teeth. "Like a squad of starved Hsktskt?"

The environome simulators were programmed not to allow living users to be terminally injured by a simulation, but the parameters certainly allowed for serious injury. Ilona looked up at the snake-soldier hissing over her head and blanched.

"She can't do this, Salo," I said, rising to my feet. "That thing will cut her to pieces."

He put a restraining hand on my arm. "If you interfere, Darea forfeits the challenge."

"Why?"

"You are a member of her HouseClan."

I sat down. "Great." Another reason to burn the adoption records. "Why doesn't this work like

ClanKill, where a member of the family can talk some sense into the bloodthirsty hothead?"

He made a shushing sound. "The challenge commences."

Unlike the physical challenge I'd once gotten into with Squilyp during my first tour on the *Sunlace*—not one of my finer moments—Darea made no announcements or declarations. She merely tossed a long, single-bladed sword to Ilona, then took up her own and launched herself at the Tingalean in front of her. Darea was warrior trained, and used the blade deftly to hack and slash at the toothy bola it flung toward her.

The assembled Torins—some forty crew members—began cheering as purple and green blood splattered the deck.

The other simulation began approaching the Terran girl, who backed up slowly. She looked too terrified to do much more than bleed, I thought, then got pleasantly shocked when Ilona dropped to the deck, rolled to avoid the bola, then thrust her sword at the Tingalean's lower extremity. The simulation easily avoided the blow, and knocked the Terran girl into an interior panel with one solid thunk of its tail. Ilona scrambled to her feet and ran a circle around it, dodging the whiplike limblets and slashing at it whenever she could get close enough.

Not bad for a humble weaver.

Darea quickly downed her snake-soldier, then tossed aside her blade and executed a flawless death strike by plunging her newly emerged claws into the Tingalean's upper torso and wrenching out its heart.

I'd once glimpsed Xonea after he'd done that to a mercenary's intestines, and the image still haunted some of my nightmares. Watching the mother of my daughter's favorite playmate do that to a living being—okay, simulated living being—made my skin crawl.

She stood, held the heart above her head for a moment, then tossed it to the deck. The dark blue claws that sprang from the tips of her fingers gleamed dark purple with simulated Tingalean blood. "I prevail."

Ilona had nearly finished off her soldier by then, and looked bewildered as the simulation disappeared. Slowly, she wiped some sweat from her face with the back of her hand. "Agreed." She tossed the sword aside.

"What happens now?" I asked Salo.

"Darea will initiate the challenge of agility."

I expected a couple more simulated killers to appear, but the environome produced a pair of what looked like elaborate rose trellises that stretched from the floor to the upper deck, some twenty feet.

"What are those things?"

"*Hatlakin.* They must climb them."

My vocollar didn't translate the Jorenian word, but I figured it was some sort of garden thing. Their homeworld was literally paved in a gazillion different types of flora. "Interesting."

The symmetrical silvery slats that formed the *hatlakins'* diamond-shaped structure were pretty, but hardly any sort of a challenge. In fact, the slats were so close together even Marel could have climbed up one of them.

"Let me guess." I peered at the simulations. "Whoever gets to the top first, wins?"

"There is more involved, Healer."

I saw what Salo meant when Darea and Ilona began climbing the trellises, and the innocuous silver slats began undulating as if they were melting. While both women hung on, pointed spikes of various sizes began extruding from the slats, directly at their hands, bodies, and feet.

Ilona yelped as she changed handholds to avoid being stabbed. "Unfair!"

"Then you must concede." Darea grunted as a spike punctured one of her hands before she wrenched it free.

"I will not." The Terran girl began dodging the spikes, moving quickly toward the center portion of the trellis.

If the spikes weren't bad enough, the trellises began drooping over, twisting into strange shapes as if attempting to shake off the women.

I leaned toward Salo. "And you use these things on Joren for *what*?"

"Protecting HouseClan property."

Attack trellises. "No wonder nobody ever steals anything from you people."

Somehow Ilona proved more adept at avoiding the spikes, and slowly made her way up the length of the writhing *hatlakin*. When she reached the top, she was ahead of Darea by a couple of inches. She was also hanging completely upside down.

"I prevail," the Terran girl called out, and then dropped onto the deck as the trellises abruptly disappeared. She grimaced as she rubbed her side with a bloodied hand.

"Does this mean they're tied?" I asked Salo. He nodded, never taking his eyes off his bondmate. "You said there were three challenges."

"The final challenge is one of honor."

Darea and Ilona faced each other as a simulated crowd of children began to appear. Some were Terran, others Jorenian, and still others of alien species. All of them were shrieking.

"You may make the first attempt," Darea said to her opponent.

"I don't understand." Confused, Ilona scanned the crowd of weeping children. The imager had produced over two hundred of them. "What must I do?"

The Jorenian female spread her arms wide. "Comfort them."

I frowned and nudged Salo. "Baby-sitting is the final challenge?"

"Honoring the young requires more than supervision."

Hesitantly, Ilona went to a Terran child, and awkwardly put her arms around her. "Shhh. Don't cry." She reached for another, stroking the small alien face. "It will be all right. Do you wish to hear the story of *Yei* who fought the Whirlwind? Would that not be pleasant?"

The entire group of simulated children dissolved into even louder hysterics.

"It is not fair." Ilona stood up, clearly annoyed. "There are too many of them."

"The path is seldom fair." Darea gave her a contemptuous look. "And there are never too many kin within the House." She pushed Ilona aside, and strode to the center of the group. Once there, she clapped her hands once over her head. The explosive sound silenced the children's weeping for a brief moment. "The Mother gives us the path. We walk it alone but we can journey together. Come, embrace your kin and offer comfort. Offer and receive what is needed."

Darea went to the nearest pair of children and turned them to each other, showing them how to put their limbs around each other. She repeated this, over and over, until the other children began to hug each other spontaneously. At last they were all smiling and whispering and holding each other.

Ilona took a step back as the simulation ended and Darea came toward her. "No. I concede. You have won."

"We travel alone, Ilona Red Faun, until we Chose to journey with another." Darea's mouth flattened, but she bent down and briefly touched her brow to the Terran girl's. "I honor your path. Honor mine, and you will never journey alone."

It was the most touching thing I'd ever seen. "You're a lucky man, Salo."

He smiled at me, but his eyes never left his bondmate. "That I am, Cherijo."

I escorted both women to Medical to treat them for their various bruises and wounds. Darea remained stoic and silent throughout the treatment, then left with her bondmate, who was treating her as though she were made out of Ki-Anakaan porcelain.

Ilona did not want me to examine her. I found out why when I bullied her onto an exam table and activated an abdominal scanner.

"Mother of All Houses." I didn't bother to make an announcement. Judging by the evasive gaze, she already knew. "When were you planning to tell someone?" I yelled, tossing the scanner aside. "After Darea beat you to a pulp?"

"It is none of your concern, patcher."

Through the faint red haze now occluding my vision, I watched Qonja approach. "Is something amiss, Doctor?" He jumped a little when I thrust her chart at him.

"Figure it out, bright boy." I would have thrown in some graphic instructions on what to do with the chart, but out of the corner of my eye I saw Ilona slip inside the critical care unit. "No, Ilona, don't—" I took off running.

I found her kneeling beside Dhreen's berth, speaking to him in a low, urgent voice. He appeared even more pallid than yesterday, but grinned when he saw me. "Hi, Doc. Who is this female? A new nurse?"

"Why doesn't he remember me now?" Ilona demanded.

"I don't know, but you have to go. Right now." I took her by the arm and guided her toward to the door. "It's okay, Dhreen. Let me return Ms. Red Faun to her berth, then I'll be back."

"No."

The tone of his voice made us both turn around. His color had improved, but the look of disgust on his face was totally unexpected.

"I remember who she is now." He struggled to sit up. "She's a liar."

"No, don't do that. Wait." I had to let go of Ilona to stop him from tearing out his chest tube. "Calm down." I checked his monitors, which showed elevations in all his vital signs. I hit the nurse call button by the berth, then looked over my shoulder. "You, *leave*."

She ignored me and rushed back over to grab Dhreen's hand. "I am not lying to you. I would never do that."

Where was the damn nurse? "He can't take this kind of stress, Ilona. Get out of here!"

"She says she is having my child." He glared up at me. "Is it true?"

I sighed. "Yes, she's five weeks pregnant, Dhreen."

"Impossible." Heat poured into his amber eyes, while bright orange painted swatches of temper over his cheekbones. Somehow he made a whisper sound like a bellow. "I've been sterile all my life."

"Stop saying that!" Ilona shrieked, clutching her abdomen. "This is your child, our child!"

I gave up hitting the button and shouted, "Nurse! Get in here!"

One of the ward nurses promptly appeared, and took the now-weeping Ilona out of the unit.

"All right. She's gone, now settle down." I made note of his vital signs on his chart and dropped it on the table beside his berth. It clattered loudly in the stillness of the unit. "How much of your memory has come back?"

"Enough to know that Terran bitch is lying."

I didn't know how to break it to him any other way than with complete honesty. "Listen, I scanned the fetus two minutes ago. Half of the baby's DNA is Oenrallian."

He closed his eyes, and some of the hectic color left his face. "I told you, I can't have children."

"You're the only one of your kind on the ship, Dhreen. There's no other Oenrallian who could have gotten that girl pregnant."

He made a weak gesture with one hand. "Repeat the test, Doc."

I glanced out at Ilona, huddled on her berth. "I don't think—"

"Repeat the test!" he shouted, then started coughing.

"Fine, you calm down, and I'll run the test again." I dialed up a mild sedative on my syrinpress and injected the drug into his infuser line. "If you're wrong, you know you're going to owe that girl a pretty big apology."

"I'm not wrong." His voice grew thick as the drug took effect. "None of us can have them."

"None of who can have what?"

"Children." He let out a long, shuddering sigh. "My people are sterile."

I left a sedated Dhreen with a nurse on constant monitor, gave instructions to another to keep Ilona out of his unit, and signaled Squilyp.

"Sorry to wake you up, but I've got to contact Oenrall." I explained the incident with Dhreen, and repeated what he'd told me. "If there's a pathogen present on his homeworld that's causing this, we need to know before we sojourn down there."

He smothered a yawn with his gildrells. "There are no indications on any of the available databases that his species has suffered mass sterility."

"Maybe they don't want anyone to know," I said. "No matter how long lived they are, this kind of thing means eventual and total extinction."

"An amnesiac is not a reliable source of information," the Omorr said. "Did you scan his reproductive system to verify his claim?"

"Yep. Here, take a look at the results." I downloaded the scan data to his terminal. "His sperm count is so low it barely registers. The fact that Ilona got pregnant falls into the miraculous category of conception."

"Very well." He rubbed his brow ridges. "Advise the Captain before you signal Oenrall, and be as tactful as possible when you speak to his people."

"You know me. Dr. Diplomacy."

I sent my next signal to Xonea, who also thought Dhreen was probably delusional, but approved my request. Finally, I had Communications send a direct relay to Dhreen's homeworld, and was routed through a number of automated systems before a real Oenrallian face appeared on my screen.

"Greetings." He gave me a rather dreamy smile. "I am Plaak, planetary communications officer."

"Hi, I'm Dr. Cherijo Torin, a healer serving on the Jorenian star vessel *Sunlace*." I told him about Dhreen, and went through the explanation for a third time, adding, "It would help us treat him if we could confirm what he's told us about your people."

"He speaks of the wanting condition," Plaak said.

I moved closer to the vid screen. "I beg your pardon, the wanting what condition?"

"The wanting condition. That is all we call it."

"Okay." I pursed my lips. "Can you transmit the complete medical data on this condition to my ship?"

He looked away for a moment, then gave me another slow smile. "No, that is not permitted."

His languid, nonchalant attitude was really starting to bug me. "Then can you tell me about it?"

"I'm not a physician."

"In your words will be fine." For now, anyway.

"It began one hundred revolutions ago." He made an airy gesture. "Our people simply stopped having children. Now there are no more left."

Maybe he was intoxicated. "No children have been born on your homeworld since this wanting condition showed up?"

"That is correct."

"Everyone's reproductive system suddenly shut down overnight? Males *and* females?" He nodded, and I rubbed my palms against my trousers. "What is your current population, Plaak?"

"One moment." He checked something, then turned back to the screen. "At the last world census, two billion, five hundred and forty-three million, seven hundred and thirty-three thousand, nine hundred and twelve."

Oenrall had too large a population to have suffered long-term effects of a limited gene pool. It didn't make sense. Two billion plus people simply didn't spontaneously lose their ability to proliferate. Not unless they'd been subjected to serious planetary-scale radiation. Or I was getting the data from a less than reliable source.

I picked the more realistic of the two. "Are you sure about this, sir?"

He shrugged. "Why would I lie?"

Most species went through fertile and infertile periods during their development, but individual age was generally the determining factor. "Has there been any widespread environmental contamination on Oenrall? You know—industrial waste, biotech weapons fallout, that sort of thing?"

Another yawn, one he didn't bother to cover. "Our people don't pollute our resources, or engage in warfare."

Maybe it was part of the Oenrallian life cycle. "Has it ever happened before?" At his blank look, I added, "In the history of your planet, have your people ever experienced mass reproductive problems?"

"Not that I know of."

I dredged up one memory of reading a report on certain types of solar radiation, the unexpected increase of which had wiped out a number of inhabited planets. "What about the other life-forms on Oenrall? How are the nonsentients doing?"

"The wanting condition only affects my species."

Cross out the usual sources, which left only a few unpleasant possibilities. Genetic mutation. Plague. Other forms of natural annihilation. "May I petition your government to have the medical data on this condition sent to my ship?"

"No." He seemed a little annoyed. "I've answered all your questions, haven't I?"

That he had. Now I only had a thousand more to ask. "Perhaps I should speak to another physician. Would that be possible?"

"I don't know." He looked away again. "No, there are none available to speak to you now."

I ground my molars together. Diplomacy was getting me nowhere. Maybe telling them about Ilona's pregnancy would. "Would you ask one to signal me as soon as possible? I have a female passenger who is pregnant with an Oenrallian child."

He didn't jump for joy. He chuckled. "Sure you do."

"I'll transmit my medical data, if you need proof."

"No, that won't be necessary." He obviously didn't believe me. "You want anything else?"

Besides a blunt object to use on his head? "No, that's all for now. Thank you for your . . . assistance." I terminated the signal, and sat back to mull over what I'd learned.

I found myself pulling up the data on Dhreen's species, and checking the average life span. In both genders, it ranged between two hundred and fifty to three hundred revolutions.

Which meant the people of Oenrall only had two hundred years left before they became extinct.

PART TWO

Persuasions

CHAPTER SIX

Remnants of Battle

I temporarily put aside the problem on Oenrall and went back to working on a way to keep Dhreen's liver functioning. There was little I could do without hard data, and I got the impression the physicians on his homeworld weren't in any rush to consult with me.

The Lok-Teel had actually been helping Dhreen's failing liver by removing toxins from his blood, and more. After I read through some unusual notes on his chart, I called the ward nurse who made them into Squilyp's office.

Savetka, a new addition to the staff, seemed a little nervous as she stood before the desk. "How may I be of assistance, Healer?"

I held up Dhreen's chart. "You recommend we investigate using the Lok-Teel for wound management. Why?"

"They seem to sense what needs to be done." She shifted her weight and dropped her gaze to the deck. "Initially, I noted how they were drawn to the patient's surgical site whenever I changed his dressing. Then the patient dislodged the chest drain, which I discovered shortly after during my hourly monitor. I found a Lok-Teel adhered to the drain site. There was no fluid buildup, and his vitals improved greatly over the course of the remainder of my shift." She met my gaze.

"If I have exceeded my authority with this recommendation, Healer, I would ask your pardon."

"Exceed your authority anytime you like, Savetka." I got up and handed her the chart. "I'd like you to work with the surgical residents and compose a treatment schedule using Lok-Teel application for direct wound drainage."

Her eyes rounded. "To initiate therapy?"

"Uh-huh. I also want your recommendations on how the therapy can be used for other postsurgical patients. You'll need to set up some trial runs, see if your idea works on other types of wounds. Arrange a testing schedule with the residents, and copy your findings to me and the Senior Healer."

She seemed dazed as she cradled the chart between her big hands. "Yes, Healer."

"One more thing." I gave her a megawatt grin. "Excellent work, nurse."

Duncan was waiting up for me when I came off duty, and Marel's room was dark. I checked the late hour on the wall terminal and nearly groaned as I recalled his request from the morning.

"Sorry." I went over to kiss him, and collapsed on the sofa beside him. "I had the best intentions in the world, until I started trying to reconstruct an organ."

"It does not matter."

But it did. I could tell. I sat up. "What did I do now?"

His arm pulled me close, and one of his hands touched my face. The link was immediate and shook me. Not from the suddenness of Duncan in my thoughts, but the state of his emotions. He was beyond angry.

I found something in our bedchamber last night. Reever pulled me from the sofa and led me into our room. *Pretend we are retiring as usual.*

I tried to joke my way out of my nervousness. *That would mean tearing your clothes off and throwing myself on top of you.*

His mouth curled on one side. *Not this time.*

I didn't have to fake a yawn as I stripped down and lowered the optic emitters. Reever did the same on his side of the room, then we both climbed into bed. I snuggled up beside him, trying to figure out how I was going to see what he wanted to show me. *Well?*

Roll over and look at the wall panel above your head.

I rolled and looked. Something, a tiny something, sparkled against the polished alloy surface. As what it was sank in, I forgot to feel tired. I reached up, but Reever grabbed me and rolled me under him.

You can't remove it.

The hell I can't. I tried to push him off.

Squilyp signaled me about Qonja. Joren may be planning to enter the League/Hsktskt conflict. If they do, they would be fools not to make use of you and me, and our particular knowledge of either side.

I went still as the implications of what that meant flooded inside my head. *No. They wouldn't. Xonea wouldn't do that to us.*

Recording drones don't implant themselves. He stroked my arm. *Unless . . . are you sure Joseph is dead?*

I watched him die. My numbness wore off as I looked through the door panel toward Marel's room. It would be simple to use our daughter to ensure our cooperation—but I couldn't believe the Torins would do that. The Ruling Council, on the other hand . . . *We have to get off this ship.*

Reever lifted his head and looked down at me. *Not until we know who did this, and what they want.*

* * *

The next day, Reever found seven more drones, using some kind of structural analyzer he "borrowed" from Engineering. They were in every room, even Marel's. We decided to do nothing immediately—actually, Duncan decided that. I was personally in favor of ripping them out and stuffing them down Qonja's—or Xonea's—throat.

His argument was logical: *If we don't learn why they have us under surveillance, we may walk into another trap.*

Fine. Just remember, until those things are out of here, we don't get to do anything but sleep.

Alunthri stopped by our quarters to see Juliet and Jenner's new family a few days later. Marel, who had appointed herself both godmother and guardian to the kittens, warned the Chakacat not to handle the kittens just yet.

"Makes Juweeyed berbous, Mama says."

"Your mama is right." Alunthri crouched down beside the storage unit and peered into the kittening box. "A fine litter. My small sibling must be proud."

"Your little brother keeps trying to crash the maternity ward," I told Alunthri as I brought over a server of its favorite beverage, café au lait, heavy on the au lait. "I had to reprogram the door panel to keep him out."

Hearing that made Marel demand to go and console the sulking Jenner, so I signaled Fasala and asked her to come by and pick up my daughter for a visit. Already a few inches taller than me, Darea's daughter had grown back the hair she'd lost from radiation exposure two years before, and was turning into another Jorenian beauty.

"How's your ClanMom and ClanDad?" I asked her when she arrived.

"Very well, Healer, but perhaps more fatigued than

is usual." She wrinkled her nose at me. "At least, they tell that is the reason they spend so much time in their bedchamber of late."

I hid a smile. "Old people like us get tired easily."

After the girls left, Alunthri lingered, talking about its work on cataloguing the different types of artistic expression from around the galaxy, and the anticipation it had for our sojourn on Taerca. It inquired about Dhreen, and I filled it in on his condition, Ilona's pregnancy, and the whole strange conversation with the Oenrallian communications officer.

"Why would he reject his own child when it obviously represents a solution to his people's dilemma?" Alunthri's confusion made its ears flick back and forth. "And why would Plaak show no interest in your information about Ilona's pregnancy?"

"Beats me."

We sat for a time in silence, until I noticed my friend's colorless eyes straying back to the storage unit. "Is something bothering you, Alunthri?"

Whiskers twitched. "Oh, no, Cherijo. I was simply . . . thinking. It is good that Jenner bred Juliet. Many of the crew would enjoy having domestic companions of their own."

"Nice try, but that's not it," I guessed.

Alunthri grimaced, baring its small, sharp teeth for a moment. "You know me too well."

"Might as well get it over with and tell me now."

It regarded me with evident discomfort. "Cherijo, I— I wonder, if I wished to have elective surgery, would you be willing to perform it on me?"

I put down my server. "How elective?"

"As you are aware, my species is hermaphroditic. I am nearly of breeding age myself. Your tale of Dhreen reminded me of a decision I must soon make." It paused, and stroked a paw across the rim of its server. "I have been considering sterilization."

"God, why?"

"I was born free, but my life in the wild only lasted a few weeks. The Chakaran pelters who captured my parent terrified me. I almost did not survive the incarceration." It gazed across the table, and that haunted expression nearly broke my heart. "Cherijo, I could not bear that to happen to my own young. The thought of my children being hunted and sold into slavery appalls me."

I reached out and covered one of its paws with my hand. "You're not on Chakara and you don't have to go back. We won't let anyone hurt you or any young you might have."

"Xonea would say, 'Much changes along the path.' "

"Xonea is not a philosopher. He told me so himself."

Its whiskers twitched. "You had Squilyp perform a tubal ligation on you after you miscarried Marel."

"I didn't have any choice." After Squilyp had transferred Marel's fetus to a prototype embryonic chamber, he'd performed the procedure to assure I'd never get pregnant again. "My immune system won't allow me to carry a child full-term. You don't have that problem."

"Even if I breed, you cannot guarantee our safety, Cherijo. If I am captured by slavers again, I will be sold on the open market, to the highest bidder. So, too, will any progeny I possess." It paused. "Surely now that you have Marel, you understand how I feel."

The Chakacat and I had always shared a special bond. Being declared a nonsentient piece of property had that effect on people, I guess. I may have gambled, having Marel, but obviously Alunthri wasn't willing to throw the dice. And yet I couldn't bear the thought of sterilizing my friend. "Then don't breed yourself."

"After a certain period, the choice will no longer be mine. I will reproduce, whether I wish it or not."

So Alunthri was in the same boat as Squilyp. Nothing like Mother Nature to throw a wrench in your single life.

"We still have a certain time frame to work within, right?" I asked, and Alunthri nodded. "Then I want you to really think about what you're asking me. If you're still bent on doing this, then I'll perform the sterilization."

It gave me a small, feline smile. "Thank you, my friend. It is a comfort to know that in this, I have a choice."

Some choice.

"To breed or not to breed. That is the question."

Squilyp looked up from the electroniscopic scanner. "What is that? Chaucer?"

"Shakespeare, slightly corrupted." I tossed an instrument into the tray and sighed. "All right, scratch hypercellular batch number two-oh-seven. Microcellular breakdown initiated at"—I glanced at the display—"fourteen hundred hours, twenty-two minutes."

The previous two hundred and six attempts to replicate the hypercells had also failed to remain cohesive, and the ineffectual results made me want to drop kick a few cultivation containers across the lab.

If Joseph Grey Veil had achieved hypercellular cohesion, then surely I could duplicate his success. After all, I was practically *his* duplicate.

The Omorr hopped over and studied the slowly liquefying glop in my culture dish. "Your report detailed a description of how the cells began replicating once they had been injected into Reever's kidney. How long did it take?"

"It was instantaneous—as soon as the seed cells were implanted, new ones started popping up, right under my scope." I shoved the dish aside. "Okay, we need to switch gears. What are we doing wrong?"

"It could be the extracorporeal testing." Squilyp's gildrells undulated as he scanned the dish. "Why are you making puns about breeding?"

"Seems like that's all everyone on this ship wants to talk about—you're arranging a marriage so you can be a dad, Alunthri wants to be fixed, Dhreen claims his entire planet is sterile, and Ilona's pregnant with a baby who shouldn't exist. I feel like I'm running a maternity crisis advisory service."

He transferred the data from the scanner to a chart. "The Chakacat wishes to be sterilized?"

"It's the potential slavery thing. Can't blame it. Happily, sterilization seems to be very low on everyone else's priority list."

"We all envy you your child, you know that." He studied the scan results. "Why don't we try injecting the cells into a training torso?"

"Using real cells on simulated flesh won't do it. The cellular foundation crumbles unless we employ simulated hypercells, and I don't trust fake versus real. We need to know exactly what the actual cells are going to do to Dhreen." I frowned. "I can't figure out why everyone is jealous of Marel. You should try keeping that kid clean and in one spot." I gnawed my bottom lip. "Wait a second. How many spare parts have you got stockpiled in the transplant bank?"

"Several hundred, mostly Jorenian. Why?"

"What if we take a common, cloned organ, deliberately injure it, then introduce hypercells extracted from

Reever's kidney?" I grinned as his dark eyes widened. "It would be as close to experimenting on a live subject as we can get."

The Omorr shuddered slightly. "I can't imagine any sane physician actually consenting to experiment on living organisms."

Since most of the medical progress on Terra until two centuries ago had been achieved exactly via that method, I grimaced. "Let's try this with a Jorenian liver."

I left Squilyp to set up the next stage of the experiment, and performed quick afternoon rounds with Adaola. Yarek was ready to be discharged, and promised to return for follow-ups and stay away from bladed weapons for the time specified in his release orders.

"Don't make me block your access codes from all the environomes," I warned him as I handed him his tunic.

"Do not fear, Healer." Yarek gave me a broad grin. "My bondmate has assured me she will do the same, should I become reckless."

I smiled back. "Who do you think gave her the idea?"

A signal came in from Command as I was preparing to return to the lab. Reever's expression remained blank, but his grim tone spoke volumes.

"Cherijo, we have found a number of ships disabled and floating in space. Energy signatures indicate a battle recently took place in this region. Our sweep has picked up multiple weak life signs from five of the vessels."

Weak meant wounded. "What kind of ships, and how many still alive?"

"Military. Four League attack strafers, and the remnants of a Hsktskt scout ship. Perhaps two dozen wounded." He patched through the readings to my screen. "Advise the Senior Healer to prepare two medevac teams."

"Only two?" Eight people couldn't cover five different ships in a hurry.

"Armed security teams will escort you."

Normally I would have given him a hard time about that, but we were entering the aftermath of a battle. The wounded were soldiers and almost certainly prepared to defend themselves. "Remind them we're there to help, not slaughter. I need you with us."

"I'll meet you in launch bay." He paused. "Be cautious, Cherijo."

Squilyp and I swiftly put together the medevac teams, handed out protective vests and communication headsets, and only argued briefly about who was going on the shuttle. I put Vlaav in charge of one team and took command of the other myself.

"I can assess the wounded as well as you can," the Omorr pointed out in a huff.

"Yes, but I can't organize triage here as well as you, and neither can Vlaav." I wouldn't insult his Omorr-hood by reminding him that if a soldier shot me, I'd survive, while he likely wouldn't. "Besides, I haven't seen my husband all day."

"Very well, but take Wonlee with you."

The Esalmalin was already hoisting my field pack over his spiny shoulder. "We should wear side arms."

"That sort of defeats the purpose of medevac, Won." I picked up a thermal proximity scanner, in case some of the wounded were hiding. "Better have the nurses start synthesizing some Hsktskt plasma; we haven't got any stocked." I watched Qonja preparing a pack, and my mouth tightened. "See you in a little while."

Both teams departed the *Sunlace* on the same shuttle,

which was the largest one the Jorenians had available. Xonea manned the helm himself, while Reever explained the flight plan.

"We have broadcast a stand-down signal to all the ships, and shall dock with each in order of largest concentration of wounded on board." He projected a thermalscan showing the meager life signs of the wounded and the ships they were on. "Once we establish that the vessel environment is intact, we will drop off one team, deliver the second to the next ship, then return to transfer team one's wounded on board." He turned to the security guards, who were carrying plenty of bladed and pulse weaponry. "Security will take point, locate the wounded, and disarm them, if necessary, before the medical team facilitates treatment."

"That means no killing," I said at once.

Qonja eyed the ruined vessel we were approaching through the viewport. "There may be traps set for intruders."

"Remind me to steal one if there are," I muttered to my husband.

"We performed a sweep for energy, chemical, and biological agents, and found no indicators. Remain alert." At a call from the Captain, Reever went to the helm, then took over the controls while Xonea came back toward the passenger compartment.

He spoke to both security team leaders in a low voice, then came over to me. "I want you to carry this." He pulled a lethal-looking dagger from his vest and handed it to me.

I tried to give it back. "I appreciate the thought, but no, thanks."

"ClanSister." He closed his fingers over mine, pressing them into the ridged hilt. "You have no claws. Humor me."

I glanced over at my one-man fan club, who was strapping a pulse rifle over his shoulder, then heaved a sigh. "This really isn't necessary."

"I disagree."

I wedged the blade in between the syrinpress and scanner hooked to my own protective vest. "But if someone tries to attack me, Won will give them a big hug. Right, Won?"

The orderly's spines bristled. "A tight hug, Healer."

Reever docked with the first ship, a Hsktskt scout vessel that had seen better days. Whatever kind of fight it had put up had been prolonged, judging by the patchwork of scorch marks left behind by League pulse fire. Nearly the entire stern was missing, along with the stardrive.

"Team one, packs and breathers." I took off my harness as soon as Reever finished docking and pulled my mask over my face.

Security went in first, as ordered, then I followed with my team. As I emerged into an interior corridor, prickles of sweat broke out on my brow and upper lip.

I'm providing medical care to a bunch of wounded, eight-foot-tall, six-limbed monsters who lost twenty thousand valuable slaves and an entire base of operations because of me. Cherijo, you have got to find another job.

Flickering optics barely illuminated the way, which wound through a gauntlet of smashed equipment and collapsing structural panels. The smell of displacer discharge stung my nose. Console alarms droned incessantly, while the more ominous crackle of overloaded circuitry snapped behind every wall.

"Hold." The security team leader's voice came over my headset, low and urgent. "Healer, take your team back to the docking bay."

I pressed a hand to my earpiece. "Why?"

"These wounded indicate they do not wish our assistance."

He hesitated, as if choosing his words carefully. "Nor do we wish to add to the injuries they have already sustained."

As usual, the Hsktskt were giving everyone a hard time.

"Wait." To the medical team, I said, "Stay here." Then I went ahead alone, easing past security guards until I approached the back of the leader, who was using his body to block an open doorway. I tapped his shoulder. "Let me see."

He glanced down at me, then moved to the left. Beyond him was a large area equipped with diagnostic equipment, oversize tables and berths, and everything an onboard physician would need to treat wounded.

There were also ten Hsktskt, in various physical conditions, who had taken positions around the medical bay. They held large, activated displacer rifles pointed directly at the security team leader and me.

I stepped forward, but as soon as my foot crossed over the threshold, one of the Hsktskt fired at the deck, making me jump back with a yelp.

"*Stoikkkass avarillna!*" the Hsktskt centuron snarled at me.

I pressed a key on my vest pad. "Reever? You're needed."

My husband's voice answered a moment later. "What is wrong, Cherijo?"

"What does '*stoikkkass avarillna*' mean?"

"Unpalatable fodder that should be disposed of at once."

That would be us. "Okay." I blew out a breath. "Here's our problem. We've got ten Hsktskt here who need immediate treatment. They're holding us off with guns and, judging by your translation, would like us to leave."

Qonja stepped up behind me. "Healer, we should go."

"Shut up, resident, I'm not asking for your advice." To Reever, I said, "What do you think?"

"Repeat the following words to them. '*Gggdssskka osssjal varreenikk.*'"

I looked at the centuron. "*Gggdssskka osssjal varreenikk.*"

The centuron stared at me as if I'd gone completely insane. Then he turned to his comrades and made a sinuous gesture with one of his six limbs, snapping the end toward me. "*Varreenikkolla Gggdssskka.*"

The other Hsktskt seemed to relax a little.

I repeated all that to Reever, who said, "Excellent. Now put down whatever you're holding and walk forward slowly. Hold out your hands so he can see they're empty."

"And you're sure he'd not going to shoot me?"

"You just gave him your rank in the Faction. He can't shoot you, unless he wants to attempt to do the same to your Designate's entire bloodline."

I put down my medical pack, but before I could enter, Qonja grabbed me and spun me around.

His handsome face had gone powdery blue. "No. I cannot allow this. You will be killed."

I jerked the blade out of my tunic and held it against the side of his throat. "Forgive me for attacking you and shield me. Out loud. Now."

He gulped. "I forgive your transgression and shield you, Healer Cherijo."

The security guards, who would have declared ClanKill or shot me for holding the blade to my one-man fan club's throat, lowered their weapons.

"Take your damn hands off me." I waited until his paws fell away before stepping in closer, and rising on my tiptoes. "You and I are going to settle this when we get back to the ship. Understand me?" His chin bobbed, and I removed the blade. "Now back off, or we'll do it here."

The Hsktskt, who had seen the entire thing, watched as I dropped the knife and moved into the chamber. "Don't they have some kind of translation devices on them?" I asked my husband.

"They are prohibited from using them in battle. Hsktskt soldiers are not interested in talking to their enemies."

"Obviously." I stopped a few feet away from the centuron, who was watching me without blinking. "Okay, now what?"

"Now he will test your claim. Whatever he does, don't move, and say nothing."

The centuron limped forward, revealing a terrible wound on one of his lower appendages that was still oozing blood onto the deck. He raised his displacer weapon and circled my head with the business end, all the time keeping his saucer-size yellow eyes fixed on my expression. I tried to look like I did this every day.

"Goinnnat ehhhar capcom crikk crikk."

"Duncan?"

"The centuron thinks you're an infant who has been allowed to creep away from inattentive parents. Slap him with your hand, palm down, in the center of his upper torso."

"What?"

"Slap him, and do it hard. He's insulted you; he expects you to do it."

"I hope you're right." I reached out and smacked the centuron on the chest, bruising my palm on the octagonally tiled scaly surface under the metallic uniform. The centuron froze. "Um, he's not moving."

"He will in a moment. Be patient."

At last, the big Hsktskt male bent down until his eyes were on a level with mine. His lipless mouth opened, displaying many rows of jagged teeth. *"TssVar ehhhar."*

"Reever, I think he just said something about Tss-Var."

"He's heard of you. He knows you belong to Tss-Var's line." My husband didn't sound too happy about that.

"That's a good thing, right?"

"Wait."

The centuron slowly released a breath, which blasted me in the face. I tried to look nonchalant and kept my gaze locked on his. A heavily taloned hand dropped onto my shoulder, then the centuron allowed his head to fall back, exposing his throat.

I knew what that meant. "He's submitting. Son of a gun."

"Call the rest of your people in and get started."

When I didn't rip out his throat, the centuron slowly straightened and lowered his weapon to the deck. The other Hsktskt reluctantly did the same.

"Okay, people." As the team entered the bay, I led the big male over to a treatment table. "Let's get them prepped to transfer back to the ship."

Xonea decided to move the Hsktskt back to the *Sunlace* on a separate shuttle, mainly on Reever's advice.

"We must keep them apart from the League survivors," Duncan said as he flew my team to the next ship. "I have notified Squilyp, and he has set up a temporary treatment area in one of the cargo holds."

I checked the position of the other shuttle, which had nearly reached the Jorenian ship. "I thought we were all pals now."

"The Hsktskt hold no treaty with any warm-blooded species. They will not attack your medical staff, but I cannot predict what they will do when they see their enemies being treated as well."

"You might have mentioned this before, Duncan."

"Hsktskt almost always commit suicide before allowing themselves to be captured." He shrugged. "I was not sure you would get any of them back to the ship alive."

The reptilian soldiers were in excellent shape, compared to the League troopers we were finding. Their ships had been hit much harder than the scout, and two had actually been boarded by Hsktskt infantry teams. More than half of the humanoids needed major surgery, three of whom were critical.

The business of evacuating the League wounded went much faster. The soldiers put down their weapons as soon as they saw my physician's tunic and the blue faces of my security guards.

"They left us here," one dusky Vinasta told me as I checked the tourniquet it had lashed on a half-severed limb. "I could not believe it when they abandoned us along with the ship."

"Wartime conditions," a Cordoban snarled at him. "Wounded are only a burden on Command. They should have destroyed our ship."

"Lovely job you guys have." I grimaced as I replaced the tourniquet with a pressure dressing. "Stay put, we'll move you on a gurney." I moved to examine the Cordoban, a major with a minor head injury and several broken ribs. "You're the ranking officer here?"

Cordobans were fierce-looking beings, with narrow

faces that seemed crowded by their slitted eyes and beak-shaped nose/mouth orifices. "I am. Major Brlety, Cordoba Fleet, Commander of the Fifth Wing Regulars."

"Nice to meet you, Major. Do me a big favor, and don't upset my patients anymore, okay? They've been through enough." I checked my scanner, then bandaged his head, and slipped a brace around his thin torso. "I'm going to give you something for the pain—"

The major shoved away the syrinpress. "No. No drugs."

"Your ribs, not mine."

We found a total of twenty-three League survivors, and were able to convey them back to the *Sunlace* in short order. I accompanied the Vinasta's gurney to Medical, where Squilyp had every staffer on board working triage and treatment.

"Where do you want me?"

"Down on eighteen, with our other guests." He handed me a chart. "You have the most experience dealing with their injuries."

Major Brlety appeared, dragging a Jorenian nurse along with him. "I demand to speak to your Captain."

"I'll relay your request," Squilyp told him. "Return to your berth."

The Cordoban scowled. "I must speak with him immediately."

"Nurse, hand me your syrinpress." Squilyp held out a membrane for the instrument, then calibrated it for a massive dose of tranquilizer. "You will return to your berth now, or I will sedate you and drag you there."

"This is unacceptable." Brlety gestured around him. "We cannot remain on this vessel. Joren has terminated their treaty with the League—to collaborate with the Hsktskt, no doubt."

Squilyp's gildrells stiffened. "You will remain until we can adequately treat your troops' injuries. Whether you do so awake or asleep is up to you."

The major stomped back to his berth without another word.

"Keep them off level eighteen, Squil. Qonja, too." I rounded up a couple of nurses and left to deal with the lizards.

Unlike our League guests, who were loud and frequent complainers, the Hsktskt sat waiting silently in the makeshift treatment area Squilyp had prepared for them. I handed out vocollars to the nurses, who went around and gingerly placed them around the wide, scaly necks of our patients.

The one I'd spoken to on the scout ship limped over to me. "I am Centuron RrissVar. You are the Designate of OverLord TssVar's brood?"

"That's me." I indicated a treatment table. "Hop on there and let me have a look at that limb."

"Why have we not been taken to your medical facility?"

He was Hsktskt. I lied. "Because it's filled to capacity, and you guys aren't exactly space-saver sized."

His black tongue flickered out, tasting the air. Reever once told me that the Hsktskt could tell someone was lying by the change in their odor. Hopefully, the centuron hadn't sampled many deceitful Terrans before.

At last, he said, "I wish to know your intentions."

"I intend to stitch up that big hole in your leg." I folded my arms, trying to look a little tough. "Unless you would like to continue bleeding all over my nice, clean deck?"

"Are we to be held as hostages?"

Reever entered the cargo hold, and joined us. "Centuron. I will answer your questions."

"HalaVar." RrissVar's tail appendage lashed out like a whip, snapping in the air. I'd never seen a Hsktskt look more astonished. "You have command of this vessel?"

"No, I serve as ship's linguist." Reever reached out and clasped the Hsktskt's limb with his hand. "It is good to see you, old friend."

Old friend. I winced. Xonea was going to *love* this.

"I thought you dead, many times over." After that blunt little statement, RrissVar looked at me. "So this is your female. We heard of your joining at the last *KressTak.*" He gave me the once-over. "She has no substance to her. Are you certain she can breed?"

"I can breed fine, thanks." I pointed to the table. "Climb up there."

Reever stayed with me, distracting RrissVar as I worked on his leg. The jagged gash had innumerable shrapnel lodged within, which I had to fish out before I could make some minor muscle repairs.

"It is time the Faction considered entering into peace talks with the League," Reever said.

RrissVar grunted as I pulled a rather large chunk of alloy from his flesh. "Doubtful. Not enough have died yet to suit the Hanar."

As the two males continued to talk about the war in low tones, I noticed the nurses were getting some resistance from the other Hsktskt troops, especially when they tried to administer medication.

"Centuron," I said, interrupting them, "would you

be so kind as to tell your men to stop giving my nurses a hard time?"

RrissVar snapped a limb, and the cracking sound made every Hsktskt in the hold stand at attention. "Allow the females to do their work, or submit yourself to me for discipline."

The big lizards abruptly became as meek as little lambs. I'd witnessed Hsktskt discipline firsthand, and calling it brutal would be a conservative description.

I irrigated RrissVar's leg and sutured up the wound, then bandaged it, and strapped on a limb support. "You'll need to stay off this for the next rotation. I'm going to infuse you with some antibiotics, but if you experience increased pain or swelling, let me know." I glanced at my husband, who was staring off in one direction. "What's wrong?"

"Who was left in charge of Marel?"

"Darea was going to watch her for me after school, why—" I turned to see what he was looking at, and my heart nearly stopped.

Our daughter was perched on an exam table next to one of the Hsktskt. It had two limbs wrapped around her and was bending its massive head down toward her little face.

"No." I automatically dialed a lethal dosage of heart stimulant and went after the Hsktskt. Or would have, if Reever hadn't grabbed me.

"He will not harm her."

I struggled. "He'll *eat* her!"

Reever gave me a good shake. "Walk over slowly with me and don't frighten her or the centuron."

As if I was the threat here. Reever kept his arm wrapped around me and guided me over to the exam table. The Hsktskt was sniffing my daughter's blond hair, the way he would a raw haunch of meat for freshness. I gripped the syrinpress tighter and eyed his jugular artery. Two, maybe three seconds, and he'd be dead. But he could easily snap my daughter's neck in half that time.

No problem. I'd simply have to kill him faster.

"Daddy, see?" Marel held up an odd-looking hunk of metal. "Sendron give me dis."

The Hsktskt spotted the syrinpress in my hand, saw my face, then wisely removed his limbs from my child. "I intend no harm toward your brood, physician."

"Yeah." Genetically altered blood could still boil. "Like you intend no harm toward the kids of every other species you've attacked, right?"

His brow ridges furrowed. "Our commander has capitulated to you."

"That's supposed to make me feel better about you touching my child?"

"Mama, why you mad?" Marel looked from me to her father to the lizard, then back to me. "Sendron my friend. See?" She held out the hunk of metal again.

It was the Hsktskt's rank insignia from his uniform. Which, in a moment, was going to be lodged down his throat.

"Cherijo, he will not harm her." Reever sounded so calm. "RrissVar yielded to us so that his men could have medical treatment. As long as Faction soldiers are on board, they will not harm any member of the crew."

Marel cried out suddenly, and I jerked. The sharp edge of the insignia had left a small scratch across the tiny palm of her hand. When I saw the blood, something inside me snapped, and I grabbed her away from the Hsktskt.

"Take her home." I thrust her at my husband. No matter what Reever said, I'd seen firsthand what the

Hsktskt did to helpless children. I'd watched a couple hundred of them die of it.

He gripped my collar and yanked me close. "Don't provoke them."

I could have killed him, right then and there. "You shut up and get her out of here, *now.*"

My husband displayed his infinite wisdom by taking Marel in his arms and walked out the door panel without another word.

CHAPTER SEVEN

Attitude Adjustments

Xonea came down to level eighteen just as we were finishing up with the last of the Hsktskt wounded. I had been working in utter silence, furious with myself for not finding a better way to safeguard my baby, outraged that Reever had even considered allowing our child near one of these killers.

"Cherijo, I would like to have a word with you, please." The Captain drew me out into the corridor. "Duncan informed me of what happened. Are you well, ClanSister?"

"How many times am I allowed to divorce the same man under Jorenian law?" I stalked off.

He followed. "Cherijo, wait."

I didn't wait. He'd have to catch up. When he did, I went off on a rant that I'd been biting back all day. "Maybe I'm not the world's best wife, but I think I've been pretty flexible where Duncan's concerned. Don't you?"

"It is not for me to say—"

I raised a hand. "Please. You're supposed to be my brother; act like one and listen." He nodded, and I pushed some hair out of my face. "I've had to take a lot, being with him. I've accepted his past with these lizards. I even forgave him for selling me to them. But this isn't about me anymore. He's not endangering my daughter like that. I won't have it." I hesitated at the panel to the gyrlift. "Where is he?"

"He took Marel to Medical to have Squilyp look at her hand." Xonea reached as if to pat my shoulder, then pulled his hand away. "She wished the Omorr to bandage it."

"It was just a scratch." Saying that made me feel slightly ashamed, because I was acting as if she'd had a limb amputated. Then I recalled the dying children on NessNevat I'd treated when I'd served on the *Sunlace* before, and my heart hardened. I'd performed plenty of amputations, thanks to the Hsktskt.

Xonea accompanied me to Medical, but wisely refrained from reasoning further with me. A good thing, too, because one more voice of reason would have pushed me over the edge, and he'd end up with his head rammed through a gyrlift panel.

"I must return to Command. I will speak to you later, ClanSister."

"Uh-huh."

All was quiet inside Medical, which bothered me until I saw why. Reever, Vlaav, and half a dozen nurses had been gagged and tied to various berths.

I ran to untie my husband, forgetting instantly how ticked off I was at him. "What happened? Where's Marel?"

Duncan had a number of facial contusions, and when he yanked the strip of linen from his mouth, it was stained with blood. "The League soldiers know about the Hsktskt." He rolled off the berth and went to release the Saksonan. "They're on their way to kill them now."

Dread seeped into me as I looked around. "And Marel?"

"They took her and the Omorr as hostages."

I went automatically to a setup tray and grabbed a handful of instruments. Almost everything a physician used to heal could also be employed as an effective weapon. "Vlaav, signal security, tell them what happened. Duncan, let's go."

"Wait. Cherijo!"

I was already out the door panel and halfway to the gyrlift before Reever caught up with me. "How long ago did they take her?"

"Ten minutes."

An eternity, considering what they could be doing to my baby. I keyed level eighteen on the gyrlift access panel and slipped through the door panel before it slid all the way open. When it closed, Duncan pressed the stop-hold key.

"What are you doing?" I swatted at his hand. "Come on, let's go! I want to get there before security does!"

"Vlaav didn't signal security."

The words didn't make sense, but there was a lot of buzzing in my ears. "Excuse me?"

"I ordered him not to signal them," my husband said. "It would put RrissVar and his men at risk."

The shock was momentary. The outrage wasn't. "You're *worried* about your *lizard* buddies?"

"Cherijo, we cannot charge in there."

"Maybe you can't." I tried to reach around him for the panel. "I can."

"If the Jorenians learn of this, they'll kill everyone."

"Which I will enjoy watching." I shoved him back, disabled the stop-hold, and rekeyed the lift for eighteen.

He hustled me aside and re-enabled the stop-hold. "Listen to me!"

"No!" I threw a hemostat at him, which smacked into his left cheek and left another contusion. "You son of a bitch. They took *our daughter.* You come with me now and you help me get her back!"

"Through you she is kin to the Torins. As soon as they know, they will declare ClanKill and slaughter everyone on that level." He didn't touch his face, but he didn't let me touch the panel. "Think, beloved. What if Marel is caught between them?"

"No." I felt the blood draining from my face. "No, they won't hurt her."

"The Torins will not. The League will use her. You know they will."

If the Hsktskt didn't grab her first. I took out a pair of razor-sharp scissors, and held them pointed at his heart. "You have another idea?" He nodded, and I placed the scissors in his hand. "We'll do it your way. Let's go."

He touched the panel, and the lift began to descend.

"About the Hsktskt." Despite the pleasure I would have taken in screaming at him, I kept my voice at a reasonable decibel level. "If it comes down to a choice between your pals and my daughter, I won't hesitate. I'll even help Xonea rip some intestines out. Yours and theirs."

Frigid, cutting thought blasted into my mind. *Do you think I would sacrifice our child for the Hsktskt?*

You seem a hell of a lot more concerned about them than Marel. When nothing came of that, I closed my eyes and felt him edge even deeper inside my head. *What's the matter? Trying to figure out how you're supposed to feel about this by using my emotions?*

You've already made your anger toward me plain. Allow me the same courtesy.

Instead of sifting through my thoughts, Reever funneled his into my mind. I staggered back and slammed into the interior lift panel as a deluge of savage, homicidal desires poured over me. League soldiers being ripped apart, tossed about like bits of junk, blood on Reever's hands. Blood everywhere.

I opened my eyes, saw him standing over me, hands on my arms, lips peeled back in a ferocious snarl, superimposed over the murderous fantasies. *Duncan. Duncan, stop it!*

The flux of thoughts abruptly shut off, and he released me as swiftly as he'd grabbed me. *Tell me now I care more for the Hsktskt than our child.*

I didn't know. On top of my frantic terror over Marel, his fury proved too much. I started to crumble, and tears welled in my eyes as I remembered how tiny she'd seemed, sitting next to the centuron. *She's so little, oh God, Duncan, what if—*

She is the daughter of Faction members. RrissVar will protect her with his life. He paused another moment, as if composing himself. *We have to stop at level seventeen.*

"Why?"

"They will have guards blocking all access routes except one."

The gyrlift came to a halt, and as we stepped out into the corridor, I heard the sound of pulse fire below our feet.

"No." My stomach surged up into my throat. "They're shooting at each other."

Duncan seemed to concentrate for a moment. "The League are trying to force their way into the cargo hold. The Hsktskt are keeping them at bay."

I knew his telepathic abilities were miraculous, but this was new. "How do you know that?"

"I will explain later. For now, we must go through one of the maintenance passages."

"I'm not playing hide-and-seek with them. They're *shooting* around my *kid*."

I whirled around to go back, but Reever stopped me by taking over my brain. *I will control you, if I must.*

I couldn't move. *Don't.*

Then do as I say. He released the mental hold, lead me to a maintenance panel, and opened a hatch in the floor. *Quickly.*

I climbed down after him to the next level's access hatch.

Be silent now. He opened it, then lowered himself into the hold beneath and helped me down. I went to the door panel and listened. Everything outside was very, very quiet.

I can sense Marel's presence nearby. Reever went to the door panel, pressed his ear against it, and listened. *The Hsktskt have barricaded themselves in a hold across the corridor.* He went to a console and called up the level's environmental controls. *I'll shut down the optic emitters on this level, then open the door.*

Brilliant. How am I supposed to find Marel in the dark?

Use this. He handed me a small proximity detector. *Squilyp put a transmitter wristband on her yesterday.*

I tightened my fingers around the unit. *Hurry up.*

I'll go first. Stay low, and if anyone shoots, drop to the deck. Ready? I nodded. *One, two, three . . . now!*

All the lights went out, then the door panel slid open and I blindly followed Reever out. Angry shouts and pulse fire erupted all around us. Something hit me on the arm, sending me sideways just as a blast passed directly by my head. I hit the deck, smelled burnt hair, and slapped a hand to my skull. A few singed strands came away in my fingers.

I hated being burned almost as much as I feared it, but I shoved my pyrophobic anxiety aside. *Can't lose it now.* With a shaking hand I held up the proximity detector, which showed a signal nearby. I started to crawl, feeling along the deck with my hands.

"Marel? Baby?" I whispered. "Where are you?"

"I have her." Qonja knelt beside me. "Here."

The sweet smell of vanilla filled my head. "Mama?"

I snatched her out of his arms. Someone barreled into Qonja, knocking him into me.

"Go!" he yelled.

I rolled, cushioning her against me until I found enough space to stand. Marel hung on, her face buried in my hair.

I felt something warm and wet on the front of her tunic, and pulled back. "Baby?" I felt my heart drop into my stomach. "Are you hurt?"

"Widow, Mama."

The soldiers were still shouting and running all around us, while weapons fired over our heads. I became oblivious to it as I pulled Marel's tunic open and ran my hands down her torso. Beneath my fingertips, I felt three shallow, parallel gashes that followed the line of her right ribcage from back to front.

The buzz in my ears became a roar. *Someone hurt my baby.*

A familiar membrane landed on my face. "Cherijo?"

"Thank God." I caught Squilyp's hand with mine. "Marel's got some torso lacerations." I guided his membrane down so he could feel them. Then something dripped on my arm. "Are you bleeding, too?"

"Ruptured some gildrells. It's nothing." From the mumbling I could tell he was lying. "We have to get her out of here."

"Come on, baby." I shielded her with my arms and body as best I could. "Squilyp, hold on to me."

"Mama, get 'Sawa and kiddies?"

"What?" I stopped in the doorway to the cargo hold.

"'Sawa bawd kiddies for Uncwip check. Dose bad men dook dem do."

Could things possibly get worse? "Where is she, Squilyp?"

"The Hsktskt grabbed her away from the League soldiers. She's in with them."

Of course, it could get worse. "All right." I carried Marel and led Squilyp into the cargo hold and put my daughter in my best friend's arms. "There's a hatch in the upper deck, over here. I'll find something for you to stand on. Grab the ladder rungs inside and haul yourself up. Get her to Medical." To my daughter, I said, "Hold on to Uncle Squilyp, baby."

"Yes, Mama."

I groped until I found an empty utility cart and shoved it under the hatch. "Climb on. I'll brace it."

The Omorr grabbed my arm. "You're coming with us."

"I'm going back to get Fasala and my cats." And Qonja, but only if I tripped over him.

"Use this." The Omorr pressed a surgical instrument in my hand. I felt the outlines and realized it was a suture laser. "It's calibrated to the lowest setting."

I adjusting the beam width to the widest possible application, which transformed it into a weapon that would leave a huge, nasty burn on any flesh I pointed it at. "Thanks."

My second trip into the corridor only took a few seconds, because I ran and lasered anything that got in my way. I had to pry the door panel open with my hands, then shoved through the narrow gap, and directly into a huge, scaly body.

"I want the other girl."

Powerful limbs lifted me off the deck. "Your kind send physicians into battle, HalaVar?"

The lights came on a second later, and I saw all the Hsktskt standing armed and ready to shoot something. Reever was leaning over one of the exam tables, where Fasala Torin lay stretched out and unconscious. Three tiny silvery bodies huddled beside her, and my husband's hands were stained with green and red blood.

I looked into RrissVar's huge yellow eyes, and pointed my suture laser at the spot in his skull where his optic nerves were located. "Down, or I blind you."

"I can see why they do." He set me down, and I ran to the table.

"Out of the way." I pushed my husband aside and began assessing Fasala, who had a huge purple bruise on her face and green blood in her black hair.

"Squilyp said the League soldiers saw PakVar's insignia in Marel's hand, and Brlety asked her where she got it." Duncan handed me a sterile pad and a bottle of saline solution. "She told him. A few minutes later, they took hostages, and left the rest of us in Medical."

"Which one of these bastards clawed my daughter?" I demanded.

PakVar appeared at my side. He looked ready to eat something that was still breathing. "She was wounded by one of the League fodder when we took her from them."

"And Fasala?" I found the shallow cut beneath her hair and cleaned it. "Did they do this to her, or did you?"

Now RrissVar came over. "We did nothing to the young."

"I'm not going to thank you."

His tongue flickered out for a moment. "No, I can see you will not."

The door panel opened behind us, and Xonea and a team of security guards strode in.

"Weapons down on the deck," the Captain ordered in a harsh voice. It deepened into a low rumble when he spotted Fasala. "Out in the corridor. Now."

The Hsktskt looked at RrissVar, who inclined his head, then slowly obeyed Xonea's orders and filed out of the hold. Reever picked up Fasala while I quickly checked the kittens. They had some minor cuts and bruises, but otherwise were fine. I emptied my tunic pockets, put the kittens inside, and followed him out.

Thirty Jorenian warriors, including the Captain, Qonja, and Salo, each had a Hsktskt or League soldier in front of them. Every blue hand had claws out and curled for a death-strike blow.

"Hold it!" I turned to Reever, who was carrying Salo's daughter like a baby. "You wanted peace talks? Time to start talking."

Reever shifted Fasala in his arms as he approached her ClanFather. "Salo. Your child needs your attention."

"Take her to Medical, Linguist." Salo's claws gleamed as he lifted his hand. The League soldier he was holding against the wall panel by the throat stared up with terrified resignation. "This business requires my attention."

Obviously, the males were all too emotional to get a handle on this situation. Reever was never good at this stuff to begin with. Which left me, the outraged mother, to call a halt to the hostilities.

"Some father you are." I went over to Qonja, and swatted him on the arm. "And you. You took an oath. Show some professional restraint."

He turned his head to look down his patrician blue nose at me. The friendly, handsome face was etched with blind rage. "Kin have been injured. Leave us to our work."

"Kin will be just fine. Take the rest of the day off." Seeing that that wasn't working, I tried my Clan-Brother. "Xonea. Don't."

Reever handed Fasala over to one of the nurses who had entered the corridor with a gurney, then came to stand beside me. "I shield these soldiers."

Thirty pairs of white eyes went from me to Reever, and if the stares had been any hotter, his face would have been scorched off. After heaving a mental sigh, I slipped my hand in his. "Me, too. Consider everyone shielded."

Xonea released the soldier he had pinned. "Our children have been injured."

"We know." I saw Fasala's father digging his claws into the chest of the man he held, and blood running down his arm. "Salo! Stop it!"

"You dare lay your filthy hands on my child," Salo said through clenched teeth. "I defend my House."

"Blood fever is upon him," Qonja said, while Reever held on to my hand. "He must have taken the herb. He will not listen to you."

Blood fever meant Salo had ingested jaspforran, a Jorenian botanical with chemical properties that enhanced aggression and blanked out pain in the natives. AKA "Beserker Herb."

"Reever, turn me loose. Salo!" I grabbed Fasala's gurney and pulled it over until the unconscious child was right next to her ClanFather. "Release that man and take your child to Medical."

The sight of his daughter distracted him for a moment, then he dug his claws in deeper. The alien blood that had been trickling down his arm now became a small stream, and the League soldier uttered a weak moan.

"Salo, damn it, get your claws out of him!"

The warrior's knot in his hair gleamed as he turned to look at me with rage-blind eyes. "You betray our HouseClan."

"You swore to me on Joren that your life was mine." I hated reminding him of that, but when this berserker state fell over them, very little could stop them from tearing their victims apart. "I'm calling in that favor now. A life for a life."

Appealing to his sense of ritual and formality worked. The herb-induced insanity slowly cleared from the big warrior's face, and the soldier fell from his hands and slid to the deck.

When Salo flicked the blood from his claws, it was with the same contempt that coated his voice as he spoke to me. "You dishonor our kinship." Then he took Fasala's gurney and pushed it toward the gyrlift. After giving me a strange look, Qonja went with him.

I knelt down and pressed my hands against the soldier's chest. "Reever, somebody, give me a hand here."

We dealt with the wounded, including the trooper Salo had nearly divested of his heart. Qonja for once had nothing to say to me, and left Medical as soon as one of the nurses stitched him up. I dealt with Squilyp, who had made light of his injuries, but proved to be in no shape to stay on his foot. After I bullied him into a berth, Vlaav and I took care of the mostly uncomplicated surgical cases.

Adaola kept watch over Marel for me, and brought regular updates. Her lacerations were only minor, but I had the Jorenian nurse put my daughter and Salo's into an isolation room, well away from all the League soldiers who had hurt them.

Fifteen hours later, I left my sleeping daughter in the

care of my staff and went to take care of the last of the day's business.

Qonja didn't seem surprised to see me this time. "Yes, Healer? Are my services needed?"

I walked past him into his quarters and pointed to a chair. "Sit." After a moment, he sat. "Tell me what's going on."   •

"I don't know—"

"You've been watching me since I came on board. Following me. Taking notes. Trying to insinuate yourself into my life. Today you saved my daughter." I tapped my foot on the deck. "Why?"

He seemed tired, and wouldn't look at me. "I admire you."

"I've had other people admire me. They don't put recording drones in my quarters."

His head snapped up. "You found them?"

"Uh-huh. I checked Jorenian law. I can have you imprisoned for what you've done. And I will, so convince me not to."

A minute of silence passed, then he said, "I cannot."

"All right." I went to the door. "As soon as your wounds heal, report back to Medical."

Then came the confrontation I wasn't looking forward to. I was exhausted as much from the marathon of patching and suturing as from the emotional overload, and the bizarre calm I'd enjoyed for the last shift seemed to be dissipating fast. Duncan and I had been through plenty, and I was prepared to trust him with my life.

My daughter's life was another matter.

He seemed to be waiting for me, I saw as I walked in, as he sat on the chair facing the door panel. Jenner was in his lap, but not for long.

My darling pet took one look at me, and sat up. *Uh-*

oh. He jumped down and hightailed it back to Marel's room. *I'm outta here.*

I said the first thing that came into my head. "You didn't come to Medical to see how our kid is. What, you were too busy checking on the lizards?"

He just sat there and watched me. "I signaled one of the nurses to apprise myself of her status, several times."

"You're such a good daddy." Hands clenched, I went over to the prep unit and briefly rested my brow against the polished alloy upper cabinet. "This isn't going to turn into yet another screaming match between us."

"I never scream."

"True." My fingers jabbed the console, and something hot and liquid poured into my empty server. "I'd feel better if you would, once in a while, but then, one can't pick one's destined life mate."

"I agree." He made a casual gesture. "Will you hear what I have to say, or would you prefer to vent your frustrations first?"

I was a surgeon, a mother, a survivor. I could be a mature adult. For a few minutes. "Oh, please, be my guest."

"RrissVar and I served the Faction together. He is an honorable soldier who deserved better than to be slain by some disgruntled incompetents embittered by their own failure."

"Those failures you're talking about would be the League soldiers, I hope."

He ignored that. "You have always been prone to act first and think later. It is not an attractive quality, but one I accept. That I think first and act later is equally unattractive to you. I ask only that you do the same and accept me as I am."

He had yet to get acquainted with some of my other unattractive qualities, but I let it slide.

"I can do that." I nodded and sipped some of what had to be the worst tea I'd ever made in my life. "That it?"

"I was trying to protect her, as much as you were. The fact that I was rational and you were not makes no difference. My choice not to signal the Jorenians was the logical one, as you saw when they later arrived."

"Yep." My fingers tightened around the server handle. "Rational. Logical. You're right. Is *that* it?"

He got to his feet and made a careless gesture. "Go ahead and vent. Doubtless you need to."

"Got me all figured out now, don't you? That's nice." I set the server down carefully and folded my arms. "We've done some stupid things to each other in the past, Duncan. I admit, I'm as guilty of that as you are. We didn't communicate well and we still have problems in that department."

He gave me an uncertain look. "And?"

"And I'm your wife. I know we have a long way to go before we work out all the kinks of what constitutes *us*. We need to talk more about our different attitudes about parenting and protecting our child."

Now he seemed mesmerized. "You mean that?"

I gave him a gentle smile. "Of course, I do. I love you. I love Marel. I want us to be a family. Can we do that, together?" I waited for his slow nod, and took a deep breath. "Excellent. I look forward to making that work." He started to walk toward me, but I held up one hand and reached down for my server. "All I want to say is one more thing."

"What is it?"

I threw the server at him, deliberately missing his head by an inch. It smashed into the far interior wall of our quarters and burst, sending a shower of terrible tea all over the deck and furniture.

"I don't care how many alien pals you've got wandering around this galaxy. Protecting our baby is more important than all of them. You think about that, because you're a father now and you're damned well going to act like one." I was shouting, but no one ever said I was perfect.

He stood his ground. "I did what I thought was best."

"It wasn't. And here's another little news flash for you, just so that we're communicating openly and clearly: If you *ever* put our child at risk again like you did today, I won't think twice. I'll take her and I'll leave you and you will *never* see us again."

Then he said what I didn't expect at all. "I know you will."

It should have taken me aback, but my anger was boiling every other emotion I possessed. "Good. Now, I'm going to take a walk around the ship a few times and punch a couple of walls. You find a way to get these damn soldiers out of here, and do it fast."

I didn't go back that night, but spent three miserable hours sleeping on the incredibly uncomfortable seating unit in the games room. A few crew members came in and out, but wisely left me alone. I went back to Medical for primary shift, feeling like a wrinkled rag, and caught a swift shower there before checking on my daughter, then going back to work.

After all the fireworks, Squilyp had refused an exam, and I'd been too upset with Reever to argue with him. Now I made him hop onto an exam table and scanned his face.

"You look about as good as I feel," I muttered as I

checked the condition of his ruptured gildrells. All but one were healing, and I applied a topical anesthetic to the one that had become slightly stiff and inflamed. "Have the girls been behaving?"

He looked over at the isolation chamber, where Marel and Fasala were playing bentaka, a complicated Jorenian board game that was sort of like chess and Chinese checkers, with a little poker thrown in. "For the most part, yes. Marel seems incapable of sitting still for very long intervals."

"That's her job."

As we performed rounds, I felt Squilyp giving me these speculative looks. Finally, I said, "What?"

"Duncan was here earlier." He handed me one of the League soldier's charts. "He sat with Marel until he had to report for duty."

"How sweet." I hummed under my breath as I studied the chart's display. "There's a buildup of fluid around the upper limb wound. We'd better have one of the nurses aspirate the joint before he goes edemic."

"Duncan said you were furious with him."

Now my husband was confiding in my boss. Since they were both male, they'd probably gang up on me or something.

"Furious, no. I got all that out last night." I noted my prognosis on the chart and handed it back to the Senior Healer. "Now I'm hovering an inch between leaving him and not leaving him. Let's go see the girls."

Although they were low priority on the rounds schedule, seeing to Marel and Fasala went a long way toward soothing my frazzled temper. My daughter could barely contain herself long enough to sit on her berth so I could remove her patient gown.

"You see kiddies, Mama?" She pointed to a small container in the corner of the room, where the abducted trio were napping, exhausted no doubt from playing with my kid. "Dey bedder now." One hand latched on to the edge of my tunic as she scratched at her dressing with the other. "Off?"

"What's the matter with it, sweetie?" I tugged her hand away and checked the bandage adhesive to make sure it wasn't irritating her skin. "This bothering you?"

She nodded. "Off?"

"Let me have a look first." I carefully peeled back one edge of the dressing. Beneath it, what had been raw gashes were now rapidly shrinking rows of pink skin. I removed the bandage and examined it. On the inside of the dressing were a couple of scab fragments that Marel must have dislodged with her scratching.

I glanced across the berth. "Squilyp, look at this."

He nodded, then scanned Marel's torso and showed me the display. "Healed completely."

"Good news, baby, you don't need this anymore." I discarded the dressing, then helped her down from the berth. "You keep Fasala company for a few minutes, okay?"

"Okay, Mama."

The Omorr and I went into his office, and stood there in silence for a few seconds, before I dropped down in the chair and rubbed my aching head with my fingers.

"It's good she heals fast. Little kids are always scraping and bumping themselves, aren't they?" I removed a syrinpress from my tunic pocket and toyed with the calibrator. "So she won't ever have to suffer pain. Not for very long, anyway."

"You knew when you became pregnant the child would have an equal chance of inheriting your genetic characteristics as well as Duncan's." Squilyp touched my shoulder. "We will test her and determine exactly how she differs from a standard Terran."

"No, we won't." Sudden, hot rage flashed through me. "No tests. Erase the scan—erase *all* the scans. From this point on, we falsify her records."

"I don't think that's necessary—"

"Oh yeah? What happens if the League finds out my daughter has the same immune system as I do? You think they're going to pass up the chance to capture the second-most valuable lab rat of all time?" I took Marel's chart from the stack and set the controls to erase all records. "Nothing goes into the permanent database about her from here on out."

"Wait." He reached for the chart, and did something to it. When he turned it around, I saw the patient name and information had been changed to that of a Jorenian child. "We'll encode the real data behind the false readings. That way, we can keep track of her development."

"Just what do you think she's going to develop into?"

"Someone wonderful." He smiled. "Like her mother."

CHAPTER EIGHT

Rendezvous Round

"We must make the transfer quickly," I heard my husband say as I walked into our quarters. Greeting me were my extremely nervous cats, two of the kittens and the delightful sight of Reever and RrissVar working together on our personal console.

"Hello, Duncan. RrissVar, you can leave."

"I need him here," my husband said.

"For what, other than making the cats paranoid?"

"We are in the midst of negotiations." He turned back to the terminal.

Knowing his concept of negotiations had been formed while serving as a slave to the lizards, I went over to have a look. On the screen was the image of a trader with a tattooed, dark face, similar to the mask Reever had used to disguise himself as Noarr on Catopsa. The trader was uttering something in his species' whirring, tonal language, one my vocollar didn't translate.

"Let me guess." I gestured to the screen. "Another of your friends."

Reever gave me a bland look and hit a few keys on the console. The trader's language abruptly transitioned into stanTerran.

"—I will want guarantees filed before one of them steps foot on my vessel."

"You shall have whatever you require," RrissVar said.

I nodded toward the screen. "You're sending the lizards off with him?"

"No. The others will go with them."

Personally I'd be happy to see the back of all the League soldiers, but the trader would have to rendezvous with the *Sunlace* in order to off-load them. "What if they've got contacts with the League? Or the local mercenaries?"

"Niat-Nuom'dain do not trade information. Only goods."

"You're sure?" I asked, and he arched a brow. Of course, he probably knew every spy within a million light-years. "Right. How did you get RrissVar out of detainment?" Given Xonea's decree that both the Hsktskt and the League soldiers would be detained until he could unload them on the first suitable planet we came to, the lizard should have still been in the brig.

"I requested permission."

The Niat-Nuom'dain addressed him once more. "We will transport the League soldiers to the closest outpost. The price is forty thousand stancredits."

I cut the audio feed on the console. "That's highway robbery."

"We don't have a choice."

"Yeah, but where are you going to get that kind of currency?" I frowned as I realized just how poor Reever and I were. All our needs were met by the Jorenians, so credits simply hadn't been a priority with us. "I doubt Xonea will finance our little venture."

RrissVar tossed something on the console. Something small and green and glittery. "This will satisfy the trader's transport fee."

I picked the gem up and studied it. It was a perfect

sphere, the center of which had an odd, bewitching glow that seemed to intensify at my touch. "Nice sparkly. What is it?"

"A verdant pearl from a Rabbat bivalve."

I rolled it over my palm. "And this is worth forty thousand stancredits?"

"Twice that." RrissVar took a pouch from his tunic and opened it. Inside were at least a hundred more green pearls. "Make the counteroffer, HalaVar."

The trader's eyes lit up at the sight of the gem, and he quickly agreed to Reever's terms. My husband arranged a rendezvous point and terminated the signal.

I wasn't quite satisfied with the whole deal, though. "Why would you pay the League soldiers' transport fee, Centuron?"

RrissVar replaced the pouch. "It will satisfy my blood-debt to your mate."

Reever had saved the Hsktskt's life yesterday, so that made sense. Until I saw my husband's expression. "What?"

"We must signal the other trader in privacy."

I sat back in my chair. "You want me to leave?"

The Hsktskt's lower eyelids slid up. "It would be best."

He couldn't be serious. "Excuse me, but I think the fact that I saved your big green tails entitles me to a little trust here."

Reever's mouth curled on one side. "It is best you know nothing of this transaction. This trader handles living beings."

Slavers. They were going to contact slavers. "Well, I certainly know how to take a hint." I stomped out of our quarters.

*   *   *

When I entered Command, Xonea barely spared me a glance. "Has Reever been successful?"

"If you mean in getting rid of our unwanted cargo, he's found transport for them." I couldn't exactly tell the Captain Reever was calling his old buddies, the slave traders. However much I was tempted to do just that.

My ClanBrother frowned. "Your bondmate plays dangerous games."

"Tell me about it." I thought of how furious Salo had been, added my husband's penchant for dealing with the scum of the universe to the mix, and sighed. "But it's better than letting them stay on the ship. One more incident and you know we'll end up with a variety of viscera strung over every door panel. It'll drive the sanitation crews nuts."

Xonea set aside the data pad he was working on. "Are you here to defend your bondmate to me, Cherijo? It is not necessary."

If only he knew. I'd been mentally rehearsing what I wanted to say, but actually getting the words out was much tougher. "Xonea, is there a difference between loyalty to the HouseClan and loyalty to one's Chosen?"

"Not for Jorenians. They are one and the same."

"So no one has ever messed up and been loyal to one over the other."

"One's Chosen always belongs to the HouseClan."

I held up my left hand and studied the silver band engraved with alien symbols. "Not always."

"The House is greater than any one of its Clan. Even one whose Chosen does not belong to Joren." He got up and came around the desk. "Allow me to be Clan-Brother instead of Captain now. What say you tell me what is troubling you?"

"Qonja. He's here on orders to watch me, or study

me, or something. You know why. You'd have to know—you're in charge." When he stiffened, I clenched my hand into a fist. "Tell me why, or I'm getting off the ship at Taerca with Reever and Marel."

Xonea looked away. "I cannot."

"That's what Qonja said. I didn't think you'd do the same, ClanBrother, but I was wrong." I squared my shoulders. "I'll start packing."

He seemed stunned by that. "Cherijo, you cannot leave us."

"Watch me."

That was when a signal came in over his console. "Captain. Trader vessel *Eniad* requesting permission to dock and load transport passengers."

Off-loading the League and Hsktskt soldiers went remarkably fast and without complication. Reever and his lizard friend arranged for the slaver vessel to dock with the *Sunlace* first, and I ran a quick exam on each of the reptilian soldiers after they reported to the launch bay.

RrissVar stood in silence as I lectured him on how to take care of his leg wound, and gave him a pack of medical supplies for himself and his men. "Change the dressings twice a day for the next week, and don't skip your dose of antibiotics, unless you want to try to regrow that limb."

"Thank you for providing aid, physician." He nodded to Reever, then followed his men toward the remarkably bland-looking shuttle.

Xonea had come down to watch over the transfer, and now came to stand beside me. "I do not recognize the design of the transport. Who are these traders?"

I twisted the ring on my finger absently. "Friends of Duncan's."

The Captain gave my husband a thoughtful look. Reever and RrissVar clasped arms, and spoke in low tones just before the big reptile boarded the shuttle. "Indeed."

The second trader docked about an hour after the Hsktskt left. The League soldiers were not as quiet, or polite, as we sent them off with the Niat-Nuom'dain, nor was Xonea pleased to see me hand over a pouch containing the verdant pearl RrissVar had lent us.

"They should finance their own passage," my Clan-Brother muttered.

I put my arm through his and guided him away from the second trader shuttle. "Let's just get them off the ship, huh?"

All the fireworks done with, the crew settled back into their normal routines. I noticed Salo making a distinct effort to avoid me, but left that situation alone. If our friendship was ever going to heal, it needed time without a lot of poking and prodding at it.

We were two rotations from reaching Taerca when the Captain called an unscheduled staff meeting. I covered Medical so Squilyp could attend, and got back to work on our hypercellular experiment, prepping the cloned Jorenian liver for testing.

The staff meeting was short, and the Senior Healer called me into his office as soon as he returned. He handed me a data pad with a copy of a direct relay from Joren.

"The Captain received this earlier today. Read it."

I skimmed through the text, then set the pad down on the edge of his desk. "Joren intends to mediate peace for the League and the Hsktskt? Talk about a complete three-sixty."

"It gets better." Squilyp sat down and rubbed a

membrane over his eyes. "We've been ordered to rendezvous with the *CloudWalk,* HouseClan Jado's ship. The Jado ClanLeader wants to be briefed on all the events that led up to the Varallan conflict with the Hsktskt and the League before they initiate peace talks."

"In other words, my life story." I sat down and propped my chin on my fist. Had my ClanBrother somehow arranged this to keep me on the ship? No, even I wasn't important enough for an entire species to reverse their political stance during an intergalactic conflict. "What does Xonea think about all this?"

"The Captain believes in aggressive defense, as you well know. Cherijo, I don't believe the Jado or anyone on the Council fully understands the danger to Joren. In matters of interstellar war, these people are remarkably overconfident. I would say, even naive."

"Comes from having a rep as the worst species to fool with." I sighed. "Other than the standoff in Varallan, they haven't been involved in any large-scale conflicts."

And now they were blindly walking into the biggest one since the Hsktskt had obliterated the Nokkian Alliance. Could Reever and I really walk away from my adopted family right now?

"What are you going to do?"

"I'm going to discharge my daughter and take her to her father." I picked up the pad and tucked it in my tunic pocket. "Reever was at the meeting, right?" Squilyp nodded. "Good. That should give us something new to argue about."

I didn't argue with Duncan in front of our kid—much as I was tempted—but left her in his care.

"Are you going back on duty?" he asked when I kissed Marel good-bye and promised to take her to visit Fasala tomorrow.

"No, I think I'd better go see Xonea. I need to finish those program inspections, and maybe while we're sparring, I can talk to him about the Jado." His reaction was subtle, but of the disapproving, glacial variety. Not a good time to tell him Xonea was mixed up with Qonja, I guessed. "They're going to try to negotiate peace between the Hsktskt and the League, Duncan. I think they should know exactly whom they're dealing with, and why they're at war."

"You are not responsible for Joseph Grey Veil's actions on Fendigal XI."

I noticed Marel was watching us both intently. "Sweetie, do me a favor and go check on the cats for me." We'd moved Juliet and her litter into Marel's room, and as soon as she went in, I confronted the very thing we'd been avoiding discussing. "You don't care why I'm getting involved. You just don't want me involved at all."

"You already have too many emotional ties to these people." He made it sound like an illness. "If you become entangled in these peace negotiations with Xonea and the Jado, it will only make it more difficult for us to leave when the time comes."

"Xonea and the Jado didn't put the recording drones in our quarters. Qonja did." Before he could say anything, I shook my head. "I don't know why yet, but go ahead and remove them."

"The Captain doubtless ordered him to do it."

The way his eyes glittered sent chills through me. "What is the problem between you and Xonea? It can't be jealousy; whatever he felt for me in the past is over, and you know it."

"He intrudes on our lives too often."

"This from the man who has ticked me off more times than a yellow star has solar flares in one revolution." I went to stand in front of him. "I thought we agreed to communicate better. So communicate."

"I want you to stay out of these negotiations." He got up fast, and showed a great deal more animation as he pulled me into his arms. "Don't become involved in Xonea's politics."

"You *are* jealous." I pulled back a little, but his arms were locked around me. "Duncan, he's like a brother to me."

"He means to change what you are."

"Look, if it comes down to a choice between Xonea and the Torins, and you and Marel, I will personally pilot the shuttle we take off this ship. You have nothing to be worried about."

"Then you will lose nothing by doing as I ask."

I dodged the angry kiss he meant to give me, and jerked free. "How about my self-respect? That may take a few dents."

"Do what you will then." He strode out of our quarters.

Since I couldn't face off with Xonea and expect my marriage to hold together, I decided to use the opportunity to combine one problem with another, and sent a signal to Qonja, inviting him to join me for a practice session.

My one-man fan club politely refused. "It would be inappropriate for me to spar with you, Healer."

I didn't argue with him, but only waited until he went off duty before I tracked him down. I took the precaution of arming myself before overriding his security code and opening the door panel to environome two.

Inside, the psych resident stood stripped to the waist, working out with Yarek Torin. Both of them were heavily armed, multibladed swords in both hands, and dancing around each other like soundless ghosts as they defended themselves against multiple attackers.

Multiple League and Hsktskt attackers.

I cleared my throat when there was a slight pause, and both men stopped in their tracks. Yarek groaned as he saw me, then sheathed both of his swords. Qonja swore under his breath and went to the panel to shut down the program.

"Healer." Yarek tried to look nonchalant. "We were not expecting you to attend . . . my student's demonstration."

"Nice try, ClanCousin. You might want to head home and explain to your bondmate why she's going to get a signal from me later." I smiled and shook my head when he made as if to protest. With a quick bow, he hurried out of the environome.

Qonja, his back toward me, secured the door panel again.

I shrugged off my outer tunic. "Tell me who you are."

"As I have said before, I am a psychiatric resident." He turned and frowned as he watched me take out my *goreu* staff out and extend it. "What are you doing?"

"I may not know much about Joren, but I know plenty about those swords you and Yarek were swinging around. Multibladeds take years to master." I whirled the black staff between my fingers, showing off a little. "Many, many years."

"It is an exercise I am quite fond of."

"That's the thing, Qonja. Medical students don't have time to become fond of anything but medicine. You seem to have missed a few things at Medtech, but here you are, an expert with a sword. Now, it seems to me if someone wanted to impersonate a medical student, he'd have to pick the kind who has no practical medical experience. Like a psychiatric student." I tucked my staff under my arm and started toward him. "I'll ask you one more time: Who are you?"

He put one sword aside, but held on to the other. "I cannot answer your questions."

"You will before we leave this room." I kept advancing.

Qonja touched the symbol hanging from his vocollar. "You cannot mean this, Healer. Perhaps we can discuss—"

I flipped out my staff, planted one end, and used it to vault to his left. As I landed, I swept the planted end up and knocked the sword out of his hand. It clattered to the deck, several feet away.

He didn't come after me, but I moved out of range anyway and entered the first of the attack patterns Wonlee had taught me. "Who are you and why were you sent here to watch me?"

Qonja ducked to avoid my staff, then grunted as I whirled the other end around and knocked the air out of his diaphragm. When he could breathe again, he wheezed, "Healer, stop."

"Stop now?" I laughed. "I'm just warming up."

He crouched over into a defense stance I'd seen Xonea use. "This serves no purpose."

"It's certainly making me feel better." I tapped him on the cheek before he could jerk back, then blocked him from getting his arm up before tapping the other. "Come on, you're better than this."

His white eyes narrowed. "It is inappropriate for me to spar with you."

"You keep saying that— why? Because you think you're better? Faster? Oops." I slammed my staff into his right knee, forcing him down on the other, then hefted my staff up over his head. "Maybe not quite so fast as you think you are. By the way, the wood used to make this *goreu* is so hard that the Esalmalin prefer it over some alloys." I rested the end against the top of his head. "One hit, and I can split your skull in half. Tell me who you are."

"You will not kill me."

"I won't beat the information out of you." I moved the end of the staff so I could tip his chin up. "However, I will protect the ones I love, and if that means killing you, I won't even hesitate. Do you understand?"

He nodded.

"Then this session is over."

I folded up my staff and walked out.

A few days after my sparring match with Qonja, the *Sunlace* assumed orbit above Taerca. Hawk's destination was the fifth planet out from the system's white dwarf star, and the only habitable one at that. As a result, traders rarely bothered to jaunt through the region, possibly the reason for the noticeable lag time in getting a response from the planet surface.

Or so Darea theorized over tea with me and Alunthri in the galley. We had taken to meeting there since her bondmate had accused me of betraying the House-Clan.

"Salo was not particularly impressed by the quality of the relay we received from Taercal Main Transport," she said. "Their request for us to delay the sojourn for three rotations seemed rather unfriendly." She offered me a slice of morningbread, which I refused. "My bondmate may exaggerate, as he has been very irritable of late. . . ." Her hand moved in a discreet gesture meaning she wasn't sure why.

I knew better. "Since I ruined our friendship?"

The Chakacat's whiskers twitched. "Perhaps Salo needs some time to think through the situation."

"What say you Terrans? 'Don't hold your breath'?" Darea shook her head. "He remains steadfast in his opinions, that much I will grant my bondmate."

I decided to change the subject. "How is Hawk taking the news?"

"They sent no images of the surface, which disappointed him, but he found the physical appearance of our contact something of a comfort."

The native Taercal must have had some of the features that Terran doctors had worked so hard to erase from Hawk's face. "I hope these people are a little more open-minded than his mom's side of the family."

"Having two parents seems at times a disadvantage," Alunthri put in. "Darea, has there been any word from the ship we are to meet at Oenrall?"

"The Jado have signaled several times, confirming their heading. Their ClanLeader knows Xonea and Salo from their service together during the territorial conflicts." Darea watched Ilona Red Faun enter the galley, and inclined her head as the Terran girl gave her a wary glance. "If anyone can bring peace to the League and the Hsktskt, it is Teulon Jado."

After our tea, I went to see Hawk and find out how he was coping with the prospect of meeting his father's people.

The crossbreed welcomed me into his quarters, which had been cleared of most of the furnishings. A number of Ilona's brightly patterned wool rugs hung on the wall panels, along with bundles of ceremonial corn and several huge, carved masks. Four intricately woven Jorenian yborra mats formed a square on the deck around an elaborate sand painting.

"Very authentic," I said, foregoing a suggestion that

he get some regular chairs. "The sojourn is tomorrow; any last-minute jitters?"

"Some. Have you seen the signal?"

He took me over to his terminal and pulled up the replay for me. A dark image appeared on the screen, a barely discernible humanoid face shrouded in darkness from all sides.

Hawk's paternal species weren't very handsome in a Terran sense, but the aquiline features and intense, all-black eyes were certainly startling. Evidently evolved from an avian life-form, the Taercal showed their genetic heritage with their dark-feathered derma, curved beak-mouths and, of course, their wings. The native on the screen had some sort of gilded ornaments stuck all over his, what I could see of them. The official's grossly overweight body swelled to fill the screen.

"He's a pretty big bird, isn't he?" I leaned closer to hear the translator kick in.

"Star vessel *Sunlace*. This is Tadam Ortsac." The Taercal sounded a bit nasal, but that could have come from the synthetic translator voice. His face emerged into the light a bit farther, and I saw small, irregularly spaced skin growths at the base of some of his feathers. "Our governing priest will allow a party of no more than ten to visit the surface of our world, in three rotations, for a period of twelve stanhours. No trade will take place during this interval, nor will any immigrants be accepted. Acknowledge your comprehension."

You didn't get much snottier than that. "Tadam certainly knows how to roll out the welcome mat, doesn't he? Warts and all."

"Salo assures me such reticence toward unexpected visitors is not uncommon among isolated worlds," Hawk said quickly.

"Once they find out you're one of their own, they'll probably be much more congenial." I couldn't knock on wood three times—everything around us was alloy or plas. "Did your grandparents ever tell you what your father's name is? It would make it easier tracking him down."

"They used his name often, when praying to the gods to cure my afflictions and curse Father to eternity in the void." Hawk's expression became slightly bitter. "He is called Fen Yillut."

"Have we been granted access to the planetary database? Maybe you could give him a call, warn him his prodigal son is about to show up?"

"The Captain already requested permission, which was denied."

A paranoid species couldn't be expected to hand the keys to their planetary mainframe to an unknown ship in orbit, but still, there were other ways. The Taercal attitude was starting to match the Terran's for outright hostility.

"Don't worry, we'll find him. Now, why don't you let me take a look at those wings one more time? You'll likely be in the air most of the time while we're down there."

Hawk agreed to an impromptu exam, which revealed him in excellent shape. Hours of flying in the largest launch bay had strengthened the twin feathered appendages sprouting from his spine to the point of prime condition. As I scanned his musculature, I noticed the face in the center of the sand painting.

"That looks like Rico," I said, nodding toward the visage.

"It is." His mouth turned down as he studied it. "I should have a sing to guide his spirit to the next life, but I have not been able to bring myself to do it."

As *hataali* to my brother's underground crossbreed tribe on Terra, Hawk had regularly performed healing ceremonials. The "sings" were elaborate rituals involving special songs, foods, and sand paintings, and sometimes lasted for days. I had a feeling bad memories were making him procrastinate—the last time Hawk had been with my brother, Jericho had nearly beaten him to death with his fists.

On the other hand, maybe the memories were more painful than simply bad. Hawk had loved my brother so much he would have let Rico beat him to death, to prove it. Kao's smiling face popped into my mind, oddly enough, until I realized why. I had loved Xonea's brother, and yet had killed him trying to save him. In a way, Hawk had done the same. "You still miss him, don't you?"

"With each breath I take."

"I know how it feels, but I still don't understand why. Jericho may not have started out as a monster, but he sure got there fast. Why did you stay with him?"

"You know the traditions of our people. Homosexuality remains a stigma among the tribes." He went over and knelt beside the painting. One of his strong hands reached out and touched the image he'd created. "Yet Rico never feared the love of another man. He welcomed it."

I didn't have such a starry-eyed view. "Rico would have mated with a snake, if it had served his purpose." I saw the brief flicker of pain cross Hawk's face, and knelt beside him. "I'm sorry, I don't mean to trample on your feelings. I know you loved him. I wish things could have been different."

"It is done now. I must look beyond, not behind." He turned to me. "When I left Terra, I decided I would never hide what I am again. Here"—he touched one of his wings—"and here"—he touched his chest—"yet what if the Taercal have such stigmas?"

"We'll deal with it. You know you don't have to stay with them, Hawk. You have a home here." And if Reever and I stopped bickering long enough to take our kid and leave the ship, Hawk could certainly come along.

"I know, but I wish— I would so very much *like* to remain with my father's people." He inspected the sand painting again, then reached out and swept his hand over my brother's image. Rico's face dissolved into a scramble of flower petals and sand. "I cannot dwell in my memories forever."

"Then let's wait and see what's down there." I patted the top of his right wing. "It's probably such an outright nirvana that they have to beat immigrants away with a stick."

Twenty-eight hours later, I decided the stick wouldn't be required. Whatever universal powers responsible for creating nirvanas had bypassed Taerca completely.

From the air, Taerca looked a little spooky. I'm sure Reever would have pointed out the bountiful vegetation, and how lucky the inhabitants were that it paved the continental basins and framed the snowcaps of round-topped mountains. Lots of veggies and veggie-eaters to supply food.

Yet something about the planet spooked me. Random topographical patterns, I thought as I looked down at the surface, should not resemble heaps of skulls rising out of muck.

Planetary sweeps indicated the Taercal were the most highly developed species on the planet, and occupied areas of mountainous tundra high above the valleys and plains. Their cities weren't highly populated, and located far apart from each other.

"So how many people live in this place again?" I asked Reever.

"Our sweeps picked up three hundred and forty-two individual readings within the capital city." He raised a brow. "You did not review the pre-sojourn data again."

"I wanted to be surprised." For a city that was twenty kilometers across, three hundred and forty-two wasn't much. "How big are they?"

"Aside from their wingspans, their physical size is comparable to ours." Reever checked his wristcom. "It could be that the natives spend much of the time in the air. Like the Meridae."

"Uh-huh." I frowned as Xonea began to descend, and the city seemed to expand below us.

A high, glassy stone wall with outward-curving white spikes on it encompassed the place, and served as a notice to "Stay Out!" better than anything I'd ever seen. Someone had painted a strange, purplish pattern on the polished stones. Inside the city, dozens of black structures rose high above the wall, but they didn't resemble any buildings I'd ever seen. They looked more like openmouthed muzzles with protruding teeth.

Scary, nightmarish protruding teeth. "What are those ugly jagged black things?"

Hawk peered through the viewport beside mine. "Part of the mountain, perhaps?"

Reever looked, too. "Too symmetrical. They're artificial, whatever they are."

The launch touched down on a small flat plateau just beyond the all-encompassing wall, and Xonea signaled Ortsac of our arrival. There was no response for several minutes, then a crackling relay came through, audio only.

"Present yourselves at the ingress," I heard the Taercal say.

Xonea requested directions, and the impatient official snarled, "Look for Sadda's Maw!"

"The Welcome Wagon sounds real jovial." I picked up my sojourn pack and nudged a frowning Hawk with my elbow. "I'm just kidding. Once they know we're not here to invade and raid and scorch everything into dust, I'm sure they'll be much more neighborly."

Climbing out of the shuttle made me retrieve my jacket from my pack. The outside air temperature was a frosty degree or two above freezing, and our breath made white puffs in the air as we hiked across the plateau toward the city wall. A foot of mist lay over the ground, and swirled up in sluggish drifts as we moved through it.

"Ugh." Something slid under my footgear, and I lifted it to see a wide, flat smear on the bottom. On the ground lay the writhing remains of an equally attractive worm. "Sorry."

The air incongruously seemed very damp for such a high altitude, and after several hundred feet my face was wet and my hair dripping into my eyes, which should have frozen, but for some reason didn't. The frigid dampness quickly invaded my jacket and garments and increased my discomfort exponentially.

"No wonder your people are feathered," I muttered as I pushed my soaked hair back and watched enviously as water beaded and rolled harmlessly off Hawk's wings. "This place is like one big cleansing unit on continuous cold rinse."

Xonea and Reever were keeping at opposite ends of

the sojourn team, with the Captain in the lead and my husband bringing up the rear. I dropped back to see if our portable translator was being affected by the humidity.

"The housing is designed to withstand immersion in most fluids," Reever said. "Did you notice the sky?"

I looked up. There wasn't much to see, besides thick foggy clouds and a couple of patches of gray beyond that. "What's wrong with it?"

"There are no Taercal flying in it."

That *was* a little weird. "Maybe they went back to the city to welcome us." Even as I said that, a chill inched down my spine, one that had nothing to do with the water dripping down from my hair into my collar.

Reever examined the lethal wall again. "Welcoming strangers does not appear to be a social habit."

The ground, while shrouded in mist, was heavily populated by worms like the one I'd stepped on, and the sound of them squashing under our footgear only added to the ambience of the planet. Which, to me, was basically icky.

"Are these parasites?" I asked Reever as I scraped another one off my footgear.

"No, they are like Terran earthworms, I believe."

"Then why don't they stay in the earth?"

By that time Xonea had located "Sadda's Maw," which turned out to be some kind of stone door recessed in the wall. A huge sculpture formed the entrance, with outcroppings that made me think of a toothy Sword of Damocles. Each of the stylized teeth had been hewn from curved, white stone carefully shaped and polished to appear like the real thing.

Worms were one thing; fangs were another.

"Duncan, what kind of animal has a mouth the size of three launches stacked on top of each other?" I murmured to my husband as I watched the white sun's faint light glitter on the points of the stone fangs.

"One we should avoid."

I shuddered. "Amen." I stepped closer to see the painted pattern on the stone, then reached out to touch it. Flecks of sticky purple came off on my fingers, and a pungent, unpleasant smell hit my nose. "This isn't paint. It's some kind of plant."

"Fungi," my husband said.

"It stinks." I took out a sterile wipe and cleaned off my hand. "Maybe we should leave them a couple of vats of disinfectant and fungicide."

The door beneath it swung outward, scraping stone against stone as it abruptly divided itself in half and slid sideways, parallel to the wall. A small group of beings emerged, stopped several feet away, and said nothing. Their garments were a cross between robes and togas, and since their heads were shrouded with odd, cowl-like drapes, there was no way to know what they were thinking. Finally, one of them, the largest, said something.

My vocollar didn't translate the clipped, toneless words, but Duncan translated at once. "They wish us to present ourselves to them."

On closer inspection, I saw more of the purple mold staining their toga-robes, and worm-splatters around the hems. Didn't these people understand the concept of laundry day?

Xonea stepped forward to make the introductions, which he kept brief and businesslike. "I am Xonea Torin, Jorenian, Captain of the *Sunlace*. This is Healer Cherijo Torin, Linguist Duncan Reever, and *hataali* Hawk Long Knife, all of Terra."

Reever translated that into Taercal, but I noted his accent was far softer and more melodic. As the officials listened, a couple of them shuffled back a step. I could tell from the squashing sounds.

Could it be that he was interpreting this whole thing wrong?

When my husband finished speaking, the biggest Taercal pulled back the shrouding hood of his toga-robe, and revealed himself as Tadam Ortsac, the official who had contacted the ship. He looked even fatter and wartier than he had on the vid.

Large and In Charge snapped something that Duncan translated as "Why do you come here?"

Hawk stepped forward, arching his wings for the first time. "Tell him I am the son of Fen Yillut, born of Charla Long Knife."

Reever obliged, but I don't think any of the Taercal were listening. Every single one of them, including Ortsac, were staring at Hawk's powerful wings. Which made me notice the bulges under the back of their robes. I'd seen that before, when Hawk had concealed his alien blood on Terra by binding them down and pretending he was a hunchback.

Could it be that his father's people also had to disguise their own wings? Why would they, on their own world?

Xonea picked up the sudden shift in mood as well. "Duncan, what say you? What disturbs them?"

"You're intimidating them." Reever went up to Hawk and put a hand on his arm. "Fold back your wings, *hataali*."

"I mean no disrespect." The crossbreed looked perplexed. "I don't understand why my wings would frighten them."

"Neither do I, but fold them back anyway." Reever had picked up on the same thing I had, because he added, "Do not attempt to fly until we can learn why these people do not use their wings."

Once Hawk had folded his extra appendages, Ortsac uttered something short and went back through the door. After a momentary hesitation, so did the rest of the group. A trail of dead worms led to the door, which remained open.

Not much of an invitation.

"Reever, I'm getting a bad feeling about this place." I glanced back at the launch, then at the growing misery on Hawk's face. "Then again, I've been known to be wrong. Frequently." I put my arm through his. "Come on, let's go see if we can locate your dad."

CHAPTER NINE

Among the Faithful

Within the walls were some of the starkest, most unattractive structures I'd ever seen. Built from the same stone as the outer city walls, they hadn't been polished, and seemed almost heaped together. Worms and mold were everywhere, under our feet, on the walls, and seemed to increase in quantity the farther we moved into the city.

"Think they're allergic to architecture and cleanliness?" I asked Reever in a low voice.

He stopped to scrape off the bottom of his footgear. "Evidently they have other priorities."

Aside from the swirly mold, the only architectural ornamentation were crude pictographs hacked in the stone above each open doorway. They were all the same thing—an image of a stick figure with two bumps on its head. Nothing else softened the bare walls, and the ground beneath our feet was simply soil carpeted with thousands of squashed worms.

Not a drone or a glidecar or so much as a public access terminal lay anywhere within sight.

"Where's their tech?" I unbuttoned the front of my now-saturated jacket. "They have to have something, or they wouldn't have been able to signal us."

Xonea peered around. "It may be kept inside the buildings, to protect it from the environment."

Where the dirt streets intersected, triangular trenches had been dug around groups of large stone blocks. There were holes in the top of the blocks, but I wasn't tall enough to see if they went all the way through. Behind them rose the towering black edifices we'd seen from the air. Each one had four splinter-shaped towers at each corner, and only a single open entrance at the base.

Something screeched nearby, and I jumped. "What was that?"

Xonea pointed to a small, darting shadow moving around the jagged points of one black structure. "Some sort of animal."

Some sort of bloodsucking animal, I'd bet. Or worm eating. The white mist rolling around the base of those black things made me expect to hear wolves howling at any moment.

"These must be communal centers." Reever looked in through one of the entrances, but the interior was as black as the outside. "Perhaps meeting places for the local population."

I didn't know who would meet there. The city seemed completely deserted. The only sound we heard was the damp wind, the trickle of condensate running down the stone walls and, as we walked on, the regular squish of the worms we stepped on. There should have been voices, music, kids running around, whispers, *something*.

"Look at this." Xonea knelt down beside a stone channel at the base of one of the houses and waved away the mist. Condensate dribbled into the primitive gutter and was funneled toward one of the black structures. As we followed the aqueduct, I saw the water draining into regular-spaced holes in the black rock base. Worms caught in the streams slid into the holes, too.

"Maybe it's some kind of pest control." I went to step into the narrow entrance to have a peek inside.

Tadam Ortsac appeared again, this time alone, and wearing a standard League wristcom. "You will not trespass upon the ziggurat that is Sadda's abode."

"We will not." Water ran down my husband's face like tears. "However, we are ignorant of your boundaries, and request your guidance."

The official jerked his beak to one side. "Our monitors shall provide instruction." Tadam pointed behind us to another group of four Taercal. Their toga-robes had silver markings on the sleeves, and were stained purple. They moved to stand beside each of us, and smelled so moldy that I started to mouth-breathe. "Accompany your instructors to the felling circles. Until you are educated, enter no ziggurat."

"We would like to contact one of your people," Xonea began to say, but the official only turned and waddled away.

My eyes narrowed as I noticed the official seemed to be hobbling. So far, I hadn't seen anyone as hefty or as warty as Ortsac. Maybe Big Bird was ill. "Reever, ask them what's wrong with Ortsac. Aside from obesity and being covered in verrucae."

Reever relayed my question, but the monitor merely pointed to a narrow alleyway beside the nearest ziggurat. "I believe we must take instruction before we can ask any further questions."

The felling circles were a group of stones set in a circular pattern on a flat, cleared piece of ground. For some reason, the mist and the mold didn't trespass beyond the triangular boundary encompassing the circles. Neither did the worms.

If the worms didn't like it, I didn't like it. I wasn't armed, but I knew Duncan was. He was always armed. "Okay."

As soon as I stepped over the stones and stood inside the circle, I felt very strange—as if something invisible tugged at me. At the same time, my monitor lifted his thin arm and activated a wristcom.

"I am north-seventh monitor." He pulled back his shroud, showing a thin, worn face. "Address me as 'monitor' at all times."

"Sure, monitor." I tried to step in another circle, but he stopped me with a hand. "I can't move around?"

"Stand and receive instruction."

I spotted some dark stains in the dirt near me. "You know, I'm not really good at taking instructions."

North-seventh monitor removed a thin stick from his sleeve and slapped it across the back of my hand. "Remain silent."

"I don't think so." I went to grab the stick, and he hit me in the same place again. "Ouch! Knock it off with the stick!"

Xonea's claws were out, and Reever poised to jump, but it was Hawk who stepped into my circle and blocked a third swat. He said something in the native language that made the monitor shuffle back a step.

Reever took my arm. "Shield the monitor, quickly."

"I shield this Taercal male," I said loudly, to stop the Captain from attacking. "Look, friend, you'd better put your little stick away."

The monitor seemed aghast at our behavior, until Hawk said something else. With great reluctance, he put the stick away.

The *hataali* stepped out of the circle. "Cherijo, he won't hit you again as long as you don't talk."

He wouldn't be able to do anything if he hit me again, I thought, then nodded.

The monitor folded his hands in his mold-stained sleeves before addressing me again. "Vanity is a sin against Sadda. You will cover your head before you enter the ziggurat that is his abode."

Terran Catholics and Muslims once required women to do the same. Apparently their gods didn't like seeing female hair, either. I remembered the no-talking rule and nodded.

"Conversation outside of prayer within Sadda's abode is a sin against Sadda. You will not speak there unless you have prayer for the ten thousand gods."

I could respect the sanctity of a church.

"Coitus is unseemly and a sin against Sadda. You will not offer temptation to the gods' scourges."

No sex. Possibly the reason why there were only three hundred and forty-two of them. I sent out a mental S.O.S. to my husband. *I don't know about you, but I think we should go now.*

Look. They are coming out to see us.

Other natives began emerging from the speckled stone buildings. These were not as silent and sober as the monitors, or as fat and warty as Ortsac. Gaunt, careworn faces inspected us as they exchanged low comments. A few kids pushed up to the front to see, and their toga-robes seemed cleaner.

"Cute kids." I smiled at a little girl about Marel's size. "Hi, there."

She cowered back against an older female, who grabbed her and hurried away.

The stick reappeared as my monitor stepped in front of me. "You will not engage the gods' scourges in idle conversation."

"Can I ask you something without getting whacked?"

He nodded like a gracious host. "You are permitted questions regarding Sadda."

I used his metaphors. "Do the gods' scourges fast for Sadda?"

"To suffer is the price of Sadda's Promise. The gods' scourges abandon all pleasures of the flesh and earth for the coming of the great one."

"Are we"—I indicated myself and the rest of the sojourn team—"expected to do the same while we're here?"

"All must bend to Sadda's whip."

"And if we don't?"

"You wish to bring down Sadda's wrath?" Obviously horrified, he stepped out of the felling circle. That acted like a signal, and the crowd abruptly dispersed and vanished.

"No, not at all. I didn't mean to—" I stopped and swore under my breath as the monitor hobbled away. "Captain?"

I turned to see Xonea snatching the stick from his monitor and breaking it in half. White-within-white eyes met mine as the native escaped. "I dislike this world."

By then all the other monitors except Duncan's had gone. I wiped my dripping face with my sleeve. "So much for being educated."

Hawk stepped into my circle to examine the two fading red marks left on my hand by the monitor's stick. "Are you all right?"

"I'll live." I was watching my husband, who had his hand on the Taercal's shoulder. A few minutes later, Reever released him, and the native stumbled away to disappear into the fog. He looked really worried as he came over to us.

"Xonea, these people are extreme fanatics. They spend most of their time cloistered in prayer." Duncan reached over and blotted the eye I was rubbing with the edge of his sleeve. "Their speech, culture, and daily behavior is strictly governed by thousands of complex ritual laws. It would take years to learn simply how to speak to them without giving offense."

I sighed. "Maybe we should leave."

"Did that one know of my father?" Hawk asked him.

"He dwells within this city." Reever nodded toward the western quadrant. "I can take you there, but we should keep our visit brief."

The *hataali*'s face clouded. "Why?"

"If I am interpreting his warning correctly, a visit to your father could disrupt his daily prayer rituals. For that, he will be beaten. Along with us."

I heard another of those sporadic, eerie screeches, and heard a faint splash. I walked toward the sound until I came across an open pit filled with water. I wouldn't have noticed it, but for a single, decomposing object sticking up out of it. Mold had turned it a fuzzy purple, but it was still recognizable.

"Guys." It was a hand, and something had been gnawing on it. "There's a body over here."

When the men came over, their movements scattered the fog and I saw not one but dozens of bodies in the murky, shallow water. I took out my scanner and passed it over the surface before handing it to my husband. Then I rolled up my sleeve and plunged my hand into the water.

It was cold, and thick with sediment. I felt down the

arm of the exposed hand, until I found the body. A male, naked except for a heavy belt studded with stones tied around the waist. As I felt along one limb, I realized he was so malnourished the body was literally nothing but skin over bones.

I withdrew my arm and shook off the contaminated water. "Starved or drowned. He's weighted down with rocks."

Xonea stood by the edge. "An execution pit?"

The thought that this could have been deliberate made me swallow a surge of bile. "Possibly."

There was nothing I could do for the victim, so we continued on to Hawk's father's home. Fen Yillut lived near the base of a ziggurat, and emerged as soon as we stepped up to the door.

"Greetings from HouseClan Torin," Xonea said, making a gesture of peace. "You are Fen Yillut?"

"Sadda has seen fit to name me thus. You are the aliens from the ship." Fen's expression surpassed Tadam Ortsac's in the dour department. "Why do you violate my prayer time?"

"They intrude on my behalf." Hawk stepped forward.

Fen looked him up and down. "You are?"

"Hawk." He cleared his throat and tried again. "Hawk Long Knife. I'm your son, Father."

Fen's black eyes nearly popped out of his head. "You are Charla's babe?"

Hawk extended his hand. "Charla was my mother, yes."

"I had not thought you would have survived your weaning year." Fen hobbled around Hawk. His obvious pain made me take a scanner out, but as soon as I lifted it, he shied away.

"No! Do not touch me with your alien blasphemy!"

"I'm a doctor," I told him. "This is just a scanner."

His face wrinkled. "Such things are disgusting to us."

That was a reaction I'd never gotten before. "I might be able to help you feel more comfortable. It doesn't hurt."

"I am Sadda's scourge back." Fen went back to the doorway, then paused and said to Hawk, "You may enter, Terran."

"My companions as well?"

He made an irritable gesture. "If they must pollute an abode, let it be mine."

We had to walk into the dwelling single file. Mold grew on the inside, too, so thick that it resembled carpeting and wall coverings; but incongruously, there were very few worms around. Above the threshold was the same, horn-headed stick figure.

There were few furnishings inside—two chairs and a table made of spindly wood. No optic emitters, only thin gray light from one window. A small hearth where a miserable little fire burned under an alloy pot on a hook. Whatever was cooking smelled as vile as everything else on the planet.

Reever sniffed the air. "Perhaps they consume—"

"Don't even think about it." I went over to the triangular window. The ziggurat loomed a foot away, effectively blocking any view of the mountains. "Fen Yillut, we saw some bodies left in a ditch of water. What happened to them?"

"They submitted fully to Sadda's scourge."

To me, scourge meant disease. "What does that mean?"

"They gave themselves up to Sadda. It is a great honor." He scraped a couple of worms off one of the walls and went over to dump them in the pot.

I didn't know whether to be nauseated over the religion or Fen's dietary choices, but no way was I going into their churches or eating anything until we got back to the ship.

Xonea gave the old man an incredulous look. "Your deity requires lives as tribute?"

"Sadda requires much of the people." Fen picked up a pail and brought it over to the rickety table. "You may drink if you are thirsty. Food is not gathered until the eleventh hour."

"Gathered?" I hadn't seen any gardens, or anything but mold growing inside the city walls. "Where?"

"We take what grows on the mountain steppes. *Tifginni* sustains us otherwise." He gestured toward the ziggurat. "Gathering is not permitted until dark, after daily prayer has been satisfied."

Eat worms or grab what you could in the dark. No wonder the people were starving. "Surely you have some technology that could help you with food production. You couldn't have answered our ship's signal without a communications array."

"Blasphemy!" Bits of saliva flew from his mouth to frame the word.

I thought of all the equipment we were carrying, and an ominous thought occurred to me.

Reever put it into words. "Does the use of technology violate your religion, Fen Yillut?"

"Of course, it does! Did you not receive instruction from the city monitors, upon your arrival?"

We all exchanged glances.

"They forgot to mention it," I said.

He hmphed. "We maintain the sky speaker only to keep Sadda's promise."

I was getting sick of what Sadda wanted, required,

and promised. Sadda needed to give these people a long vacation.

"Father," Hawk said, "why do the people hide their wings? Why do they not fly?"

"Such frivolous activity interferes with proper prayer." He twitched his shoulders, as if he wanted to shake the bound wings from his back. "Our ancestors abandoned all such pleasures. Now they function no longer."

"They're atrophied." I forgot to be diplomatic. "Your ancestors didn't do you any favors, Fen."

That sent him into a rage. "You have never prostrated yourself on Sadda's steps, woman! Five days there and I vow you'll have more respect for the gods' scourge backs!"

"Father, please." Hawk's wings fluttered with agitation. "These people are my friends. They mean no disrespect. They brought me here so I could meet you."

Fen took an alloy ladle from the bucket and sipped some liquid, then coughed. When he could speak again, he said, "I have answered your questions. Now, go."

The *hataali* flinched, as if his father had struck him. "I had hoped to spend time with you, Father."

"Why?"

"Do you not wish to know me?"

Fen uttered what might have been a laugh. "I went to Terra to endure a suffering pilgrimage, and the water gave me brain fever. Your mother lured me into her bed. I did not wish to know her; why would I wish to know you?"

Hawk passed a hand over his eyes. "She died for you."

"None die but for the glory of Sadda."

He might have been old, but I could have slapped

him silly just then. "Have a little sensitivity, Fen. Your son's traveled a long way to see you."

"I did not ask him to." His expression turned nasty as he stared at his son. "He is not wanted here."

Two monitors abruptly entered Fen's dwelling. "Fen Yillut, you have not reported for prayer."

All the contempt left the old man's face. "The monitors speak the truth, as always." He staggered over to the door. "These aliens intruded here. The winged one is son of an alien scourge I suffered. It is no excuse, only the circumstance."

"There is no excuse to keep from prayer." One of the monitors took out a stick and struck Fen across the chest. It drove Hawk's father to his knees.

"Hey!" I lunged forward, but Hawk beat me to them.

"Don't you hit him!" he shouted, wrenching the stick away and tossing it across the room. His wings spread out, creating a twenty-five-foot curtain that completely blocked the thin light coming through the window. "He has done nothing wrong!"

"You are allotted one hour of prostration on Sadda's steps for every minute you have spent in idle conversation," the monitor said to Fen, completely ignoring Hawk. "Brook your penance, or apply yourself to the mastering circle."

"Such is Sadda's will, that I accept with joy," Fen said.

"Why am I not surprised?" I couldn't help saying.

The silent monitor pointed a thin, gnarled finger at me. "Sadda's scourge will fall upon you, woman."

I showed him some teeth. "I'll duck."

The monitors withdrew, but only retreated to the alley beside Fen's house, and watched us through the window.

"Why do you allow this?" Hawk demanded of his father. "They have no right to come in here and discipline you."

"Correction of sin is the gateway to enlightenment. Such is the purpose of having monitors among us." Fen straightened his robe and limped toward the doorway. "Already I must devote eight hours of penance for dallying with you. Begone now."

Reever intercepted Hawk's father and took his hand between his. "Give me a moment, so that I might understand better."

The Taercal and my husband stood locked in silence as Reever probed Fen's mind. Whatever he found made him release the old man quickly and step out of his way.

"Leave, and do not return." Fen trudged out.

I looked at the others. "Can we do that? Please?"

"We need more data." Reever went over to the bucket and drew a ladle of the liquid, which I saw was some kind of thin, white fluid. "Their water, I assume."

"Don't drink any of that." I activated my scanner and headed his way. "Remember what was in the ditch."

I scanned the bucket. Readings indicated a high mineral content, as well as a thirty percent diffusion of calcium.

"It's H_2O all right, only with tons of minerals in it. No trace of microorganisms, so it's been distilled or treated by someone. Okay, Duncan, if you want to be brave, have a drink."

Reever only sipped a little before dropping the ladle. "I have tasted better water from mud puddles."

Given his predilection for disgusting tastes, it must have been beyond repulsive. "Did you get anything from the link?"

"His emotions were in turmoil. He feels hunger, pain, and great anger. His mind was filled with images of the ziggurat." Duncan wiped his mouth on the back of his sleeve. "And one other. A structure in the center of the city where archaic technology is stored. He thinks of it as the Place of Sadda's Promise. We should go there before we return to the ship."

"Does he have any memories of Terra? Of the joy he knew with my mother?" Hawk asked as he took a drink from the bucket, and grimaced.

"His memories of your mother are very clouded. I could not feel any particular emotion."

My Reever-radar told me he was lying, something he hardly ever did. Like the Hsktskt, he considered it beneath him. Fen must have had some horrible emotions for him to do that.

Xonea went to the door. "The next sojourn team is due to arrive within the hour. We should meet them before they enter the city."

Reever nodded. "Then we should hurry."

The Taercals' unpleasant environment, surly attitudes, and dismal existence didn't bother me as much as the growing signs of infirmity I was seeing in the population. As we walked toward the center of the city, nearly every native we saw appeared almost crippled. I also caught glimpses of distorted hands and crooked limbs beneath their stained toga-robes.

"I've never seen so many malnourished people," I said as we watched a pair of adolescent males swerve to avoid us. Both limped badly. "Maybe Fen will change his mind and talk to us later. He's elderly; he would know what's been happening."

"My father is not old," Hawk said, astonishing me. "He has only forty-two revolutions—the Taercal life span is nearly identical to a Terran's. You can tell age by the number of short feathers, here." He pointed to a patch of feathers on his neck. "The older one is, the more one grows."

Hawk had about half the short feathers his father had. All the Taercal passing us had even less. "That can't be right, Hawk. That would mean most of these people are in their teens and twenties."

"This affliction the natives share—could it be a juvenile disease, carried on into adulthood?" Xonea asked.

"Unless it's something new, no. The last childhood diseases were eradicated by the Allied League more than a century ago." I gnawed on my lower lip. Could the Taercal have been successfully isolating themselves that long?

"Their environment and lifestyle is exceptionally harsh," Duncan said. "Perhaps that is to blame for their poor health."

"This species evolved in this environment, and developed feathers and wings as specific adaptations to it. I doubt there have been any significant climatic changes over the last couple of centuries," I explained, squashing that theory as flat as the worms under my feet. "As for the lack of comforts, it really isn't any worse here than any primitive, pretech society. The rigors should actually toughen them up, make them stronger. Not create this kind of wear and tear on their bodies."

"They seem very underfed," was Xonea's comment.

I thought of what Fen had mentioned about gathering food. "That's something—the population could be suffering from a vitamin deficiency." On Terra, outbreaks of scurvy and rickets among poor countries no longer occurred, but I'd seen history texts on them.

"Cherijo." Duncan nodded toward a young Taercal

boy, who was staring at me. A heavy bundle of sticks sat on the ground beside him.

I smiled. "Hi, there. I'm Cherijo. What's your name?"

My husband relayed that, and the child gave me a wary look. "Sadda has seen fit to name me Hyt."

"Hyt. That's nice. On my world, we shake hands when we first meet a friend." I held out my hand.

The child backed away. "To touch is blasphemy."

"For kids or grown-ups?"

"Both," he said, like I was stupid.

"Try it anyway. Come on, I won't hurt you." Slowly I got my fingers around his, and felt calluses covering the inner surface of his hand. Despite my gentle touch, he winced. "Does that hurt?"

"I am blessed by the scourge," the boy said, snatching his hand away. His gaze darted to a nearby grave-pit, and the worry lines around his mouth deepened.

"Hyt, tell me something." I kept my voice low and calm, hoping to instill a little confidence. "Why are there bodies in that ditch over there?"

"They were grievously afflicted by Sadda. They chose to sacrifice themselves for the Promise."

Sadda be damned. "Is it because they were in pain?"

Hyt hung his head. "The scourge becomes very hard to bear." At the sound of passing footsteps, he jerked around. "Monitors." With effort, he balanced the stick bundle on his back. "I must go or I will be late for prayer."

I waited until he limped out of sight before I folded back my sleeve and unstrapped the scanner from my arm. "He's moderately malnourished and, believe it or not, dehydrated. With all this water around." I scrubbed condensate off the display before checking the systemic readings. "Nonexistent white count, enlarged spleen, severe anemia, moderate to major inflammation in every joint in his body." I saved the scans and formatted them for transmission. "I've seen better readings from diseased octogenarians."

Reever exchanged a look with Xonea. "Is it a disease?"

"It could be, but I'm not picking up any pathogens or antinuclear antibodies. And his blood should be riddled with something, to cause these kind of symptoms. It's as if his immune system detonated." I transmitted the readings up to the ship, along with a note for Squilyp to see what he could make of them. "I need to get comparison stats from one of the adults. We don't have this species on the medical database, but we can use Hawk's physiology to help develop one."

Getting another scan proved much more difficult. Few of the natives came out of their homes. The older Taercal who did, refused to speak to us, and their children proved much more skittish than Hyt.

We also passed several more of the drowning pits, which were full of bodies, and the stone blocks inside the triangular trenches. Monitors seemed to pop out of the stonework whenever we paused by the pits, so I was unable to scan for signs of disease. By the time we reached the center of the city, I had yet to get my comparison scan, but had counted nearly a hundred drowned bodies.

"This is the structure." Duncan nodded toward a stone building that was three times the size of any of the dwellings. It also had the single, narrow doorway, but this one was flanked on either side by monitors. Horned stick figures had been carved all around the stone doorway.

"I don't think they're going to just let us walk in."

"Hawk may be able to help." Reever said something

low in Taercal to the *hataali,* who nodded and arched his wings before approaching the monitors.

"What's he saying to them?" I asked Reever as we watched Hawk make a sweeping gesture with both arms.

"He is telling them we wish to abandon our blasphemies and keep to Sadda's Promise."

I wrapped a protective hand around the strap of my sojourn pack. "I am *not* leaving my gear here."

"You only have to pretend to do so."

The monitors studied us with evident suspicion, then drew back from the door. As I followed the men in, I had the feeling someone was watching us. A quick look back revealed Tadam Ortsac hovering at a discreet distance.

"Big Bird is out there watching us," I muttered to Xonea.

"I will guard the entrance passage," the Captain said. "I do not think they will wait long. You three had better hurry."

The interior of the storage building would have made our ship engineers weep with fury—sophisticated hardware and assorted tech had been tossed in piles, forming a sort of cluttered maze that we negotiated with some difficulty.

"There are prep units, envirocontrol panels, energy conversion conduits—" I was no engineer, but even I could see what they'd done. "It's like they stripped out everything they had that was artificially powered or made of alloy, and threw it in here, to rust."

"Cherijo." Reever pushed aside a terminal and stepped over an ancient housekeeping drone before lifting another unit. "Is this a diagnostic unit?"

It was. "I need a table or something to set it down on."

Hawk cleared off a tool bench and Duncan placed it on top. I punched the panel and watched as the medical unit sluggishly activated.

"Hawk, I'll need you to translate."

"I regret I can only speak my father's language," he said. "Duncan?"

"I can read it. Go ahead, Cherijo."

Thankfully, the hardware was League-compatible, so it had no problem adapting to my scanner. I plugged the leads in, downloaded Hyt's readings, and waited. At last, something started to scroll on the cracked display screen.

"They identified an outbreak of juvenile infectious arthritis some fifty years ago. Commonly referred to as Sadda's scourge, according to the notations." Reever was silent as he read further. "Symptoms develop into adult infectious arthritis, with a side effect of severe bone distortion."

"That's ludicrous." I checked the leads. "We cured arthritis three hundred years ago, and it doesn't cause bone distortion anyway. What else does it say?"

"Give me a moment." Reever took off his wristcom, did something to it and the panel, and at once the Taercal readings converted to stanTerran. "Check the last readings from their medical exchange database."

I did. According to what I read, the Taercal had stopped downloading medical information from their Quadrant Surgeon General's Office almost two hundred years ago. Given that length of isolation, and their disdain for technology, the people would have quickly forgotten whatever they once knew about effective treatment.

But why would their physicians allow them to do that?

I punched up everything in the database on the condition. The notes on the initial outbreak were so brief it was criminal. "The doctors who diagnosed this did nothing about it. They had the cure, but they never administered it. They just let kids like Hyt suffer for no reason."

"We don't have much time," Hawk said. "We must discover why my father's people have isolated themselves and reverted to such primitive living conditions."

"That won't be on here." I downloaded the standard readings for Taercal physiology before I shut off the unit. "Whoever these idiot physicians were, they only recorded medical data on this unit."

Reever looked around. "They may have preserved something on their public access terminals."

We found one in another pile of junked components, but it was in terrible shape. Only a partial screen appeared when Reever finally got it working, but it was enough to show a vid of the Taercal as they stripped all the tech and hardware from their homes. These were much healthier-looking specimens, dressed in fitted garments that allowed their wings to show.

"Can you enable the audio?" I asked as I watched some of them open their mouths and shout at each other.

Reever tapped the console, and a static-filled recording crackled in the air. The Taercal sounded furious, screaming in high-pitched voices at each other.

"They say it is the end of indulgence," Hawk said, frowning as he concentrated on the crackling audio. "They beg the ten thousand gods to be merciful. More of the same from the others—prayer, pleas for leniency."

"Look at the women." I tapped the screen, where the image of a line of females carrying wrapped bundles appeared. They were sobbing and hysterical, and one of them dropped to her knees, clutching her bundle to her breast. The cloth covering it fell away from a small face contorted with agony.

"It infected their children first," my husband said.

Hawk looked sick. "Can you help them, Cherijo?"

"They could have helped themselves a long time ago—their doctors *knew* what to do. This condition can be cured with a couple of infusions and nutritional supplements. It's all on the medical console." It didn't make sense. "Why would they withhold treatment and let them descend into mass hysteria like this?"

Reever nodded to the screen. "They were otherwise occupied."

Another vid was running. This one showed a mob of outraged Taercal throwing stones at a smaller group of cowering males and females—all of whom wore white-and-blue physician's tunics.

I sat back as I watched them die. "Oh my God."

Reever showed us replays of other atrocities. Beatings. Arson. Stabbings. More stonings. In the end it was very clear why the doctors had been unable to finish recording or treat the population.

The Taercal had reacted to their "scourge" by systematically executing every physician on the planet.

CHAPTER TEN

Sadda's Price

We left the techno dump site united in the decision
that we needed to get off this world as quickly as possible.

"They must not discover Cherijo is a physician,"
Hawk said, scanning the dwellings around us. "They
will kill her."

"I don't know why they haven't tried already. It's
not like I've tried to hide it." I touched the stylized ca-
duceus on the shoulder of my tunic. "Xonea, you introduced me as a healer, and they've seen me use my
equipment."

"It has been many decades since the population
murdered their own physicians." Xonea removed a
dagger from a sheath under his flightsuit and palmed
it. "They may not recognize your insignia or even understand what a healer is."

I thought of the graphic vids we'd seen. "Let's
hope."

We entered the streets and headed for the city walls
where we had entered through Sadda's Maw. Reever
took point, having gone into his silent, alert mode.
Hawk and Xonea flanked me. We walked in a brisk,
but unhurried way, past monitors and citizens, ignoring the stares and whispers.

"I don't like this." As the carpet of worms squished

under my footgear, something occurred to me. "Xonea, how long before the second sojourn team lands?"

The Captain swore and checked his wristcom. "They have left the ship by now."

"Signal them to go back," Reever said.

My ClanBrother tried, but dropped his arm and glanced around us. "Something is jamming transmission. We are also being followed."

I turned to see a number of people and monitors trailing us at a discreet distance. "We'd better make a run for the launch."

We ran. Since my legs were shorter than everyone else's, I soon lagged behind. Xonea stopped long enough to grab me and pick me up.

"Your pardon," he said as he propped me on one strong arm. "It will be easier this way."

Reever didn't look happy about that when he glanced back, but said nothing and continued to lead us on a zigzag path through the streets. Over my Clan-Brother's shoulder, I saw a huge group of Taercal limping in pursuit. Given their physical condition, they'd never catch us, but I wouldn't feel safe until we got off this worm-ridden rock.

Just before we reached Sadda's Maw, Ortsac and his group of officials stepped out to block our exit. "Halt! You will submit yourselves to instruction and discipline!"

"Another day, perhaps." Reever whirled into one of his inhuman, rolling moves and knocked the fat Taercal out of our way. The stone door remained closed, but he took out a pulse weapon, adjusted the beam, and fired. A big hole appeared in the stone, and he ducked out through it.

I didn't think, I linked. *Reever?*

I can see the second launch landing. We must hurry.

I told Xonea, who carried me through the doors. On the other side, he flinched, then stumbled forward as something hit him from behind. I heard a stone thump on the ground, and ducked to avoid another.

They were throwing rocks at us.

"Run faster!" I shouted to Hawk.

We made it to the landing site with the Taercals lagging behind, still in pursuit. The second sojourn team was already disembarking, and as they saw us, Dhreen and Salo drew their weapons.

I couldn't believe my eyes. "What the hell is Dhreen doing out of Medical?"

"What is it?" Salo shouted.

"Get back on the ship and get out of here!" Reever yelled.

Xonea would have flung me into our launch, but the hull doors didn't open. I spotted the damaged access panel beside them and realized the Taercal had taken out some insurance ahead of time. I twisted out of his arms and staggered to my feet. "Can the other launch fit all of us?"

The Captain's muscles bunched as he watched the mob rushing toward us. "No time."

Reever pushed him toward the second shuttle. "Take her—Hawk and I will hold them off."

Arguing with that was useless, but before I could get to the second launch, a hailstorm of stones flew at us. The rocks bounced off the launch and, as they started smacking into me, I instinctively threw up my arms to cover my face.

"Polluters!" I heard Ortsac shriek. "Blasphemers!"

Hard hands grabbed me, too many to fight. I got to watch the same happen to Xonea and Hawk, while Reever barely kept his attackers at bay. Dhreen and

Salo were already being held, and the mob quickly disabled the second launch.

Monitors stripped everyone of their weapons, and there was an almost gleeful shout as two dozen Taercal finally took my husband down and held him pinned to the ground.

"They belong to Sadda now!" Tadam Ortsac shouted. "They . . . belong—" He stopped as a sudden hush fell over the crowd.

I looked over at the second shuttle, where Alunthri came out from behind the docking ramp where it had evidently been hiding. The mob stoning the launch staggered back so fast they tripped over one another.

"Oh, Jesus," I whispered, then yelled, "Alunthri, run!"

The Chakacat didn't seem to hear me, because it took a step forward. Its silvery head canted to one side as it regarded the mob. "Why are you doing this?"

The Taercals seemed riveted in place, as if frozen by those five simple words.

At last, Tadam Ortsac shuffled forward, his head bowed, his entire body quivering—but not with anger. A few yards from the docking ramp, he sank to his knees. He stretched out his arms and lifted his pudgy face to the sky.

"The ten thousand gods bestow their blessings at last! All praise we lift to Sadda!"

The mob respectfully murmured a repeat of the same.

Condensate ran down the official's puffy face like tears of joy as he prostrated himself, facedown in the wormy dirt. "We have long awaited this day, waited with patience and prayer," he said, his voice a little muffled by his position. "Now it is upon us, and we are grateful to you, oh, Sadda."

"Reever." I yanked at the hands holding my arms. "Talk to me. What's he going to do?"

"Not what you expect."

Tadam rose to his feet and shuffled around to face the mob. "Behold the profit of prayer!" He pointed back at Alunthri. "For Sadda himself is returned to us!"

It got even weirder from there.

The entire mob reassembled into straight, long rows, then dropped to prostrate themselves on the ground. Faces pressed to the worms, just like Ortsac's. A low monotone hum began and grew as each Taercal added his voice to it, until the wordless chant seemed to press in on my ears.

The only exception to this mass-prayer thing were the Taercal holding on to each of us. They watched with unblinking, reverent awe as Ortsac approached the mob.

"Sadda's scourge is everlasting!" he yelled, pacing back and forth in front of the lines, like a secular cheerleader working a game crowd. "Sadda has tested the people and found them not wanting! Praise be to Sadda for the gift of will and endurance."

Endurance, ha. Let them spend a year on a Hsktskt slave depot and then come talk to me about endurance.

The worship ceremony went on and on, until I was ready to scream. To keep from making a spectacle of myself, I tried to figure out what had triggered the Taercals' extreme response.

Evidently "Sadda" was a feline deity, doubtless responsible for the claws we'd seen decorating everything. Alunthri must have borne a close resemblance to she/he/it. A good thing, too, because I suspected without the appearance of the Chakacat, we would have all been tied up with stones and drowned in shallow grave-ditches.

Finally, the crowd rose slowly to their feet, and Ortsac lead the troops back toward the city entrance.

"Which one of the ten thousand gods is Sadda, exactly?" I asked the Taercal who were hauling me back through the wall entrance to the city.

"Silence, blasphemer." A monitor struck me with a stick. "Your lips are not clean enough to form the great one's name."

I thought about mentioning the fact that I had actually owned the great one for a brief period of time, but bit my tongue. If I blew Alunthri's cover, we might all be killed.

Ahead of us, the Taercal were ushering my friend with the kind of reverent deference one gave to a world monarch. I could just imagine what the Chakacat was thinking—as long as it went along with the religious fanatics, it could keep us alive.

At least, I hoped it was thinking that.

A dozen natives dragged Reever past me. He was still struggling and blood ran down the side of his face, and his eyes had gone that scary, colorless gray shade they got when he was really upset.

Duncan. What are we going to do? If they find out Alunthri isn't a god, they'll drown all of us.

Alunthri will shield us, long enough for us to come up with a plan. Have you seen Hawk?

I tried to look around, and got another whack from the stick. "Look, you," I said, feeling very testy, "if you don't stop hitting me, I'm going to shove that stick in a very uncomfortable anatomical location." I spotted Hawk a few yards away. Like Duncan, he was struggling wildly to free himself, and bore a number of facial contusions. "Hawk! Stop—"

Someone clubbed me over the head, and the world became a little dim for a few minutes. They kept dragging my limp body along, while I tried to muster my senses back to some semblance of order.

Cherijo!

Duncan's frantic thoughts were what pulled me back from the abyss. *I'm okay. Just give me a minute.*

Baby, we need a little more than sixty seconds, a familiar voice said.

Who is that? my husband demanded.

Hello, Reever. We haven't met yet. Maggie's voice sounded amused. *I'm the little snot's mother. In a stand-in kind of way.*

You're not my mother. Coldness seeped into my limbs. *Duncan, end the link. I don't want her infecting your mind, too.*

The world went away, and I was swept into darkness. This time, I wasn't alone, and felt Duncan latch on to me with his inexorable control.

I fought him. *Duncan, I mean it. Let go of me. You can't stop her.*

Then I'm going with you.

We ended up falling together, tangled in each other's thoughts, into the abyss that always led to Maggie. Where we ended up was a total shock.

"How did we get here?" Duncan asked me as he helped me to my feet. Although we were still inside my mind, everything appeared as genuine reality around us.

The reality of my hotel room on Caszaria's Moon.

"Maggie likes to play her little games." I straightened my tunic and looked around. "Don't worry, it never lasts long, thank Whoever Is in Charge Up There."

A tall, red-haired woman stepped in through the

door panel. She wore a waitress's uniform that was a little too tight around the chest and hips, and pushed a cart laden with champagne and trays of little cakes and desserts. Her smile was as sexy as the wiggle of her hips.

"Room service." She stopped the cart, straightened, and tucked a napkin over her arm. At the same time, she waggled her eyebrows at my husband. "Whoo-hoo. Hellooooo, handsome."

Duncan regarded her the same way he did Terran food. "This is your maternal influencer?"

"Paid companion, replacement mother, partner in crime," Maggie said in her sweetest voice.

"Personal demon from hell," I added for good measure.

"That, too." She removed a silver cover from one of the dishes with a flourish. "Let's see here, we've got Dom Perignon, chocolate eclairs, imported cheeses, oh, and those vanilla cherry whatever-they-ares you gorged on back on that jungle world where you two met." She held up a delicate china plate and looked at both of us expectantly. "Anyone hungry?"

I'd been through similar synaptic scenes in the past too often to let her rile me. "What do you want, Maggie?"

"Lots of stuff." She left the cart in the center of the room and went to open the drapes. "Nice place, for a dome world. I like the posh, but I wouldn't want to stroll through those bubble things down there."

"How are you doing this?" Reever demanded.

My childhood companion ogled my husband again as she turned. "Dunkie, you really should have done more than just kiss her when you guys were here. Consider the waste of the bed, at least."

"Dunkie?" My husband sounded mortally offended. "I beg your pardon."

"Never beg, gorgeous." As she walked past him, Maggie reached out and slapped his backside. "With a bod like yours, you should only have to fight them off."

When Reever took a step to go after her, I caught his eye and shook my head.

Maggie wasn't finished, and gestured toward me. "Take Dr. Uptight here. She's not a pushover, my Joey, but with a little effort you could have convinced her to cheat on her boyfriend, way back when."

"If that's what you think," my husband said, "then you don't know Cherijo very well."

"Oh, well, I suppose you're right. Call it *wishful* thinking."

"Maggie."

She turned her attention to me. "And you. You're supposed to be on your way to Jxinok, little girl." Maggie took the champagne bottle from the ornate silver ice bucket and popped the cork. "We need to discuss that. Here, have a drink."

"Let's not and say we did. We have to go back."

"Ah-ah-ah." She wagged a finger at me as she handed me a flute of champagne. "Remember, ten seconds in your reality equals ten hours here. You won't be gone longer than the blink of an eyelash."

When she handed Duncan his glass, he knocked it away. The crystal smashed all over the deck. "End this and release us."

"Raised with aliens, weren't you? That would explain the hostility *and* the lousy deportment. So don't drink—hell, I'm not going let good champers like this go to waste." Maggie drank from the bottle, then belched.

He glanced at me. "She does this to you every time?"

"Every time."

Taking the bottle with her, Maggie sat down to give a test bounce on the bed. "Excellent firmness. Really, Dunkie, you should have nailed her back then. Would have put a little flex in that titanium spine of hers."

"Okay, you've embarrassed me enough, fun's over now." I had my own hands clenched. "Get to the point."

"Gee, I thought I had. You're stuck on this wormball here, and you're supposed to be on my homeworld." Maggie lit an illegal cigarette and dragged the smoke in before releasing it with a satisfied sigh. "I'm not very happy with you, baby."

"You'll survive." I coughed and waved a hand in front of my face. "These people have taken us prisoner. Besides, we haven't figured out where your world is yet anyway."

"I told you back on Terra to move your little ass. You got the discs. You got the big blueberry guys to chauffeur you around and lots of big guns to guard you with. How hard can this be?" Maggie took another drink and sighed. "Jesus, Joey, just do what the hell I told you to do."

"Cherijo has no obligation to do anything for you." Duncan began pacing in front of the bed. "You don't own her any more than Joseph Grey Veil did."

"Ah, but there's where you're wrong, son. She's all mine." Maggie grinned at me as a box appeared on the bed, and she opened it. The red dress Ana Hansen had once lent me spilled across her thighs. "Yikes, what a choice little number. I know *you* didn't pick out this one."

"It was a gift from a friend—" I made a frustrated

sound. "Look, there's nothing I can do to get to Jxinok faster. We may not even make it off this planet alive." I snatched the dress out of her hands and tossed it back in the box. "Are we done now?"

"Not yet." Maggie got up and walked another circle around Duncan. "You two had better straighten out the other problem you have, because I can't keep barging in to save your backsides every time something goes wrong."

"Save *our* backsides?" I threw my arms up. "Please, refresh my memory, because I don't remember you doing a damn thing for either of us."

"Who told you to keep your mouth shut about the baby around Joseph? Who told you to tell handsome here about it, for that matter?" Maggie turned to Duncan. "And did she listen to me? No. She made you wait until you could see the kid. Is that trust, I ask you?"

"I didn't even know if Marel was *alive*," I said, snarling. "I wasn't going to let Duncan go through that, too."

"That comes with the territory, when you love someone. You share the good stuff, and the agony. It all comes down to the same thing, Joey. Trust." My former companion returned for the bottle and shoved it back in the silver ice bucket on the cart. "You and Duncan have figured out the love thing. You're halfway to figuring out the parent thing. Now you've got to deal with the trust. It's got to be total, blind, and unwavering."

"I trust Duncan."

"Honey, you haven't trusted anyone since you found out your father cooked you up in a test tube." Maggie laughed. "As for this husband of yours, he's made a living out of *not* trusting anyone. I'll leave you two to get to work on that and, oh, hurry up and get off this sticky, wet rock."

She pushed the cart toward the door, and Duncan suddenly lunged after her. He grabbed her arms and forced her around. "Tell my wife the truth."

"Ooooh, big and strong and everything a woman wants in an alpha male." Maggie felt the muscles in his arms. "Much as I'm tempted, you might want to let go of me, pal."

Duncan only gave her a shake. "You're not emanating from a subliminal implant. I can feel you. You're a life force. You're *projecting*."

"Smart boy." Maggie patted his cheek. "Let me give you some practical advice." She gently pushed one hand against his chest. Reever suddenly flew across the room and crashed into one of the walls. "Don't mess with this life force."

"Duncan!" I ran to him, but he was already pushing himself up from the deck. I whirled around and spat, "You bitch!"

"Takes one to raise one." She whistled as she pushed the cart through the door panel. "By the way, that hypercellular injector you used on the old ball and chain there has done some interior redecorating. I think it would do you both some good to take a better look at that."

"How?" I shouted. "What has it done to him? Tell me!"

"Simple, sweetheart. Use a mirror." With that, Maggie disappeared, along with the hotel room and the abyss.

My husband and I wound up inside my head, still connected by the link. I sent out a tentative feeler of thought. *Duncan? You okay? Answer me.*

I'm fine. His thoughts were strong and steady—much steadier than my own. *That female is a menace.*

Tell me about it. I collected myself. *We'd better get back to the lynch mob.*

Cherijo, what she said—

Not now, Duncan. We've got to live long enough to get back to the Sunlace *first. Then we can dissect Maggie's little speech.*

Swimming back to consciousness wasn't difficult. One of the Taercal helped by dousing me with a bucket of cold, white water.

"Wha—" I spluttered and shook my head, trying to free a hand to wipe my face. Only I couldn't.

I was pinned inside stone—one of the stone blocks we'd seen all around the city. Only my head stuck out through the hole at the top. Something soft and slimy wriggled against my body. Worms. They'd put worms inside this thing with me.

"Reever!"

"Beside you." My husband, Salo, and my Clan-Brother occupied the nearest stone blocks.

I tried to lift my arms out, but there was no room. "Where's Alunthri and Dhreen?"

"I don't know. Stay calm."

Something hopped up on the stone in front of my nose. A small animal with mud-colored fur, four stunted limbs, and translucent hide wings. It hissed at me, and displayed two rows of needle-sharp teeth.

I did *not* need my face eaten off. "Get away from me!"

It shrieked, hopped back, and took off into the air.

"Drown the demon lack-wit!"

Trying to see who yelled that hurt my neck, then something slipped down the back of my collar. I tucked my chin in and saw that the top of the stone block was heaping with worms, which were crawling into the cavity holding me.

I was going to vomit. Soon. "Duncan—"

"I know," he said. "Don't think about it."

A mob approached the stones. In front of them was a long row of monitors, Tadam Ortsac, Hawk, and Dhreen. Alunthri was nowhere in sight.

Ortsac nodded to the monitors holding Dhreen, and they jerked his head up by yanking on his orange hair. My Oenrallian patient, who should have been in his critical care berth, looked numb and pale.

"Behold the blood polluter, the defiler, the inflictor of pestilence." Big Bird lashed Dhreen across the face with a stick. Orange blood beaded along the long line of the resulting weal. "Sadda shall rend its flesh and suck from its bones!"

"Stop it!" I fought the stone box, desperately trying to work my arms free. "You can't do this. Let us go!"

No one so much as glanced at me. Everyone shouted as Ortsac struck Dhreen in the face a second time.

"Cherijo." My husband nodded at the nearest ziggurat. "Alunthri was taken within, there. They seem to believe the Chakacat is the reincarnation of their messiah."

"Space their messiah; they're going to kill Dhreen." I stopped writhing and tried to concentrate on feeling for any spare inch of room or loose spot. "Why are they beating him? He just got here. He hasn't done anything."

Xonea's head jerked as he struggled with his stone cage. "He resembles the pictographs over the thresholds."

"What?" I stared at Dhreen as they dragged him toward us. "I thought they were some kind of horned deity."

"Judging by their reaction, I think not."

"Hey, Doc." Blood stained Dhreen's smile. "I was feeling better before I got here." He grimaced as another monitor struck him on the back of the neck.

"Be quiet and keep your head down." I caught the official's eye. "Tadam Ortsac, this male means you no harm. He's very sick. Please, release him."

"His seed polluted our kind." His fat face creased with a smile. "Sadda will grind him back into the soil from which he came."

"Father!" Hawk, who was being dragged over to the stones behind Dhreen, broke free of the Taercal holding him. "Father, do not allow them to do this! My friends have only offered friendship to your people!"

Fen Yillut appeared out of the crowd, so pale and drawn he resembled a walking skeleton. The crippled hand he used to point at Hawk, however, remained steady. "Born of a pilgrimage of suffering, my son," he said to the others in the crowd.

"I am your son," Hawk said. "As your son, I beg you, stop this."

"My only son, and still you betray Sadda's Promise."

"I haven't done anything but find you." Hawk's beautiful voice broke on those last two words. "Father, please."

"You brought the demon lack-wit to our world," the old man said as he shuffled forward. "It is my place to wield Sadda's Claw, in his name."

One of the monitors handed Fen a heavy, thick wooden club. Sharp, stained stones shaped like talons were embedded in the knobby end. I thought of the bodies in the ditches, and wondered how many of them were missing the backs of their skulls.

The needle-toothed monkey-birds began circling overhead.

"Hawk!" I screamed as Fen lifted the club.

The *hataali* had been standing frozen, staring at his father in disbelief. As the ceremonial club swung down, Hawk suddenly jumped back and up.

Then Reever shouted, "Fly!"

Hawk's powerful wings swept out once, twice, and then he was hurtling up into the fog. The crowd rushed forward, trying to grab him, but he was already too high. His black wings swept through the air until the mist closed around him, and he vanished.

PART THREE

Revelations

CHAPTER ELEVEN

Sustenance

Hawk's escape stirred up the crowd, and like any angry mob they turned on who was left. The monitors managed to hold them back, but it didn't look like that would last for long.

All of this, in the name of religion?

"Really nice, Wart Sack," I said to the obese official as he waddled over to stand in front of me. "Come to Taerca, get your skull beaten in with a big stick, no extra charge."

"Sadda is returned to us." He flicked his pudgy hand at me in a snide little shoo-shoo. "You are less than dust."

Reever took his usual approach. "Sadda is returned to you, and yet you dare the wrath of the ten thousand gods by offering unworthy sacrifice."

"Why, Reever." I pretended to be offended. "You promised you wouldn't tell them we're not worthy of getting our heads bashed in. Now you've gone and ruined the entire sacrifice for everyone."

"Quiet, Cherijo." To Ortsac, he said, "A wise leader would display sacrifices for Sadda's inspection and obtain his leave to offer, now that he is here among the people. But you did not think of that, did you, Tadam Ortsac?"

Mr. Superfluity's feathers bristled. "There is no one

more devoted to Sadda than I. I have spent my life preparing for his return."

"Have you?" Reever lowered his voice to a bare whisper. "Or have you spent that time stuffing your throat and adorning yourself?"

The fat Taercal reeled back from the stone, acting the offended one now. "I am that which Sadda will need. All I have done is for the glory of the great one."

"Might want to check with Sadda anyway," I suggested. "Just to be on the safe side. Nothing like screwing up a sacrifice to bring down celestial wrath."

"No!" Ortsac blocked a monitor who was hefting a club in my direction. "Do not ply Sadda's Claw yet. We must seek Sadda's approval, now that he is come."

A ripple of unease ran through the crowd. It was apparently easier worshipping an absent deity by bashing in people's heads than asking permission for the same from one in person.

"Summon the great one from his abode," Ortsac said to another monitor. "Beg Sadda's indulgence in this, for which we need his council."

"The Terran lies." Fen Yillut pushed past the monitors and went to work with his finger again. This time he pointed at Duncan. "He seeks to preserve himself by plying persuasion. They are all like that."

"I'd much rather suture your face shut," I mentioned. "Just FYI."

"Silence. Fen Yillut, your attentiveness is admirable, but I have this situation in hand." Ortsac had puffed himself up and now stood like an enormous, overstuffed chicken. "Monitors, summon Sadda from his abode."

Off the guys with the sticks went, into the largest of the ziggurats in the city. I wondered how the Chakacat was handling godhood.

Pretty well, I found out, when the monitor returned. "Sadda summons the faithful to his abode. Sadda will inspect the sacrifice within the confines of his holy place."

"Thank you, Sadda," I said as two of the monitors came at my stone. They pressed their hands on either side, and two hidden recesses popped out. A moment later, the stone split in half, much like the door in the city wall. My confinement came to an abrupt end, but my limbs were numb and made me fall forward. A slushy pile of mostly dead worms poured out on top of me. The monitors grabbed me just before I smacked face first into the dirt.

"Cherijo?"

I swiped at the squashed bodies clinging to my garments. "I'm spending a month in the cleanser when we get back, but I'm okay." I glanced over my shoulder to see other monitors doing the same for the boys, and saw how furious my husband looked. "Keep it cool for a few more minutes, handsome."

Despite being covered in worm-puree and stiff limbed from lack of circulation, they forced us to walk over and into the ziggurat. As I passed the stone threshold with a monitor pushing me from behind, I felt the same strange, pulling sensation that I'd sensed standing in the felling circle.

Like it wants to suck me in.

A cold chill shot up my arm when my hand brushed against the black stone, and a memory snapped into focus. I'd definitely touched this stuff before, under oddly similar circumstances.

"Reever." I watched him place a hand on the rock. "Feel it?"

"Yes. It's tul, but it's . . . not alive."

The tul, a black crystal we'd encountered on

Catopsa, had been like a mineral cancer, eating into and sucking the life out of the Pel, another variety of semi-sentient crystal that formed the entire asteroid.

Whatever the Taercal had used to make their cathedrals had been tul or had been infected by it. Had it been active, we would have been in very bad shape. The black crystal had invaded the bodies of hundreds of slaves and one particularly brutal Hsktskt guard. It had crystallized within their bodies, insidiously eating into the nervous system, causing serious brain damage and, in the case of the guard, insanity.

The dead crystal seemed inert, but the Taercal still may have contracted some form of the tul disease by long-term exposure to it. That would certainly go a long way to explaining why they acted like complete psychotics.

The ziggurat's interior rose around us, a huge cavernous area that stretched hundreds of feet above our heads. Sheer walls draped with hundreds of yards of dense, dull-colored fabric were illuminated by what appeared to be urns of burning sticks, set all around the base of the cloth hangings. The air smelled stagnant and acrid with old smoke, so thick that it made my eyes and lungs burn.

"Someone ought to open a window in here."

It looked like any church in the galaxy, with one exception—it didn't *feel* like a church. Something else was going on inside these walls, and considering what they were made of, it had to be bad.

There were no pews or chairs, as one might expect to find in a place of worship, only a series of steps leading up to an elevated platform. Another sculpture hung suspended above the platform, this one rendered in the same silvery alloy Ortsac had used to ornament his stunted wings.

A forty-foot-tall, silver replica of Alunthri.

"I take it that's Sadda," I said, nodding toward the huge feline icon.

That got me a whack between my shoulder blades from my monitor. "You will not speak in Sadda's abode."

There were other ways to communicate. *Duncan, do you see Alunthri?*

Over there.

My husband inclined his head toward a small chamber at the base of the north set of steps, from which the Chakacat emerged. Everyone except the monitors fell to their knees. This included Tadam Ortsac, who made sure to drop directly in front of Alunthri.

I felt like bobbing a curtsy myself—they had dressed up the big alien kitty cat in a midlength, elaborately ornamented toga-robe which shimmered and glittered with every move it made. More ornaments, similar to the marks the monitors wore on their sleeves, encircled its wrists and ankles. Faceted oval gems studded the polished silver like dark stars.

"Oh, great one," the official crooned. "We have brought the sacrifices into your abode, as you directed. Find favor with our offerings, that we may spill their brains and glorify you in their blood."

"Bring them to me." Alunthri, the gentlest and most unassuming creature I'd ever known, lifted both front paws and made a perfectly regal, come-hither gesture.

The four of us were dragged over to the steps, and shoved down on our knees several yards from the Chakacat. I bowed my head, but lifted my eyes to meet Alunthri's.

My friend gave me a slow but deliberate wink.

"These sacrifices are not worthy of me. They are

alien, not of the people." Alunthri's whiskers twitched once as it drew back. "I refuse the offering."

"We will take them away from your blessed sight and drown them at once, great one." Ortsac hurried to assure it.

"No." Quickly hiding its alarm, Alunthri snapped out another order. "You will take them to my chamber, so that I may inspect them further. They may be of use to me in other ways."

"Other ways?" What might have been suspicion crossed Ortsac's fat face. "But, great one, surely—"

"You dare question me?" Alunthri tensed, and bared its teeth. "You, who are less than a grain of sand in my eye?"

Big Bird threw himself down on his face again, talking to the stone floor. "No, great one, I beg your forgiveness, your indulgence. You are the scourge and I am your back."

The Chakacat waited a couple of beats before saying, "Very well, I will indulge you this once. Now, bring them to my chamber."

I could tell the Chakacat was enjoying its roleplaying, as it had when it pulled off a feral act among the Hsktskt. I only prayed it would be able to keep it up long enough for us to figure a way off Taerca.

The monitors hauled us to the small chamber at the base of the steps, and shoved us inside. When they would have followed, Alunthri stepped in and waved them away.

"I will speak to them alone."

That caused a few looks to be exchanged, but the monitors bowed and shuffled back.

Since there was no door, and no way to know if the Taerca were listening in on our conversation, Reever addressed the Chakacat in its own native language.

Alunthri responded, at length, then gave me a reassuring grin.

"You, small Terran. Attend me." It held out a brush, then shrugged out of the heavy toga-robe. I started brushing its fur. In a scarcely audible whisper, it said, "Sorry. They expect everyone to worship me."

"I already do, pal. What's the plan?" I watched as Reever quietly spoke to Xonea and Salo.

"I will conduct a short service for the natives. Then, with a bit of luck, do as Duncan says and ascend into the heavens with my offerings." The Chakacat purred with pleasure as I drew the brush through its short, gray fur. "That feels wonderful."

"You're as bad as Jenner." I put down the brush, and picked up one of the strange arm-cuffs. They might have been designed as personal ornamentation, but they resembled manacles a little too closely for my taste. "Pretty things."

The Chakacat took one and traced the outline of the gems imbedded in the silver. "They displayed chests of them for me. I think they've been saving them up for years."

I checked the door to see if anyone was watching. "Have you found out anything about this god they think you are?"

"I'm not a god, exactly. From what I've gathered, Sadda was a feline alien whose vessel crashed on this world many centuries ago. It taught them how to build and gave them some of its technology as prototypes, to create their own. The alien eventually was deified for the enlightenment it provided." It curled a paw around the ornament. "What's so provocative is that my species may actually be descended from that alien's people."

"I thought Chakacats lived in the wild on your world."

"There have been many technologically advanced civilizations on Chakara. Over time, war and outside conflict consistently decimated the population. It is possible that at one point in our history, my kind were the dominant species on our planet."

I couldn't help a slightly evil chuckle. "Now that would be proof enough to get Chakacats sentient status within the League."

Alunthri beamed. "I believe it would."

"Then we'd better grab some evidence, if we can."

The Chakacat held up a small disc. "Presented to me with all due ceremony. It contains all known accounts of the origins of Sadda. They want me to check it and make sure their ancestors recorded the facts correctly."

The monitors hovered outside the doorway, making discreet noises, and Reever nodded to Alunthri.

"My rainments." It swept its paws outward so I could put its toga-robe on. "Come. You have been instructed and shall attend me at the ceremony for my people."

The ceremony was as pretentious as any I'd ever seen. Hundreds of Taerca poured into the ziggurat, and formed living chains by standing with arms linked on three sides of the steps leading up to the central platform. Alunthri and the rest of us climbed the fourth set of steps, which had been left empty for the holy procession.

Tadam Ortsac prostrated himself again and asked if he would be worthy to conduct the ceremony.

Alunthri took a minute and pretended to think about it. "Are you the best the people can do?"

"I am, great one. I have been preparing myself to

serve you since my birth." The official rubbed his bulging stomach. "You will find no fault with my oration or my sustenance, I promise you this."

"Very well."

On the platform, Alunthri stood calmly in the center of the rest of us, and Ortsac only hissed at us to kneel before addressing the assembly.

"Sadda is indeed returned to us, surrounded by his sacrifices, benevolent and gracious in all things."

The chains of devoted worshippers swayed as the Taercal sighed and murmured their pleasure.

"Our ancestors allowed themselves to be seduced by the power afforded to them by that which was not of Sadda. We were wise to eradicate those who would have kept us in thrall to false gods." He turned to the Chakacat. "Behold, great one, your gifts intact still."

All around us, the monitors went to the walls, and jerked down the immense drapery. Beneath them wasn't more black, tul-infected stone, but vast interior alloy panels that began to flicker and glow with lights and color. At the same time, there was a distinctly recognizable rumble beneath our feet.

The ziggurat wasn't a church.

"Reever." I stared at the panels. "Are you thinking what I'm thinking?"

"Yes." He scanned the walls slowly. "It's a vessel of some kind."

There were more than thirty ziggurats inside the city. "All of them?"

"It is possible."

Even as the rumble of engines faded away, I rubbed my arms. "They aren't going to try to fly this one, are they?"

"I don't think so. They're just displaying the fact that they've kept the ship in working order. Something the original Sadda probably helped them build and taught them to maintain."

Even Xonea, who had been exposed to myriad alien tech over the years through trading, looked a little dazzled. "Why didn't they destroy the ships when they divested themselves of technology?"

"It was their own technology, developed by the Taercal themselves, that they destroyed. The configurations of this vessel do not correspond with any I have ever seen before." Reever studied one of the nearby panels. "It may be from a former civilization."

"Watch the fat one," Dhreen said. "There's something wrong."

He was right. Wart Sack looked so happy that I blinked. So did all the other Taercal.

"You have the evidence of our faith before you now, Sadda," the official said, waving his beringed hands around. "We have endured your scourges and remained steadfast and unwavering. We welcome your indulgence, so that you may lift the holy affliction from us, your devoted and suffering." Ortsac folded his arms and bowed again. "Enlighten us now. Remove our burden, feast on your sustenance, and restore the people to our former joy."

Uh-oh. Lifting holy afflictions and restoring people to former joy hadn't been in our game plan. And what was this "sustenance" business Big Bird kept yammering about?

Alunthri hesitated, long enough to make Ortsac's grin droop a bit. Finally, it nodded. "I am pleased by the evidence of your faith and suffering. I shall remove the scourge from the people from the heavens, as I ascend."

"Ascend?" Ortsac looked confused. "I do not understand, great one. You are among us; you belong to us now. As you promised, you have returned. Your strong backs are here. Your sustenance is here. You have no reason to leave us."

"I am not leaving you," Alunthri lied. "In order to lift the suffering from so many, I must perform the proper ritual in the air. The air from whence the people came down, and bore the scourge for my sake." It stroked its facial fur with one paw, then added, "Surely you do not mean to delay the alleviation by bombarding me with questions as to my methods, Tadam Ortsac."

That was enough to send the official into a momentary panic. "No, great one, of course not. I would never— I would not even think of performing such blasphemy!"

"Excellent. I am pleased with your obedience. Now, you will escort me and my offerings to the place beyond the city where my ascension vessel awaits."

We all held our breaths as Ortsac digested that, then turned to the assembled people. "This day we walk in Sadda's favor! To the plateau beyond the city!"

"Keep looking like you're going to bite someone's head off," I murmured to Alunthri as we passed through Sadda's Maw. "Once we're on the ship, we'll do a sweep and locate Hawk."

The Chakacat halted for a moment as it studied the sky. "We may have another problem."

I looked up, and my jaw sagged. A third launch was descending at a dangerous angle, rocking and shaking as it came down through the atmosphere too fast. "Who is that?"

"Someone who does not know how to fly," Xonea said, in low outrage.

Since every member of the crew had undergone

pilot training, there was only one person left on the ship who fit that description. I pressed a hand over my eyes and watched through my fingers. "Dhreen, I think your girlfriend's here."

Despite her lack of piloting skills, Ilona Red Faun somehow managed to pull the vessel's nose up just before she hit the surface. Sprays of crushed worms and dirt repelled the mist as the bottom of the launch bounced once, then twice, before skidding to a noisy halt.

"You could use some of those attack trellises in the launch bays," I said to Salo, who was shaking his head.

Reever was more practical. "We had better take her launch, and abandon the other two."

The Captain hadn't been pleased by the idea of leaving behind one, and I could almost hear his teeth grinding. "She reports to me as soon as we return to the ship."

I wouldn't want to be in her moccasins in a couple of hours. "Someone had better go get her."

While all this was happening, the Taercal were trying very hard to look worshipful and affronted at the same time. Xonea and Reever didn't quite reach the shuttle in time, and the exterior hull panel opened.

Ilona Red Faun didn't bother with a docking ramp but jumped out. She brandished a pulse rifle under one arm and one of the Captain's multibladed swords in her hand.

"Dhreen? Dhreen!"

She spotted him a moment later, dodged the men, and ran directly at me, Alunthri, and the object of her affections. Behind us, the Taercal made a collective, unpleasant sound.

Reever grabbed the weaver from behind and, despite her struggles, held on. Salo quickly disarmed her.

Frustrated, yet unable to free herself, Ilona began ranting in Navajo.

"All we need now are some Hsktskt," I murmured to Alunthri. "Or some popcorn."

It stopped being funny when Dhreen pressed his spoon-shaped fingers to his chest and began gasping for breath. I braced him with one arm and checked his vitals.

My smile faded. We had to get off this rock.

"Ilona, listen very carefully," I said, walking with Dhreen toward her, but keeping my eye on the mob. "You've just blown our escape plan. Kneel in front of Alunthri and beg forgiveness."

She stopped swearing in Navajo. "Why should I?"

"Because if you don't, two things are going to happen. Those people will attack us, and your boyfriend will go into respiratory arrest." I beckoned with my free hand to Reever, who turned the weaver loose and came to help me support Dhreen from the other side.

"How do I know you speak the truth?" Ilona demanded.

"Don't do it, and find out."

"Why must I kneel?"

I closed my eyes for a moment. Stuff like this always happened with the lovesick. Usually while I was trying to keep them from getting their heads bashed in. I looked at her again. "Because these maniacs think Alunthri is one of their gods."

"They're insane."

"I guess you'd know." I adjusted my grip on Dhreen. "Now do it, and remember to call it Sadda in a nice, loud voice."

Ilona scowled as she performed the obeisance. "Honored Sadda, forgive me . . . I meant no offense to you."

The Chakacat gestured for the Terran girl to rise. "Return to the vessel and await my judgment."

Before Ilona could move, Tadam Ortsac approached Alunthri and sank down on his knees in what I was beginning to think of as Sadda's Position.

"Great one," he said, wringing his hands, "please, I beg you, enlighten us."

The Chakacat glanced at me. I shrugged—I was no religious expert—and rolled my eyes toward the launch. To Ortsac, Alunthri said, "What is it now?"

"These polluters, great one. Surely they but interfere with your alleviation of our suffering." Wart Sack gave me the usual you're-not-worthy glare. "Let us drown them for you, and offer you proper sustenance before you ascend."

Again with the "sustenance." Did Big Bird intend on force-feeding Alunthri?

"It is not your place to question my decisions, scourge back." Alunthri adjusted a fold of its toga-robe. "These aliens will accompany me on my ascension. That is final."

"But . . . why?" Ortsac finally burst out.

My friend produced a chilling snarl.

"Forgive me, great one, but I do not understand. Your need is my provision."

I leaned in to whisper, "He wants you to eat. Tell him you're going to eat us up in the sky."

"In order to alleviate the suffering of the people, I require sustenance. You have said so yourself. These aliens will do nicely."

"But that is what *I* am to do, great one," Ortsac whined.

Uh-oh. Suddenly, the official's pathetic obesity took on all new and gruesome overtones.

He went on. "I have been fattened specifically for

you, Sadda." The official tore open his robe, exposing his flabby, feathered body. He disrobed so fast he knocked over two other Taercal around him. "Behold your sustenance, Sadda. Feed upon me."

No one moved or spoke. What could anyone say? Don't offer yourself as a twelve-course meal for the local god? Luckily, Alunthri recovered and thought of another stall.

"Perhaps if I am still hungry when I return, then I shall feed on you." Alunthri made a grandiose gesture at the official's robes. "Cover yourself."

"No!" Ortsac clawed at his swollen neck, tearing feathers out by the handfuls. "No, I am ready, I am yours, I will be your sustenance!"

He was determined to be a martyr. We had to get out of here. "Alunthri, let's go. Let's just go."

Two of the monitors came forward, clubs in hand, as Ortsac's clawed hands drew blood from his own throat. Alunthri hissed out a furious order for him to stop, but it was too late. Both clubs hit Ortsac's head from either side, and crushed his skull.

Ilona screamed as Taercal blood splattered all of us, and Ortsac fell over, dead.

Alunthri's colorless eyes closed. As it stood closest to Ortsac, it had been drenched. Slowly, it lifted trembling, bloodstained paws to its face. It had always been a sensitive creature, unable to tolerate violence in any form.

"Don't pass out," I muttered. "Not now."

"Reject the offering," Reever said.

With great reluctance, Alunthri licked one of its paws, then spat bloody saliva on the ground. I could tell from the way its nostrils flared that it was fighting the urge to vomit. "This sustenance . . . is not . . . worthy of me. Take it . . . away."

The two monitors grabbed Ortsac's body by its stunted wings and dragged him off into the crowd. Monkey-birds circling overhead began diving down, trying to get at the body.

The Chakacat was visibly shaking as it turned to us. "All of you, enter my ascension vessel." It even managed to growl at the crowd when a couple of them shuffled forward, "No more delays! I must ascend now!"

From there, we walked as fast as we could into the launch. Dhreen's lungs were straining by the time I got a breather strapped on him and switched it to pure oxygen feed. His pulse skittered beneath my fingertips, then he slumped forward, unconscious.

I held him up, but he was deadweight. "Duncan, give me a hand, will you?"

Reever helped me strap him in, and Xonea went to the helm. Alunthri paused in the door panel to lift a paw and wave to the crowd. As soon as the panel closed, it stumbled over to a disposal unit and vomited.

I felt a terrible sympathy for my friend, but I couldn't leave Dhreen. "Ilona, go help Alunthri. Xonea, can we leave before the demon lack-wit dies on me?"

The Captain spared me a glance. "We must locate Hawk."

"Oh, hell." I'd forgotten about him. "How are we going to find him?"

"I know where he is," Reever said. "Captain, if you would, ascend to two hundred feet and head seventeen degrees north."

"Make it fast, unless you don't want Dhreen around much longer." I frowned at my husband. "How do you know where he is?"

Duncan gave me one of his enigmatic looks. "Where would you go if you had wings?"

"Some place where the people who can't use theirs won't get at me." I glanced through the viewport. "Those peaks, right behind the city."

"Exactly." Reever went to sit copilot beside Xonea. "We will find him as quickly as we can."

I wiped Dhreen's face and started an infuser line with saline. "You'd better hurry up, or Sadda is going to get its first alien sacrifice."

It didn't take long for Reever to pick up Hawk's thermal signature, or locate the exact cave he'd decided to hide in. Landing was impossible, but Xonea kept the launch on hover while Reever opened the exterior panel.

"Hawk!" He had to bellow to be heard over the roar of the wind and the launch's stabilizers. "We're going back to the ship! Come out of there!"

The *hataali* emerged, his scarred face drawn and his black eyes rather wild. "Leave me!" he shouted back. "I don't belong with you!"

So he was feeling sorry for himself. I left Dhreen and joined Reever. "Hawk, you get on this shuttle right this minute!" I shrieked.

"Cherijo." His dark eyes filled with tears. "I can't! I might become like they are!"

"Not a chance! We won't make you eat worms and go to church!"

He only shook his head and started to move back in the cave.

Reever grabbed Ilona's pulse rifle and pointed it at Hawk's head. "Board the launch or I will shoot you!"

The wind made his long dark hair whip across his eyes, while a ghost of a smile appeared on Hawk's scarred face. "You wouldn't do that!"

"I have a patient dying in here! If he doesn't, I will!"

I didn't blink as Reever activated the weapon. "Please, Hawk. Let's go *home*."

"I am home! Look at my home! Look at it!" He pointed down at the city. Then he turned away, his wings drooping.

What had I done, letting him come here?

Reever aimed the rifle. Behind me, Dhreen's breathing got worse. Ilona sat beside him, rocking and chanting prayers in Navajo. Alunthri was slumped over in a harness, trying in vain to wipe the drying blood from its pelt. Xonea couldn't leave the helm.

I put all my faith in my instincts, leaned over and kissed Duncan. "Don't be mad at me for this."

He swiped at me as I jumped out into thin air. "Cherijo, no!"

"Hawk!"

Plummeting down the side of a mountain is about as much fun as being burned, I soon discovered. Wind tore at my tunic and face as I dropped, and the ground started rushing up toward me at an alarming rate.

I tried to look up, but I couldn't see him. "Hawk! Remember I can't fly!"

I couldn't take my eyes off the rapidly approaching ground after that. A few hundred yards before something very unpleasant happened, I felt two heavy sets of talons latch on to my shoulders and yank me up into the air.

I flung my head back to see Hawk soaring up toward the launch. "What took you so long?"

"I had to lift Duncan first."

"Oh." I swallowed. It was one thing for me to try to commit suicide, knowing my immune system would repair the damage, whatever it was. But Duncan was only human, and still, he'd jumped out after me.

He really loved me. And would probably never speak to me again.

"Your husband has that rifle in his arms again," Hawk said as he reached down and pulled me out of his talons and up into his arms. His body jerked as his wings worked against the air. "He looks as if he intends to use it."

"He won't," I assured him. Until I saw the look on said husband's face as we approached the launch. "Not on you, anyway."

CHAPTER TWELVE

Too Much

Duncan settled for completely ignoring me for the entire jaunt back to the ship. As soon as Xonea shut the engines down in launch bay, he opened the hull doors and walked out without a single glance my way.

Which was fine. Jumping out of the shuttle had seemed like the logical thing to do at the time, and even if Hawk hadn't caught me, I wouldn't have died on impact. I would have been really, *really* uncomfortable for a few days or weeks or however long it took my immune system to heal the damage, but it had been essentially a safe bet either way.

I wondered if using that argument would work as a defense, or if I'd find Reever packing his bags when I returned to our quarters.

Unfortunately, my marriage problems had to wait. As soon as we disembarked, I rushed Dhreen to Medical. After a quick cleansing to remove the dead worms from my skin and hair, I spent the next several hours working to restabilize the Oenrallian's condition. His weakened respiratory system had not responded well to the high humidity on Taerca, but his liver was stable and functioning.

Savetka hovered across the exam table from me until she caught my eye. "Healer, there is something you should know."

I infused Dhreen with antibiotics to combat the pneumonia forming in his lung/heart. "What?"

"Pilot Dhreen's body absorbed one of the Lok-Teel." She indicated the area above his liver. "At least, I think it did."

I scanned the site, but found no evidence of any foreign substances. "Did you see the mold enter his body?"

"No, but it disappeared while it was cleaning his torso. The critical care unit was sealed, and there was no place for it to go, so I assumed it entered him somehow."

"Okay." I rescanned Dhreen's liver, and found it had doubled in size. I was tempted to take him in for exploratory surgery, but with the condition of his lung/heart I'd be pushing my luck. "Set up to insert another chest tube."

Once Savetka had everything prepared, I injected Dhreen with a local, then reopened the drain site and inserted the tube. Almost immediately, the putty-colored pseudopod of the Lok-Teel appeared, filling the tube and oozing out onto Dhreen's stomach.

I looked at the nurse, who was wide-eyed. "Found your missing mold."

Another scan showed Dhreen's liver had shrunk again, but was still functioning normally. I had Savetka run a full series of blood and tissue scans while I helped Squilyp finish examining and treating the remainder of the sojourn team for minor injuries.

Squilyp listened as I described the absorption of the Lok-teel, and agreed more tests would be needed before we could assume the busy little mold had actually gone inside Dhreen's body and healed his liver. He didn't seem happy about it, though, and I found out why when he ordered me into his office.

"I ought to relieve you of duty for a week," the Omorr said. "Jumping out of a launch in midair. Have you lost whatever is left of your senses?"

"Hard to say. I haven't exactly relocated them yet."

"Don't you make jokes about this, Doctor. You know exactly what kind of damage a fall like that would have done to you!"

I sat down in the uncomfortable chair. After two days on Taercal, it felt like a cloud. "I would have healed."

"Indeed." Squilyp dropped some charts on his desk and stood behind it. His expression and tone reminded me a little of Tonetka Torin, our former Senior Healer. She'd yelled similar things at me, many times. "You take your gifts for granted."

"Squilyp, you've seen third-degree burns disappear from my skin. It wouldn't have hurt me."

"Even if your immune system can heal the physical damage, what if you had sustained a head injury? Can your creator's genetic engineering cope with the neural results of massive brain damage?"

There was more to the brain than neural tissue. It was entirely possible I could become an immortal vegetable, under the right circumstances. I'd never considered that before. "All right, so it was a little stupid."

"It was a consummately idiotic thing to do."

"I wasn't abandoning him on that god-awful world. You weren't down there; you didn't see what those people are like." And the worms. And the mold. And their crazy religion. "I can't imagine what Hawk is going through, after meeting those demented freaks. He didn't belong on Terra, and now"—I sighed—"now he's got nothing left to call his own, except us."

"We will provide counseling, if necessary, to see him through this." My boss pulled a data pad out and read the screen. "He hasn't reported for his follow-up exam. Schedule it for the morning."

I'd already signaled Hawk's quarters, but he hadn't answered. "Can we give him a few days?"

"I'm not inclined to do anything for you but find my own stick and beat you with it." He rubbed a membrane over his gildrells. "What has Duncan to say about this?"

"I don't know." I'd also signaled his duty station, but his console had been programmed to block incoming relays. "He's not talking to me."

The Omorr nodded. "A sensible man."

"Yeah, maybe he should beat me with a stick, too."

"I'll suggest that the next time I see him. Now, go home."

My husband and daughter had gotten home before me. Marel was happy to see me when I came in, but a still-silent Duncan only handed her off to me and left. My daughter didn't enjoy her bubble bath as much with only her mother in attendance.

Her little face grew serious as I dried her off and got her into her night tunic. "Daddy mad ad you, Mama."

"I know he is." We'd never fought in front of Marel before, and all Duncan was doing was giving me the stone-face treatment, but she wasn't stupid. "I did a silly thing, trying to help Uncle Hawk. Daddy didn't like what I did."

"Tell Daddy sorry you noddy," was my daughter's suggestion. "He give you dime-owd."

"I will, sweetheart." I held her close. My conscience kicked me even harder than before as the feelings of love and protectiveness welled up in me. I owed my life to Reever, a couple of times over. I owed it to Marel to be a good mother. Not something I could do if I was hooked up to life support with a drool-bib tucked around my neck. "Don't be upset. Daddy will forgive me, in a few years."

"I not 'sed." She patted my face like she was the indulgent parent. "You good mama."

"I'm working on it, baby."

Alunthri came to see me later that evening, after it had been discharged from Medical. Its miserable, pink-rimmed eyes met mine. "Cherijo, I know it's late, but may I come in?"

"Sure." I stepped aside from the open panel. "If you're looking for Reever, I guess he's either walking around the ship or working out in one of the environomes." Or punching out a wall somewhere where the dented alloy wouldn't be noticeable.

"No, I wish to speak with you." It sat down, and refused my offer of a drink. So I sat down across from it. "I've been thinking about that native. You know, the one they . . ." It coughed, then struggled to regain its rocky composure. "Was there something I should have done?"

"Believe me, Alunthri, there was *nothing* you could have done. I don't understand why, but that man's whole purpose in life was to sacrifice himself. He thought you were his god, and he did what he was trained to do."

"Perhaps it is as you say." It made a small, wistful sound. "I still find it very hard to accept, knowing even indirectly, I was responsible for his death." It blinked a few times. "I have never harmed anyone."

"You didn't harm anyone. You tried to stop them."

"I should have been able to prevent it. They believed me their god—why couldn't I prevent it?" Alunthri studied one of its paws. "I spent hours in the cleanser, trying to get the blood out of my fur. I— I think I can still see it."

"Oh, no, Alunthri. No."

It held the paw up for my inspection, new tears making dark streaks in its silvery facial fur. "Can you? Can you see it?"

My heart constricted as I got up and went over to the sofa, and sat down beside my friend. Carefully, I took its paw between my hands. "There's no blood on you, pal. I promise."

Alunthri curled up against me, making that low, wretched sound all felines do when frightened or lonely. "I am so sorry this happened, Cherijo."

My eyes stung, too. "It's okay. Everything will be okay." I stroked my hand over the Chakacat's back and murmured to it, until it fell asleep. I eased up and found a blanket to cover my friend with, then turned out most of the optic emitters and sat in the dark, waiting for Reever to come home.

Sometime in the middle of the night, I woke up to find my husband holding me against him with one arm, his hand stroking my hair. We were on our sleeping platform, so I surmised he must have come home and carried me there.

"Hey." I propped myself up on one elbow and smothered a yawn. "Can't sleep?"

"No."

"Want to hear how sorry I am about today?"

"No."

"Okay." I tentatively touched his bare chest. He slept naked, something I thoroughly enjoyed. Maybe there was another, better way to show him how much I loved him. "I guess anything more than sleeping together is out of the—"

His mouth landed on mine, not hard enough to bruise, but with the lightest of touches, just enough to shut me up and make me forget what I was going to say. He rolled over with me until I was on my back and his long body covered me.

He entered my mind a moment before his legs parted mine.

Waenara. His hands found the edge of my tunic, and pulled it slowly up over my head. The air in our quarters felt cool against my skin, almost as good as his touch. *You feel so good under my hands.*

I smiled against his neck as I stroked my fingers from his waist to his shoulders. *So do you.*

His long hair trailed across my face as he moved his mouth along the line of my jaw and down my throat. *I can feel your desire. I can see it.* He lifted his head, long enough to kiss me again, opening my mouth, gliding his tongue against mine. *I can taste it.* He left my lips tingling and moved lower.

Intense need knotted inside me as I wriggled under him and tried to close the little gaps between our skins. I could feel his erection nestled almost exactly where I needed him, and lifted my hips from the mattress to urge him in. *Duncan . . .*

He used the flat of his tongue on my breasts, stopping some of the ache. *You like this.*

I'd like more. I cradled him with my thighs, but he kept holding back. It seemed like forever since the last time I'd felt him inside me. I dug my fingernails into his shoulders. *Don't tease me.*

His touch changed as he took me by the wrists and pulled me up until we were both sitting up, with me straddling his lap. He held me suspended by the arms, his hands bruising. *Do you still want more?*

Occasionally, we got a little rough with each other, but not like this. *Thanks, but I think I'll take a rain check.* I tried to free myself, but he wasn't letting go. At the same time, I realized that although we were linked, I couldn't feel a single emotion coming from him. *Duncan?*

If you love me, you'll say you want more.

I didn't like being manhandled, but I was no coward. *Okay. More.*

He reached under the pillow and pulled out something that he held against my neck. It was cold, thin, and sharp. *Don't worry.* He pressed it in, and warm blood flowed down my neck. *You'll heal. You always heal.*

Marel appeared by the side of the sleeping platform. "Daddy?"

I jerked my head back, and fought to free my hands. *No, Duncan, don't!* The blade in his hand glinted as he lifted it over my head. *Stop it!* Afraid he wouldn't, I looked at my daughter. *Marel, get out here!*

She smiled at me. "Everybody afraid of Mama bud Daddy."

Reever. I looked wildly up at him. *Don't do this in front of our baby.*

Why not? You won't die. You'll never die. So I can keep killing you—he stabbed me in the chest—*and killing you*—he yanked the knife out—*over and over and over and*—

"Cherijo."

I screamed and threw my hands up over my face.

"Cherijo."

No blade. No blood. Only Duncan, fully dressed, standing over me. Not stabbing me. Shaking me.

Waking me.

He smoothed some hair out of my eyes. "You were having a bad dream."

My hands shook uncontrollably as I reached up for him. A moment later I lay safe in his arms, pressed to his heart as I wept. I cried so hard I couldn't catch my breath. I cried for what I'd done to him that day, and all the other stupid mistakes I'd ever made since falling in love with him.

In between sobs, I tried to tell him how sorry I was.

Time passed, I don't know how much. He didn't complain, didn't try to push me aside or tell me to shut up. He held on to me until I'd sobbed myself out, then reached for something. A soft cloth touched my face, drying my tears, wiping my nose.

"Better?"

"Let me wash my face and mop up a little more." I eased out of his arms and stumbled over to the lavatory. When I emerged, cleaned up but still shaky, he sat waiting in the same spot. "I'm sorry about what I did today. I didn't think of you, or Marel. It was stupid and reckless."

He held out a hand. "Come here."

I went to him. In the dim light from the bedside emitter, his face seemed full of shadows. The kind I'd thought I'd banished.

"You're really mad at me, aren't you?" I ducked my head. "I don't blame you. I deserve it."

"I was walking on level ten, and I felt a terrible fear. Your fear, from your nightmare. I came as quickly as I could. When I entered our chamber, I heard you begging me not to kill you." His fingers tightened on my waist. "I would never harm you, wife. No matter how angry I become."

"I know." I moved my shoulders. "It just seemed so real."

"Lie down with me."

No dream could equal the real thing. At first we touched each other with tentative, gentle caresses, helping each other out of our garments, soothing each other's still-frazzled nerves. Heat bloomed on my skin wherever Duncan's fingers traveled. A mist of sweat sprang up when his mouth followed.

When I worked my fingers into his shaggy mane and tugged, he lifted his head. For some reason, I had to say the words. "Don't tease me."

He moved up over me, gathering me up against him as he lodged his hips between my thighs. I lifted up, caressing the smooth head of his penis while aligning myself to him. His fingers laced through mine at the same moment he sank into me.

His mouth touched mine, his tongue mimicking the gentle thrust below.

"You're going to make me cry again," I murmured against his lips.

"Yes." He lifted his head, looking down at where our bodies lay joined. His voice went low and deep as he added, "But not the way you think."

He rolled to his side, taking me with him. With our faces only an inch apart, he cupped my backside, and began to move inside me. He used slow, steady movements as I pushed back, trying to reach that place he'd taken me so often. As he watched me, he cupped my breasts in his hands and stroked them with the same, unhurried deliberation.

"Whenever I look at you, I think of this," he whispered against my ear. "I think of being inside you, a part of you." He buried his face in my hair. "I won't let you go, *Waenara*." He turned over, moving on top of me, pushing in deep. "I never will."

The leisurely, gentle lovemaking turned into something fast and frantic, with clutching hands and eager mouths and straining bodies. He kept his promise and made me cry out, more than once, and caught the sound with his mouth as he took me.

"Duncan, please!" I arched my back as I hovered just

on the brink, suspended between desperate need and mind-blowing pleasure. "I need . . ."

He moved faster, harder, working deeper with each thrust. "Come to me, beloved. Now, come to me now."

The darkness exploded with a thousand unseen lights as I pulled his head down to me. As I fell into the cascading sensations, I kissed him with all the passion and longing he'd wrung out of me. His thoughts poured into my mind at the same time he came, and I rode to another peak on those twin sensations, holding him as tightly as I could, saying his name over and over.

Reever and I made love most of the night, and although we were both tired the next morning, I felt as if we'd healed a lot of old wounds. My only regret was knowing that I'd caused most of them.

"Good morning, Cherijo." Alunthri was up and playing with the kittens when I dragged myself out to the kitchen. "Forgive me for overstaying my welcome last night."

"Your welcome and staying privileges have no time limit." As I smothered my yawns and prepared breakfast for all of us, I noticed my usually up-and-at-'em daughter hadn't made her usual early appearance. "Marel still asleep?"

"I down here, Mama."

A glance under the table revealed my daughter feeding a bowl of her favorite creamed wheat to one of the kittens. "Hey, that's supposed to go in your tummy, kiddo."

She grinned at me. "Kiddy wikes id do."

Reever came out of our room, which made our kid and the kitten emerge. He swung Marel up in his arms and endured a neck-wrenching hug. "Good morning, *avasa*. Did you sleep well?"

"Pree good."

He bent down to pick up the bowl of cereal. "How did this get under here?"

"I make did."

I'd assumed Alunthri had prepared the cereal for her, and turned to measure the distance from the floor to the prep unit. Unless she'd grown two feet overnight, there was no way she could have gotten to the menu panel. "How?"

Marel giggled and hid her face against Reever's tunic.

"Okay, be mysterious about it." I went over and safeguarded the unit with a pass protective code. I didn't mind Marel getting food, but she might accidentally spill something hot on herself while climbing up or down or however she'd gotten to the panel.

After breakfast, I dropped my daughter off at school and heard from one of the instructors that Xonea had confined Ilona Red Faun to quarters. No one was sure how he would deal with her stealing a launch and inadvertently causing the loss of two more.

"What usually happens?" I asked Marel's teacher.

"I do not know, Healer." She made a helpless gesture. "We do not steal things. We ask permission to use them instead."

With that new worry on my mind, I reported for duty and went over the results of the post-sojourn physicals. In addition to all the trouble she was in, Ilona's latest scans showed two distinct fetal outlines.

Dhreen and his girlfriend were having twins.

"Two of them." I sat back in my chair at the console. "God help us."

When I signaled the weaver with the news, she

didn't seem very interested in that, or the follow-up physical I'd scheduled for her. "I cannot report to Medical. I am told I must stay in my rooms."

"The Captain will make an exception for a prenatal exam." Although she'd brought it on herself, I felt a reluctant sympathy for her. I knew how boring it was to be confined to quarters. "Listen, Ilona, if you need anything, why don't you—"

"Thank you, patcher. I am fine." She abruptly terminated the signal.

Life on board the *Sunlace* settled back into its normal routine quickly enough, but I began to get the feeling it was a calm before a storm.

Alunthri began dropping by Medical more frequently to volunteer its services. Knowing the benefit hard work had in dispelling feelings of guilt, I gave the Chakacat several administrative tasks, including updating our database by downloading all our recent chart entries.

Squilyp seemed to have a lot on his mind, too. When he wasn't hopping around Medical trying to sterilize everything in sight, he was sniping at me, the residents, the interns, and the nursing staff. After a particularly nasty remark over the way I'd put together an instrument tray, I reminded him I'd already kicked his Omorr backside in a challenge and I'd be more than happy to repeat the exercise.

The Senior Healer had the grace to look a little ashamed. "Forgive me. The waiting seems intolerable."

"Waiting for . . . ?" I trailed off, raising my brows.

He only shook his head and hopped off to clean something else.

I found out soon enough. The signal came down from Command one day while the Omorr was in the middle of routine surgery on one of the crew members who had complications from a previous knee injury.

"Inform the Senior Healer that the Omorr vessel *Naquorekan* has docked at launch bay four. His guests await his presence."

Squilyp had *guests*? Since when?

I scrubbed and went into the surgical suite, and waited until the Omorr had powered down the laser before I told him the news. And watched the Senior Healer overturn an infuser rig and knock a setup tray to the deck.

"She's here? Already? That's wonderful." He looked down at his patient. "No. That's terrible. I can't go."

I held up my gloved hands. "I'll take over for you."

"Yes. No. I mean—" He stopped and took a deep breath. "I must finish here, and prepare myself. Yes. That is what I should do." He gave me an uncertain look. "I am anxious to make a good first impression. It is very important that I do that."

I bit back a laugh. "Tell you what—I'll go meet your friends while you finish. And change. You look like you've just murdered someone."

He looked down over his mask at his blood-spattered scrubs. "Yes. I will finish here and I will don more appropriate garments."

"One more thing—who are these friends of yours?"

"She is not a friend. She is Garphawayn of Cestes— Lady Cestes."

I made a rolling gesture with my hand. "And this lady is . . . who?"

"My *adorlee*." Under his mask, his gildrells writhed like a bunch of thin, white snakes. "My mail-order bride."

*   *   *

I changed into a clean tunic and went down to launch bay four, feeling a little like an older sister determined to make sure the new addition to the family was worthy of her fiancé.

She'd better be wonderful. He deserves the best.

The Omorr passenger starshuttle *Naquorekan*, being too large to actually fit inside the bay, was docked outside. A sealed passenger ramp had been extended between the two interiors, and as I entered through the launch bay doors, I saw five Omorr hop out of it.

Xonea and a number of the Command crew were already on hand to welcome Squilyp's guests, and the Captain made an elegant bow. "Welcome to the *Sunlace*. I am Xonea, of HouseClan Torin." He introduced the other members of the crew, ending with me as I joined them. "May your stay with us be a pleasant one."

"Pleasant is far too much to expect, Captain," a high, rather querulous voice said. "I dare only hope for tolerable."

The Omorr who spoke hopped forward with an abbreviated version of Squilyp's natural bounce, all the while holding her spine so straight she seemed as tall as the much bigger Jorenians. Her lean form was encased in a feminine version of Squilyp's native, one-legged garment. A long, sweeping cloak hung from her narrow shoulders. Both were made from fabrics dyed with an eye-popping assortment of colors. The other Omorr in her party were less gaudily attired, and seemed a little older.

Chaperones, maybe?

From what I could see, there wasn't much outer physical difference between the Omorr genders. Not that anyone would mistake the younger female for a male, given the number of personal ornaments she wore. An odd number of golden, feathery protrusions were all over the top of her dark pink skull, but I wasn't sure if they were hers, or more embellishments. Cosmetics enhanced her round, dark eyes, and a number of her gildrells had tiny, sparkling rings on them.

One of the older, more conservatively attired Omorr bounced over to stand beside the first. She looked directly up at Xonea, her face stern as she gestured to the younger female. "This is the Lady Cestes, Garphawayn, here to negotiate a contract of marriage with Squilyp of Maftuda."

"You are very welcome, Lady Cestes." Xonea stepped forward to give her a Jorenian kiss of welcome, thought better of it, and bowed instead.

"You may address me as Garphawayn." Lady Cestes's gildrells became straight white sticks as she looked around. "None of you are Omorr. This is completely unacceptable. Where is he? Lemesen, have we arrived on the correct vessel?"

"Mama?" My daughter appeared beside me and put her hand in mine. "Who dad parkwy wady?"

I picked her up and leaned close to whisper in her ear, "This is Squilyp's friend. Her name is Lady Cestes." I cleared my throat and took a few steps forward. "Um, excuse me, I have a message from Squilyp for you."

"You do?" The female Omorr hopped down the line to inspect us, then reared her head back a bit. "Why is this infant here?"

"This is my daughter, Marel." I kissed the top of her head. "She tends to pop up in unexpected places."

"You allow children to run about this vessel, unsupervised? What sort of mother are you?" Squilyp's intended didn't wait for an answer, but sniffed in my face. "Children must be safeguarded by a proper caregiver. Something like this would never happen on Omorr."

"We take care of our kids, too," I replied, showing her some teeth. "It's just sometimes we get distracted by visitors."

"Your attention span wants improvement, then. Now, where is this *adoren* who sent for me? Has he not the simple decency to greet me upon my arrival?"

"Whad dad?" Marel asked her.

Garphawayn peered down at my daughter. "It speaks?"

"*She* speaks, yes."

"It is impossible to tell the difference between your genders. You should wear markings on your garments." To Marel, she said, "Of whom are you speaking, infant?"

"Whad dad 'doren?"

"An *adoren* is an unmarried male who seeks to contract matrimony with an unmarried female." The Omorr female seemed offended by my darling daughter's wide grin. "Your name is Marel, infant?"

"Dad's me."

"I see. Someone"—she gave me another snotty look—"should instruct you on the proper behavior to use when greeting visitors for the first time. You are far *too* precocious."

Marel cocked her head to one side. "Why?"

I closed my eyes briefly. Ms. Congeniality had no idea what she'd just set off.

Lady Cestes lifted a membrane and made an imperious gesture. "On my world, children also do not speak to adults unless they are spoken to."

My kid rubbed the back of her hand across her nose, then asked, "Why?"

Garphawayn took a breath. "They are taught by

their parents that such behavior is disruptive and inconsiderate." Another haughty look came my way. "You should learn better manners as soon as possible."

Marel gave her another, ingenious smile. "Why?"

Squilyp's intended wasn't going to give up easily. I had the feeling she liked having the last word. "Children are more presentable when they have had the opportunity to develop proper social skills."

"Why?"

"Because without them, you display a lack of consideration for those who are older and superior to you." The female Omorr held up one of her three arms, and flared her membrane. "Do not ask me to explain further."

My daughter frowned. "Why not?"

"Do not ask—"

Xonea coughed, probably to cover a laugh, then said, "Forgive my ClanNiece, Garphawayn. Her curiosity is as endless as her mischief."

"I beg your pardon, sir. You may be the commander of this vessel, but that does not give you the right to interrupt me." As Xonea's big hands clenched, Garphawayn turned to the other Omorr. "Lemesen, attend me. I would have your opinion on this pathetic state of affairs. Aside from the criminal lack of breeding and civility displayed by the *adoren's* absence."

The older female came over. "It does not appear as unfavorable as we feared, *adorelee*. They are an unmannerly lot, but seem otherwise agreeable." She sent me a pitying look. "Certainly there is no competition apparent."

I kept Marel on my hip and a smile pasted to my face. *Squilyp, you owe me big time for this.* "Right. Well, as you may know, Squilyp is our Senior Healer, and ship's surgeon. He—"

Lemesen interrupted me with a titter, then said, "I assure you, Terran, there is no need to inform us of these details. We know *everything* about Squilyp of Maftuda."

"Including his unfortunate choice of occupation." Garphawayn didn't seem to think anything was funny. "I cannot fathom why he would desire a position here, either. I see nothing of merit about this vessel, except for its size, which is of exceedingly vulgar dimensions. The exterior design reminds me of a certain soil-boring parasite we regularly exterminate on Omorr. And all this blue about . . . are these beings color-blind?"

The Captain leveled a look at Garphawayn that would have sent half the warriors on the ship running for cover. "The *Sunlace* has traveled extensively through hundreds of civilized systems. It has safely conveyed and protected my HouseClan for over three decades, and is the envy of the Jorenian fleet."

Garphawayn drew herself up like a hissing snake. "Then apparently the Jorenian fleet has as little taste as you do."

"Um, about Squilyp." I stepped between the two. "He would have been here, except he's in the middle of an operation. As soon as he finishes with his patient, he'll be on his way to meet you."

"Indeed? How long does this operation take?"

"Another hour at the most."

"I must loiter here for another hour until it is convenient for the *adoren* to make an appearance? Among all these impertinent savages? This is too impolite to be endured." The younger female gave me the once-over. "Why does Squilyp of Maftuda entrust his messages to you? Are you his personal valet?"

"I'm beginning to feel like it," I admitted.

Xonea put a hand on my shoulder. "Healer Cherijo

is one of the physician surgeons who works with the Senior Healer."

"He should have sent his representative," Lemesen said, sounding very righteous.

"Another oversight on his part. We shall have to make do with this underling." Lady Cestes fingered one of her many ornaments and studied the deck overhead. "I am fatigued and hungry. Spending *too* many days in space is tiring, particularly when I am called upon to stand and wait on an unmannerly laggard who thinks himself a proper *adoren*, yet sends enormous barbarians and inattentive stuntlings to stand in his place."

"Barbarians?" The tips of Xonea's claws appeared. *"Stuntlings?"*

I nudged my ClanBrother with a discreet elbow. "Like the lady said, she's fatigued. And obviously has had no contact with Jorenians prior to today. I'm sure with a little time we'll all get to know and become accustomed to each other." God, I was becoming such a consummate liar.

Xonea retracted his claws and somehow produced a strained smile. "Allow me the pleasure of showing you and your party to your quarters." His tone indicated extended torture would have been preferable.

"I think not, sir." The female Omorr somehow stared down her flat nose at the Jorenian towering two feet over her. "You are *too* large, *too* loud, and *too* blue. I dislike being in close proximity with beings of improper size and coloring."

"Then you're not going to be very happy on this ship," I muttered under my breath, before adding in a louder tone, "I'll take you." As I saw the skin over his cheekbones darken, I handed Marel to Xonea. "Go with your ClanUncle, sweetheart." I gestured to the door panel leading to the main corridor. "Follow me, if you would, Lady Cestes."

"You may address me as Garphawayn," she said as she led the procession out of the launch bay. "On my world, only social equals address each other by formal title."

I had a couple of things I would have liked to call her. "Good to know."

We didn't make it to the Omorr's assigned quarters. Not surprising—by the time we'd worked our way through two levels, Garphawayn had managed to insult every crew member she met on the way. And she refused to use the gyrlifts, despite my repeated advice that it would speed things up.

"They look far too flimsy to be trusted with my person."

"I promise, they're very safe—"

She plucked at the line of her cloak. "When I require your assurances, Terran, I will ask for them."

"When you want to leave, be sure and mention that, too." I wanted to pop a few bottles of champagne.

"Greetings," one of the engineers passing us said, and stopped to offer the usual Jorenian warm welcome. "You are Omorr, like our Senior Healer."

"So these barbarians do have functioning mental organs," Garphawayn observed aloud. "I was convinced when I looked in their eyes I could see the back of their skulls."

Another pair of Torins working on one of the corridor panels paused long enough to say hello and be insulted over their choice of garments.

"What is the obsession with blue?" the female Omorr asked me as she declined the traditional Jorenian kiss of welcome from the workers. "Is it not bad enough their skin resembles that of an asphyxiated corpse?"

"Omorr have such an edgy sense of humor," I said to the workers as I hustled the harpy and her friends past them. "Half the time you think they're serious."

"I am!" Garphawayn said. Then she added in a tight voice, "*What* is *this* thing?"

Alunthri had come around the corner. In its arms were two kittens, who were batting at each other with their paws. "Small nephews, you must not fight with one another." The Chakacat lifted the kittens up to its shoulders, where they began batting at its whiskers. "Hello, Cherijo. I tracked these two for Duncan. He said they slipped out of your quarters this morning."

Lady Cestes sneezed explosively. "Take them away! At once."

So much for making more introductions. "Would you mind taking them home for me, Alunthri?"

"Of course. Fare you well, Lady Omorr." Politely, it whisked the cats in an opposite direction.

"Lady Omorr." Garphawayn made a contemptuous sound. "I thought Chakacats were well-versed in proper forms of address. Why does it not wear a collar and leash? It should be in an animal carrier, along with its litter." She made another grand gesture. "Go and lock it up immediately. We shall wait here."

"Garphawayn." I took a deep breath. "No matter what you've heard, Alunthri is a free and sentient being. We treat all sentient beings with equal respect on this vessel. I hope I can count on you to do the same."

Her brow ridges elevated. "You can actually count? I am astonished." She stomped past me. "I trust in your tireless pursuit of respect and equality that you will not feed us from a bowl on the floor."

Alunthri appeared from around the corner, and beckoned to me. "Is that Squilyp's bride?"

I glowered. "If she lives that long."

I barely got them to Medical before half the crew considered declaring group ClanKill. Luckily, Squilyp was not only finished with his surgical case but had changed into his finest garments. He looked handsome and nervous.

No way is he marrying this bitch.

"Senior Healer." I stepped aside and gestured toward The Harpy from Hades with a casual hand. "The Lady Cestes, Garphawayn."

Flushed nearly purple, my Omorr colleague barely kept his gildrells from flaring as he surreptitiously tugged at the front lines of his tunic. "Greetings, *adorelee*, negotiator. Honored members of the Cestes household." He bobbed a couple of swift bows, then stared at Garphawayn as if she were a goddess.

"Hmph." The goddess looked him up and down a few times, then turned her back on him and whispered something to her negotiator.

"You were not present when the *adorlee* kindly graced this vessel with her presence." Lemesen tucked her three arms into a complicated, huffy mesh. "Not an auspicious beginning to negotiations, Lord Maftuda."

Lord Maftuda? In spite of myself, I choked back a laugh.

"Forgive my tardiness and neglect." Squilyp was almost stammering. "In my duties I am sometimes required to step outside protocol and treat the suffering. I will take measures to assure it will not happen again."

"Speaking of inauspicious beginnings, Senior Healer"—I did a little arm-folding of my own—"it would go a long way in smoothing things over with the crew if you explained Jorenian protocol to the *adorlee*. In detail."

He leaned over to murmur, "She's already insulted someone?"

"Everyone she's spoken to so far. Including me."

"Surely we are not going to be required to remain in this facility?" Garphawayn regarded the patient berths with faint horror. "In communal sleeping areas?"

"No, this is only for patients. I would be honored to escort you to your quarters," the Senior Healer assured her.

As the Omorr delegation bounced past me, Squilyp following up behind, I leaned over to murmur, "Don't kick her in the heart. You'll break your foot."

That got me a dirty look. "She's only shy."

"Right. So are bone saws."

"Adoren!" The female Omorr stood waiting beside the door panel to the main corridor. "I should like to see my quarters *today*, if it would not be too inconvenient."

I watched as my boss hurried off after his highly displeased intended, and wondered how much return postage it would take to send back this nasty little package.

CHAPTER THIRTEEN

Gains and Losses

Garphawayn of Cestes decided to remain on board for a grace period of several weeks, while her entourage returned to Omorr to negotiate the marriage contract. Apparently, the final round of talks were held between their families, while the two lovebirds got to know each other.

The Senior Healer apologized to me for doubling up on shifts so he could allot the proper time for their courtship. "I will compensate everyone once the matter is settled."

We'd just finished morning rounds, and I'd been away from his fiancée long enough to feel a little charitable. "Yep, you're going to owe me big time. So how is it going, anyway? She loosening up a little?" Personally, I didn't think that would happen without dunking her in an immersion tank filled with mechanical lubricant, but miracles were known to happen.

He looked pained. "Omorr females are not as . . . informal . . . as you Terrans."

I nodded. "So she's still complaining about basically everything that moves."

A reluctant chuckle left him. "Or doesn't."

My husband surprised me a little later that shift by reporting for his next series of kidney screens. "As you said, I have put this off long enough."

"He must be ill, boss. He's actually listening to me."
I prepped an exam table and checked Reever's vitals
while Squilyp scrubbed to perform the biopsy. "I don't
know why I'm even bothering to check your stats. Your
readings hardly ever vary more than a few points, either way."

"Neither do yours."

"Yeah, but I'm genetically engineered to be perfect,
while you . . ." An image of Joseph's underground lab
flashed through my mind, and I froze. "Chameleons."

Reever peered down around the table. "Where?"

"No. Not the lizards. I need to do a molecular thermal spectrum. Squilyp!"

The Senior Healer appeared, freshly sterilized and
masked. "Is something wrong?"

I pushed Reever down and sterilized the extraction
site above his mysterious kidney before infusing him
with local anesthetic. "Take the biopsy."

As soon as the Omorr had retrieved a sample of
Reever's kidney cells, I grabbed the biopsy needle and
headed for the hemoanalysis unit. Over my shoulder, I
yelled, "Reever, keep that tunic off. Squilyp, do a deep
systemic scan, see if his renal vein or regional lymph
nodes are enlarged. Check the perinephric space for
nodules and soft-tissue attenuation, and have a look at
the inferior vena cava and the main renal vein while
you're at it."

"What is it, Cherijo?"

"I think I know where the kidney came from."

Performing a spectral analysis of Reever's renal tissue down to the molecular level seemed to take forever,
but gave me time to think about my extremely wild
theory.

Did you actually do it, Joe? Did you create a chameleon?
My creator had rarely talked about it, mostly be-

cause the lack of apropos technology and cohesive organic material rendered it basically theoretical. By varying the characteristics of the organic solvents encapsulated within a bioartificial organ—the kind he grew in his laboratory on copolymer scaffolding—he had reduced the time it took for the transplant recipient's own cells to replace the neo-organ. In the process, he'd also stumbled across an interesting side effect: Transplanted "stem" cells, which stimulated the regrowth process, were in fact not replaced, but incorporated as part of the resulting engineered tissue.

"I found no criteria to support carcinoma," the Omorr said as he hopped in.

"It's not carcinoma. It's a chameleon."

"I am not familiar with that term."

I told him about my creator's original experiment, and went on from there. "If the remnant stem cells were programmed to release themselves from the copolymer prior to incorporation, they'd enter the bloodstream and reattach themselves to another diseased organ, continuing the replacement process."

"But that would only work on twin organs."

"Not necessarily. Take a look at this." I pointed as the molecular data began scrolling onto the vid. "See the variations in ten percent of the cell sample? Those aren't kidney cells. They're the chameleons. Bioengineered to alter their molecular structure to match whatever organ they attach themselves to. Reever was born missing a kidney, but he apparently had enough remnant renal cells to attract the chameleons."

"What you're talking about is medically impossible."

I reminded him about the Core, the sentient pathogen which had nearly wiped out the colony on K-2. That single-celled organism had possessed the ability to mimic their host's native cells, down to the chemical signatures. "And, aside from xenobiological examples, the Terran body cannibalizes millions of cells every second. We grow a new gastric lining every four days, new skin every four weeks, and regenerate our livers in six. Even our skeletons are completely replaced every revolution. It's not hard to believe Joe found a way to replicate, then alter the natural process. God knows, I'm a shining example of that."

The Omorr studied the vid screen. "How long do these chameleon cells remain viable?"

"I don't know. The original plan was to have them degrade like blood cells. Feasible for one hundred and twenty days, tops."

"Then they should not be present in my body."

We both turned around to see my bare-chested husband standing behind us. When I saw the color of his eyes—the same shade ice crystals had when they formed on steel—I swore under my breath. "Reever, we don't have conclusive evidence of any of this. I need to do more tests."

"You have the biopsy sample." He pulled his tunic over his head. "I must report for duty."

"Duncan—" I got up from my chair, but he was already gone. "*Damn* it. I didn't want him to hear it that way!"

"*Adoren!*"

Garphawayn hopped through the main entrance to Medical and planted herself in the center of the bay. Squilyp sighed before going over to greet her, but she was having none of that.

"Do you realize it has been two hours since we were to dine together in that communal trough area?"

Adaola came over to stand beside me. "The Senior Healer's Chosen?"

"Uh-huh." I finished downloading the remainder of the data on Reever's kidney. "Looks like something that would eat her own young, doesn't she?"

"Healer!" The intern tried to sound scandalized, but ruined it by giggling. "She is very loud with her opinions, I think."

"Yeah. The sonic cannons are getting jealous."

The female Omorr was still ranting about proper meal intervals and how much she disliked being kept waiting while I tried to signal Reever. His assistant in Command promised to pass along my messages, so I concluded he was actively avoiding me.

Finding out Joseph had experimented on me had made me run away from Terra. What would it do to my husband?

In frustration, I went to work on the other scheduled cases, and noticed that one member of the sojourn team had still not come in for his physical. "Signal Hawk for me, if you would, and have him report to Medical immediately."

"I tried to do so, several times this week," Adaola told me. "He has not responded to any of my relays."

I hadn't seen him around the ship lately, either. Stubborn Terran males were almost as annoying as their female Omorr counterparts. "Okay, let me go round him up. I'll be right back."

Politely, I waited until Squilyp's fiancée paused for breath before I let the Senior Healer know where I was headed.

"Very well," Squilyp said. "I will wait until you return."

"I have been kept waiting long enough! Send one of the servants!" Garphawayn motioned toward the nurses.

"They're not servants," I said through gritted teeth.

"Why don't you sit down for a few minutes until I get back? I'm sure your mouth could use a rest."

"How dare you!" The pink-faced Omorr went purple. "I refuse to take that sort of insolence from you, you—"

"Rude, ungracious, unpolished, discourteous, and impolite Terran female. I know. You've told me. Frequently." I stalked off to the door panel. "Good thing we're not getting married, huh?"

I calmed down by the time I reached Hawk's quarters, and even felt a little ashamed of myself. My personal dislike of Garphawayn wasn't making things easier for Squilyp, who had evidently fallen head over heel for her. It was possible Lady Cestes was feeling defensive, being alone on a ship surrounded by strangers. I pressed the door panel chime, wondering if some candid girl talk might help make the Omorr lady feel a little more at home.

If that doesn't work, I can always sedate her.

No answer from Hawk. I checked the panel, and saw from the interior sensor sweep that he was inside. Why wouldn't he answer the door? I punched in audio, and said, "Hawk? It's Cherijo. Let me in. I want to talk to you."

There was no response. Fearing the worst, I input my emergency medical override code, and manually keyed the door to open.

A faint waft of smoke swept over my face as the panel slid to one side, revealing complete darkness. I squinted, trying to see. Were the optic emitters malfunctioning? "Hawk?"

The door panel slid shut, about the same time a strong hand grabbed me by the throat and hauled me inside. "Did they send you?"

I clawed at his fingers, trying to get enough oxygen to reply. "Hawk . . . let . . . go. . . ."

Abruptly he released me, muttered something, then switched on the lights.

I rubbed my throat and blinked. The *hataali* stood naked but for a stained piece of linen wrapped around his hips. He'd yanked out most of his chest feathers, judging by the condition of the swollen, bleeding follicles, and smeared himself with a moldy-looking yellow substance. The smell of that, combined with his body odor and oily hair, told me he hadn't deconned since returning from Taercal.

I should have checked on him days ago.

The interior of his quarters matched his filthy, haggard appearance. Remnants of meals had been left out to rot. A huge dry painting covered most of the floor, but this one had been formed from bits of his own feathers and—was it possible? his own blood.

"Hawk? It's Cherijo. Are you feeling sick?" I took out my scanner as I went toward him.

"You're one of *them*." His arm lashed out, and knocked my scanner out of my hand. The instrument clattered to the deck. "I'm not going to let you eviscerate me." He whipped his head to one side and addressed an empty space. "Quiet!"

"Okay. No eviscerating today. Got it." Warily I backed up and grabbed my scanner. "Hawk, do you know where you are?"

"I am at the beginning of the end of the world," he told me. "Abandoned to the *yei* of the water and the fire."

The *yei* were Navajo demons and monsters. Was he hallucinating? "You don't remember being on a Jorenian star vessel?"

His hoarse voice lowered to a whisper. "That is what

the *yei* wish us to think." He reached up to his chest, and plucked out a feather, handing it to me as if bestowing an expensive gift. "That is the trap of the water and the fire. You are very small for a *yei*."

"I'm not a monster, but I know they come in all sizes." The doctor inside me started taking assessment: limited or no contact with reality. Disordered speech. Self-inflicted wounds. I had to keep him talking. "These *yei*, why are they doing this to you?"

"They hate me." Tears ran down Hawk's dirty face. "They intend to sacrifice me on the altar to their gods." He backed into a wall, then slid down it to sit on the deck. His voice went flat. "This is the way of the end of the world." His lips continued forming the words silently: *the way of the end of the world, the way of the end of the world.*

"Why would they do that? You haven't done anything wrong." I moved closer, activating the scanner. "You're a nice guy."

"They took me from my father and my people." He looked over at the empty space again. "Stop whispering!" Then he spoke to me again. "They thirst for my blood because it is the key to everlasting life." Hawk watched me pass the scanner slowly over him, this time showing no fear and only perfunctory interest. "What is that?"

"A protection against the *yei*," I told him as I studied the display. No fever, though his dopamine and serotonin levels were off the grid. No injury to the frontal cortex lobes—yet. "Are you hearing these demons, or can you see them, too?"

Suddenly he straightened and gave me a haughty look. "I see all the *yei* gathering here. I have heard their plans for destruction of the universe." He slumped back and went back to saying/mouthing words. "I keep watch over them, because I am the only one who can stop them." *The only one who can stop them, the only one, the only one.*

"How do you feel about that?" Without a comprehensive blood series, I couldn't determine if he'd resorted to drugs. They were a very real possibility—he may have brought something with him from Terra, for ceremonial purposes. "Does it make you angry or sad?"

"No." He sounded remarkably calm, for a man who was in the throes of a severe psychotic episode. "I feel only resolve."

Hawk had all the classic signs—delusions, false beliefs, multiple-sensory hallucinations, thought disorder, and blunted emotions. With time and a few tests, I might be able to determine whether he was suffering from organic psychosis or had developed a functional schizophreniform disorder.

If he doesn't kill himself or me before we leave this room.

Casually, I went over to the console, standing in front of it as I keyed in an emergency signal to Medical, leaving the channel open so Squilyp could hear what was going on.

"What are you doing now?"

"I have an idea." I quickly couched everything into terms he would respond to positively, and carefully drew out my syrinpress. "There's a place I know where the *yei* can't see or hear or come after you. I want you to go there with me, right now. You'll be completely safe, I promise."

He lurched to his feet, and snapped out his wings. Handfuls of feathers were missing from them, too. "You are trying to deceive me."

"I never lie about being safe." I held my ground. Without sedation, I had no means to control him. If I couldn't get the drugs in him, I'd have to leave and secure the door panel. "This place is a sanctuary for others like you—"

"There is no one like me!" he screamed.

Time to get out and lock him in. I whirled, only to see a small figure standing a few feet from the closed door panel. "Marel? How—?"

"Hawk?" She toddled over until she stood between us.

"Back, child!" The *hataali* jumped on me, knocking me to the deck. I grunted as all the air left my lungs, and my syrinpress skidded away across the deck. He straddled me, and tried to wrap his hands around my neck. I fought back. "You will not devour her, I will not let you!"

As I wrestled with him, I twisted my face toward my daughter. The medevac team would arrive any moment, but I wasn't taking any chances. "Marel, sweetie— I want you to— go see Fasala. Hurry and go— right now— for me."

She did the exact opposite, and walked toward the madman sitting on top of me. "Hawk? Doan hurd my mama."

Hawk seemed determined to choke me. I kept my arms up, blocking his hands, but he had the strength of psychotic desperation backing him. "Go, child. I will keep the *yei* from harming you."

"Mama not monster." A little hand gently patted Hawk's tattered wing, distracting him as she slipped the syrinpress into my hand. "Mama heawer. Wike you."

He hesitated, struggling to focus on the little girl. "What?"

"You sing heaw peepoh. Mama hands heaw

peepoh." Marel made it all sound very logical. "Mama
heaw you."

"She will make the *yei* leave me alone?" he asked,
still suspicious.

"Sure." Marel's smile widened. "Everybody afraid
of Mama."

"You lie!" Hawk rolled off me.

Somehow, Qonja appeared, and threw himself in
Hawk's path just before he got his hands on my daughter. The two men went down, and began slugging each
other.

"Healer!" the resident shouted, struggling to hold
his own against the *hataali's* fury. "Now!"

I hurried over and administered a fast-acting sedative, then closed my eyes as Hawk slumped back, unconscious. Marel was already in my arms before I
straightened.

I held her tightly and looked down at Qonja's bleeding face before extending a hand to help him up.
"Thank you."

We moved Hawk to Medical, got him cleaned up,
and ran a full series scan, but I had to sedate him
again. Qonja treated his own cuts and bruises before
disappearing into the Senior Healer's office. A few
minutes later, the Senior Healer emerged and announced a staff meeting to determine diagnosis and
treatment.

It wasn't the way I would have handled it, but
Squilyp was in charge, not me. What bothered me was
wondering what Qonja had said to him.

As we gathered in the conference room and waited
for the rest of the senior staff to arrive, Adaola asked
me to fill them in. "And if you would, please describe

the patient's condition and behavior as you witnessed it."

I covered what had happened in Hawk's quarters, adding, "I tried talking him down, but he showed very limited response and ignored almost all my verbal cues. I'm not sure he even heard everything I said."

"What is the current status on the patient?" the Omorr asked as he closed the conference room panel, and came to the table.

"We've ruled out brain tumor, temporal lobe epilepsy, autoimmune responses, Huntington's, liver malfunction, and allergic or substance reactions." I handed copies of Hawk's chart to the residents and interns, feeling a bit like a secretary. When I reached my boss, I leaned over. "Where is Qonja? Shouldn't he be in on this?"

"He had to speak to the Captain." Squilyp cleared his throat, then addressed the group. "So we have no viable reason for this patient's delusional state." He gave me a brief glower, then switched on his chart. "Questions, thoughts?"

Adaola took the first shot. "His history indicates he is biologically vulnerable for acute functional psychosis. His condition could be the end result of years of severe mental and physical abuse, exposure to perpetual conflict, and poor adjustment to social conditions, and personal loss."

"I'd be inclined to agree." I sat down and took a sip from my server of water. "However, I know this patient pretty well, and prior to this episode, he has displayed no functional maladjustments whatsoever. We're talking about a normal twenty-four-year-old male suddenly developing crippling mental illness. It just doesn't happen overnight—we would have seen behavioral changes and other warning signs for months."

Vlaav was next. "Cellular degeneration within the frontal cortex lobes is not apparent, but from the patient's lethargic reaction to rysperidyne therapy, I'd say he's suffering organic psychosis resulting from increased stimulation of neurotransmitter receptors. Perhaps a form of Pick's Disease."

Squilyp shook his head. "Something triggered the endocrine response, and there are no signs of prior neurological disease."

"We can't continue receptor-blocker therapy without risking extrapyramidal side effects, like suppression of bone marrow production and seizures," I pointed out.

"We cannot continue sedating him," Iolna added. "Already he requires five times the standard Terran dosage of valumine. Repeated infusions will only build up toxic levels in the bloodstream and possibly cause permanent systemic damage."

"That leaves only one option—sleep suspension, until we can tag the source and develop a viable regimen." I wasn't happy about putting my friend in a deliberate coma, but we had no other choice.

"That will make him unavailable for further psychiatric testing," Vlaav said.

"In his present state, he could hardly provide cognizant test responses." The Omorr made a notation on the chart. "Very well, we shall put the *hataali* in sleep suspension. Adaola, you and Vlaav work on the organic sources. Test for every known neurological and endocrine disorder. Iolna, I want you on strict monitor. Advise the team of any changes in his condition, however minor." He glanced at me. "Cherijo and I will cover the other possibilities."

"It's not functional," I said. "It has to be pathogenic."

The Senior Healer nodded. "If it is, we'll find it. That's all for today. Thank you and please keep me updated on your progress."

I waited until the rest of the staff cleared the room before closing the door panel and leaning against it. "Okay, Squid Lips, tell me what's going on here. We have our first psychiatric case, and Boy Shrink disappears?"

He got busy stacking charts. "I don't know what you mean."

"You're a surgeon, not a group practitioner. What's the deal? What did he say to you in your office?"

His gildrells drooped. "I have orders from the Captain."

Xonea getting involved with Medical—never a good mix. "Orders, I take it, I'm not supposed to know about."

"He mentioned throwing me in the brig a few times when he was issuing them."

"So live dangerously and tell me what the hell is going on."

"I need everyone working on this, not just me and you. We have to find out what caused Hawk's episode, and quickly."

"*Why?*"

The door panel slid open, and someone even madder than me hopped in the room.

"You liar." Garphawayn threw a handful of photoscans at the Senior Healer. "I demand we resolve this disgusting matter at once!"

Squilyp bent down and picked up the images, which were of a beautiful, smiling Jorenian female. Inwardly, I groaned.

It seemed Garphawayn had just found out about the other woman in her fiancé's heart.

*   *   *

"I will not accept your solicitation," the Senior Healer said as he finished picking up the photoscans and handed them to me. "We are contracting marriage, not seeking to kill each other."

"*You* are contracting marriage under false pretenses. It is *too* revolting to even think about." The female Omorr's gildrell rings clinked together. "I demand satisfaction for your blatant insult to the Cestes name."

My boss seemed to snap. "You have insulted it yourself by searching my quarters, you harridan!"

"That's enough." I decided it was time I stepped in, before membranes started swinging. "Both of you, shut up for a minute."

Malicious dark eyes shifted to me. "Stay out of this, Terran, or I will solicit you next."

"Since I've already kicked your fiancé's backside once in a solicitation, I wouldn't recommend it." I pulled out a chair and pointed to the seat. "Park yourself for a minute. You, too, Squilyp." When they didn't move, I raised my voice. "Now, or I call security and tell them to bring weapons!"

The Omorr chose opposite ends of the table and refused to look at each other.

"Good. Now we're going to straighten this out. Squilyp, tell Garphawayn who the female in the photoscans is."

"Lalona Torin, one of my patients. She was badly burned in a fire on the ship. I performed the reconstructive surgery that restored her facial features and proper respiratory functions."

"Ha! She has no scars on her face!"

He planted two membranes on the table and leaned forward. "I am an excellent surgeon."

"If what you say is true, then why do you keep only

her images? Where are those of your other patients?" The female Omorr tossed her feathered head. "Produce them, and I will retract my accusations. I am willing to be understanding. This once."

"Oh, someone needs to record this moment and preserve it for posterity." I sighed. "Garphawayn, you can't go through marriage asking for proof every time your spouse tells you something. Marriage is about faith and trust in each other."

She gave me a shut-up look. "Very well. *Adoren*, tell me you have no feelings for this blue female in the images, and I will withdraw my solicitation."

"I loved her," Mr. Honesty felt compelled to say.

"You see?" She gave me a triumphant glare. "His heart is not open. He is not suitable for marriage. And yet he deceived me, brought me to this wretched vessel, compelled me to waste my time negotiating a contract which could never be fulfilled—"

"Right. Okay. Shut up." My boss was maintaining a mutinous silence, so I decided to explain the muddle. "In the first place, Lalona Torin and Squilyp could never be together. Jorenians and Omorr are not physically compatible. He knew this, which is why he never pursued her."

"That makes little difference." She thumped the table. "His heart was to be mine by contract!"

"Lady, if you think a signed document is going to make this guy love you, you're existing in another dimension." That wasn't enough, I saw from her expression. I'd have to get creative. "Besides, Lalona Torin died as a result of her injuries. You're jealous of a ghost, nothing more." When Squilyp made as if to protest, I silently stomped on his foot under the table, and he subsided.

Garphawayn looked a little thunderstruck. "She's dead?"

"That's what I told you," I said. "Now, I think you'd better withdraw your solicitation and go spend an interval under a cold cleanser port. What do you say?"

"I withdraw my solicitation." She rose on her leg, looking even more regal than ever. "As for the marriage contract, I will have to consider this new codicil. Perhaps, Squilyp, you should ask yourself if you truly desire a wife, or merely a substitution for a deceased love." Out she stomped.

As soon as she was gone, Squilyp exploded. "Why did you lie to her? Lalona is not dead; she's on Joren!"

"Uh-huh. And when do you think your future bride is ever going to visit *that* particular planet?"

He sat back down. "Likely never."

"I rest my case."

My boss still looked miserable as he sorted through the photoscans. "She's right, you know. I'm still infatuated with a female I can never have."

"I didn't think too much of this one, until she came in here demanding to beat the hell out of you." I smiled. "Squilyp, Garphawayn has been acting like a refrigeration unit since she got on board. Now, suddenly, she's insanely jealous. In my mind, there's only one reason for that."

"Hormones," he said in a morose tone.

"No, you idiot." I patted his cheek. "She's in love with you."

The Omorr's behavior lingered in my mind as I went to check on Hawk and see how well the sleep suspension was working. Savetka reviewed his vitals with me, then pointed out some minor fluctuations in brain activity during the transition phase.

"It was much the same when we began administering the additional sedation. I have little hope that he will be able to remain in suspension for an extended period of time."

"He's as ticked off as Squilyp's girlfriend is," I joked, then nearly dropped the chart. "That's it."

The nurse looked mystified. "Your pardon, Healer?"

"Pull up all the hematological results for the patient, and sort out the hormone and protein levels." I pulled back the suspension shroud, and felt under Hawk's neck. There was a distinct bulge indicating an abnormality in the thyroid gland, and I scanned it before replacing the shroud. "No growth, but definitely enlarged."

Meanwhile, the nurse had collated the data I needed and handed me the chart. "He has a number of hormones out of balance, including several that the database cannot identify."

"He's only half-Terran, so it would make sense that he has some Taercal glands." I'd already downloaded what few readings I'd taken from the native population, and went over to a console to pull them up. Hyt only had a couple of matching secretions in his blood, but the dead adult male I'd scanned had all of them. "Bingo."

Savetka studied the screen. "Without a comprehensive database, we cannot determine which glands are affected."

"I'm way ahead of you." I signaled Communications. "This is Healer Cherijo. I need to relay a signal back to Taerca." When the Communications officer looked at me as though I'd lost my mind, I glowered. "It's a medical emergency; put me through."

"Yes, Healer."

The response was immediate, and the officer

patched it through to my terminal. I didn't know the face of the official who answered, but I certainly recognized the hostility.

"What do you want, polluter?"

"I have one of your people on my ship, and he's dying," I said, deciding blunt was best. "I need you to upload your standard medical database to me."

"We do not blaspheme Sadda."

"I have Sadda on the ship, remember?"

"Then the great one will tell you himself. If you or your kind ever come within our space again, we will destroy all of you."

The signal terminated, and there were no further answers to the other dozen relays I sent.

CHAPTER FOURTEEN

Celebration City

If it wasn't frustrating enough that I couldn't get the medical data I needed to save Hawk's life, or find out what Qonja was doing, the Captain decided to get all Jorenian on me about going down to the surface of Oenrall.

"Until I know what's making these people sterile, it's idiotic to send anyone else but me!" I shouted at the terminal.

"I shall not debate this, Cherijo." My ClanBrother was using that no-nonsense tone with me, which the console relayed perfectly. "I refuse to allow you to so-journ alone."

"I won't be alone. Dhreen is going with me."

"Dhreen is injured and has severe memory loss. He is also in no condition to help you, should the situation deteriorate, as it did on Taerca. Command out."

That left me fuming as I prepared to jaunt down to a planet full of people who had been rendered barren by an unknown cause. Naturally, I was going to vent, and Reever just happened to walk in our quarters at that moment.

I said a few uncomplimentary things about Xonea, ending with, "Who does he think he is, telling me how to do my job?"

"The Captain." Duncan seemed faintly amused.

"Perhaps having a big brother is not the delight you once thought it."

"Have you looked at the sojourn roster? Why does Squilyp have to come with us?"

"I believe the Omorr wishes to have some time away from the female he is considering as a mate."

I gave him a baleful look. "I know how he feels. Especially when my husband walks out in the middle of a medical procedure on me and doesn't answer my signals."

He went to the viewer. "I was preoccupied."

"You were dodging me." I could see the tension in his shoulders, but my supply of patience was running low. "These chameleon cells are serious business, Reever. The theory alone went way beyond risky—I'm not even sure they'll remain cohesive. We need to talk about what we're going to do."

That was when he pulled one of my tricks. "After the sojourn," he said, and walked out.

To assure himself there would be no monkey business, Xonea piloted the launch down to Oenrall Main Transport. I was too angry at being overruled to say much to him, outside my affirmative snarl to his greeting when we arrived in launch bay three.

Dhreen and Squilyp were already there, waiting to board as an Engineering crew gave the launch a final preflight check. Reever took my medical pack and placed it next to the others waiting to be stowed.

"Don't juggle this around too much," I said, handing him the cryogenic carrier.

"What is inside?"

"The Jorenian liver we've been working on. I want to show it to one of the native doctors."

Qonja watched me from his position by the entrance ramp, his eyes intent. The entrance to the bay opened behind us, and I glanced back to see Garphawayn and Ilona Red Faun walk in together.

Great. All we need are the Hsktskt and we can have a party.

Garphawayn hopped over to stand beside Squilyp. "So this is the vessel you will jaunt in to the surface? It is *too* cramped. Tell the Captain to fly a larger shuttle."

"Dhreen." Ilona's voice wasn't as loud, but commanded as much attention. The Oenrallian watched her approaching him, and just as she reached him, turned his back on her. "Dhreen, please."

"Leave me alone."

I hissed my impatience. "Dhreen, don't be an ass."

"Attend to your own lookout, Doc." Now he turned around to confront her. "I informed you, there is nothing further to converse about. I don't remember you. I don't know you."

The Terran girl wrapped her arms around her torso. "I am pregnant with your children."

"They aren't mine!"

Garphawayn, who had been bickering with Squilyp over launch sizes and Captain's prerogatives, snapped her head up. "You, orange-haired one. Do not speak to her like that. It is absolutely *too* indiscreet to make such statements in front of others."

"They're his," Ilona told the female Omorr, her voice breaking into a sob on the last word. "His children."

Garphawayn turned to me. "You. Bad-tempered Terran. A DNA test has been performed?"

"I have a name." I gave her the eye. "And it's not 'Bad-tempered Terran.' "

"I cannot remember it." She went over and placed a comforting membrane on Ilona's shoulder. "Well? Is he responsible for the female's pregnancy, or not?"

"This is not the time or place to discuss this matter."

Reever squeezed my arm when I would have aired my opinion. "Perhaps, Lady Cestes, you could escort Ilona Red Faun back to her quarters?"

"If I must." Garphawayn sniffed. "*Adoren*, this subordinate of yours has failed to reconcile this distressful matter. You will personally attend to this situation when you return."

"Yes, *adorlee*." For once the Senior Healer sounded sick and tired of being told what to attend to. "Until we return."

"Another thing—do not allow these Terrans to agitate the indigenous species on *this* world. I would dislike having to accompany a rescue mission to retrieve you."

As the female Omorr led Ilona from the launch bay, I sighed. "You know, those two may actually be the only ones on this ship who get along without a problem."

"Thank you for the prediction," the Senior Healer said, obviously miffed.

We boarded the launch and departed from the *Sunlace* a few minutes later. In the passenger compartment, Reever and Squilyp got into an intense discussion about gathering specimens of indigenous botanicals. Qonja seemed preoccupied with staring out the viewport. That left me to sit and monitor Dhreen.

The Oenrallian had rallied a second time from his injuries, but he was still pale and thin. I told myself I wasn't being overly cautious, even as I ran a scanner over him for the third time since leaving the ship.

His amber eyes narrowed with speculation. "Uneasy about me?"

"Since the day I walked into that New Angeles tavern and fell for your first scam," I said, checking his heart/lung rate. "You still can't remember Ilona or the time you spent together on Terra?"

"Those children are not mine."

Okay, scratch talking about the kids. I expelled a breath as I studied his readings. "You're not going to be able to run around down there. If I see you try, I'm going to sedate you and have you brought back to the ship. Got that?"

"Absolutely."

I looked through the viewport at the planet we were rapidly approaching. It was a mottled swirl of blue oceans and green land masses, with a few dark ribbons indicating areas of high elevation. The capital, Valsegas City, was located in the center of the largest continent. "Can you remember anything about your home-world?"

"I read what was on the database," he admitted. "It's comparable to your homeworld, negligible depreciated gravity, oxygen-nitrogen atmosphere. The oceans aren't as salty, and they don't eject saliva on visitors or shape their botanicals into geometric structures."

In spite of my disgruntled mood, my lips curved. "Sounds like you remember a little about Terra."

"I have flashes, sometimes." He sat back and closed his eyes.

Since he looked tired already, I left off grilling Dhreen and went up to the helm. Xonea was entering coordinates for final descent and nodded when I pointed to the copilot's seat.

"Any problem with Valsegas?" I asked, watching the planet fill the front viewer.

"I do not understand what you mean," the Captain said.

"Problems, you know—mandatory quarantines,

triple decon scans, a mob gathering to chuck some stones at us?"

"None so far." My ClanBrother shot me an amused glance. "You will not persuade me to believe you could have accomplished the sojourn successfully by yourself."

"Give me time, and I will."

Main Transport outside Valsegas City was a busy place, filled with trader ships landing and lifting off all around us. I got a chance to witness real pilot savvy as Xonea hovered until a gap on the docking pad opened up, then squeezed in under two other vessels vying for the space. The standard biodecon scans only took another minute.

"Valsegas Main Transport, *Sunlace* launch five pilot, all scans negative. Request permission to disembark."

Someone laughing stopped, coughed, and barked over the audio, "Sure, come on down!" More laughter, this time from others in the background.

While the guys assembled the sojourn packs, I woke Dhreen up. "Rise and shine, pal. You're home."

Whatever subconscious fears I'd had about walking into another Taercal-style mess instantly evaporated as we left the launch. Beyond Main Transport, a busy metropolis sprawled out in all directions. There were Oenrallians rushing in and out of buildings, crowding around ships, dealing with traders, and constantly talking, gesturing, and laughing. Dhreen's native language was being bantered around us nonstop, and had a staccato sound to it that reminded me of heels tapping with impatience.

"Productive place," I said to Dhreen as we passed a group of squat, blocky Ramathorran traders hauling containers from an off-ramp into an open cargo hold. "Anything jogging your memory yet?"

He regarded the workers, then rubbed his horns/ears. "Not them."

Valsegas reminded me a lot of Dhreen's old trader vessel, the *Bestshot*, only on a city-size scale. Apparently the waste-not, want-not attitude was a cultural thing, as every structure appeared to be constructed of a conglomeration of materials, and every mode of transport that passed us displayed recycled and salvaged parts. As Oenrall's red sun set, a bewildering amount of photo-sensor optics began lighting up. Some were in the oddest places, too: strung from wiring hung out of doors and windows, floating on autonomous hover units, and in transparent panels on the walkways under our feet.

I squinted up at a flashing red rectangle floating overhead. "Someone afraid of the dark?"

"Valsegas is the city that never takes a sleep interval," a deep, pleasant voice said behind me.

We turned to see a group of Oenrallians following us, led by a towering Amazon with a shaggy mane of sun-bleached hair and brightly ornamented yellow garments.

Qonja stepped in front of me. "May I be of assistance?"

"If I wasn't already mated, you could." She gave him an admiring once-over. "You're from the Jorenian ship, am I right?" Without waiting for an answer, she held out a hand that was bigger than my face. "I'm Mtulla, Rajanukal of Handler Row. Welcome to Oenrall."

"Qonja Torin." He took her hand briefly, waited a moment, then stepped aside to let her do the same with me.

"Hi. Dr. Cherijo Torin." I gingerly accepted the clasp, but all she did was squeeze my fingers gently before letting go. "What does 'Rajanukal' mean?"

"I run the row's business." She tapped her brow. "And get most of the head pains that go with that."

I grinned, liking her already. "I know how that is. Let me introduce you to the rest of our sojourn team. Captain Xonea Torin, Senior Healer Squilyp of Maftuda, Ship's Linguist Duncan Reever, and—"

"Dhreen! Son of an Abboreul dream snatcher, it's good to lay eyes on you." Mtulla went to seize him in a less cautious embrace, then stopped short when he drew back. "What's the matter with you, boy? You look like a cabbuna chewed you up and regurgitated what it couldn't belly!"

Reever stepped in and said something in low, fast Oenrallian, too low for our wristcoms to translate.

At once Mtulla's happy expression faded. "Oh, child." She tried to touch Dhreen's face, but again he avoided her hand. "Well, at least you're onplanet now." She cocked her head, making the tiny bells woven in her bleached hair chime. "It's been sixty years since I last routed you out of my dwelling."

"We were friends?" he asked her, still looking suspicious.

She shook her head. "Worse. We were neighbors, before most of the domains changed hands."

"We'd like to take Dhreen to a familiar place, maybe his home," I said. "It might help trigger some memories. Could you direct us there?"

"Direct you?" She laughed. "I'll transport you there myself." As she saw Xonea take out some credit chips, she added, "No payment is necessary, Captain Torin. I'd be gratified to help the boy."

Mtulla turned and snapped out some orders in

rapid Oenrallian to the group, who abruptly took off in different directions.

"I'll give you the tour of the city on the way, if you don't mind a few stops," she said. "Got to keep a grip on my crew, if I'm to handle the business and stay out of Debtor Row."

I frowned. "What do you handle, exactly?"

"Goods, buying and selling." She produced a thin card with a view square that displayed various tech, garments, and jewels. "We handle anything—fast and cheap, found and lost."

"What are lost goods?" my husband asked.

"Whatever needs someone to find it." She gave Reever a faint, lascivious wink. "Come on, friends, let's cruise the rows."

Valsegas's domains were huge areas of the city devoted to a particular family, Mtulla explained as we followed her to her personal transport. Each family specialized in some industry, rather like a guild, only they referred to the family residence and business as one in the same—their "row."

"We've got every kind of row an offworlder could want—tech, trade, data, raw and processed materials, transport, labor of any kind, you name it. Here's my ride." The Rajanukal went to a huge heap of modular hoverlifts fitted to at least three separate glidecar bodies that had been welded together, and yanked open a door panel. "Hop in, friends."

"Wait." Qonja stepped forward and had a long look inside. "Very well."

"If I needed a security guard," I told him as I climbed in, "I'd have brought one from the ship."

The interior of the vehicle had a number of odd-looking interior seams, but plenty of seats, harnesses, and viewports to accommodate all of us comfortably. Mtulla eased her big frame in behind the modified driver's console and hammered on the panel to initiate ignition.

"Now I see where you got your ship design from," I muttered to Dhreen as I arranged my footgear around some wiring sprouting from the floor panel. I checked out the main viewpanel. "Mtulla, how long does it take to get to these rows?"

She pointed at the buildings surrounded the docking area outside. "You're in the middle of one now—this is Transit Row."

Xonea leaned to one side. "Those structures at the left appear to be residences."

"They are." Mtulla started the ignition sequence, and a powerful engine rumbled to life. "Transit Row workers and their families live where they do their business. All of my handlers, for example, live with me in Handler Row."

Qonja leaned forward. "How many rows are there in your city?"

"A thousand, maybe more." She shrugged. "No one really counts."

The Captain and the psych resident exchanged a glance, but Qonja only sat back and subsided into silence.

We got the five-star tour as Mtulla drove us through the city, and pointed out the features and specific rows within each domain we passed through.

"East seventh domain, Artisan Row on your right, Quarry Row on your left." She handled the vehicle as deftly as she pointed out the attractions. "Coming up on Textile Row, for anyone looking to invest in some new garments or bed coverings."

Each row seemed to include a miniature open-air

marketplace, displaying wares in front of each structure. Some of the buildings, our guide explained, served as businesses by day and residential housing for the row's occupants by night.

"Are the workers governed by separate guilds?" Xonea asked.

"Nah. Everybody works for the Rajanukal of their row, but they're expected to govern themselves."

Everybody appeared to be actively employed, at least from the number of Oenrallians I saw walking around the streets. Something didn't seem right, until I realized that everyone I saw working *wasn't* Oenrallian, but members of offworld races. The natives themselves were everywhere—laughing, talking, gathering in groups—but doing nothing else. "Is today some kind of holiday?"

Mtulla glanced in the rear viewer. "Don't know what you mean, Doctor."

I decided to press the point. "There are Tingaleans selling paintings over there, and a pair of Aksellans hauling stone to that transport glidetruck. I don't see any of your people actually doing the work themselves."

The row leader's smile faded a bit. "We delegate to subcontractors. You know how it is—why do the grunt work yourself when you can pay another to acquire the aching muscles?"

It sounded reasonable. So why did I get the feeling she was putting me on?

I thought I saw some familiar-looking shadows disappear into one of the building entrances and peered over my shoulder through the back viewpanel to see if they'd come out again. They didn't.

What is it?

I felt Reever's unease even before his thought became clear. He was more worried than I was. *I don't know. I could have sworn I just saw a couple of Bartermen.*

Look to the right. Do you see the beings in the helmets and brown fitted garments?

I spotted them right away. *Yeah. Who are they?*

Akkabarrans. Now disgust blended with his unease.

Something about their appearance nagged at me, but I couldn't identify precisely what is was. *Never heard of them.*

You might have seen a few of them on Catopsa, during the slave auctions.

Now I remembered. *They're slavers?*

Living beings are only a side enterprise. Their main commerce is weaponry of any kind.

Noise and activity outside the transport seemed to elevate, the farther we got in to the city. By the time we reached what had to be the center, it appeared as if the entire population was having a wild party. Everywhere I looked, natives behaved with perpetual, almost manic hyperactivity. Singing. Dancing. Throwing colored strips of glowing paper up in the air.

"Not exactly shy, are they?" I said to Xonea, who like me was mesmerized by a group of Oenrallians tearing off their garments and jumping into a huge basin spraying water hundreds of feet into the air. They splashed each other like a group of mischievous kids.

"A pleasant contrast to Taercal," my ClanBrother said.

Mtulla worked her vehicle through the crowded street and parked beside a towering structure. "Excuse me for a moment, friends." A light appeared on her console and she took out a strange-looking headset and fitted it over the two horns on the top of her head before moving a connected transmitter unit in front of her mouth.

"Rajanukal." She listened, then sighed. "Expected as much. All right, see what you can do to locate it." She took off the headset. "Sorry about that. We've gotten as far as we're going, friends. I've got some business to attend to on Traders Row, just ahead. Everybody out."

Traders Row took up both sides of the wide street beyond the next intersection, and spilled out onto it from every direction. As soon as we stepped down from Mtulla's vehicle, we were surrounded by a horde of excited Oenrallians.

"Terran, beautiful footgear from your homeworld!" one young Oenrallian male with soulful yellow eyes called to me. He held up a pair of skimpy, black-strapped sandals. "They'll make your feet look smaller and yourself taller!"

Qonja stepped between us. "She is not interested, peddler."

"Thanks," I said over the resident's shoulder, before poking him in the back. He turned around. "Do you mind? I can speak for myself."

Another, older male grabbed Xonea, who shook him off like a troublesome flea. Jorenians dislike being mauled as much as Terrans. The native only grinned and gestured at him like an old friend. "Come and drink at my tavern with your friends, pilot."

Even Squilyp wasn't safe. A female flung a handful of squirming crimson bugs up under his gildrells. "Look, sir! Fresh cephalopods from Omorr!"

For people who liked to subcontract, the natives were awfully eager to sell things to us. I noticed no one approached Dhreen or Mtulla—apparently the peddlers preferred aliens—then saw a gorgeous female latch on to Reever.

She jumped on him, winding her arms around his neck and her legs around his waist. "Pleasure from my body, Terran. Any act you prefer." She undulated against him.

"Hey." On closer inspection, I saw she was hardly more than a kid. "Off my husband."

Reever untangled himself and set her on her feet. "Thank you for the offer, but I am exclusive to my wife."

"I will pleasure you both." She beckoned to me. "Let me service you together."

Mtulla stepped into the middle, then bellowed, "Rajanukal Handler Row! Leave off my friends and clear out!"

The crowd groaned, but gradually backed away from us. I watched, horrified as the young prostitute began bargaining with a pair of leering, furry humanoids twice her size.

Furious, I went after her, only to come up short and find my wrist in Reever's hand. "For God's sake, Duncan, she's just a kid!"

"She's seventy, if she's a day."

I sighed with frustration as I recalled how slowly Dhreen's people appeared to age. "Terrific. Next thing you know, we'll be accosted by infants."

He released me. "There don't appear to be any."

Which confirmed Dhreen's claim—since we'd landed on this world, I hadn't seen a single child.

While Mtulla completed her business, I got out my scanner and ran a routine check on the sojourn team. Everyone seemed to be maintaining, except Dhreen, whose blood pressure remained at slightly elevated levels. Pathogenic sweep indicated negative, which meant we hadn't contracted anything.

Our guide returned, but thought it would be best if we went the rest of the way to Dhreen's home on foot.

"I take my ride down these streets"—she swept a hand toward the mass of pedestrians—"someone will end up under the hover ports."

As soon as we began walking, I saw what the Oenrallian woman had been driving by too fast for me to spot before.

"I knew it. Mtulla." I pointed to a group of the dark-robed beings. "What are those creeps doing here?"

"Creeps?" She followed my gaze. "Those are Bartermen; they administer Traders Row. Most of the other rows now, too."

"I thought you said the Rajanukal ran the rows."

"We run them, but we work for the Bartermen. They like to trade." She didn't seem to think it was a big deal. "So do we."

"Fresh, new stock here," an Akkabarran said through a wristcom as we passed. "Collar trained, eager to serve you."

"They're *people*, not stock," I told him.

"Strong and obedient slaves, they are." He patted a coil of stim-cord on his hip. "I trained them personally."

"I thought Oenrall didn't traffic in slaves," I said through clenched teeth.

"I guess they do now," Dhreen said.

Reever grabbed me and forced me to keep walking. *Not here and not now. We have to find out why this is happening. It's not only the slavery. These people are in trouble.*

"What's your problem, Healer?" Mtulla wanted to know. "There aren't any Terrans in that bunch. Why be concerned?"

I grabbed the Rajanukal by the front of her tunic. Qonja tried to step in, but I glowered. "I spent a year as a slave, Mtulla. I don't like seeing people being sold like cattle."

She held up her big hands. "Sorry, I didn't know."

I let her go. "God, Taercal is starting to look good."

I saw more Bartermen skulking around, making their secret deals. Akkabarran and Garnotan slave traders worked out in the open, offering beings for rent or purchase. By the time we'd reached Dhreen's block, Reever had his arm clamped around me.

"All I wanted was a couple of minutes with that Garnotan piece of slime," I muttered under my breath.

Squilyp was so angry he was purple. "We have to stop this."

Jorenians only show claw when they were furious, and Xonea displayed all twelve of his. "Agreed."

"You can't stop the slave trade," Mtulla said.

I laughed, once. "You don't know who you're talking to."

"There is no law against it." She gestured to one of the slave pens.

Reever turned his cold gaze on her. "Do you have *any* law on this world?"

"Only one. You can't murder anyone." She scanned our faces. "If you kill, you'll be put to death immediately. No trial. No defense. A life for a life."

Mtulla's revelation kept us all silent for the remainder of the walk to Dhreen's home.

"This is it." She led us into a shabby, empty-looking building at the end of Traders Row.

Inside, dim lighting veiled everything in shadows, but I could smell stagnant water. Gnatlike insects swarmed around us briefly, driven off as soon as Mtulla switched on a hand-held emitter. A thick layer of dust and dead insects coated every surface. I'd half expected lots of clutter, but the furnishings were minimal.

"I don't like this," Dhreen said, his face gleaming with sweat. "Can we go back to the ship?"

"About your launch." Mtulla cleared her throat. "It's been appropriated."

Xonea turned on her. "What say you?"

She tapped her horns. "Got a signal from my Transit people. I sent a crew to safeguard it, but apparently they didn't get there in time."

"I wish to speak to someone in authority. At once," my ClanBrother said.

"We'll track down what happened to it," Mtulla told him. "Could have been a couple of my own handlers who took it."

"I can't stay here," Dhreen repeated, and headed for the entrance. "Something bad happened here."

"Hey." I caught his wrist. His skin felt clammy, but his pulse was normal. "If this place is helping you remember, maybe we should stick around for a few minutes."

He seized my hand and held on to it with a bruising grip. "What about the launch? What if we can't get off here, like Taerca?"

His paranoia was starting to worry me. "Mtulla will find it, or the Captain will send for a replacement." I tugged him toward another room. "Come on, let's see what's in here."

"I'll take a look at the database." Reever went over to a console and dusted it off.

I followed Dhreen over to where he stood, looking out a filmy window. "Hey."

He gripped the sill so hard the flat ends of his fingers whitened. "I don't like it here, Doc."

I put an arm around his waist. "Give it a chance. What do you think of, when you look out there?"

His eyes took on a faraway gleam. "That they're worse than when I left."

Silently, I took out my scanner and ran a brain sweep. "Who's worse?"

"They said it was a just a temporary reaction, you know." He murmured the words in such a soft, anguished voice that my eyes stung. "Only it was all part of the wanting."

"Tell me about it."

"They can't sleep or rest. Seeing a dim light is like staring into the sun. Hearing whispers as loud as screams." He swallowed. "If I stay here, it will happen to me."

I finished my scan and saw Mtulla hovering behind Dhreen. "Is what he's describing true?"

She shook her head. "We have medicine for it now."

I left Dhreen at the window and hauled Mtulla into the next room. "What kind of medicine?"

"Sensblok. It's the only thing that stops the symptoms."

The slang term sounded ominous. "What kind of drug is it?"

She took a vial from her pocket and handed it to me. "It calms and blunts the senses."

I scanned it. "This is neuroparalyzer—you can't use something like this; it'll kill you."

"No one has died of it yet."

When I found the physician who prescribed this, I'd have their license burned. "How often are you taking it?"

She shrugged. "When I can afford to buy it, every hour."

Neuroparalyzer on demand. Mother of All Houses. "Do you have any idea what kind of nerve damage you probably have, right now?" I dropped the vial and crushed it under my footgear, and saw blind rage flash across Mtulla's face. "You're addicted to it, aren't you?"

She bent down and got in my face. "Do you know how much Sensblok costs, you stupid female?"

"Bill me," I snarled back.

"Mtulla." Qonja appeared in the doorway, holding an energy pistol leveled at her. "Do not touch the Healer again."

"Knock it off, Qonja. She isn't threatening me." To Mtulla, I said, "Neuroparalyzer accumulates in the body. If your people are taking it hourly, they'd have toxic levels in their organs within a few weeks. No one gets to be an old chill-juice junkie. How many people have died?"

"None." Mtulla ignored the pistol and, after a moment, heaved a deep sigh. "I shouldn't have shouted at you, but you don't understand. Don't get involved in this."

"I'm a doctor. It's my job to get involved in this." I left her and went back in to the men, and brought them up to date. "I need to find someone in charge of medical, and talk to them. These people are addicts, and that's got to be involved with the sterility problem. Let's go."

"You're wrong, Doc," our guide said as she joined us. "My people became sterile long before we started taking Sensblok."

CHAPTER FIFTEEN

Eternity Row

Our guide agreed to take us to the Rajanuk, a kind of council made up of leaders from all the domains in the city. They decided on matters pertaining to the people, and relayed data on larger issues to the planetary Rajan, who governed all the Rajanuk from Oenrall's cities.

"I thought the Bartermen owned everything," I said.

Her lips curled. "They are only interested in trade. The rest is left to the Rajanuk and the Rajan."

As she drove us from Dhreen's home to meet with the city's officials, I sat behind her and took a couple of discreet scans, comparing the results to what I had on Dhreen. Allowing for the differences in size and body weight, they were essentially identical.

So why was Dhreen able to impregnate Ilona while the rest of his people remained barren?

Mtulla took us out of the boisterous Traders Row to a quieter domain with rows of silent, vacant-looking structures. She parked in front of one and nodded to the entrance. "Rajanuk convenes in there."

Dhreen frowned. "This isn't Governance Row."

"Things change, child." Mtulla shut down the engine and released the door locks. "The Rajanuk meet where the Bartermen tell them they may."

Mtulla led us inside, to a large room sectioned off on

the sides with small interview areas. What had been a working facility, probably an office, was now a void echoing with our footsteps. At the other end of the room, someone had set up a table, and behind it sat six smiling Oenrallians.

"I've brought the visitors," our guide announced without ceremony, and identified us by name. "They come from the ship in orbit."

All six smiles widened, and one of the males stood. "Welcome to Oenrall. We are so grateful for your generosity."

"We have not been asked to be generous as of yet," Xonea said, walking toward the table. "Perhaps you would explain your needs first."

The young official held out his hands, palm up. "Our people suffer from the unbalancing disease. If you could spare some medical equipment and supplies, we could prepare a treatment facility and begin addressing the population's present needs."

"Oenrall has hospitals," I said. "Plenty of them."

"Unfortunately, all treatment facilities have been acquired by the Bartermen Association." The young male put on an aggrieved air. "The equipment they contained has been removed, along with the medical database, and sold."

That sounded like the Bartermen. "Why?" I asked.

The earnest amber eyes grew damp. "The people will do anything to get Sensblok."

"Perhaps we can spare a few diagnostic units," the Captain said.

I couldn't exactly see refusing them myself, until Reever came to stand beside me and curled his fingers around mine. *Cherijo, he's lying.*

Startled, I looked at him. *How can you tell?*

His body language, the tone of his voice, choice of words, everything indicates he is being deceptive. My husband inclined his head toward Dhreen. *I have observed the same behavior from your friend in the past.*

So what do we do? We can't just accuse the local government of being liars.

Can't we?

Duncan stepped up beside Xonea. "Official, what is your position within the Rajanuk?"

"I am Moaan, the primary speaker," the Oenrallian said, "here to—"

Reever interrupted with, "What are the names of the members of the current Rajan?"

Moaan looked at the other natives at the table. "I am not acquainted with their names, but—"

"How often does the Rajanuk convene?" My husband paced the length of the table. "You— do you know at what time they convene?" To a third, he said, "What was the last issue you decided on?"

"We convene every six rotations, at— at the same time." The Oenrallian lost his grin, and added, "I cannot discuss our past decisions with offworlders."

"But you can accept our technology." Reever began pacing up and down the table. "When does the Rajan meet? How do you communicate with the planetary government? Where is it located?"

"These are also confidential matters," another of the officials blustered.

"A convenient answer," Mtulla said, and moved toward the table. "I am Rajanukal of Handler Row. You may answer to me on these questions."

One by one, the officials exchanged glances with each other, then rose out of their chairs. "Another time, perhaps," Moaan said, easing back away from the table. "This meeting is over."

"You're not of the Rajanuk," Dhreen said, startling everyone. "I know them. Who are you?"

Xonea removed the dagger from his tunic. "Answer him."

Moaan grimaced, then swept a low bow. "Moann of Players Row."

Dhreen made a disgusted sound as the other "officials" scattered. "They're role-players. Actors."

Mtulla made a sad, pointed comment on how some enterprising Sensblok addicts apparently would do anything, including impersonating government officials, to get their fix.

"One does what one must for Sensblok." When Xonea eyed Moaan, he backed away with his hands up. "No heat, friends. We take whatever work we can get."

I frowned. "Someone hired you?"

Moann didn't answer, but grinned before he raced out the back way.

Mtulla apologized before she sent a signal to her row to locate the "real" Rajanuk. "I should have run a check on them, but it's been so long since I've had dealings with the government that I took it for granted they were genuine."

That seemed a remarkably naive statement from someone in her line of work, I thought. Then again, maybe acquiring all those "lost" goods made her avoid the authorities.

"I thought you said row leaders regularly reported to the Rajanuk," Squilyp said.

"We did, before the unbalancing. Now little matters beyond doing whatever is necessary to acquire Sensblok." Her eyes dulled. "You've seen how our people are caught in its grip—no one can work or eat or sleep without it. Our society has fallen apart."

"Is it the same in other cities?" I asked, and took a deep breath when she nodded. "If this drug addiction is on a planetary scale, then it is directly related to the infertility problem."

"I told you, we stopped bearing children long before we discovered Sensblok, Healer." Mtulla stopped the transport and rubbed the sides of her temples. "It brings us no pleasure to medicate ourselves into a stupor, but the alternative is much more disagreeable, I assure you."

Something in her voice made me activate my scanner, and run it over her from behind. "You're in pain."

"Handler's pride," the Rajanukal admitted with a wry smile. "I only take a full dose at night, so I can sleep. I was due for a partial three hours ago, but you smashed it under your heel." She looked down at the scanner's display. "You can tell what I feel on that thing?"

"Your pulse, blood pressure, and body temperature indicate the stress." I saved the readings, and glanced up at her. "There's so much adrenaline in your bloodstream that I wouldn't be surprised if you jumped up and punched a hole through the roof."

"That's why I stay on foot, Healer." She patted the surface above her. "To preserve the interior."

I took out my medical case and sorted through it. "I can't give you neuroparalyzer, but a tranquilizer might help, temporarily."

"I'm grateful, but I have to stay on edge now." She nodded toward a building seething with activity. "That's my place. Come on in. I'll arrange a meal for us."

Mtulla's handlers moved constantly in and out of the building, like a living tide, bringing reports of goods being acquired, sold, and relocated. No word on our launch, but the Rajanuk assured us we could arrange transport from a local trader or signal the ship to send down another shuttle.

"I've got a signal out to the real Rajanuk, too. We should be receiving confirmation any moment."

I didn't apologize for scanning the food before allowing the team to sit down with the handlers, and refused everything but a server of water and a couple of thin rounds of cooked grain that tasted a little like rye bread. Qonja paced around me like a guard dog.

"Resident, go sit down over there before I thump you." I turned to my husband, who, like me, wasn't hungry. "What's wrong?"

"We need to leave this place."

"I haven't found anything that explains the symptoms I'm seeing in the population or the mass sterility." I took a sip from my server. "Chill-juice addiction will wipe them out, though. If anything, I should set up some kind of treatment facility to wean them off it."

Across from me, Dhreen reached for the pitcher of water between us. When he caught my interest, he filled, then lifted his server. "To finding a cure."

I completed the toast and watched him drain the water in a few swallows. "How are you feeling?"

He shrugged. "Better."

His color had improved, I decided, and he was definitely moving easier. "Is your memory improving? Any desire to go dancing in the streets?"

"Things feel familiar here, but I don't want to dance." He grimaced as someone bumped into him from behind—a pair of young men, who grinned and went back to chasing each other and a hoverball. "Mtulla's nephews." He grinned. "I remember them. Tiilm and Fduuv."

I scanned the room. "Are any of these people her kids?"

"I remember a daughter, but I don't see her." Dhreen turned and caught the hoverball. "Take it outside, boys, will you?"

We visited with Mtulla's extended family and employees, who all seemed to have their symptoms under control. Several seemed a bit sluggish, but responded readily to whatever I asked them. We kept the conversation light and inconsequential. It was obvious that the Rajanukal commanded a good price for her services, and treated her people well, because everyone under her roof seemed devoted to her.

"Mtulla is the best handler on the planet," a young woman confided as she passed around what equaled tea and cookies. She looked across the room at the Rajanukal, and smiled. "We'd be on Beggars Row, without her."

"Are you her daughter?" I asked after I refused the treat.

The young woman nearly dropped the tray in my lap. "No, I am one of her nieces. Forgive my clumsiness; it is time for my Sensblok."

Mtulla left us for a brief interval, and returned to inform us that the launch had been located, and the Rajanukal of Peddlers Row had sent a pair of representatives to speak with us. "If you want it back, you'll have to bargain for it."

"What do they want?" Reever asked.

She glanced at me. "Sensblok."

The representatives met with us in one of Mtulla's central row buildings, this one in slightly better condition than the others we'd seen. No conference table this time, only an older Oenrallian male and female dressed in clean but slightly ragged garments.

"Mtulla told us you were subjected to a ruse by some of the Players," the man, who identified himself as Loaj, said. "We will not subject you to that. We are honest traders."

"Indeed," Xonea said. "Yet you stole our launch from Main Transport."

"We acquired the space vessel to satisfy an existing debt," the female said. "Under Bartermen ordinance, we were entitled to take it."

"And now you want neuroparalyzer in exchange for it," I said. The male nodded, and both looked eagerly at my sojourn pack. "We came here to try and help your people find a cure, not supply you with more drugs."

"That is very commendable," Loaj said, "but there is no cure."

"Whatever rendered your population sterile is not being helped by drug addiction. If it continues unchecked, it will wipe out your species." Both averted their eyes. "We're willing to provide what assistance we can," I added in a softer tone, "but we can't give you more drugs."

"Then we must settle the existing debt with what you do possess." Loaj fumbled in his garment pocket before extracting a data pad.

"What debt do you refer to?" Qonja asked.

"Payment for services provided to Dhreen's family while he was offplanet," the female said. "A large outstanding balance still exists."

"What family?" I asked Dhreen, who only shook his head, perplexed.

Loaj began reading off a list of supplies and services that seemed to go on forever.

I finally lost my patience. "Look, we don't have time for bookkeeping right now. Why don't you tell me where the nearest medical facility is, and we'll go there and initiate a treatment schedule for the population."

"The family member, Lkooy, is unable to settle the debt," Loaj said. "Even when it is stripped down and sold, the vessel will not satisfy the account."

Dhreen jerked back, bumping into me and Reever. "Lkooy. I remember him." His face went pale, but his voice grew furious. "I left more than enough credits for his care."

"Inflation has risen several hundred times since you departed our world, Dhreen. The Bartermen have been caring for Lkooy during your absence. You made yourself answerable for all his debts before you left, and you remain accountable for them now."

Beside me, I heard Reever murmur to Xonea, "We must contact the ship and arrange for another launch to be sent down, Captain. Immediately."

I was all in favor of that, but I had an oath to uphold. "Can someone just point me in the direction of a medical database? Because this is a complete waste of my time."

The female shook her head. "That database now belongs to the Bartermen Association."

My jaw sagged. "You *sold* your medical data to them?"

In the meantime, Loaj put aside the data pad. "Restitution must be made immediately, of course. The Bartermen have already been more than generous to allow the debt to exist for so long." He turned as an immense alien wearing glittery, tight-fitting garments entered the room. "Bkof, you may remove your property."

I looked from him to the officials, lost. "What property?"

Xonea grabbed me, and pulled me behind him. Qonja flanked me on the other side. "They've sold us to that slaver."

"Hold on." I refused to believe I'd just been sold into slavery. Again. To Loaj, I said, "We're not for sale. You can't do this. We came here to help you." When no one even blinked, I yelled, "We're not even citizens of this planet!"

Mtulla appeared, holding what had to be the biggest pulse rifle on Oenrall. "Sorry about this, Doctor. You two Jorenians, place your weapons on the floor, or die." She turned her head a little. "I wouldn't do that, linguist. I can shoot you in the back just as easily."

I saw Reever, tensed to spring, and watched Qonja adjust his grip on the pistol he'd taken out. "Guys. Do what she says."

"No one makes slaves out of my crew," Xonea muttered as he enabled his own weapon.

Qonja was even more upset. His claws had sprung out, and he had that everybody-gets-disembowelled gleam in his white eyes. "Release us or die."

"Captain." Reever made a strange gesture, and Xonea nodded his head minutely. Then he glanced at me. *When we do this, run.*

You'd better be right behind me.

"Stay out of this, linguist," my ClanBrother said, his lips peeling back from his teeth.

"There is no need for violence." Reever stepped up to Xonea and put himself in front of the weapon.

The Captain gave him a shove. "Follow my orders!"

"Put it down." Reever glanced at me, then punched Xonea in the face. My ClanBrother reeled back, then lunged at my husband. Somehow the slave trader got caught between them, and all three of them went down.

Something fired, and Qonja collided with me. He held on for a moment, then looked down.

Green blood began darkening the front of his tunic.

I jerked as Reever's thoughts blasted into my head. *Now, Cherijo, go!*

"Come on." I braced him with my arm and stumbled along half-supporting him to the entrance. Dhreen had already disappeared, I saw, and Squilyp was hopping over to help.

He grabbed Qonja just as the big Jorenian sagged. "We must take him to a medical facility."

"We've got to get out of here first."

Between us, we dragged him to the entrance. Mtulla, who was mesmerized by the three men now rolling and grappling on the floor, looked up just as we reached the door panel, and fired her weapon. A section of the wall vaporized as we stumbled through the entrance and hauled Qonja down the corridor.

"We've got to get to a relay station, signal the ship for medevac," I panted out the words as we hurried to the street. "We'll take Mtulla's vehicle, out to Transport maybe, then—"

Waiting for us by the glidecar was Dhreen. He had a weapon trained on the entrance and was holding the door open with the other. "Get in! Cherijo, you drive."

I slid behind the controls and started the ignition sequence. Squilyp plopped in the back with Qonja, then I felt something touch the back of my neck.

"Dhreen," I said in a very soft voice. "That isn't your gun I feel, is it?"

"Drive straight, four kilometers." When I didn't touch the controls the pressure of the weapon's business end increased. "I know you can't die, but do you want to live without a head?"

"If you harm her," Qonja said, his voice thready with pain, "I will tear your limbs off, one by one."

"Thank you, resident. Dhreen, I don't know what's going on, but I'm not leaving the others behind." I sat back and folded my arms. "So go ahead and blow my head off. I'll probably just grow a better-looking one."

He moved the gun away from my head, then slid over and pressed it to Squilyp's skull. "How about the Omorr? Do their heads grow back?"

Qonja made an odd sound as I jammed my foot down on the accelerator and took off.

Dhreen didn't take us to Transport, as I'd expected, but forced me to drive deep into the heart of the city.

"We need to take Qonja to a medical facility, before he bleeds to death."

"You can treat him where we're going."

"Really. And where would that be?" I asked as I avoided another happily manic group of Oenrallians dancing in the street.

"Just drive, Doc."

I drove. "I take it your memory has come back completely." He didn't respond. "Are we headed for another League troop freighter?"

"No. I'm finished with the League."

"How comforting. Is it the Hsktskt, then?"

"I'm going to show you why I brought you here."

I knew there was something fishy about the planet-wide sterility story. "So now I get the whole truth, and nothing but the truth?"

"I didn't lie to you. I didn't remember until I heard Lkooy's name."

"Pilot." Squilyp shifted, then winced as Dhreen

jammed the weapon harder against the back of his head. "Whatever assistance you need is not going to be provided at gunpoint. Not when we must attend to this man's injuries."

"He will not live long enough to require anything," Qonja muttered.

Our patient and hijacker made a rude sound. "When you see what the wanting is, you'll change your mind."

Dhreen instructed me to take a series of twisting turns. As I drove, I noticed the buildings grew sparser, and what there were seemed abandoned.

"This part of the city seems pretty dull," I commented.

He made a harsh sound. "My people abandoned it decades ago."

"Any particular reason why? Other than the lousy accommodations?"

"No one wanted to live here."

"But you thought we couldn't wait to visit." I could have spit, I was so angry. "So what is this? More slaver houses? Brothel Row? What?"

He didn't answer, and my attention was dragged back to the road as we came to an abrupt, dead end.

"This doesn't look promising." I stopped Mtulla's vehicle beside the walled-in end of the road and shut down the engine. "This doesn't look like a medical facility, either. Where's the hospital, Dhreen?"

"Get out."

I climbed out of the glidecar, and watched as Dhreen did the same, still keeping his weapon trained on my boss. "Look, Dhreen, we're your friends. Don't do this. Take us somewhere so I can get Qonja some help and signal the ship."

"In there." Dhreen pointed to a corner of the wall, where a small, narrow gap appeared in the masonry.

I eyed it, then him. "You really think we're going to fit through that little hole?"

"Move."

Between us, we got Qonja through. Squilyp muttered obscenities in Omorr as the back of his tunic tore on the rough edges of the hacked-out space. "This is ridiculous," my boss spat out. "This man needs attention, Dhreen!"

"Keep walking and shut up."

We walked in near-total darkness, toward a dimly lit interior chamber. Some old abandoned medical equipment sat in neglected piles on either side of a sealed entrance. A complex locking mechanism secured the panel on all three sides, and the floor had some kind of grid spread over it that didn't look too friendly, either.

"You have the combination for this?" I nodded toward the lock. "Whatever this is?"

"It is keyed for Oenrallian DNA." Dhreen went over to it, avoiding the grid, and stuck a finger in a slot. The lights changed color, and the heavy alloy bars screeched as they pulled back from the door panel. "This is Eternity Row."

I had the feeling that we weren't going to like the "Eternity" part of this place as soon as we crossed the threshold. Maybe it was the way the air felt—cold and dry, like the way old bones felt. Or the stillness, which was so complete our footsteps sounded like sledgehammers pounding against the floor.

"What is this place?" I asked again as we came to an intersection. "A prison?"

"You could call it that." Dhreen pointed to the right. "That way."

Squilyp hopped beside me, and nodded at my glance. I pretended to lose my footing, and swung around in front of Qonja. My boss slipped something into my tunic. "Sorry, resident."

Qonja managed a smile. "Watch your step."

"Pilot, is it your intention to incarcerate us here?" Squilyp demanded.

I put my hand in my pocket, and curled my fingers around the syrinpress. "Yeah, what crime are we guilty of, other than saving your life and helping you get back your memory?"

"No crime." Dhreen only walked up to another, unsecured door and opened it. "This is why you're here."

Inside the door was what looked like a medical ward. One that smelled as if it hadn't been sterilized in years. The sporadic lighting from overhead emitters cast deep shadows over everything, which made it hard to see, but I wasn't concerned with my vision. I was too busy cringing from the noise.

Hundreds of voices rolled at us like a wave. All of them were, in various degrees, weeping or crying out with pain. From what I could make out, every single bed was occupied.

An epidemic ward?

"Squilyp, get Qonja out of here." I looked at Dhreen. "He can't be exposed to this—whatever it is."

"He won't catch it. Put him on that bed, over there." Dhreen pointed.

Reluctantly, Squilyp and I got the resident over to the empty bed and, after shaking out the dusty linens, lowered him on it. A quick exam revealed he'd been shot high in the back, thankfully to one side of his spine. The exit wound on his torso indicated his liver was involved.

"We should run a hepatic special this month." I straightened and looked at our abductor. "Dhreen, this man needs surgery. Right now."

"You can do it in the operating room."

"So this is really a hospital? What's wrong with these people?" When he didn't answer me, I strode to the nearest bed, on which lay an odd-shaped bundle of linens over a huddled body. Squilyp did the same thing on the other side of the room. I tried to pull the linens back, but the person beneath them wouldn't let go. "Dhreen, what is going on here?"

A glance over my shoulder revealed that our abductor still stood by the doorway. He had gone a sickly color of yellow, and his weapon hung loosely by his side. "I can't. I can't look at them again."

"Cherijo." Squilyp stood over the other bed across from me. "You'd better take a look at this one."

I debated on whether to wrestle the gun from Dhreen or sedate him, then found I couldn't do it and went to join my boss. "What have you got"—my eyes widened—"here . . . ?"

The patient on this bed was very still, and did not protest as Squilyp drew the linens back. Mostly because the patient didn't have a head, or arms, or legs. Even more bizarre, some form of skinseal had been applied to the points of amputation.

This wasn't a hospital. It was some kind of a *morgue*.

"Why hasn't this body been attended to?" I looked around. "Where are the people who work here?"

Squilyp lifted his membrane and touched the chest. "The derma is still warm." He jerked back, then reached down and splayed his membrane flat against the patient's chest. "Gods. I can feel a heartbeat."

I had to feel that for myself. Sure enough, I felt the strong, steady pulse of life beating within the dismembered torso.

"Are they keeping it alive?" I looked for infuser

lines, something to explain how the body was being sustained.

There was nothing but the bed and the linens.

"No." I went to the next bed, pulled back the linens, and stared at the form under them. This woman had a head, and arms, but nothing else from the lower chest cavity down. Skinseal gleamed over exposed edges of organs. I stumbled back when the patient opened her eyes. "Oh, God."

"Please," she said, her voice so hoarse it barely rose above a gasp. "Make it stop. Please."

"Dhreen!" I turned and ran to the door, and grabbed his tunic with my fists. "What have you done to these people?"

"Nothing, nothing." His eyes avoided mine, and he was nearly hyperventilating. "Our doctors couldn't help them. They tried—they tried everything—"

"Let him go." Squilyp came over and took my hands away. "You'd better see the others."

After making sure Qonja was stable enough to spare us, we made rounds of the hospital ward. Every bed contained a patient who had been horribly mutilated or injured in some way. Missing limbs, heads, huge gaping wounds in their torsos. Burn victims with no features left, and only charred, withered appendages. All of them were Oenrallian. Men, women, and children.

Worse, every single one of them was still alive, with normal body temperatures and strong, vital heart rates.

The only treatment given evidently was sealant to whatever portion of their anatomy that had been amputated or wounded. By the time I made it to the end of the ward, tears were running down my face. The ones who could talk pleaded and begged for us to help them. To end their pain. To stop whatever was happening to them.

The ones I couldn't bear were the bodies without heads. The ones who could never plead or beg for anything again. And yet somehow they knew we were there. Their torsos moved. If they had hands, they clutched at us.

"It's medically impossible for every person here to be alive," I said to Squilyp as we made our way back toward the entrance. Our Oenrallian pal was slumped down on the floor, his face buried against his arms. I took the weapon out of his limp hand. "Get up, Dhreen. Get up and explain this to me, right now."

He raised his face, which was wet with tears. "You're the doctor. You tell me."

"These people should be dead. Why are they still alive?"

"They won't die."

I yanked him up on his feet and snarled, "Why won't they die? What did your doctors do to them?"

"Nothing. They put something on them to stop them from bleeding. That's all." He swallowed, and wiped his face on his sleeve. "They never die."

"You are not being clear," Squilyp said. "They have to die. These people cannot survive these injuries."

"They want to die." Dhreen's voice went soft. "We want them to die, but they don't. They live. They live if they're chopped into pieces or burned or lose their heads. They never stop living, no matter what happens to them."

I let go of him as if I'd been scalded. "That's why you call it this. Eternity Row."

He nodded. "We don't die anymore, Doc. No one has died in over a hundred years. My people have become immortal."

*   *   *

The operating room hadn't been used in at least a hundred years, and prepping it to accommodate Qonja took time. Dhreen had retreated into silence, staring out at the ward, so Squilyp and I did the work.

"I don't like the look of the exit wound." The Omorr checked our sojourn packs, pulling out what we needed. "We must return to the ship."

"We don't have time to wait for another launch," I said. "Even if we can find a way to signal them."

Once we had established a reasonably sterile field and the instruments we needed for surgery, we transferred Qonja from the gurney to the procedure table. Squilyp scrubbed while I prepped the resident.

"Your pardon for this, Healer." Qonja made a wry gesture. "I did not intend to make more work for you."

"Thank you for shielding me from that blast."

He reached up suddenly and seized my wrist. "The Captain is my Speaker. When he tells you—"

"Not going to happen. You just concentrate on staying alive." I adjusted his infuser line, then initiated the anesthesia. "Go to sleep, pal."

His hand went limp and slid away from my arm as Squilyp changed places with me. While I scrubbed, I wondered just what the Captain would say, if Qonja died on our table.

He's not going to die.

Dhreen refused to leave, so I made him scrub and gown. After discovering the surgical unit's power cells had died sometime in the last decade, I made do with the suture laser from my pack and some antiquated scalpels.

"You're very good with those," Squilyp commented.

"I had to use them on Terra." I examined the instrument with mild disgust. "Give me a good laser rig any day."

Once we opened his chest, things went from bad to worse. His liver, unlike Dhreen's, had not survived the blast. Jorenian physiology ensured he'd live for another twenty-four hours, but beyond that was doubtful.

Playtime was over. "Dhreen, I have to get this man up to the ship. As soon as we close."

"There is no way to leave now."

I left the table and went at him, my gloves up, covered with Qonja's blood. "He needs a liver transplant. And I can't do that here. Signal the goddamn ship!"

"You can use this." He produced a familiar container.

It was the Jorenian liver we'd brought down. He must have retrieved it from Mtulla's vehicle.

"I'm not putting that into this patient!" I yanked down my mask. "It's part of an experiment, not a viable transplant organ!"

"You're not going back to the ship," he said. "If anyone in the city finds you, they'll turn you over to Mtulla or the Bartermen."

"Dhreen, he's going to *die*."

"Then you'd better hurry up and use it." He shoved the container in my hands.

Squilyp vetoed my idea of using our scalpels on Dhreen, and quietly performed a tissue match. Incredibly, the experimental liver was an acceptable replacement for Qonja's ruined organ.

"He'll need some antirejection therapy until we can clone another liver from his own cells, but it shouldn't present a treatment problem." The Omorr prepped the liver, then noticed my preoccupation. "What is it?"

"This." I turned Qonja's head to one side, and revealed what his hair had covered. A small HouseClan symbol, one shaped like a dagger.

"It is one of their birthmarks, isn't it?"

"Uh-huh. But look." I pointed to the mark on my own neck, which was shaped like the upswept wings of a bird. "This is the Torin symbol."

"Well, *that* isn't." Squilyp shook his head. "Why would the crew pretend Qonja was a member of their HouseClan?"

"To cover up what he really is." I checked the transplant site and changed my gloves. "Are we ready?"

"Yes." He brought over the basin containing the liver. "Cherijo, whatever is happening, you can depend on me."

"Good. Because I don't know who else to trust."

PART FOUR

Solutions

CHAPTER SIXTEEN

A Price for Everything

Some six hours after we entered Eternity Row, I closed Qonja's chest with the last in a long vee of sutures, and stepped back from the table. "We'll need to run a blood series every fifteen minutes, and watch for signs of rejection." I saw Dhreen still standing against the entrance panel, watching us. "We're done here. I need an isolated berth for him."

"There are none. Leave him here."

I stripped out of my gown and went to cleanse. "Fine. I want to see the other patients being kept here. Squilyp will stay with him."

Dhreen took me through the first ten wards on Eternity Row. Every ward was interconnected and crammed with Oenrallians who should have died of their injuries, but evidently couldn't.

"How many more of them are there?" I asked, my voice tight after we'd walked through the fourth.

"I don't know. There were hundreds of wards when I left. Now there may be thousands."

As I continued my nightmare rounds, I saw living bodies in conditions that defied description. One ward had been stocked with rows and rows of open specimen containers, which held a gruesome collection of severed limbs and detached heads. Since they were no longer connected to their bodies, they couldn't function, but the limbs reacted reflexively to any touch, and the decapitated heads watched us, their eyes following our every movement, their mouths forming soundless pleas.

Along the way, Dhreen kept his eyes averted from the inhabitants of the wards, and described what had happened a century before. "The first to come here were multiple amputees, involved in a transport crash—miracles, we thought—until it became apparent no one would ever die, no matter what happened to them."

"The decapitations would have done it." I felt a deep, aching sorrow creeping over me.

"When our doctors realized the head and body still functioned apart from each other, then we knew." He cleared his throat. "Something terrible has happened to our people."

"Why did you put them all here?"

He looked slightly defensive for a moment, then his shoulders slumped. "First they were given the finest care. When there was still hope. Years passed. They didn't die. They didn't even age—none of us do. No cure, no hope of finding one. There were so many of them, you see."

"So you made this Eternity Row."

"Our doctors gave up. Families couldn't bear to see those they loved existing like this. Now no one comes here, unless it is to bring someone to stay."

I looked through the door panel viewer, and saw the next crowded ward waiting on the other side. "How many buildings are there?"

"Mtulla told me they cover three domains now."

"How many people?"

"I'm not sure. Maybe ten thousand."

With a population of two billion, more than that

should have died in any given revolution. "And in the other cities? Is it the same? Are they warehousing the bodies, too?"

"It is the same everywhere on the planet."

I did the math. If forty to eighty thousand people could have been expected to die each year, then the number reached into the millions.

"You've just been stacking them up here, year after year. This isn't eternity, Dhreen. It's Hell."

"They are given Sensblok once per cycle. It is all the people can afford to do now."

"Your people could stop taking the drugs themselves and use them to put these poor bastards out of their misery!" I shouted.

"We've tried." Dhreen bowed his head. "Nothing kills them."

I took the syrinpress Squilyp had put in my tunic and strode out to the ward, stopping at the bed of a mangled Oenrallian male who was literally encased in sealant. I broke the seal over an intact blood vessel and dialed up a fatal dose of narcotic that would kill him within ten seconds.

"It won't work," Dhreen said behind me.

My hand faltered as I pressed the instrument against the vessel. *It's not murder. Not like this.* Something inside me snapped, and I administered the lethal dose.

Ten seconds went by. Then twenty. Then forty. The patient only stared at me with the one eye he had left, and made low, moaning sounds through the open gaping hole in his throat.

Shaking now, I infused him with a second dose. Then a third. I was dialing up the fourth when Squilyp appeared at my side and took the instrument from my hand.

"Give it back to me." I swiped at it.

My boss held it out of my reach. "You're wasting it, I've already tried it on another patient myself. He won't die, Cherijo. Dhreen's right. None of them will die."

"They have to," I said, and my voice cracked. "Oh, God, Squilyp, we can't leave them like this. Not like this."

"Now you know what I feel, Doc." Dhreen joined us, and took the hand of the patient in his. The mangled man's two remaining fingers curled around his. "This is Nojan. He and I grew up together on Traders Row. His glidecar malfunctioned and crashed into another. It took them hours to pull him out of the crushed alloy." Gently, he lowered Nojan's hand back down to the bed. "He deserves better than this. They all do."

Something struck me. "This is why you kept denying Ilona's pregnancy."

"Yes. Even when I couldn't remember they were mine, I knew I didn't want them."

"But it should have given you hope."

"Hope? For my children to end like this?" He gazed steadily at me. "Could you bear to see Marel here? Strapped to some bed, suffering for eternity?"

"No." I wiped the tears from my face. "We're not letting these people suffer any longer, either. Let's get started."

Scanning the total inhabitants of Eternity Row was impossible, so we performed comprehensive exams on patients showing a variety of terminal conditions, due to injury, disease, or old age.

Initial scans revealed completely normal readings, with one major exception: None of the living dead showed any metabolic activity, which explained why their bodies no longer needed to be fed. It also created a new problem—if they didn't require caloric intake, what *was* keeping them alive?

"It's as if they're in some kind of stasis," I said to the Omorr as we finished with a young male who had been exposed to massive radiation. He'd been on Eternity Row for so long that his blistered body no longer contained any traces of the toxic heavy metals that should have killed him. "No digestion, no excretion. But they're sustained by something."

"How often do you go without eating?"

I scowled. "Not years, that's for sure. And I still lose weight if I skip meal intervals."

"But not as much as before. I've noticed that." Squilyp hesitated, then added, "This could happen to you, couldn't it?"

I started to deny it, but the potential was there. "I hope my friends would make sure it never did."

He nodded, and hopped away.

Squilyp's comment haunted me for the rest of the day. As I went from bed to bed, I thought about my own dilemma. My creator had engineered my body to withstand any biological assault, and repair itself so perfectly that I never even scarred. I'd been subjected to repeated severe trauma, so I knew something of my own physical limits.

As far as I knew, I had none.

Whatever Joseph Grey Veil had done to me, the process was also getting faster. Right after I left Terra, a wound I sustained might take several days to heal. Now I could almost watch any injury I received knit itself back together within an hour or two.

"Help me," a woman's voice begged.

I went over to the next bed, and found an elderly female covered with cancerous tumors. "Here, let me take a look."

"Doc." Dhreen came over, then quickly turned around. His voice choked as he asked, "Anything you need?"

"More of this sealant." I peeled back a layer to scan the surface of an enormous malignant tumor that had erupted through the dermis over the old woman's torso. The voracious mass was spreading over her entire body, but seemed to be growing on top of her rather than consuming her own cells.

"I'll go get it for you."

"Has Squilyp gone to check on Qonja?" When he nodded, I straightened and shut off my scanner. "I also need to know what's happened to Duncan and Xonea."

Dhreen had the grace to look slightly ashamed as he brought me the topical sealant applicator. "They will be taken to the slave pens, and prepared for auction."

"We need to get them back, Dhreen." I glanced at him. "Can you find out exactly where they are?"

"I will." He left.

I moved to the next patient, a small girl whose bones had been pulverized after a terrible fall from the top of her row house. My hand shook as I drew back the linens, and saw the sealant gleaming over the jagged edges of the bones sticking through her flesh.

Someone had been caring for her, judging by the clean condition of her linens. A small vase of fresh flowers sat on a table where the child could see them. Her hair had been carefully brushed, and her face washed.

Amber eyes met mine, and what I saw in them made me swallow, hard. "Hi, I'm Dr. Cherijo. What's your name?"

"Gerala." She didn't grab at me, but lay quiet as I scanned her. "Are you going to hurt me?"

"No, honey, I'm going to help if I can."

That was when she latched on to me, crying as her broken hands grasped my arm. "Can you give me the medicine to make me sleep? I've been trying to wait for my mother, but it's been so long."

I had already tried different compounds on other patients, desperate to find something to ease their pain. Nothing had worked. Then something my first-year Medtech instructor had lectured on came back to me. "Sweetie, I have a very powerful medicine here. If I give it to you, I have to be careful. It's a hundred times more powerful than Sensblok."

"Please." Her shattered fingers dug into my arm. "Please, may I have some?"

"All right. As soon as I infuse it, you're going to feel very tired. Then you'll sleep and you won't wake up for a long, long time." I brushed her hair back from her face. "Ready?"

She nodded, and I injected her. Squilyp came over to observe, and went still as my medicine began to work.

"I feel it," Gerala said, her ruined voice in awe.

"It makes the pain go away very fast, doesn't it?" I watched as her eyelids drooped and she yawned. "There you go. Don't fight it, just let the medicine work. That's my girl. Go to sleep now." I pulled the linens up over her, motioned to Squilyp, and returned to the research unit.

He shut the doors and secured them. "You infused that child with saline solution."

"I know." I went to the storage cabinet and began sorting through it. "There are some other syrinpresses in here. They're old, but I think we can make them work."

"Cherijo!" Squilyp jerked me around. "You injected that child with salt water!"

"I *said* I *know*." I pushed a syrinpress in his membrane. "You're going to help me do the same thing to all of them."

"This is sheer insanity."

"No, it's a placebo. Look." I took out my scanner and switched it to display Gerala's brain imaging. "Watch her chemoreceptors—they reacted immediately to the infusion. The salt makes it sting, like a real drug would. As long as the patient believes what I'm giving them will stop the pain, the brain reacts accordingly."

"But not in all cases. Placebos have only be shown to be effective in less than seventy percent of most humanoids."

"That's better than nothing."

Squilyp listened as I coached him on how to "talk" the patients into accepting the lie, then we went back out to start treating the patients. An hour later, we had nearly everyone in the ward sleeping.

"Better than ninety percent," I said as we went to recharge the synrinpresses. "And all it takes is ten cc's of saline."

"Doc." Dhreen appeared. "I've got a line on where they're holding Duncan and Xonea. How did you do that?" He waved back at the silent ward.

Squilyp answered for me. "It is a highly technical procedure that will take too long to explain. We must retrieve the others and return to the ship as soon as possible."

"But you have to stay, and help the others," Dhreen said. "I'll find a way to get Duncan and Xonea back to the *Sunlace*."

"We cannot help them without an analysis of our scans, and the equipment here no longer functions. Will the Bartermen allow us access to the medical database?"

"Not without turning us over to slavers." Dhreen made a face. "They want their credits pretty bad."

"Then either return us to the ship"—the Omorr hopped over to Dhreen, and smacked him in the chest with a scanner—"or figure out what to do yourself."

I silently applauded my boss. "We'd better take a couple of specimen containers along with us, too. We'll need the tissue samples." I gathered up the dusty, ancient charts left behind by the Oenrallian doctors. "And no heads, please."

After we retrieved what we required, and moved Qonja on a litter to the back of Mtulla's vehicle, Dhreen drove us beyond the city to what appeared to be a secondary, abandoned Transport site. No Oenrallians rushed toward us as we climbed out, but my skin prickled.

Someone was watching us.

"Where are Duncan and Xonea?" I said as we carried the resident's litter toward a small pile of junk parts left beside the stripped-down hull of an archaic League starshuttle.

"We're going to get them now." Dhreen reached into the salvage heap and pulled. The parts began rolling away, revealing a small, battered launch beneath. "Get in."

"That?" I stepped back. "No. I don't think so."

"It's all I could steal on short notice." A sound made Dhreen whirl around. "Get in, or we're not making it out of here."

I glanced at what had grabbed his attention and groaned. A cluster of glidecars were headed for the launch area at full speed. "Will I ever leave a planet without being chased down by the locals?" I said as I helped Squilyp carry Qonja up the docking ramp.

"Probably not," the Omorr replied.

Dhreen got in behind the helm controls while Squilyp and I strapped our patient down and climbed into the crude harnesses hanging from the interior wall panels. There were no seats, and from the look of the rewired components powering the launch, we'd be lucky not to fry in a flash fire before the Oenrallian got us off the ground.

Shots smashed into the outer hull, making me throw a protective arm over Qonja. "Dhreen!"

"Hang on!"

The launch shuddered violently, then lifted off. Shots fired from below still smashed into the deck under our feet, and Squilyp closed his eyes.

"Going to hover over the auction pens," Dhreen said as he flew back over Valsegas. "When we're in position, dump the lower cargo container."

"What's in it?" I said as I untangled myself from the harness.

"Something to distract the crowd."

I went back to the cargo hold controls and manned them. Squilyp went up to the helm and took over from Dhreen, who came back and strapped on some weapons. "If everyone on this planet is immortal, those won't work," I said.

"The slavers aren't Oenrallian." He activated a pulse rifle, then slung it over his shoulder before facing me. "Don't worry, Doc, I won't kill anyone. I'll stun whoever gets in my way." He checked the viewport, then called to Squilyp, "We're here. Assume hover position ten meters above the central complex."

"What about me?" I jerked my chin toward the control panel.

"As soon as I lower myself out, dump the hold." Dhreen wrapped a hoist cable around his waist and secured it. "I'll signal you, then pull us back up. Be prepared to fly out of here fast, Senior Healer."

I wanted to jump on the cable, too, but someone had to handle the controls. I settled for reaching out and touching his arm. "Be careful."

He grinned. "Ceaselessly."

I waited until the loading access panel slid to one side, and Dhreen jumped out, then I dumped the cargo hold. Whatever fell out made the launch jerk up, then back down into position. I ran over to the edge of the access opening to look down.

In the streets below, Oenrallians were scrambling and fighting with each other over a hundreds of small, sealed packages. Some ripped them open immediately and applied the coin-size items inside to their skin, then slumped over or fell into a stupor.

"Sensblok!" I forgot all about how much I loved Dhreen. "He's showering them with *drugs*?"

The diversion worked. Dhreen landed on the top of the building below us and went inside. A short time later, he emerged with Duncan and Xonea, and fired a shot directly in the air. I ran back to the controls and initiated the hoist lift.

The launch bucked again as the cable began reeling in. I went over to the access opening and reached down, grabbing the back of Reever's tunic as he climbed hand over hand up the cable.

"Duncan." I pulled until he got over the side, then wrapped my arms around him. "Thank God you're safe."

He kissed me, hard, then helped Xonea and Dhreen back in. More shots were fired, and one burst up through the opening and exploded on the interior ceiling, showering us with sparks.

I rolled over and covered the resident's body with my own. "Squilyp, go!"

My boss gunned the controls, and the launch started a vertical climb away from Valsegas City.

Squilyp switched places with Dhreen so he could watch over Qonja while I examined Reever and Xonea.

"Stop complaining and let me have a look at you," I told the Captain. "It's here or in Medical, as soon as we get back."

Xonea wanted a full report on what had happened since we'd been separated, so Squilyp filled in the details while I ran the scans. Both my husband and the Captain had sustained some minor injuries, mostly nasty contusions from fighting with the slavers, but were otherwise unharmed.

"How many of these people are suffering in these death-hospitals?" my ClanBrother asked me.

I shut off my scanner and replaced it in my medical case before relating my estimates. "This is based on what Dhreen told me, and the natural death rate among this level of civilization and population. It could be millions, plus or minus a few hundred thousand, but even one person suffering like this is too many."

Reever brushed some hair out of my face. "Are you all right?"

I nodded briskly. The last thing I wanted to do was get all weepy and helpless. I owed the people on those wards more than that. "We can't leave Oenrall until we try to help them." I turned to Xonea. "I know Dhreen's abduction wasn't exactly the best way to get us there, but I understand why he did it."

The Captain wasn't convinced. "His people could have applied to their quadrant governors for assistance."

"You've seen how the League pursues me, and I'm just one person who may or may not be immortal. Can you imagine how valuable an entire planet of people who can't die would be? The slave traders alone would descend in hordes. The League's scientists would have subjects they could experiment on forever."

"I regret they suffer as much as you do, Cherijo." His face grew stern. "However, serious harm has been inflicted upon our House."

"Please, Xonea. Please don't retaliate against him or his people. If you'd seen how they were . . ." I stood up quickly and straightened my tunic. "If the placebo worked, then the key is in the brain activity. All we have to do is figure out how to shut it down. I can do this."

"I'm not as convinced," Squilyp admitted. "There were numerous bodies disconnected from their cerebral organs. They were as alive as the others. More indepth investigation of the condition is required."

"Oenrallians have nerve clusters, all along their vertebrae. I'm betting those are doing the same job as the brains would." I sighed. "But you're right—we need to do extensive analysis of our data, and that's going to take some time." I turned to the Captain. "It's the right thing to do, Xonea. That's all I can say to you. I hope it's enough."

He nodded. "For now, it will be."

Dhreen angled the launch to dock with the *Sunlace*, and set down inside the bay. The decrepit hull seemed to tremble as he went through decon and opened the outer door. "We're clear to disembark."

On the deck below a small group of Command officers waited, along with Squilyp's intended. She was dressed in her usual gorgeous finery, and looked ready to throttle the first one who stepped down.

Which was me. "Gee, you didn't have to come to meet us. I'm touched."

"You will be more than touched when I am finished with you, Terran." She hopped up to me and gave me a little push with one of her membranes. "How dare you accost my *adoren* and force him to remain on that wretched planet, with all those drug addicts! Have you no respect for the institution of contract marriage under negotiation?"

"I shield you," I said quickly, to protect her from the Jorenians' wrath. "Squilyp, come and put a leash on your female, will you?"

"I am making a solicitation, you greedy, dishonorable woman! You will submit yourself to my challenge!"

"No, she will not." Squilyp hopped slowly down the docking ramp and over to us. "I apologize for Garphawayn's behavior, Doctor. And you." He turned on his fiancée. "You will return to Omorr, as soon as I can signal a ship to come and get you."

He hopped out of launch bay, leaving both me and his ex-fiancée staring after him.

"I refuse your solicitation," I said, just to make it official. Despite my intense dislike for the Omorr female, I felt a wrenching pity as I watched her haughty face dissolve into disbelief. "Maybe you should go talk to him."

"Mind your own affairs!" she snapped, then stomped out of the launch bay.

Our Senior Healer might have been eager to dump his girlfriend, but it turned out not to be quite so simple—as I found out when I reported for duty the next day.

Squilyp had finished rounds already, and I found

him sulking in his office. "Hey. You could have waited for me. I'm not even late this time."

"Sit down." As I did, he handed me a stack of charts with Dhreen's on top. "I've reassigned your cases to the resident staff, so you and I can concentrate on researching the Oenrallian quandary. Make your final notes and pass them over to Adaola and Vlaav. I've readmitted Dhreen as an inpatient."

I switched on the chart. "Problems with the Lok-Teel shunt?"

"No. I want to run comparison analysis between the specimens we brought back and his cellular composition and physiology. Whatever is happening to those people down there hasn't affected him, or has worn off since he left Oenrall."

Now that was something I hadn't considered. "It might be coming from something indigenous."

"Exactly." He sat back in his chair. "There is another problem: time."

"Time?" I frowned. "I know we want to work fast, but those patients on Eternity Row aren't going anywhere."

"I signaled Omorr last night, to send a ship for Lady Cestes. They refused." He punched up a relay on his screen, then turned it for me to see.

"We regret we are unable to enter an active war zone to pick up your passenger. Please relocate your ship to an unconflicted area and relay your coordinates."

I stared at the dignified Omorr face on the screen. "We're not in a war zone."

"Keep listening," my boss said.

A second relay appeared. "We have received your inquiry. At this current time, a faction known as 'Sadda's Justice' have declared war on Oenrall. The Locias Quadrant forces have declined to take part in this aggression, as it involves theological differences. They have additionally refused to provide protection to any ship which enters the specified war zone."

I frowned. "Why have they declared war on Oenrall?"

"According to what they told quadrant officials, removing Alunthri from their world gave them cause enough to reinstitute the use of their abandoned technology—and they know more about it than they led us to believe. They tracked the *Sunlace* here, and tapped into quadrant databases to learn more about the planet."

I recalled their reaction to Dhreen. "And the minute they saw what the Oenrallians looked like, they probably went nuts." I watched the screen's sad image fade away. "So that's it? They just announce some holy war and we're cut off?"

"That's not all." Squilyp handed me a data pad, which displayed a star chart with a cluster of objects approaching the Oenrall system. "They haven't simply declared war. They're on their way to invade the planet."

With the ship on full alert, Squilyp and I prepared the staff and Medical for the worst. We brought our contingency plans to the emergency meeting of department heads the next day, and reviewed a multistage method by which we would be able to convert storage space and run triage stations to handle minor injury cases from each on four different levels of the ship.

The Captain approved of our strategy, and the others presented by various departments. "Engineering is to be given priority on each level. Be prepared to initiate these procedures immediately upon notification from the helm." He cleared the center holoprojector and punched up a new image, one of an immense Jorenian research vessel. "The *CloudWalk* is en route to Oenrall, as you know, to meet with us regarding the League/Hsktskt conflict. I notified ClanLeader Teulon yesterday and apprised him of the intelligence the Omorr passed along to us. This was his response."

A strong, intelligent blue face replaced the image of the ship. "Our thanks to HouseClan Torin for relaying news of the Taercal intentions within the quadrant. After consultation with the Ruling Council, it has been decided to postpone first negotiations with the Allied League and Hsktskt Faction. Instead, we will attempt to establish reasonable dialogue between Taerca and Oenrall."

"He'd better bring plenty of guns and tranquilizers," I said under my breath.

The young ClanLeader continued. "As we remain several days from our rendezvous point, the Jado request that the Torin arrange a meeting between representatives from both worlds at a neutral site agreeable to both. Please advise us of your status as soon as possible. Our thanks once more for your assistance in this matter." The head inclined, and the image disappeared.

Squilyp stroked his gildrells in a thoughtful way. "He doesn't want much, does he?"

"Senior Healer, what is Hawk's status?" Xonea asked. "Will he be able to assist us in communicating with the Taercal?"

"Not at this time. Hawk Long Knife is suffering from acute paranoid schizophrenia, and must remain in sleep suspension until we devise a treatment plan." Squilyp didn't have to say that the occupants of Eternity Row took precedence over that. Xonea knew what we were dealing with.

The Captain turned to the end of one table. "Alunthri, these people equate you with the deity they worship. Are you willing to assist us in communication and negotiation with them?"

The Chakacat nodded, but it didn't look happy.

Xonea turned his head. "Ship's Linguist, have you completed your surveys?"

"Yes," my husband said. I smiled at him, then rolled my eyes when I saw who he had on his lap. "There is a planet in the solar system between Taerca and Oenrall which would suit our purposes." He removed a disc from Marel's hand and placed it in the table console, producing a holoimage star chart. "Surface sweeps indicate the indigenous population was exterminated by war many millennia before this quadrant was colonized."

"Pree dars," my daughter said, pointing.

The pretty stars dwindled as the imager zoomed in on the world. The heavily cratered surface still showed signs of multicolored zones that indicated something was still living on it.

"Does it have a name?"

"At present"—Duncan shifted Marel back away from the console—"it has only a numerical designation. However, I believe my wife knows its name."

"I do?"

"Mama's dar," my kid said, and smacked a key. The imager zoomed back out, and she crawled up on the table to stick her finger in some of the lights. "See? Two dars, one big dar, four widow dars. Make a fwower."

"Honey, please get down, you . . ." I stopped and slowly rose to my feet. I didn't have to look at my husband to know what he was thinking. "No, Duncan. Pick another planet."

He was already signaling someone. "Relay the data

up to here." A moment later, another, very familiar chart came up and superimposed itself over the original.

"They match." Xonea studied the grids. "What say you, ClanSister?"

"I say, no way." I took my daughter down from the console and tucked her on my hip. "So some of the stars match. That doesn't mean this planet is the one."

"Captain, this is the same world recorded on the discs given to Cherijo by the alien female." Reever didn't look the least bit ashamed as he wrecked my whole day. "It is Jxinok."

"Tell me something, sweetie," I said as I tucked Marel in for her nap that afternoon. "How did you know about that star chart your daddy showed us?"

"Pree dars." She blinked, and nestled down into her pillows. "Make fwower wid pree dars."

I left her sleeping and went out to where my husband was manning the console, still studying Maggie's star chart. I reached over, shut down the file, and popped out the disc. "Why are you doing this to me?"

"If we are ever to live free and unafraid, we must discover who Maggie is and what she wants."

"She's a ghost who's stuck in my head and nothing else."

"That's what you want her to be." He got up and tried to pull me in his arms, but I was still too angry to do the kiss-and-make-up thing. "Cherijo, why are you so afraid of knowing the truth about yourself?"

"I'm not afraid. I'm a mother now. It's not just me this affects." I looked at Marel's room. "What happens if we find out everything Maggie has said is true? That I'm not human, that I can't die, that there's some other reason I was created? It's bad enough I can't tell her about her grandfather, the sadistic bastard, or any of her uncles, until she's old enough to know what monsters are. How much more do you want to dump on this kid?"

"Marel is not your clone, and she also deserves the truth." He got up and walked away.

I followed him. "Why, so she can have a bounty put on her head? So some scientist can wrap her in nerve-web and see how much pain she can take? So she can watch people she loves die trying to protect her? Look at me, Duncan!" His eyes went from blue to gray as he met my gaze. "This isn't your decision to make, it never was. And yet you go right ahead and push aside my wishes so you can satisfy your curiosity. That's really what this is about—you can't stand it, not knowing. Well, I can."

He stroked my cheek with his fingers. "If you wish, I will not go to Jxinok. You never have to tell me what you find there."

"That was the only good argument I had," I said through gritted teeth. "Thanks for blowing it away."

"The first thing I loved about you was your courage," he said in a very soft voice. "You would crawl through fire to save another's life. I have seen you shot and stabbed and burned and beaten and none of it stopped you. That is what Marel needs—her mother's courage, not her fear."

I gave in, and stepped into his arms. "You're going with me. I need you to go with me."

He rubbed his palm over my hair. "Always."

After a few moments, I stepped back and handed him the disc. "Let's look at it again."

Duncan pulled the charts back up, and the data coming in from a long-range probe he'd launched the day before. "The environment appears innocuous, and the atmosphere amenable for the Jorenians. The higher nitrogen content may make you feel light-headed, until you adjust."

"The Captain wants us to revive Hawk tonight, see how he reacts." I looked at the ancient star chart from Maggie's disc as my husband superimposed it on the more modern version from the ship's database. "Why aren't they identical?"

"Some of these stars are now novas, or black holes." He tapped a couple of unmatched pinpoints of light. "Others have formed in the interim between surveys."

"How long does that take?"

"I'm not certain." He stared at the console. "My best estimate is at least two million years."

"How could she have a star chart that old?"

"There is only one way." He met my gaze. "Her species, like you, is immortal."

"Don't start that with me again." I grabbed my work tunic and shrugged it on.

"Cherijo, she's alive."

"No." I swiveled around. "She's not. I watched her die. I buried her. She's decomposing in a hole in the ground on Terra."

"Why didn't she choose to be cremated? That is the standard funerary disposition of bodies on Terra now."

"How the hell do I know?" I threw up my hands. "She was a strange woman. Practically everything she did was socially unacceptable!"

"And yet Joseph kept her on staff and allowed her to supervise you for eighteen years." He switched off the terminal. "Joseph, who you will agree was more conservative than most Terrans."

"She told me they were lovers. Maybe he kept her because she was good in bed." I finished fastening my tunic and headed for the corridor. "I'm going to work."

"Wait."

I waited. He came up behind me, and rested one hand on my neck. "What?"

"Don't change your mind about going down to the surface."

"I won't, but I'm going to complain about it," I said, and went out the door. "Frequently."

In Medical, Squilyp and the nursing staff were prepping to remove Hawk from sleep suspension. I didn't say anything as I joined them, still in knots over Duncan and Marel and Maggie's stupid discs.

"We've already observed a tolerance for rysperidyne," the Senior Healer said as he removed the suspension shroud and deactivated the support unit. "Given the serious prolactin elevation, conventional drug treatment is out of the question."

"The obvious choice would be a dibenzodiazepine," Qonja said. He had recovered in record time from his transplant surgery, and showed no signs of rejecting the bioengineered organ. "Clinical studies on Joren have shown that drugs such as clozapyne increase delta and theta activity, and slows dominant alpha frequencies. They also exert potent anticholinergic, adrenolytic, antihistaminic, and antiserotonergic activity."

"Yeah?" I turned on him, glad to have a direction to vent. "Last time I was in Medtech, clozapyne use was strictly limited to totally nonresponsive or highly intolerant patients. Maybe because it causes agranulocytosis, tachycardia, and seizure in most patients. Or did you forget to attend that class, resident?"

"The patient has been given two courses of chemically unrelated, conventional antipsychotic drugs and responded to neither." Instead of being miffed, Qonja sounded almost amused. "What other course of action remains unexplored, Doctor?"

"Why don't we wake him up first and see what we've got to work with?"

"I agree," Squilyp said, before the psych resident could protest. "Administer the neutralizer, nurse."

Savetka administered the mild stimulant, which roused Hawk within minutes. His eyelids fluttered, then opened as his drowsy eyes tried to focus. "Patcher?" he said, his voice raspy.

"So far so good," I murmured to the Omorr as I moved in and checked Hawk's vitals. "How are you feeling, *hataali?*"

"Strange." He looked from me to Squilyp, and then turned his head toward Qonja. "What happened to me?"

"You've been ill, so we've had you in sleep suspension for a couple of days." His pulse jumped under my fingertips, and I felt sweat dampening his skin. "Easy, now. Everything is going to okay."

"I want to go home." He sounded like a scared little boy. "Please take me home."

The expression on his scarred face made me fold his hands between mine. "I wish I could, pal."

The next thing I knew Hawk had clamped his hands around my neck, dragging me across the berth, while Squilyp and Qonja struggled to free me.

"I am the lifeblood of the world!" he screamed in my face as he choked me.

Qonja did something fast with his hands. I heard bones snap, then Hawk howled with pain.

"Sedate him now!" the Omorr shouted, wrestling down one free arm and pulling me off the berth. I fell to the deck, holding my throat and coughing, my eyes fixed on Hawk's spasming hand as my boss strapped his arm in restraints.

All the fingers on one of Hawk's hands were broken.

CHAPTER SEVENTEEN

Mirror of Confrontation

Qonja didn't bother to duck my signal when I came off duty. Nor did he raise any objections to accompanying me to an environome.

I ignored him at first, warming up the way Wonlee had showed me a few days before—what he called "a quick start after a long lull." I wasn't sure what I was feeling, outside of a determination to get to the truth, but I had no intentions of leaving that environome until I got what I wanted.

My target politely refused to arm himself against my *goreu*, and spent the next hour expertly dodging my attacks.

"This serves no purpose," he said, just like he had the last time.

"You be sure and tell my husband that. I signaled him right before I came to get you."

The door panel slid open behind us. "Cherijo." It was Reever, and he didn't sound happy.

"Hello, honey. Qonja here was just getting ready to tell me who he is. Aren't you, Qonja?"

The psych resident looked past me and his expression went from strained to relieved. "Captain."

Xonea approached us from the side, clearly upset himself. "ClanSister, what are you doing?"

I twirled my staff. "I'm going to beat some answers out of this man, if he ever holds still long enough."

"I shield the representative," Qonja blurted out. "This was not her doing. I— I provoked her by my actions, and I beg forgiveness of her for doing so."

Reever took the staff from my hand, and threw it across the room. "Does this satisfy you now, Xonea? Or would you see her kill him?"

I ignored that, and stared hard at Qonja. "What representative? What are you talking about?"

He remained on his knees, until Xonea made an impatient gesture, then Qonja rose and gave me a formal bow. "You, representative. I was ordered not to reveal this information to you by our Captain, until the Jado arrived."

"What information?" I turned to Xonea. "What is he babbling about?"

"A vote was taken some weeks ago, by the people." My ClanBrother put a big hand on my shoulder. "Qonja was sent to guard you until we could transfer you to the *CloudWalk*."

"Why?" I shouted.

What he said then was something so bizarre it barely registered. "You have been appointed to serve on the Ruling Council, Cherijo. You are now one of the leaders of Joren."

Before I could say anything, my husband dragged me back away from Xonea. "You are responsible for this."

My ClanBrother slowly nodded. "I made the recommendation to the other ClanLeaders. She will be taken back to Joren and kept safe from the League and the Hsktskt. No one would dare attack a world leader."

Which made sense out of the whole mess. Of course, Xonea would think having me appointed to the Council would protect me. He lived on a decent world, where people respected the rights of others.

I doubted my newly elected status would impress the League or the Hsktskt one bit.

"By doing this, you have attempted to violate the bond between me and my mate," Reever said, in flawless Jorenian.

"Wait." Panic made me grab him. "No, Reever, Xonea didn't violate anything."

His eyes, which had lost all color, shifted to my face. "He cages you with his politics, the same way Joseph caged you like a specimen. I will not have it." To my ClanBrother, he said, "I challenge you. Here, in one hour."

"I accept." The Captain made an eloquent, terse gesture. "One hour."

Somehow we had gone from me pretending to want Qonja dead to Reever and Xonea fighting over my future. "No. I won't let you two do this."

"I protect what is mine, too," Reever told me softly.

Qonja came to stand beside me as both men strode out of the environome. "Healer, I apologize. Perhaps if I had been permitted to tell you sooner, this might not have happened."

"No, Qonja." I stared at the door panel. "I think this has been brewing for a long time, and I'm just now seeing it."

I couldn't track down Reever or Xonea, so I ended up in Medical, wandering around the inpatient ward trying to figure out how to stop the two men I loved from killing each other. I was staring blindly at a patient's chart when I noticed a couple of the nurses having some trouble at the other end of the ward, and went over to help.

Dhreen lay on the berth, laughing and swatting at them as they attempted to take his vitals. "I'm fine, I'm fine." He saw me, and sat up. "Hey, Doc! What say we get out of here and play some whump-ball? I've got credits burning in my pocket, just waiting for you, how about it?"

"Dhreen, calm down." I took out my scanner and passed it over him. His heart rate and blood pressure were spiking.

"I told you, I'm fine." His eyes never stopped scanning our faces, and the nurses had to grab him again as he tried to climb off the berth. "Come on, Doc, lighten up! Let's have some fun, I'll spot you twenty points; what do you say?"

He didn't stop talking, but I tuned him out as I prepared a syrinpress. "How long has he been like this?" I asked one of the nurses.

"Most of the day. One of the engineering staff brought him in when he was found toying with a prep unit in the galley."

"Toying?" I injected Dhreen with a mild tranquilizer.

"I believe the crewman said the pilot was offering to prepare traditional Oenrallian dishes for everyone who wished to use the unit."

I checked the time, and saw the hour was nearly up. "All right, keep him quiet, and monitor his vitals closely." As Dhreen settled down, I unfastened his tunic to check the shunt, but the mold was gone. "Put another Lok-Teel on him and strap him down, if the dose wears off before I get back."

Squilyp caught up with me in the corridor. "I heard the news. What provoked Reever into challenging the Captain?"

"I've been elected to Joren's Ruling Council. Whether I like it or not."

The Omorr grimaced. "That would do it."

I quickly briefed him on the latest development with Dhreen, while he updated me on Hawk. As we entered the environome with a crowd of crew members, Squilyp said, "It seems visiting their homeworlds did neither of them any good."

"You can't go home again," I agreed, then stopped. Someone bumped into me and apologized, but I simply waved them on. "That's it. That's the connection I was looking for."

"I don't understand."

"They both visited their homeworlds after an extended absence. Think about it." I led my boss to the gallery seating, and pulled him down on a chair beside me. "Hawk had never been to Taerca, and Dhreen's been away for about the same amount of time. Their immune systems couldn't cope."

"The biodecon prior to landing on both worlds would have identified any bacteria detrimental to them."

"I don't think it's bacterial. It's something else."

Squilyp's dark eyes narrowed. "We will have to obtain biosphere samples to test—food, soil, air, and water. I doubt, however, that either species shall willingly provide us with them."

"Reever sent a remote probe to Jxinok. He could do the same thing again for Oenrall and Taerca." I looked out at the warriors quad, where my husband and Xonea stood facing each other. "God, I've got to stop this."

"Yes, you must." Salo came and sat down on the other side of me. When my brows rose, he added, "Qonja came to me and explained what has happened. I think I can help, if you'll allow me to do so." He placed an ancient Jorenian book in my hands. "These are the very first laws created for our people."

I was afraid to open it, it was so fragile. "And there's something in here that will keep them from killing each other?"

"Yes." He opened it to a central passage, and pointed to a heading mark identical to the pictoglyph Qonja wore on his vocollar. "Listen, and I will translate for you."

It took a few minutes for Salo to interpret the symbols for me. As I listened, I watched both men warming up. Xonea seemed even more enormous than ever, his muscles bulkier, his entire frame emanating sheer, animal power.

Reever, who would never be as tall or muscular as the Captain, had other advantages—speed and agility, which he demonstrated by going through a number of those odd, inhuman moves the Hsktskt had taught him.

Watching them made me realize for once just how dangerous both of them were.

"That is all that is written, but I believe it is enough," Salo said when he finished translating the passage.

"I can't do this unless I say okay to the whole deal, right?" Which was going to make my husband furious, but would keep him alive.

My friend made a cautious gesture. "You must assume the appointment in order to take advantage of the law."

"An appointment for life—a life for two lives." My lips twisted. "Not a bad deal, really."

"Are you certain?" Squilyp asked.

The gallery fell silent as Xonea turned to address the crowd. "Ship's Linguist Reever has challenged me, by the right of bond. I have freely accepted, thus no retribution will be taken against Reever, should he prevail."

Reever only stood, silent and waiting. I nearly got out of my seat then, but Salo clamped a hand on my arm. "Patience, ClanCousin. It must go to the point of death-strike, and only then can you act."

"You'd better be right about this, Salo."

Xonea returned to his position in the quad, and nodded to Reever. An eerie silence fell over the gallery as both men entered the central quad, circling each other. They seemed to do that forever, until Xonea feinted to one side and slammed into Reever from the other. My husband pivoted in the same direction of the blow to his abdomen, and returned the favor.

Then the gallery exploded with shouting voices, and the two began to literally beat the life out of each other.

My chest tightened as I watched, and waited. I couldn't help the sounds I made when either of them took a fist or kick to their body, couldn't help the tears that welled in my eyes as I saw the first splatters of red and green blood stain the quad's surface.

"I can't wait," I said to Salo, my voice cracking.

"You must." He put an arm around me. "Be strong for them now."

The fight went on. At first it seemed Xonea had a greater advantage, with his superior size and strength, but slowly Reever began moving faster, working up to that blurry, frightening speed he had used in the past. After fifteen minutes, both men were covered with bruises and contusions, and panting from pain and exertion, but Reever seemed to be holding his own.

I kept flinching and jerking as each blow landed, almost feeling them on my own body. The tears in my eyes now streamed down my face, and I couldn't smother my sobs. Salo's arm tightened, and he placed the book in my hands.

"Now it comes," he murmured.

The crowd fell silent as Reever flipped down on his stomach, almost completely prone, then vaulted up and back when Xonea tried to straddle him. Somehow he got the Captain facedown on the quad, one strong arm locked around his blue neck. The Jorenian thrashed and writhed under my husband, but it was obvious he wasn't going to get out of the hold.

"Now." Salo thrust the book into my hands, and I jumped up and ran for the quad.

"Ruling Council intercedes!" I shouted as loudly as I could, to be heard over the now-roaring crowd. "Stop the challenge and adhere to what I say now!"

Duncan looked up, his face a battered mask of blood. He frowned, as if not quite sure it was me. Reluctantly, he released Xonea, and got to his feet. "What are you doing?"

The Captain slowly rose, rubbing his throat. "You cannot stop us."

"I just did. According the First Laws of Joren"—I held up Salo's book—"a member of the Ruling Council can and will intercede in any matter pertaining to the welfare of the HouseClans. Xonea, you yourself had me appointed to the Council, and know that I may speak for them in their absence."

"That is only during times of conflict, when the Council members are separated."

I deliberately gazed around me. "I don't see any Council members around here, do you?"

"They can be signaled," the Captain insisted.

"Our communications array is not functioning, Captain." Salo came down to stand beside me. "I believe it will take several days to perform the necessary repairs."

"We are not in the middle of a conflict," Reever pointed out.

I'd anticipated that, too. "HouseClan Jado goes to negotiate peace in the League/Hsktskt conflict. By doing so, Joren enters the war and under those conditions, I am obliged to protect our people."

"Say what you will, wife." Reever wiped some blood from his eye. "You are not joining their Council."

"By announcing the intercession, I already have." I shook my head at him when he would have responded, then turned to the crew. "Duncan Reever has prevailed, and by doing so has the right to divert ClanLeader Torin's path. However, our people must have a ClanLeader who understands the war we have entered. As there is no Torin with more experience in dealing with the League and the Hsktskt, Xonea cannot be replaced. The law reads that the needs of the Clan are more important than any one of the House, and by that law, I declare this challenge is ended."

Reever stared at me for a moment, then limped out of the environome.

"What would you have said if I had prevailed?" Xonea asked me.

"The HouseClan also needs allies willing to help them prevail over their enemies," I said, and handed the book to Salo before slipping my arm around the Captain. "In case you haven't noticed, Reever is the best ally we have."

His pain-filled eyes met mine. "I knew you would not wish to join the Council. Why did you do this?"

"You left me no choice, and we'll talk about it later. Let's get you to Medical."

"You will serve Joren well," one of the crew said as he passed us.

I smiled, only a little bitterly. "Now that I have no choice, I guess I'd better."

I confined the Captain to a medical berth and a dermal regenerator for the night. "You're not scaring my kid by letting her see you like this," I said when he objected. "Sleep. We can discuss the hows and whys of this tomorrow, when you're apologizing to me."

He took my hand in his before I pulled the regenerator over him. "I regret my actions provoked your bondmate, ClanSister."

"Me, too." I bent over and kissed him. "Good night, champ."

I had the feeling Reever wouldn't go back to our quarters looking the way he did, so I took my medical case and went to his second-favorite place on the ship. It meant taking a gyrlift all the way down to level thirty-five.

Beneath the transparent panels of the observation dome, a lone figure sat in the dark, staring at the stars. He didn't turn around when I stepped off the lift. "What are you doing here?"

"I came to watch you sulk." I switched on the lights, then sat down beside him to survey the damage. "And bleed." I pushed his head to one side to get a better look at a nasty gash above his ear. That and a dozen other small wounds were still oozing, so I opened my case. "Xonea looks worse, if that helps."

"Xonea *lost*." There was some deep, primitive satisfaction in the way he said those two words.

"You would have killed him out of jealousy over me."

"No. But I would have killed him for changing who you are."

I stopped blotting up blood and sat back. "What?"

He lifted a swollen hand, and brushed a piece of hair from my face. "Xonea is a warrior. He wishes you to become a warrior. To be truly Jorenian, like his people. He wants you to lead them, to fight for them."

I chuckled. "Boy, is he going to be disappointed, because I don't have to—"

He pressed his finger against my mouth. "He will teach you to kill for them, beloved. That is the truth of why I challenged him. That I cannot allow."

It hurt me, oddly, to hear him say that. "Don't you trust me to do the right thing?"

"When I was enslaved by the Hsktskt, I tried to do the same. Each time I prevailed in the arena, I refused to kill. The centurons forced me to watch as they executed my opponent, then they beat me for defying them." He looked out at the stars. "The Hsktskt do not encourage disobedience, and the beatings became increasingly vicious. After several bouts, I knew I would not be able to physically endure another and prevail again in the arena. I wanted to live. So I killed my next opponent, to save myself." He closed his eyes. "I felt his blood on my hands for years."

I wrapped his hand with a sterile dressing while I tried to conceal my horror and think of how to reassure him. All I could come up with was, "I'm not a slave anymore, Duncan. I'm a physician, and I won't kill."

"There are many types of enslavement, and many ways to kill." He got up and held out his bandaged hand to me. "Let's go home."

The *Sunlace* left Oenrall space and headed for the planet we now assumed was Jxinok. I didn't have much time to contemplate what would happen when Reever and I went down to the surface during that interval. Hawk's psychosis wasn't responding to dose-limiting him on antipsychotics, and Dhreen had become so manic that restraints were required around the clock.

"The latest series of toxicologies show no sign of pathogenic infection," Savetka said as she handed me the lab results on our two patients. "No similarities between the cases have been identified, either."

"There has to be something that triggered this. Something in the environments." I thought for a moment. "When do the probes get back?"

After I explained my theory, Reever had supervised sending off the remote drones to Oenrall and Taerca. Like Squilyp, he wasn't sure my environment theory was viable—biodecon always took care of native bugs—but didn't offer a debate. Neither did the Captain when I requested permission to launch the probes. In the aftermath of the bout I'd stopped, we were all trying to be extremely civilized.

"I believe they were programmed to return within the week." Savetka stared at the chart in my hands. "Is something amiss, Healer?"

"No, why?"

She nodded at my hands. "You are leaving marks in the casing."

I glanced down and saw my fingers were digging into the chart so hard that I was leaving nail marks in the plas. "Sorry." I handed it back to her. "I think I'll take a break. Signal me in the galley if I'm needed."

Walking down to get a cup of tea—I wasn't hungry—didn't seem to burn off the extra energy I was feeling. Neither did three games of whump-ball or beating the two administrative assistants who played against me.

I found myself standing in front of an exterior viewer, watching as the ship assumed orbit above a small, sandy-colored world.

Go home, Cherijo.

The server I'd absently carried from the galley slipped from my fingers, and smashed on the deck. My hands were up and pressing against the plas panel separating me from the cold, instant death outside the ship, and still I heard my fingernails screech across the unyielding surface. A vague throbbing started in my temples as I pressed my brow harder and harder against the viewer.

Go home, just go home—

"Healer?"

I snapped out of my self-induced trance and looked to one side. "Yes?"

Qonja, who now had no reason to hide his real job as my personal advisor and all-around bodyguard, bent down to pick up the pieces of my ruined server. "You seem disturbed."

"Impatient," I corrected him, and knelt down to help. "I want to get to this over with as soon as possible."

"The Jado will arrive shortly, as will the representatives from Oenrall and Taerca." He took the shards from my hand and carried them over to a nearby disposal unit. "We should discuss how it will go for you, as a Council representative."

"I thought all I had to do was listen."

"You will be Joren's final authority. An open relay with the remainder of the Council will be maintained, of course, but there is no guarantee any signal will go through without mishap."

"Then I may get to decide the fate of two or three worlds." I went back to pressing my head against the viewer. "They didn't cover this in Medtech."

He looked as upset as I felt. "We can review historic precedent, if it will make you feel more at ease with your duties."

"Narcotics wouldn't dent my discomfort at this point." I eyed him. "How would you feel about doing some sparring with me?"

"Will you be using that staff of yours?"

I grinned. "Not if you give up your swords."

Sparring with Qonja helped release some of the odd tension I'd been feeling, and made me more receptive to the news Duncan brought home from work that day.

"Sensor sweeps show no indications of past conflict on the planet's surface," he told me as I stepped out of the cleanser. "It is also a very ancient world. More than six billion years in existence."

I took the towel he handed me, and rubbed my face in it. "So when we go down there, we won't see some wasteland of blasted, lifeless rubble?"

"There are some very old ruins which appear to be the last traces of whatever civilization occupied the world. They are slowly being reclaimed by the rising water table." He took another towel and began to dry my hair. "Other than a variety of small mammals and benign botanicals, the planet is uninhabited."

"When do we go?"

"Tomorrow." He stopped rubbing and moved my hair to one side, away from a bruise on my shoulder. "You've been sparring again?"

"With Qonja. He knows almost as much as Wonlee does, and I don't have to worry about stumbling into him and getting spiked." I turned in his arms, and rubbed my cheek against his bare chest. "He's only teaching me self-defense."

He was quiet for a minute, then he tossed the towel aside and lifted me up into his arms. "Someday I want to see all these new moves of yours."

We nearly made it to the bed when the door panel chimed. By the time I was dressed enough to answer it, Marel had woken up and gotten to the panel ahead of me. Garphawayn stood on the threshold.

My daughter yawned as she pointed up at Lady Cestes's unhappy face. "Parkwy wady here, Mama."

"Thanks, sweetie. Go back to bed for me, okay?"

Reever appeared, and led our kid back to her chamber.

"I do not wish to intrude." Squilyp's ex-fiancée swept her hand to the side, making ornaments jingle. "I will come back tomorrow."

Normally I wouldn't have argued with that, but something told me she was in trouble. "No, that's okay. Come in."

She declined my offer of a drink, and sat down gingerly on the edge of my favorite chair. Since it was his, too, Jenner came over to sniff at her foot and give her the eye. Strangely, his close proximity didn't make her sneeze.

I rubbed a hand over the back of my neck before sitting across from her. "What can I do for you, Garphawayn?"

"Lord Maftuda has refused to reinitiate contract negotiations." She adjusted one of her gildrell rings. "I find I cannot bear to linger on this vessel another day."

"From what I understand, the Omorr can't come and get you until we leave this quadrant."

"They cannot. That is why . . . I would like to

know . . ." She paused as Reever came out of Marel's bedroom, and moved to stand behind me. As he placed a hand on my shoulder, her expression became even more miserable. "I wish to accompany you and the sojourn team tomorrow. Would you permit that, Council representative?"

Although she might prove more of a hindrance than anything, I didn't have the heart to turn her down. "Duncan, have we got room on the launch for one more?"

"We can accommodate several passengers. Lady Cestes is welcome to join us."

I nodded. "There's one thing you should know—Alunthri, our Chakacat friend, will be going with us."

"I shall take another dose of antihistamine prior to launch." Garphawayn rose majestically. "I extend my gratitude to you both, and will intrude on your privacy no longer."

I beat her to the door panel. "Are you all right?"

She kept her head up and her spine straight. "In time, perhaps, I shall be." She looked down at me. "Your concern is unnecessary, Lady Torin. I do not believe I deserve it."

"I disagree," I said, smiled, and opened the panel for her. "Try to get some rest."

After she'd gone, I noticed Reever was smiling, too. "What's so funny?"

"You despise that female, and still you offer her sympathy."

"She may be the biggest pain in the posterior I've ever met, but she's hurting. And she took an antihistamine before she came over." I went to check on Marel, then took Duncan to bed. "She's in love with Squilyp, you know."

He rolled me over on top of him and held me against his chest. "I know."

I lifted my head. "We difficult females have to stick together. Especially when we fall in love with difficult males."

"I'm easy," Duncan assured me.

"If you only knew." I bent down to kiss him.

From the moment the launch left the *Sunlace*, my nervous tension escalated, until I had to slip out of my harness or start shrieking. Garphawayn watched me curiously as I paced the interior passenger cabin.

"Are you well, Lady Torin?"

I knew she was paying me a compliment, addressing me as an equal, but I was no lady. "Cherijo, please. I'm fine. Just a little jittery."

The female Omorr looked down at the other end of the cabin, where Alunthri was sitting, and sniffed. "As I have already taken the required dosage of allergen medication, perhaps you could convince your feline friend to join us."

"Alunthri." I gestured, and pointed to a seat on the opposite side of the female Omorr. "She's taken medication, so it's safe. Come on over here."

The Chakacat smiled as it slipped from its harness and joined us. "I was hoping to have an opportunity to speak with Lady Cestes regarding art on her homeworld."

"You are an admirer of art?" This was said with a certain amount of skepticism.

"I have devoted several years to the study of it." Alunthri went on to describe some of the cultures and art forms it had collected photoscans, recordings, and other data on.

"I had no idea a—a feline entity would have such

an awareness of the subtleties involved with self-expression," Garphawayn said. "I must tell you about the many forms of personal embellishment we have cultivated on Omorr."

That discussion would have put me to sleep, but Duncan was busy calculating the proper trajectory angle to enter the atmosphere, so I didn't bug him. Something else was wrong, though. I'd gotten to the point where I felt like I might jump out of my skin.

"How much longer is this going to take?" I muttered.

"It is a routine planetary expedition, Doctor." The female Omorr covered her face with a membrane, and sneezed. "Forgive me, Alunthri, but due to the amount of dander in the air, I believe I must have another dose of medication."

The Chakacat sniffed the air, then slipped out of its harness. "That is not from me." It tracked whatever it was smelling to one of the lower storage containers, and opened it.

"Hi, Wundri!" My daughter crawled out, holding Juliet and two kittens. "Surprise, Mama!"

"Marel." My jaw sagged, then snapped closed. "How the hell did you get in here?"

"I wan come wid you."

I swiveled toward the helm. "Reever."

Duncan looked over his shoulder, then made an abrupt turn. "I'm heading back to the ship."

"Good." I grabbed my kid and strapped her into a harness. "I don't know you managed this one. Sweetie, what were you thinking? Do you know how dangerous this is?"

"Daddy said room for more."

I rubbed my brow. "Oh, boy."

"She must have overheard us speaking last night."

Garphawayn hopped over and sat down beside my daughter. "You have frightened your parents, child. You should apologize for your impulsive behavior; it is not good to distress those you love."

My little girl almost gave her The Pout, but Garphawayn only raised her brow ridges. Marel bowed her small blond head. "Sorry I noddy, Mama."

"It's okay." I glanced at the Omorr. "Teach me how you did that."

"It has been my observation that children as precocious as your daughter respond well to firm authority. You would do better to establish that with her yourself." Garphawayn covered her face and sneezed. "Alunthri, if you would be so kind?"

The Chakacat took all three cats from Marel and secured them in a container at the back of the launch. I went to the helm to see how far we had traveled.

"Fifteen minutes, and we'll have her back on the ship."

"And grounded for another week," I said. "Duncan, you performed a pre-launch inspection, didn't you?"

"Yes."

"Then would you mind telling me how in blazes she got in here?"

"I have some ideas." He didn't look too happy about them, either. "We'll discuss them with our daughter after the sojourn."

When I went back to the passenger cabin, Alunthri was still securing the cats' container, and the female Omorr was listening to Marel as she prattled on about the "pree dars" and "fwowers." The launch shook, then the engines made a strange sound.

"Watch her," I said to Garphawayn, then returned to the helm.

Reever was struggling to stabilize the launch, so I

strapped into the copilot's harness and activated the board. "Duncan, we're losing power to the engines."

He performed another rolling manuever and turned the launch back toward the planet. "I'll have to land it on the surface. Signal Command."

I tried to relay our status to the *Sunlace,* but the communications array had also lost power. "Transmitter's down. I can't get through to them."

Neither one of us said anything, but we were both thinking the same thing: *All these power failures were way too convenient for mere coincidence.*

"Prep for emergency landing."

I went back to do what needed to be done in the passenger cabin. The ride into the lower atmosphere was bumpy, but Marel only giggled and bounced in her harness.

Garphawayn noticed my expression, and reached over to touch my hand with her membrane. "Your husband is a skilled pilot, is he not?"

"Yes, it's just—" I glanced down at the tiny blonde between us. "She's the only kid I'll ever have."

"I envy you her." She sat back. "I doubt I will have any now."

The interior of the launch turned dark as Duncan shut down power to all unnecessary systems, to prevent flash fires. Finally the surface swelled up to fill the viewports, and we landed with a series of jolts and crashes beneath our feet.

Something crackled over our heads as we unstrapped ourselves and Marel.

"Take her for me," I said as I ran to help Alunthri retrieve the cats and grab my medical pack. I glanced back to see Garphawayn bounce out, holding Marel firmly clasped in her three arms. "Are you okay?"

"I am fine." The Chakacat looked out through the hull doors. "We are stranded here?"

"For a while. Let's get out of here before something blows."

Duncan secured the helm, then met us at the docking ramp. "Any injuries?"

"I don't think so." I hurried down to make sure of that, then took a deep breath of cool air and finally noticed our surroundings. If the sky had been green instead of bluish-white, we could have been back on K-2. "So far so good. Duncan?"

My husband had ducked under the launch, and reappeared a few seconds later. "Power conduits to the engines are fused."

Alunthri straightened. "Can you signal the ship?"

He shook his head. "The transmitter is in the same shape. I'll get the survival gear from the cabin."

CHAPTER EIGHTEEN

From the Repository

Maggie's world was, in fact, a milder version of Kevarzangia Two, with thick forests interspersed with rolling plains. None of the native botanicals looked familiar, but none scanned as poisonous to us, so we set up a makeshift camp in a clearing a short distance from the launch. The temporary shelters would serve as our home away from home until the rescue team from the ship arrived.

"How long?"

"They won't be able to activate our receiver, so they'll assume the communications array has been damaged." Reever gazed up at the sky, then back at our disabled launch. "Xonea will send a rescue team for us in two rotations."

"With the negotiations between Taerca and Oenrall scheduled to begin, won't he come after us any sooner?"

"Perhaps."

"Mama?" Our daughter darted between us, and grabbed my leg. "Caw Uncwip come down see?"

"Not yet, honey. Daddy has to fix the transmitter."

Garphawayn declared she was famished, and Alunthri called Marel over to help it prepare an impromptu picnic for all of us.

I led Reever off a short distance, and kept my voice low. "There's nothing else we can do?"

"No." He kept staring at the launch. "This was intentional." At my blank look, he explained, "The power failures, the conduits fusing. And the transmitter. The only cause of that kind of damage is a massive energy surge."

"I don't remember an energy surge."

"There wasn't one. All systems were functioning at optimum levels from the time we left launch bay."

I noticed some small eyes watching us from the ground cover and nodded in their direction. "Someone is interested in us."

Reever took out a proximity device and swept the area. "Four of them, six kilos in weight, warm-blooded." He knelt down and removed his wristcom, rolling it so that the sunlight flashed off the shiny surfaces. At the same time, he made a low, whirring sound.

Slowly, a diminutive creature crept out of the foliage, and approached, its attention fixed on the wristcom. Short brown fur covered its six-limbed body and long tail. The shape of its head reminded me a little of a cat, with the pointed ears and slanted eyes, but the body and mouth were completely alien in structure. Three more near-cats of similar sizes followed.

Once it sniffed Reever's hand, it looked up at both of us and made an inquisitive, chittering sound.

So far Marel hadn't noticed them, but she loved anything with fur. "Do you think they bite?"

"Let's find out." Reever carefully stroked a finger under the near-cat's chin, and it made a high-pitched squeal and undulated with pleasure against his hand.

"Wook, Mama!" Marel toddled over, holding a pair of her own. They crawled up onto her shoulders, and licked her face while making more of the squealing, happy sounds. Alunthri followed, holding a couple more in its arms. "New kiddies!"

More near-cats emerged from the forest, until there were nearly a hundred in our camp. Jxinok's only inhabitants proved too good-natured to resist, and we spent most of the afternoon watching them play with Marel, Alunthri, and each other. Garphawayn at first kept her distance, but their fur didn't seem to aggravate her allergies, and the near-cats ended up crawling all over her, too.

"They appear to be very healthy," I said after scanning the largest of the horde. "Stomach contents indicate they're herbivores, and have at least six distinct gender variations. I'd love to know how they reproduce."

"Perhaps they are like me," Alunthri said, stroking one small near-kitten with its paw.

"Cherijo." The female Omorr divested her lap of felines and rose on her foot. "Would you care to walk with me a short distance? I feel in need of some exercise."

Alunthri agreed to keep an eye on Marel, so Garphawayn and I took a tour of the bushes around the clearing. She didn't seem to notice the strange and beautiful varieties of flora, and only answered me absently when I commented on them.

"That's pretty much it for my supply of small talk," I said after a few minutes. "Is something on your mind?"

She plucked a flower and studied it intently. "This is rather like the tafar blossoms we grow on Omorr, but it is too red." Without skipping a beat, she added, "I am not certain how to go about it, but I would like to renegotiate my position with Lord Maftuda."

"Okay." I knew as much about Omorr marriage contracts as I did the flowers. "How can I help?"

She stopped hopping. "I rather expected you to persuade me to return to Omorr. You have made your
opinion of me only too plain."

I spotted a couple of shiny pebbles and picked them
up, Marel loved pretty rocks. "Squilyp is my best friend.
I wasn't sure you were good enough for him."

"And now you do?"

I smiled. "When I first met Squilyp, he drove me
nuts. He was so picky and snotty and thought he was a
better doctor than I was. We spent more time arguing
than we did consulting. I couldn't stand him. And then
I had to fight him."

"He told me about forcing you to make the solicitation. He is not proud of what he did."

"Neither am I. Still, it changed things. We apologized
to each other, and started over. We learned to respect
each other and became friends." I glanced at her stiff expression. "Maybe you and I could do the same."

"I have never had a Terran friend." She tossed the
flower away. "I have never had many friends at all."

"So we'll practice."

She made a *hmmmming* sound. "That may work for
friendship, but Squilyp is a different matter."

"The relationships may be different, but the same
theory works both ways."

"You have an advantage that I do not. You share your
calling with Squilyp, while I know nothing about medicine."

"It doesn't matter. Garphawayn, he's a good man.
Yes, he's one of the best surgeons I've ever seen. It was
his skill that saved many lives, including my daughter's. But that's not all he is." I met her dark gaze. "He
wants to share his life with someone. He wants a child."

Her rings clinked as her gildrells curled and un-
curled. "I am well-acquainted with that feeling."

I turned to her. "Then you're going to have to fight, too. Fight for him. Don't let him go."

Her skin turned a faint purple. "He does not love me."

"What have you done that would make him love you?"

She thought about that for a moment. "I see your point. Yet I fear it is already too late for me to begin negotiations again."

"Let me tell you a story about me and my husband," I said, as we headed back across the clearing.

When we arrived back in camp, Juliet and the kittens were yowling in their container.

"They wish to come out and play," Alunthri said as it tried to soothe the Terran cats with some dried salmon bits. Juliet, who had never been one to refuse food, only kicked them back out through the screened panel.

The near-cats were curious about them, to the point of crawling all over the container, but that didn't mean the two species would get along.

"We can't let them out, I'm afraid. If they take off into the forest, we might never find them again."

My big mistake was not explaining any of that to my daughter. A few minutes later, as Garphawayn and I were debating how to arrange the sleeping pallets, I heard Marel shout.

"Juweeyed!"

Through the opening in the shelter tent, I watched the former stray female dart through the camp, followed by her two kittens, and disappear into the forest. My daughter ran after them, calling for them to come back.

"Oh, hell, she let them out. Alunthri, help!" I ran after her.

Fallen branches snapped under my feet and leaves whipped my face as I ran through the forest. The Chakacat ran much faster than I did, so I wasn't surprised to see it flash by a few moments later. Distantly, I heard Duncan and Garphawayn following me, but was too busy keeping my eyes on the small blond head bobbing through the foliage to pay attention to my back. Then I lost sight of her, and started yelling.

"Marel? Marel! Answer me! Marel!"

By the time I heard her little voice call back, I was deep in the forest. I found her sitting at the base of a tree, holding a panting Juliet in her arms.

"Mama, see?" She held up Jenner's mate, making the two kittens sitting at her feet meow. "I caud her!"

I snatched the cat from her hands. "Don't you ever run away from me like that again!"

I'd never yelled at Marel before, and she looked as if I'd slapped her. "Mama? You mad ad me?"

"Yes!" I took a breath. "No, no I was just scared." Then, seeing how upset she was, I caved in. "I'm sorry I shouted at you, baby."

She flung herself into my arms. At the same time, something hit me in the side of the neck and stung me. I slapped my hand up and came away with a small, green insect squashed over my palm. "Ugh. Let's go back now, honey."

Going back proved to be more of a challenge than I thought, as I hadn't paid attention to landmarks or direction while I'd been chasing down my kid. After a few minutes of yelling for Alunthri and Reever and wandering around, I began to feel a strange, heavy lethargy creep over me.

I reached up and felt the small bite on my neck. It was starting to swell, which meant a reaction. My immune system would respond efficiently, but I might not be able to stay conscious in the interim.

"Marel, listen to me." I turned her face toward me with my palm. "I've been stung by something, and it's making me sick. We need to find a place to wait for Daddy, and you have to stay by me. Even if I fall asleep, okay?"

"Okay, Mama." She curled her little hand in mine.

I looked for a relatively safe place, but the forest was thick and my legs weren't working properly. I staggered over something bumpy and tripped, falling forward into some moss. Under the moss was something hard, cold and smooth, and I tried to roll away.

The ground seemed to open up, and I dropped down six inches. "Marel!"

My daughter leaned over the recess, her small face smiling. "Sleep now, Mama?"

I held up my arms, which felt like lead piping. "Come to me, baby. Take a nap with me."

She climbed down and curled up at my side, one arm across my stomach. "Daddy come soon?"

"Soon . . ." I pulled her up on top of me, and wrapped my arms around her. Juliet and the kittens jumped down, and nestled around my legs.

I watched through bleary eyes as Marel fell asleep, all the while trying desperately to stay awake myself. Whatever poison was in me was having a direct effect on my brain, as I began to see a faint, hazy glow creeping up around us. I managed to turn my head, and saw a patch of stone through the moss, also glowing brightly.

Is it some kind of weapon?

Above us, something rustled. I blinked as dozens of the near-cats came to the edge of the recess, and sat down. They were no longer making the funny chittering sound, and seemed to be waiting for something.

Then the glow intensified, and something hurtled me, still clutching my sleeping daughter, into an abyss.

For a time I dreamed of nothing but darkness. Unfamiliar, weighted darkness that seemed to drain the energy out of my entire body, making me a part of it.

Am I dead? Did she lie to me? Is this death?

There was no tunnel of light, no voice to guide me. I fell deeper, growing weaker until I nearly lost all sense of myself. Then an incredible warmth enveloped me, like a heated blanket, and life seeped back into my limbs.

"You're not dead, Joey. Wake up."

For once, I almost happy to hear that voice. "Maggie?"

"Come on, baby. Up and at 'em." Hands lifted me, touched my face, shook me lightly.

I didn't regain consciousness so much as I jerked back into it, feeling absolute panic. Light blinded me as I opened my eyes. "Marel!"

"She's right here."

As my vision adjusted to the light, I saw I was still holding my daughter's sleeping body. "Thank God." I rested my cheek against the top of her head, then looked around. "Maggie?"

"So this is the little demon."

My former maternal influencer appeared in front of us, in the tailored gray-and-white uniform Joseph Grey Veil had made her wear while she cared for me. It only emphasized the brassy blaze of her red hair and hinted at the voluptuous curves underneath. Whenever we'd gone out in public, men had practically tripped over their tongues, watching her saunter around.

As she stepped forward and reached toward Marel, I stepped back. "Don't."

"Jesus Christ, Cherijo, I'm not going to hurt the little rug rat. Wow." Maggie smiled down at my daughter. "She's really cute. Much prettier than you were at this age. Must take after Dunkie."

Everything was different than it had been before. I had no idea or even a sense of where we were. It was just me and Maggie and Marel, hanging in the midst of a glowing, soft white light.

This wasn't like any of the subliminal, implanted memory-whatevers she'd sprung on me before. "Where are we? What is this?"

"You're in the planetary repository." My former companion lifted a hand, and beyond the glow I saw vague outlines of stone walls and huge machinery. "Give it a minute; it's been quite a while since it started up."

"Are we really here, or is this inside my head?"

"We're really not in Kansas anymore, Dorothy." She looked down at my daughter. "Which reminds me. Much as I would love to hear all your mom war stories, she's got to go back for a little while." She snapped her fingers, and my arms jerked as Marel vanished.

"No!" I whirled around, searching the now-solid stone chamber we stood in. I turned and lunged at Maggie. "What did you do to her?"

I hit an invisible wall, and went down, hard. The weakness returned, and for several seconds I thought I'd passed out again.

"Joey, Joey." Strong arms lifted me up on my feet and held me steady. "She's perfectly safe. I've made sure of it. The repository requires a level of tolerance, and she needs to grow a bit more before she can visit her Grandma Maggie."

Her voice was louder, stronger. I opened my eyes,

and focused on her face. "All right. I'm here. I did what you wanted. Now tell me everything—what you want, why you got me involved, everything."

"And make it snappy?" Maggie chuckled. "I will, baby. Just let me slip into something more comfortable first."

She stepped away, leaving me to find my balance. The nearest wall was more than fifty yards away, and covered with intricate panels of alloy and crystal unlike any mechanism or device I'd ever seen. Some parts of the panel seemed to vibrate, operating at a blur, while others gave off varying degrees of the glow. There were no pictographs or alphabet to indicate the language of whoever had built it, but from the shape of some of the parts it would take a wide, dexterous hand to work them.

A hand with five articulated joints.

Maggie's form changed, blurring from a the voluptuous Terran redhead to another being altogether. One with straight, dark hair streaming from a long, high skull with slits instead of ears. Bejeweled yellow ribbons hung in a diagonal fringe over her slanted, dark eyes. The companion's uniform lengthened to a strange gown made up of knotted folds. The fabric glowed, then brightened to the same shade as the ribbons.

Unearthly serenity settled over her expression. "Does it disturb you to see this form?"

"I'm not crazy about the screaming-yellow outfit," I said.

"As Maggie would say, this is the real deal, so get used to it." The slim, elegant alien moved her hand an inch to the right, and the wall devices seemed to go into a frenzy. "Physical form has its limitations, but my kind have always been enchanted with its possibilities."

"Who are your kind?"

"Language also has its restrictions. To phrase it at your level of understanding, we were, are, and will be the Jxin."

"Congratulations." I made a slow circle. "And this place? You called it a repository. Can you phrase that a little better for the dumb Terran?"

"Wherever the Jxin dwell, we create storage places. That is all this is. Unfortunately, only modified beings such as yourself can access them." Before I could reply, she smiled. "You want to know what 'modified' means and why you would access a place like this and what is stored here. Perhaps it would be better to do this in my Maggie persona." An instant later, she had returned to the redheaded Terran female form. "Better?"

I had the feeling I was supposed to be in awe of these transformations. I wasn't. "Nice magic tricks, but could we move along now?"

"Always anxious to cut to the chase, huh?" Maggie laughed. "Okay, baby. Here we go." She put two fingers in her mouth, and let out a loud whistle.

The repository disappeared, replaced by the forests of Jxinok. Not the Jxinok I had come to, though. Huge trees sprang up around us, growing thick and lush from a primordial black soil. Leafy fernlike bushes as big as star vessels hung in midair. Flowers crowded each other, growing in wild disarray and studding everything from the tree canopy to the moss under our feet.

"This is what Jxinok looked when my kind moved in. Gorgeous, isn't it?" She took my arm and led me forward, following a natural path through the dense trees. "This is just one of great spots—you should have seen the valley of waterfalls over on the northeastern continent. We fell in love with this place at first sight."

"You're not from this planet?"

"Um, no. We don't know where we're from. Actually,

we've never exactly come from anywhere. Existence is—" She shook her head. "Let's skip that part for now. It's one of those concepts that takes a few centuries to figure out."

We left the tree line and I nearly choked as a huge, towering city of pure crystal pushed up from the earth, as if growing under the yellow sun.

"My place is right over there," Maggie said, pointing to a particularly beautiful transparent column. Inside, several other elegant aliens were occupied with various domestic chores. "I really miss the view. From there you can see the whole valley."

Light glittered through the transparent structures, spinning moving rainbows through the air. I could smell flowers and hear laughter drifting on the air. "Must have been a real job, washing windows."

She laughed. "We had a little help."

"Those machines I saw in the repository?"

"Something like that, only bigger, and in orbit. We used our . . . machines . . . to build a couple of thousand cities here, like this one. The Jxin would have happily stayed here forever."

"But?"

"Smart girl." She rubbed a hand over my head. "We found out we couldn't stay." She walked over and touched her hand to one outer wall, and an opening appeared. "Come on, you'll really like this."

I followed her, gawking at the beautiful people and wondrous sights inside. "Why would you want to leave?"

She nodded toward a couple who were embracing each other. "Watch."

The same glow that had enveloped me and Marel in the recess formed around the couple. Slowly, their bodies fused together, then dwindled, leaving only a pool of light hanging in the air. A few seconds later, that disappeared.

"It's what we called transcending, but we only did it when we wanted to before we came here. Something in this reality triggers it. We're still trying to find out what."

"What happened to those two people?"

"They're existing in another dimension. At least, we think they are. We've gotten pretty scattered over time, and lost track of each other."

What could I say? "Oh, not good."

"Really not good. Despite all our efforts, remaining corporeal became damn near impossible for us. We found a way to control the transcension, but we couldn't stop it." She frowned as she paused by a crystalline fountain, and trailed her fingers through the water. "I sure liked being solid, too."

"You're not solid after that glow gets you?"

"No, baby. We've always moved through different dimensional incarnations, but none of them could be permanent. Not even when we wanted to stay that way."

I covered my head as something exploded nearby. "What is that? What's happening?"

"That? Just some raiders." Maggie made a shoo-shoo gesture toward a group of vicious-looking beings storming the structure. They shot down everyone in sight. "They attacked us after we visited their world and improved their technology. Happens all the time with inferior life-forms—stop by, say hello, give them some presents, and they think they can invade your planet."

Acting on instinct, I ran to an injured female, then jumped back as my hands passed right through her.

"Sweetheart, I should have explained—you're only

seeing recorded memory patterns. You can't do anything for them."

I watched the raiders taking captives and dragging them off to huge star vessels designed to hold thousands of slaves. "They're not even trying to escape."

"Why should they? We wanted them to come and get us." Maggie gently put a hand under my chin and closed my mouth. "The raiders didn't understand why we wouldn't fight back, but they got over it fast enough. Never look a gift slave in the mouth."

I stopped watching the raid. Unreal or not, I couldn't stand seeing those brutes dragging the not-so-helpless Jxin to their ships. "Why would you want to be slaves?"

"We didn't feel like building our own ships. All the alloy and laying power conduit and creating light-speed propulsion—too boring for words." She covered a yawn with her hand. "They wanted slaves; we needed serious transportation. Simple as that."

I was starting to get a headache. "That makes absolutely no sense."

"We had better things to do, Joey. Wherever we've lived, we leave something behind. Repositories, like the one I showed you. Sometimes only the structures that housed them—what you call ruins—with some interesting stuff chiseled in the stone. A couple of artifacts here and there—only our garbage, really, but it wouldn't do to leave functional items where you kids could play with them."

"What did you expect we'd do with this stuff?"

"We figured if anyone ever evolved enough to tolerate exposure or decipher our graffiti, what we left would help them with future changes. In the case of your reality, however, we knew we had to do a little more than leave our trash behind."

I gnawed my bottom lip. "Why do I get the feeling you're leading up to what happened to me?"

"You're a bright girl."

I wasn't so sure of that. "Go back to the part where you became slaves so you could travel. To where?"

"Anywhere with a viable species to be developed—a species evolved enough to own slaves. Lots of those up there." She gestured to the sky. "Being sold and taken to other worlds gave us the access we needed. Once we had settled on a planet, we began our real work."

Putting it together didn't take a genius. A powerful, superior species, spreading themselves across a galaxy they couldn't stay in. Why else would they waste their time? "You seeded the native DNA with your own."

"Bingo." She produced a cigarette, lit it, and blew out some smoke before giving me a singularly sweet smile. "But we went a little further than that, baby. We created you."

Hearing my darkest suspicion confirmed wasn't as bad as I'd thought. I didn't want to tear out my hair and wail to the heavens for being the result of an alien conspiracy.

I wanted to knock her on her ass.

Absently, I noticed we were back in the Jxin repository, and the wall devices were still whirring and vibrating away. "Then Joseph had nothing to do with my creation, and you only worked for him to get access to the DNA you needed."

"Actually, I took advantage of his primitive progress, as it was convenient for my purposes."

"What about my brothers?"

She lifted a brow. "What about them?"

"Did you do them, too?"

"Ah, no. They were all his work, not mine." She smirked a little. "Which is why they were all failures."

I let out a bitter laugh. "You weren't helping him at all. You were competing with him."

"Please, Joseph? He never had a chance. All I got from him were the raw materials, and the equipment. You can't just diddle with a species' DNA and not expect some flack from the original models, you know."

I'd never realized it before, but she was as arrogant as Joseph had been. "Why didn't you just skip the test tubes and breed with these species?"

"Do you have any idea what a crossbreed between a multidimensional life-form and a corporeal would turn out like? Not that we even considered it." She snorted. "No offense, Cherijo, but humanoids to us are like the Date from Hell That Never Ends."

"Right." I suppressed the urge to slap her. With effort. "So you put a few surprises in the gene pool. How did you manage to cross whatever barrier there is between our life-forms?"

"We discovered by experimenting with the raiders that we could alter the native DNA by injecting select chromosomes from our corporeal selves into a developing fetus." She went to one of the walls, and tapped something. A three-dimensional projection of a Hsktskt soldier appeared between us. "These guys are descendants of the original bus drivers we used to get off Jxinok."

"Bravo." Not even the Hsktskt had been safe from tampering. "And you're still doing this?"

Maggie threw back her head and laughed. "Oh, honey. I'm sorry, but the look on your face is just priceless. No, we're not 'doing it' anymore. I was the last to leave. There aren't any of us left in this reality."

I felt like tapping my foot. "So how long until more super-physicians start popping up all over the galaxy?"

"There's a little more of a time line involved." Maggie fiddled with the wall again. "Let me show you what Terra looked like when I was captured by the pre-Hsktskt."

The room around us melted away, and we returned to the darkness. Stars began popping out around us, and in the distance I saw a star in the final stages of formation.

"That's Sol," she said, then turned and pointed to a swirling mass of dust solidifying in space. "And that's your homeworld."

"You're telling me you witnessed the formation of Terra."

"Uh-huh."

I watched time speed up as the planet became whole. "Was Reever right about the subliminal thing?"

She smiled. "He does have some bright moments."

"You never implanted anything in my head. I'm communicating interdimensionally with you." I should have slapped her before, now I wanted to pound her head into something. "Where the hell are you, anyway?"

"The place seriously defies description, baby. Its pathways are very similar in structure to the synaptic thought patterns of your brain." She patted my cheek. "We can talk any time you like, now."

My headache swelled to new, hammering intensity. "If you became a slave when Terra was forming, then I know who you are."

"Taa-daa!" She stepped back and bowed low. "The one, the only, the fabled founding race."

CHAPTER NINETEEN

Housekeepers

We returned to Jxinok, to walk through the forest around the now-smoldering ruins of the crystal city. I had a lot of questions, and for once, Maggie seemed only too happy to answer them.

"What about the blood disorder you supposedly died from?"

"Faked it." She yawned and examined her fingernails. "Well, not really faked it. My cellular cohesion had deteriorated to the point that it really looked like my blood was rotting. The real challenge was altering the tissue and blood samples so all those doctors your father made me see didn't freak out."

I wouldn't remind her what watching her die had put me through; my pride wouldn't let me. Still, superior life-form or not, Maggie needed some sensitivity training. "How many planets did you hit in my galaxy?"

"By the time the Tagbno—that's what the Hsktskt used to call themselves—got through selling us, we bounced around as much as we could." She started counting on her fingers by the hundreds, then tossed up her hands. "I don't know, three, four hundred thousand worlds. It was fun, spending all those millennia moving from planet to planet and discovering new species."

"I'll bet." I did a quick mental tally on the number of explored, populated quadrants within the galaxy. Adding what I estimated was still out there to be discovered, I concluded that she and her DNA-happy species had likely meddled with most of the inhabited planets in existence. "You ended up on Terra when?"

"I think it was the fifteenth—no, sixteenth century. I wasn't sold to your species. I escaped this really dreary little drift-colony as it passed by Terra." She made a rude sound with her lips. "Then all I had to do was sit back and wait for you to get over the Black Death, the Renaissance, and the Industrial Revolution."

I'd already seen a few holes in her story—epic and grandiose as it was—but decided to push her on a few more points. "What about the other Jxin? No one had a problem with this plan? No one objected to it? You were all in agreement?"

"We're not like you, squabbling like mammals, honey. We knew we only had a few million years to play with. What else was there to do, but modify what looked promising and watch them grow?"

I could think of a few things. "So you picked Joseph Grey Veil as one of your victims."

"One humanoid is as good as another. I needed the correct political situation." She shrugged. "When I discovered Joseph was trying to crack the genetic limitations of your species, I knew he was the Terran I'd been waiting for."

"So you came to work for him, and switched me for whatever he was working on." I thought of what Jericho had told me—that I had eight more clone-brothers scattered around the galaxy out there—and wondered if she'd tampered with their development, too, no matter what she claimed. "Why did you make me female?"

"Oh, that was his idea. I only added some Jxin DNA

to his experiment and corrected his mistakes. You were special, little girl. I couldn't let him muck it up."

But she had no problem with watching him ruin the lives of eight little boys. "Why? Why am I special? Just because you and I share some cellular material that you couldn't hold on to?"

"I worked with what I could get." She shrugged. "My kind would have done a lot more if we'd been able to stick around another hundred billion years, but you know how time flies when you're trying to stay solid."

"You said I can't die. Is that true?"

"For the most part. Oh, you can kill yourself by tossing your body into a star, or staying immersed in molecular acid, but aside from that, you're immortal."

We were finally getting to the part I needed to know. "There's a reason you needed me to live forever, right?"

"Right." She bent over, plucked a blue flower, and handed it to me. "You're going to continue the work."

"Your work?"

"Not exactly. It's more a housekeeping job."

I laughed. "A what?"

"We can't come back and fix anything that breaks, Joey. And given the possibilities with the modified species, well"—she rolled her eyes—"somebody had to take the job. So while we were out there founding all these new species, we also created some very special kids, like you."

Kids. Not kid. "To clean up your trash?"

"Sometimes. Mostly you've got to do what you were trained to be—a doctor. Make some house calls, or rounds, or whatever you want to call it. You've got to monitor what happens on these worlds."

"That isn't housekeeping. That's baby-sitting."

"Works for me. But if it makes you feel better, just think of how you heal the sick and injured, and apply that on a galactic scale. Voilà, instead of one patient, you get to treat millions."

"I can hardly wait." I was nearly finished. I just needed a little more information. "How do I do that, exactly?"

"You're already doing it, baby." She tucked another blue flower in my hair. "Identify problems like the one Dhreen's people are having, go in, gently manipulate certain aspects of it—you'll know which ones as you run into them—and preserve as many of our seeded species as you can."

"And that's it? That's the whole job?"

"Well, if any promising new species crops up out of some primordial sludge, you'll need to introduce Jxin DNA to their gene pool." She made a casual gesture with one hand. "Just to keep all the humanoids on the same page."

"Do I get any retirement? Or do I turn into a big glow somewhere down the road?"

"Your native DNA assures you won't suffer our fate—it prevents you from making the final transcencion." She kissed me on the brow. "You're going to do a great job, I know it."

"I'm positive I would," I assured her, "if I bought your sad little story."

Superior life-forms don't rattle easily, I discovered.

"Sweetie, what are you saying? Haven't I explained it right?"

"Oh, you explained it just fine. It's certainly a grand plan, and my part in it, to say the least, is impressive." I eyed her up and down. "Just how long did it take you to think up this waste?"

She gave me a slightly pouty, sorrowful look. "Here I thought you were so bright."

"What I can't figure out is why you wouldn't have pulled me to the side while we were both on Terra and do the big revelation scene there. Would have saved me all kinds of grief, not to mention light-years of travel."

"Why would I lie to you about something as important as this is, Joey?"

"I can think of a couple of million reasons." I watched her expression, but she didn't give anything away. "I'm sure some of it is true—you definitely did something to my creator's experiment—but the crystal cities, the benevolent superior life-form, the founding-race thing? Come on. If you had idealized anything else in this little fairy tale of yours, I'd have dropped into a hypoglycemic coma."

"Well, this has been totally nonproductive." Maggie made a careless gesture, and a moment later we were back in space, with galaxies whizzing past us and stars exploding at distant points. "I've given you immortality and the guardianship of this galaxy, and all you can do is cling to your idiotic human suspicions?"

"Guess you picked the wrong experimental fetus." Now I patted her cheek. "Better luck next time."

"I've given you proof!"

"You've shown me exactly what I needed to see to believe you. Beauty and wonder on an epic scale. Only the scale isn't balanced, Maggie. No superior species is going to live in crystal cities, or sell themselves to slavers, or mess with inferior life-forms. That's ridiculous. If your kind is as powerful as you say you are, you'd play volleyball with this galaxy first. We would mean zero to you because we'd be nothing to you."

"And now you're going to tell me your theory, I suppose."

I had one, but I wasn't going to show her my cards. "No. I don't have one and I don't care. I don't care about you, the Jxin, your plan, or anything else remotely connected with you. Now, if you're done playing with me, I'd like to go back to my life. I'd also like you to stay out of it. Forever. Any questions?"

She gave me a speculative look. "No. But—"

"But nothing. Wave your wand, send me back, whatever you have to do to end this." I rubbed my aching brow. "I thought finding out I was a clone was bad. Then finding out my father/brother/whatever had made me to be his wife was worse. But this? This really takes the cake."

"It's the truth, Cherijo."

I looked at her. "Why am I still here?"

"This has to be done." She changed her shape, transforming into the Jxin female again. Her voice struck my ears with the full force of its terrible beauty. "There must be cohesion, order."

Which confirmed part of my working theory. This wasn't about benevolence. It was about control. "I know a couple of Terrans who would agree with you. Like Hitler. Or Hussein. Or my father."

"Your role in the order must be carried out."

"I'm not falling for it. Go find someone else. You're not God, and you'll never convince me that you are."

She rose to her full height and extended her arms. Wind began to blow around us. "The Jxin are your God."

Now came the celestial fireworks, apparently. "Then I just became an atheist."

The Jxin female laughed. The wind died, and I could hear the ghost of Maggie laughing with her. "Of all my special ones, I have loved you the most, girl. Now I know why."

She loved me, all right. The way Joseph had loved me. For reasons that made me want to throw up. "Yeah, well, get over it, because I am not doing anything for you."

"Don't you see, child?" She smiled. "You already are."

I didn't have a clear memory of what happened after Maggie/Whoever smiled at me. One minute, I was ready to scream, the next I sat up and groaned.

Sunlight filtered over my face, warm and gentle. My back felt like someone had taken one of the Taercals' clubs to me.

"Mama?" Marel was perched on my legs, playing swat-the-grass-blade with some cats sitting overhead on the edge of the recess.

Both the Jxinok and Terran felines seemed determined to shred the thin green stalk into ribbons, so I took it from her. "No, baby, they might claw you by accident." I coughed and rubbed my throat—my voice sounded terrible, like a rusty drone's.

"Healer!" A terrified Omorr face filled my vision. "You are awake, thank the gods. I have been attempting to revive you for more than an hour."

"I'm fine." I checked my daughter over, but she seemed none the worse for wear. "How long have I been out?"

"We found you last night. Linguist Reever could not revive you at all." Remembered fear clouded her eyes. "The child refused to leave you."

"I'm sorry I scared everybody." I set Marel aside and got to my knees. "Did someone kick me?"

"It must be from sleeping on the stone. Here, let me help you." I handed Marel up to her, then climbed up out of the recess.

Garphawayn helped by tugging with her three upper limbs. "I cannot recall a time I have been more frightened. I would not want to undertake your profession for all the drell rings on Omorr."

I thought of Maggie. "There are worse jobs." I looked around. "Where's Reever?"

"He and the Chakacat decided to return to the launch to retrieve some medical supplies and repair the communications transmitter, if possible."

I scanned the skies, but there was no sign of anything but some fat, lazy clouds. "I guess if they'd had any luck, we'd be rescued by now."

"Your spouse was quite concerned about someone he called Maggie having some manner of hold over you," she added. "I was not aware there were any inhabitants here to be concerned with."

"There aren't, and it's a long story."

I didn't want to wait until my husband and the Chakacat returned, but the Omorr refused to go anywhere.

"We are exactly where we are supposed to be, and I can't remember the way back to the launch. Can you?"

"No," I had to admit. I paced around the recess, feeling the uncontrollable desire to put as many miles between me and Maggie's world as was possible. Instantly. "How long did he think it would take?"

"It took no time at all."

I turned and ran to Reever, who caught me in a fierce embrace. "Duncan."

When he managed to wrench his mouth from mine, he cradled my face between his hands. "What happened? I couldn't even link with you this time."

"It was Maggie. Or whoever Maggie is. What she told me— well, you're not going to believe it. I certainly couldn't."

"Will you link with me?"

I opened up my mind, letting Reever see everything that I had experienced while under Maggie's trans-dimensional spell. It felt as if we were linked closer than ever before, and he felt every one of my emotions.

Finally there was nothing more to remember. *Duncan, I don't know why she tampered with Joseph's experiment, but she created me for a reason. Just not the one she was trying to sell me this time. What I do know is, if she went to this much trouble to get me to believe this story, then maybe it's better that I never know the truth. I have the feeling there aren't any crystal cities in the real story.* I reached for him, with my hands and my thoughts. He was so quiet and still that it shook me. *Say something.*

I love you.

We emerged from the link. "Are you sure? I don't think she will hurt anyone besides me, but I don't want to take chances with you and Marel."

"We will deal with Maggie together."

I felt the invisible weight on my shoulders evaporate. "Then you'll stick by me, no matter what?"

All he had to say was one word. Lucky for me, it was "Yes."

The rescue team was on the way to rendezvous with us at the launch site, so we gathered everyone together and trekked back through the woods. A veritable herd of near-cats escorted us, and seemed particularly drawn to Alunthri, who was carrying Juliet and the kittens in its arms.

"I'll speak to Xonea when I get back to the ship," I said to Reever. "I have to resign from the Council as soon as possible."

"Do you think that's wise?"

"Given this new turn of events, yeah, I do." I looked

back through the forest, and shuddered. "I want to stay as far away from positions of world domination as possible."

"Perhaps the Jorenians will assist us in getting a ship of our own." My husband stopped for a moment, listening for something. "Wait."

Garphawayn came up short behind us. "What is it?"

"Someone is already at the launch site."

"Xonea's a fast worker." I started forward, but Reever held me back.

"The rescue team won't be here for another thirty minutes." Reever turned to Alunthri. "Can you identify their scent?"

"I have smelled them before, on Oenrall and K-2." The Chakacat stepped back into the foliage. "It is the Bartermen."

Weapons suddenly appeared all around us. I took Marel from Reever and held her close, and saw Alunthri vanish into the undergrowth.

A small, robed figure stepped out in front of us. He yanked back his cowl, displaying a gaunt, gray-skinned face that was as attractive as the odor coming from his dusty robe. "Bartermen have appropriated this vessel, and all its contents."

"We have no quarrel with you. Take it," my husband said.

The end of a pulse rifle nudged his chest. "All of its contents, including escaped slaves."

As we were forced inside the Bartermen's appropriated Oenrallian vessel, Garphawayn decided to vent some of her pent-up frustrations.

"I refuse to believe that a sentient species who also belongs to the Allied League of Worlds would violate the treaty between the League and Omorr by selling my person to slavers." She turned to the Bartermen's head trader, and rapped him on the arm with her sojourn pack. "I am speaking to you, sir. You will rescind this reckless decision and return us to the *Sunlace* immediately."

"Bartermen not change trade agreement." He pointed to a corridor. "You go there."

"I certainly will not!" The female Omorr moved her head from right to left, then back again. "Who is in authority here? I demand to speak to that person, at once!"

"Bartermen speak for Bartermen." Our escort jabbed his hand toward the corridor again. "You go there now."

"I will not."

Then Lady Cestes did something I never expected. She thumped down on the deck, folded her hands in her lap, and refused to look at the Bartermen.

"You get up and go there," the Barterman said.

"I cannot hear you." Gildrells stiff, pink skin blazing with patches of purple color, the Omorr turned her face away.

By unspoken agreement, Reever and I sat down on the deck with Marel between us. Garphawayn thawed enough to give us a curt nod of approval.

The Barterman took out his weapon. "You get up and go there or Barterman will shoot you."

"Bartermen have a trade agreement for live, unharmed slaves," my husband said. "Understanding your professional reputation as I do, I seriously doubt you will use that on us. It would nullify the entire deal, would it not?"

Our escort turned to me and Reever. "You tell Omorr female to get up and go there."

"No, I don't think I'm going to do that. Reever?" My husband shook his head. "Sorry. Can't help you out."

Clearly frustrated, the Barterman grabbed Garphawayn by two of her arms, and tried to pull her to her foot. She responded by screaming at the top of her lungs and beating him over the head with her sojourn pack.

"How dare you! I am the first daughter of the Cestes line! I will have you stripped and flogged for daring to put your filthy hands on me!"

I tried to hold Marel close to me, but she was too fascinated by the spectacle of Garphawayn pummeling the smaller Barterman with her pack.

Reever also got up, assuming that stance he used just before he began wiping up the deck with someone. "Release the Lady Cestes. Now."

My daughter buried her face in my tunic. "Mama, Daddy's mad."

"I know, honey."

"I doan wike id when Daddy mad."

I rubbed her back. "Me either."

More Bartermen came back into the compartment, doubtless to see what all the racket was about.

When more weapons appeared, I got up and held Marel close. "That's enough, Lady Cestes."

Startled into silence, the female Omorr let her sojourn pack sag. "What—"

"I appreciate what you're trying to do, but this isn't the time." I looked straight into my husband's eyes. "Or the way." To our escort, I said, "We will cooperate as long as you allow me to transmit a signal to the *Sunlace* first."

"You belong to Bartermen now," I was told.

"Whatever." I mentally crossed my fingers. "If I

don't send them a signal, they will fire on this vessel as soon as you enter the upper atmosphere."

Our escort and the other Bartermen formed a huddle and discussed my warning in their native tongue. Reever came over and took Marel from me, to show her he wasn't mad anymore. She held on to him with tight hands and, incredibly, fell asleep in his arms.

He stroked the back of her head. "They will try to separate us."

"We're not going to let that happen. I have a plan, but I need you to promise you won't interfere."

Before he could say anything, one of the Bartermen came forward and spoke to me. "Bartermen will permit a brief signal. Bartermen will punish deception harshly."

I wasn't going to risk them taking out their ire on Marel, so I stuck with my story as I raised Xonea on the Bartermen's transmitter.

"We've decided to take a little trip with some friends," I said. "You might want to stop by this planet. There are all kinds of cats down here. Big ones who talk, as a matter of fact."

His expression changed. "Cherijo—"

"The Taercal and the Oenrallians will be here in a day, right?" I spoke quickly, to keep him from blurting out anything that might provoke the Bartermen further. "Make sure the Jado get them to call a truce before they decide to blast Oenrall to smithereens. Duncan and I will take care of our friends as well. Talk to you soon."

As the Bartermen's vessel made the jaunt back to Oenrall, we were herded into a confined, empty compartment and locked in. Reever immediately began looking for weapons and a way out, while I held my sleeping daughter and spoke quietly with Garpha-wayn.

"They will do whatever they want to secure a trade agreement. In our case, we've already been sold to a slaver on Oenrall. In their eyes, we really are nothing more than misplaced property."

"*I* was not sold to anyone." The female Omorr stared with great indignation at the locked door. "But still, surely I can pay these little creatures enough credits to release us. My family is quite wealthy."

"You can offer, but I don't think they'll accept anything but hard currency." I thought of the impending war. "Also, no one will jaunt into this system until the Jado get this peace treaty hammered out."

More unpleasant news arrived when our escort came back to inspect us.

"You." He pointed a skeletal finger in my direction. "Bartermen remember you. Bartermen never forget one who corrupts the flow of trade."

They'd sworn never to forget the way I'd shut down their brisk trade business during the Core plague on K-2. Just my luck, they'd stuck to their promise. "I'm touched."

"Bartermen will substitute the Omorr female for you to the Akkabarran slaver on Oenrall. You will bring much greater trade from the Allied League. The Hskt-skt also wish to make trade for you."

"So which one are you guys going to sell me to? Whoever makes the best offer?" I shook my head sadly. "The minute you offer me to one of them, the other side is going to attack you."

"Bartermen have trade agreements with both sides. Bartermen will be protected by them. You eat, drink. Bartermen will transport you to the surface shortly."

He dropped some ration packs on the deck, then departed, securing the door behind him.

"I hope the Hsktskt really slam these guys."

Garphawayn looked thoughtfully at the door panel. "I suspect what he claims is true."

I rubbed circles into my throbbing temples. "If they try to play the League off the Hsktskt, or vice-versa, someone is going to blow up Oenrall in the process."

"They do not appear to be concerned with anything but trade," the female Omorr said. "It does not matter to them what happens to any of us."

"They have nearly drained Oenrall of all its assets," my husband said as he joined us. "They must be planning to abandon the planet as soon as they finish this transaction for Cherijo. She is the most valuable item they possess."

"I can give them something even more valuable." I looked up at Duncan. "The ability to trade forever."

When the Bartermen escort came the next day to check on us again, I made my radical offer.

"You release my husband, my daughter, and the Omorr female. In return, I will give you the C.H.E.R.I.J.O. experimental data."

The Barterman folded his hands in his sleeves. "Bartermen do not know of this experimental data. Give Bartermen details."

I told him exactly why the League and Hsktskt were after me, skipping several key facts, but leaving enough of the truth in to make the offer irresistible.

After I finished, he nodded and held out a hand. "Give Bartermen experimental data to examine."

I shook my head. "That's not how it works. I don't have it on me. I have it in me." When he came forward as if to search my body cavities, I held out my hands. "I memorized it before I left Terra. Everything"—I tapped the side of my head—"is up here."

He left the compartment, only to return a few minutes later with some of his buddies. "Bartermen wish to see a sample of the experimental data. You come with Bartermen."

I was taken to a terminal, where I entered the beginning sequences of a number of genetically engineered alterations, and identified what they altered. I didn't give them enough data to use for anything but verification of my claim, then returned to the compartment.

"Cherijo, you must not do this," Garphawayn said, as soon as we were left alone. "If you are as you say, they shall auction you off to the highest bidder. Someone will take you to a laboratory and experiment on you, or lock you up in it until you produce a clone like yourself."

I fought a grin. "They've already done that, twice. Reever and I are pretty good at escapes, aren't we, handsome?"

My husband was equally unenthusiastic. "I will not be able to help you if you do this, *Waenara*."

"I know." I pretended not to see the ice crystals forming in his eyes. "I know you trust me, and you won't give me a hard time about it, and you'll take our kid back to the *Sunlace*, where she'll be safe."

"Please reconsider," the female Omorr said. "These creatures may not adhere to the terms of your trade agreement."

"Oh, if it's one thing I know about the Bartermen, it's that they stick to their deals."

The Bartermen checked out the data with someone, then came to the compartment en masse. "Bartermen accept your terms. Cherijo Torin will provide the experimental data, in return for the release of husband, daughter, and Omorr female."

I nodded. "Agreed."

"There is a Jorenian vessel in orbit above Oenrall. The male and females will be released to this vessel."

Which was exactly what I wanted. "Nice doing business with you."

Duncan couldn't let it go at that.

"I am not leaving you," he said as the Bartermen docked with the *CloudWalk.* "Garphawayn can take Marel over. I will stay with you."

"I need you to protect our daughter first and worry about me later." *Please, Duncan. Don't make this more difficult than it already is. Trust me.*

He kissed me. "I trust you. I would do anything for you."

"Great. When this is over, put me down for a long vacation." I lifted my daughter and held her between us before handing her over to Duncan. "Just you, me, and the kid."

From the one viewport in my compartment, I watched the transfer take place, then was taken to a terminal to receive confirmation from the Jado Clan-Leader, Teulon.

"Your kin have arrived, and we will keep them safe, Council representative." He looked ready to use claws on someone. "Allow my kin the honor of being of further assistance to you."

I took it that *further assistance* would arrive in the form of enraged warriors to take the shuttle by force and eviscerate every Barterman in sight. Also, Teulon had to get moving if he wanted to negotiate peace between the Taercal and Oenrall, who would soon be arriving on Jxinok.

"Thank you for the offer, ClanLeader, but I will take it from here. Please continue on your assignment, and may the Mother watch over you all."

Since the Bartermen didn't have the kind of medical database on board their vessel I would need to handle all of the C.H.E.R.I.J.O. experimental data, they took me down to the planet, where they had plenty.

Their headquarters had been established on, fittingly enough, Bankers Row, where most of the goods they had bilked out of the natives were being prepped for final shipment. I was taken to a huge room of medical diagnostic and database equipment, and shown to one of the largest and most sophisticated computer consoles on the planet.

"Bartermen want the experimental data now."

I pulled up a chair. "I'll get right to work."

Figuring they'd be monitoring me closely at first, I began to enter formulas from the experiment that Joseph had used to create me.

"Oh, Joe." Stringing together fragments of alteration procedures and formulas which would never actually work was boring, and I yawned frequently. "If you could see me now."

It would take weeks to finish entering the bogus data—if I went slowly enough—and even more time for whoever bought the data to find out it wouldn't do anything but mess up a lot of lab equipment.

The Bartermen brought me food twice, and I was allowed a short rest period of several hours. I didn't sleep, though—thoughts of what had happened on Jxinok, and Maggie's improbable revelations kept me staring at the ceiling.

How much of it was true?

I sensed a lot of truth in what she'd told me. Truth that had been ripped apart and strung back together,

like the phony formulas I was creating for the Bartermen.

The Jxin—certainly a superior life-form, but if Maggie exemplified them, they weren't exactly perfect. I
didn't believe for a moment they'd lived on Jxinok in
crystal cities, or had invited raiders to enslave them,
but I suspected some elements of both had happened.
Perhaps they'd stopped there, and had been captured.

*Why would they need humanoids to do anything for
them?*

Maggie's epic tale of galactic genesis might have
worked, if the Jxin had stayed around to play God to
the mortals they'd messed with. But why create their
"special children" and then wink out of our dimension,
never to return? No man or woman would have a
child, knowing they would have to abandon it before it
grew to adulthood.

*What was it she said? There must be something . . . cohe-
sion . . . order. . . .*

That scared me more than anything else. A species
who could cross dimensions wanting to create order
wherever they went would go to great lengths to get
rid of anything that threatened that goal.

Had Maggie created me not to be a guardian, but an
enforcer? And how many other "special kids" like me
had she created, and where were they now?

I fell into a light doze, and dreamed of watching my
homeworld swirl into being.

Chapter Twenty

Last Rounds

Hands shaking me woke me up abruptly, and I opened my eyes to see Dhreen, Hawk, and Ilona hovering over me. I blinked a couple of times, but they didn't go away.

"What are you doing here?" I asked the weaver, struggling with the sheet draped over me. "Why are these two out of Medical?"

"We took a launch from the *Sunlace* as soon as the *CloudWalk* arrived at Jxinok," Ilona said. "We were able to get in by trading with the Bartermen. Dhreen, give her the disc."

The Oenrallian handed me a disc. "The Omorr wanted you to have this. I said you'd want a good bottle of spicewine, but he wouldn't listen to me." Dhreen chuckled and then wandered away, fiddling here and there with the medical equipment.

"He isn't any better, is he?" I asked the Terran girl, who shook her head. "Why did Squilyp send them to me here?"

"He said only you would know how to cure them."

Great to know my boss had so much faith in me. As I got up, Hawk backed away and began restlessly pacing around my pallet. "The *yei* are everywhere," I heard him mutter.

"How much tranquilizer did he give them?" I asked Ilona.

"Enough to keep them manageable for several hours," she said. "I have more, if we need it."

"Squilyp, you really owe me big-time now." I got up and went over to the diagnostic console. "Let's see what we've got here."

The disc contained Hawk's and Dhreen's medical files, as well as the results of tests performed on water samples from both worlds. The lab had found no micro-organic contaminants. My environmental theory instantly and irrevocably collapsed.

"This is zero help." I could have screamed. "Okay, so there's nothing in the water, and only trace readings in the bloodstreams and—" Something Squilyp had noted in the summary paragraph below each test made me sit up and stare at the screen.

Unidentified mineral-based compound is present in both samples.

Now, the universe is made up of a certain number of minerals, and certainly there were plenty of the same to be found on any two worlds, in various compounds. However, mineral-based meant it was something more than rock or metal, and the only thing I'd seen in that category was the black tul crystal/ships on Taerca. I'd seen tul under a scope, back on Catopsa, and whatever this compound was, it wasn't killer black crystal.

However, it contained traces of it.

I looked down at the floor, at the beautiful stark patterns of black against the white. "Dhreen?" I got up from my chair and knelt on the smooth surface as he wandered over. "Dhreen, what's this black stuff in the floor covering?"

"Rock."

"I know that. What kind of rock?"

He shrugged. "Black rock from the craters."

"What craters?"

"Impact craters. They're all over the place. The city planners used them because they didn't have to dig mines. Whatever hit way back then dug its own holes." He laughed. "Pretty convenient, huh?"

"Real convenient." I grabbed a scanner. "Come here."

"No poking now," he said as he submitted to the scan. "You want to go out? I could use some chill-juice. The sound of that hummer is starting to bug me."

"Ilona, I need more tranquilizer." After recalibrating my scanner twice, I found moderate levels of the mineral-based compound in Dhreen's bloodstream and, after dosing the Oenrallian, compared them to an early scan from his data, taken prior to our sojourn to his home-world.

No compound had been present until we had landed on this planet. Nor had Hawk shown any signs of psychosis prior to his visit to Taerca.

There were too many coincidences for this to be two separate disorders. I raised my head. "I need Hawk over here."

"I don't think he's going to help you, patcher." Ilona directed my attention to the *hataali*, who was hovering by the entrance panel. "Not without more drugs."

I grabbed a syrinpress and walked slowly over to the panel. "Hey, pal. How are you feeling?"

He only rocked back and forth on his heels and watched me, like his namesake.

"Tell you what, why don't you come over here and see what I found on the console?" I edged to one side, hoping to get a clean shot before he came at me. "You're not going to believe this, but I think you and

Dhreen may be suffering from different mutations of the same infection, and—"

The door panel opened, and a group of Bartermen walked in. Hawk went berserk.

I tried to pull him off before they used their jolt-sticks, but both Hawk and I were sent flying back through the air and hit one of the tables. Somehow I landed on top of him, my hands trapped beneath. I felt blood pulsing against my hands, lifted off him, and rolled him over.

Then I saw what the alloy frame had done. "No!"

His belly was ripped wide open, and blood poured down the front of his legs like a wide curtain.

I made a makeshift pressure bandage, and had Ilona hold it in place as I went to prep the surgical table. The Bartermen got in my way. "You've done enough. Leave."

"Bartermen give you one hour to finish."

"Fine. Go."

I had everything I needed to operate on Hawk except one thing—blood. There were no perishable supplies in this warehouse, and without blood, he was going to die.

"I can't transfuse him with mine," I said to Ilona as I took a blood sample from her for analysis. "My immunities make it poisonous." I ran the chem analysis and swore. "And you're incompatible. Goddamn it."

Dhreen ambled over and stuck out an arm. "Take some of mine."

"Knock it off, you're not even half the same species." I pushed his hand away, froze, then grabbed it again. "Hold still."

I drew the sample and shoved it in the analyzer. As the data scrolled up, I forgot to blink. I groped for the sample I had taken from Hawk, and ran a comparison.

"Can you use Dhreen's blood?"

"Yeah. They're almost identical in composition and the type matches perfectly."

"But how can that be?"

"I don't know." I faced one of my worst nightmares, all over again. I looked up at the ceiling. "If this is your idea of a joke," I told God, who I was pretty sure hadn't been my surrogate mother, "I don't think it's funny."

Giving Hawk a transfusion of Dhreen's blood went against every single thing I'd learned as a physician and from killing Kao with my own blood. Yet as I hooked the two men up, I also knew I was out of options.

"Start praying, Ilona." I initiated the transfusion, and began working on suturing the wound in Hawk's belly.

Not only did the transfusion work, it saved Hawk's life. I had his wound repaired and him resting comfortably when the Bartermen returned.

"Your hour is up—"

"I need another one."

"You do not have trade for another one."

"Here." Ilona took off the white quill collar she wore around her neck and tossed it to them. "Indigenous body ornament, Terran, North American Navajo."

The Barterman who caught it fingered the collar. "Bartermen give you one more hour." The group withdrew.

I looked across the table at Ilona. "Thank you."

"You're welcome."

Hawk's eyes fluttered open as I removed the infuser line. "Cherijo?" His voice was hoarse, but otherwise normal. "What happened?"

"You tried to give yourself a new navel." I bent over

to check his vitals, which were stabilizing at normal levels. "Still worried about the *yei*?"

He frowned. "Why would I be worried about some children's fairy tales?"

With a few more questions, I confirmed that Hawk's psychosis had abruptly disappeared. An even more radical idea occurred to me as I drew a sample of blood and turned to Dhreen.

"Ilona, hold his arm still one more time."

When I transfused Dhreen with Hawk's blood, the Oenrallian's hyperactivity also quickly disappeared.

The Terran girl sighed with relief as a rather bewildered Dhreen asked why we were sticking him with needles. "It worked, patcher."

"That's the problem—it shouldn't have. They both have the same contaminant in their blood, so cross-transfusing doesn't remove it." I drew two more tubes of blood and went to the analyzer. "It's something else I'm not seeing."

I set the unit to run a complete spectrum analysis on Dhreen and Hawk's samples, then returned to the medical database.

"Identical hematological profiles means the Taerca and the Oenrallians are cross-fertile." I pulled up a full physiological reference file on Dhreen's species, then downloaded both men's medical files into the database. "Let's see if it means something else."

As I ran comparison baselines, Dhreen and Ilona flanked me. "You can't compare me to Hawk that way, Doc. We're different species."

"Yes, you're supposed to be." I watched the results scroll up on the display. "Different species who have identical blood cells, bone cells, tissue cells, nerve cells, and brain compositions."

"But he has an independent heart," Dhreen said, tapping the screen. "I don't."

"He got the heart from his Terran mother." I asked the computer to extrapolate a conclusion I'd already reached. Ten seconds later, it printed its response on the screen.

Oenrallian and Taercal life-forms are genetically mutated variations of the same progenitor species.

Dhreen glanced back at Hawk. "We can't be the same. He has feathers, and wings."

"His race probably developed them in response to the change in environment when they left the planet. Yours didn't have to, because they stayed behind."

He frowned. "The Taercal lived on Oenrall?"

"A long time ago." I pointed to his horns/ears. "Long enough to change your people into a legend that they chiseled above the doorways."

Dhreen still wasn't convinced. "It doesn't seem likely."

"Look at the two worlds—Taercal has barely one percent of the population of Oenrall, yet both populations have equal technological development. Or did, before Hawk's people abandoned theirs. They're not indigenous to Taerca. I'm betting they colonized it."

"There's a legend my mother told me when I was a boy, about a group of separatists who called themselves The Purists." Dhreen went on to repeat the story, in which radical Oenrallians had deserted the planet in search of the perfect world to go along with their rather demanding religion. "No one ever heard from them again, and those left behind assumed they'd been lost during the journey."

"They called you a defiler and a blood polluter when we were captured, remember?" I started running a new series of comparisons, this time on matching internal organs. "Maybe they were persecuted or driven off Oenrall for their beliefs—that happens in a lot of societies. Or maybe they left voluntarily. However it happened, over time they might have villainized your people, just to keep future generations from returning here."

"We don't share the same sickness, though."

"No, you seem to be complete opposites in that." I thought for a moment. "No one dies on Oenrall, and no one lives very long on Taerca."

Ilona drew in a startled breath. "That is opposite, too."

I glanced at her. "I beg your pardon?"

"How they die. Dhreen's people live forever. Hawk's people die too soon." She turned to me. "Why?"

"Aging is a natural process, dependent on a number of factors. In some species, like ours, genetics govern aging. The programmed senescence—the rate at which we grow old—determines how long our cells function and when they die. In others, the toxins produced and accumulated by cells during a lifetime cause the aging process. Disease and environment are also major factors, as is evident in the Taercal."

"But if they come from the same planet, why are they not dying at the same time?"

"They evolved differently." Or had they? I pulled up the geriatric files on Dhreen's people. "Okay. Under normal conditions, Dhreen's people age as a result of cellular deterioration, governed by two hormones released by the iydroth gland, located at the base of the brain." I split the screen and accessed Hawk's neuroanatomy file. "Which the Taercal also have, only Hawk's is a lot smaller."

I got up and went back to the blood analyzer.

"Hawk and Dhreen should both have iydrothpin and trioiydrothyrnine in their bloodstreams." I checked lab stats on both prior to the transfusion. "What? That can't be right." I ran the blood series again

Dhreen came over to the analyzer. "What's wrong?"

"Before you swapped blood with Hawk, you didn't have any iydrothpin in your system." I waited for the scan to finish, then reread the results. "And he didn't have any trioiydrothyrnine."

"What does it mean?"

"Wait for it." I went over to Hawk, and performed a systemic sweep. Sure enough, the mysterious signs of deterioration in his organs had halted, and in some cases, had reversed. Then I scanned Dhreen, and found a tiny decrease in his organ output.

The only thing left to do was run an immersion simulation on the mineral-based compound, and the two hormones. The analyzer did that in a few seconds, and produced the same results: In Hawk's blood, it destroyed the trioiydrothyrnine. In Dhreen's, it wiped out the iydrothpin.

Then I sat down and cradled my head in my hands until Ilona touched my shoulder.

"Patcher?"

"It's okay." I was scaring them, but then, I'd just scared myself. "I know why the Oenrallians have become immortal and the Taercal are dying young." I showed them the results on the analyzer. "The mineral-based compound in the water on both worlds has gradually destroyed hormonal production. Because it attacks different sides of the hormonal combination, it has opposite effects—the Taercal experience accelerated cell deterioration, while the Oenrallians experience none."

"But why doesn't it attack the same hormone?"

"Before the compound got into your water tables and your bodies, the genetic degradation of the iydroth gland was already in progress. The compound only accelerated the natural process. Because of the separation, you've evolved into different races, but each developed the genetic flaw.

"A temporary solution would be to augment glandular production in both peoples with synthetic hormones to replace the ones that are missing," I said thoughtfully. "But in the genetic long term, the Taercal and the Oenrallians will have to get back together."

Dhreen's orange brows rose. "Interbreed? With them?"

"If both races want to survive, yeah, that's what you're going to have to do."

"But we're sterile."

I shook my head. "The sterility is a by-product. Once the hormone is reintroduced, your people will be as fertile as bunny rabbits again." I was betting psychosis was a by-product of Hawk's deficiency, too.

He nodded slowly. "Doc, can you synthesize this stuff now?"

I knew why he asked that, and looked around at the equipment. "Yeah. I can."

"Will you do what has to be done?"

"I'll need help getting out of here, and cover while I'm gone." I sized up Ilona. "You're taller, but if you stay parked at the console I don't think the Bartermen will notice. Just don't leave Hawk alone, not in his condition." I told her how to keep close monitor on him, then turned to Dhreen. "I need you to get back there, and do this right."

Pale-faced, he nodded.

Ilona went behind a stack of portable terminals with

me, and traded garments. Then I synthesized enough hormone to do the job.

"I'll be back soon." I pulled on Ilona's cloak, and covered my head, then slipped out of the complex behind Dhreen.

The trip took only a few minutes, but I would have been happy to stay on the road forever.

"I've hated death all my life," I said, watching Dhreen drive. "Fought it, like it was some kind of private demon. And now I'm going to work for it."

"If there was another way, I'd offer it to you."

"Just help me get through this."

We left the glidecar Dhreen had stolen a few yards from the gap in the wall. I took off the cloak and opened the case of vials as soon as we were behind the main security panel. "Administering it intravenously will take days. I need access to that hygiene pump you showed me before."

"You're going to spray them with it?"

"They'll absorb it through their skin. We have to add it to the water supply, too. That's all I can do for this city. You'll have to synthesize more and distribute it around the globe."

Dhreen led me to the abandoned maintenance section and valved off a supply line before prying open an access port. After adding the synthetic hormone, I muttered a silent prayer under my breath, then stepped away from the water line.

"Seal it and start the pump."

I left him to monitor the unit while I went out to make my final rounds of Eternity Row. I'd seen thousands of people die; now I was going to kill thousands.

When the overhead hygiene sprayers sputtered into life, I went from bed to bed, making sure the patients had enough derma left unsealed to absorb the hormone-laden moisture. I watched the first patient's eyes glaze over, then flutter closed. A shallow, sighed breath left the burned man's scorched lungs, then his chest never rose again.

Rest in peace.

I continued my rounds, becoming soaked myself as I opened specimen containers and watched dismembered limbs cease their century-long twitching. The worst part, or so I thought, was seeing the decapitated heads die. I wasn't sure if it was water rolling down their cheeks, or tears.

Knowing I couldn't walk the length of Eternity Row, I made my last stop at Gerala's bedside. She wasn't alone.

Mtulla held the dead child in her strong arms. She lifted her amber eyes to me, then kissed the little girl on the brow.

"She was my daughter," the Rajanukal said as she carefully lowered the body to the bed, then arranged Gerala's hair around her peaceful face. "I sold you to the Bartermen to get enough credits for her daily dose of Sensblok. I would have done anything to keep her from feeling pain."

I put my hand on her shoulder. "I'm sorry, Rajanukal."

"Do you know, I came every day. I never missed a day. Not in seventy-three years." The big woman pulled the linens up over the still body. "She once told me that knowing I'd be here every day was all that kept her from screaming and crying like the others. She never wanted me to find her like that. She didn't want me to be ashamed of her." She passed a hand over her eyes, and her shoulders shook. "I never cried in front of her because I didn't want her to be ashamed of me."

Everything I wanted to say seemed useless. "She was a very brave little girl. Brave like her mother."

Mtulla covered her face with her big hands, and wept for a long time. I put an arm around her shoulders and listened to the tears and sobs she had never allowed Gerala to suffer. Somehow, that seemed right.

After she composed herself, the Rajanukal insisted on helping me finish my work. Other handlers came and in a few hours, Eternity Row was completely silent.

Mtulla joined me on the last ward, and looked down the rows of beds. "Now we can put dearest ones to the rest they deserve. Thank you for that, Doctor. Whatever I can get for you, it is yours."

The Rajanukal kept her word. She not only helped arrange for Hawk to be transported back to the *Sunlace*, but she bootlegged one of the medical consoles to transmit my own findings to Squilyp. I emphasized the need for discretion and urgency while administering the synthetic hormone to the Taercal.

Oddly, it was that illicit signal that the Bartermen used to trace my location. They burst into Mtulla's house on Handler Row, and demanded I be turned over to them at once.

"We will not let them take you," the furious Rajanukal said. Then she shouted at the Bartermen, "Don't you know what this woman has done for us? She's freed us of the Sensblok! You will get nothing more from our people!"

"Easy, Mtulla. There's been enough death for one day." I stepped up to the Bartermen. "Just what did you have in mind, boys?"

"Bartermen want the promised experimental data."

"No, I'm not going to give you that." I crossed my arms. "Next request?"

The Barterman who spoke for the group looked aghast. "You agreed to trade."

"I know. I lied."

"Bartermen will not wait for the Hsktskt and League to arrive," I was told as a couple of mercenaries flanked me. "Bartermen have too much trouble with Cherijo Torin. Bartermen sell you to the Akkabarran slaver."

I didn't fight them, though I had to repeatedly tell Mtulla to back off.

"Right now, there are two Jorenian ships headed this way," I reminded her. "As soon as they get here, the Bartermen are going to have to hand me over, or face all those claws."

Mtulla shoved one of the mercenaries aside so she could clasp my arm. "If you ever need anything, you signal me and I will bring it to wherever you are."

I felt fairly confident of being rescued, until I was led outside and one of the Bartermen produced a jolt-stick.

"I'm being cooperative," I said, eyeing the weapon. "You don't need that, now—"

He zapped me, and I slid into unconsciousness.

When I woke up, it was in the oddest of circumstances. I was crammed into a very small space, with my legs tucked in and my shoulders pressing against what felt like a tiny console. I opened my eyes and found two small, slimy faces close to mine. "Who are you?"

"Rilken." One of the diminutive aliens reached out and prodded me with a sticky finger. "You Terran?"

"Uh-huh." I tried to sit up, found I couldn't, and swiveled onto my stomach instead. I was inside what had to be the smallest vessel I'd ever seen. A lavatory on the *Sunlace* was ten times bigger. "Why am I here?"

"We purchase you from Bartermen." One of the little guys went to an equally tiny helm and initiated some engines. "Prepare for launch."

"Wait a minute." I managed to hunch over and sit up, and immediately felt like Gulliver. I filled up half the passenger compartment, which had been designed for beings less than half a meter in height. "Where are we going?"

"We are leaving Oenrall," the other pipsqueak said. "We are mercenaries. You will be returned to the Hsktskt for blood-bounty."

Midget mercenaries. Well, why not? "You're friends with the lizards?"

He shrugged his tiny shoulders. "The Hsktskt offer more credits for you."

The tiny vessel lifted off and entered the upper atmosphere. Before the mercenaries could initiate their flightshield, something struck us.

"What is it?" The one guarding me ran up to the helm.

"A Jorenian ship, firing on us." Fear ran through the Rilken's voice. "They have disabled our stardrive."

Considering the size of the ship, Xonea must have used a peashooter. I crawled up behind both of them, and felt for the syrinpress I'd been carrying in my tunic pocket. It was gone, so I'd have to use more creative measures.

"Nighty-night, boys." I knocked their skulls together once, then watched them slide to the floor. I looked around me. "That's it? I don't get shot, stabbed, poisoned, whipped, burned, or anything else?"

The Rilken didn't make a response.

Clunking them was certainly easier than using their communications array. I had to use one of my fingernails to operate the control panel. At last I raised the

CloudWalk to let them know I was in control and all right.

"It is good to see you, Council representative," the Jado ClanLeader said, and smiled. "There are two others here who wish to relay their happiness, as well."

He stepped aside, and the welcome sight of my husband and daughter appeared on the vid screen.

"Cherijo." My husband looked very relieved. "You escaped the Bartermen by yourself?"

"Mtulla helped. By the way, if you ever want to get kidnapped, pick Rilkens. Very easy species to overpower. Marel could do it." I thought of the peace talks. "Have I ruined everything for Captain Teulon?"

"No, it appears the negotiations are a success. The Torins retrieved Alunthri from Jxinok, and it has convinced the Taercal that your cure is a divine intervention, and that their god refuses to allow them to suffer, as was prophesied."

"About time." I moved one of the sleeping Rilken out of my way and sat back against the interior hull wall. "Well, I think that wraps it up here. I'd really like that vacation, now, please."

"Come and get us."

Reever told me how to fly the Rilken vessel to rendezvous with the Jado ship, then touched the screen with his hand. "I'll be waiting for you, *Waenara*."

I matched my fingertips to his. "Not for long, *Osepeke*."